SUNSET

Weatherhead Books on Asia

Weatherhead Books on Asia

Weatherhead East Asian Institute, Columbia University

LITERATURE

David Der-wei Wang, Editor

CONTINUED ON P. 213

TRANSLATED AND EDITED BY

BRUCE AND JU-CHAN FULTON

SUNSET

A CH'AE MANSHIK READER

Columbia University Press   New York

This publication has been supported by the Richard W. Weatherhead Publication Fund
of the Weatherhead East Asian Institute, Columbia University.

Columbia University Press wishes to express its appreciation for assistance given by the
Daesan Foundation in the publication of this book.

COLUMBIA UNIVERSITY PRESS
PUBLISHERS SINCE 1893
NEW YORK   CHICHESTER, WEST SUSSEX
cup.columbia.edu

Library of Congress Cataloging-in-Publication Data
Names: Ch'ae, Man-sik, 1902–1950, author. | Fulton, Bruce, translator. |
Fulton, Ju-Chan, translator.
Title: Sunset : a Ch'ae Manshik reader / translated and edited by
Bruce Fulton and Ju-Chan Fulton.
Description: New York : Columbia University Press, 2017. |
Series: Weatherhead books on Asia
Identifiers: LCCN 2016045237 (print) | LCCN 2017003674 (ebook) | ISBN 9780231181006
(cloth : alk. paper) | ISBN 9780231181013 (pbk.) | ISBN 9780231543408 (electronic)
Subjects: LCSH: Ch'ae, Man-sik, 1902–1950—Translations into English.
Classification: LCC PL991.13.M3 A2 2017 (print) | LCC PL991.13.M3 (ebook) |
DDC 895.73/3—dc23
LC record available at https://lccn.loc.gov/2016045237

CONTENTS

PREFACE

WE FIRST MET CH'AE MANSHIK THROUGH HIS STORY "REDIMEIDŬ insaeng" (A ready-made life), as taught by the late Professor Kim Chongun in a course on short fiction from colonial Korea, while he was a visiting professor (from Seoul National University) at the University of Washington in 1982–83. But not until 1991, when we were made aware of Ch'ae's collected works through Paul La Selle, a fellow student in the Korean Studies M.A. program at the Jackson School of International Studies at the University of Washington and then a doctoral student under the the late Marshall R. Pihl at the University of Hawai'i, did we begin to appreciate the magnitude of Ch'ae's accomplishment and to translate his fiction. It is to Paul La Selle that we owe the title of our translation of Ch'ae's story "Ch'isuk" (My innocent uncle), the first modern Korean story to be included in the *Norton Anthology of World Literature*.

"A Ready-Made Life" became the title story of a collection of Korean colonial period short fiction translated by Kim Chongun and Bruce Fulton (1997). Already by then, we had been introduced to Ch'ae's postcolonial period works, having translated his 1948 story "Ch'ŏja" (The wife and children) as the lead story in a volume of post-1945 Korean fiction, *Land of Exile: Contemporary Korean Fiction*, translated by Marshall R. Pihl and ourselves (1993; rev. and exp. ed. 2007).

We have long felt the need for an anthology devoted to Ch'ae's writing. He is one of the few Korean authors to boast of a significant body of work both before and after the milestone of Liberation from Japanese colonial rule in

1945. Moreover, it makes perfect sense to situate Ch'ae amid the increasingly intertextual and intermedial prominence of the Korean cultural tradition, a consideration that prompted Ross King, with Bruce Fulton, at the University of British Columbia to undertake a project focusing on Korean parody fiction; a translation launched by King and Bruce Fulton of Ch'ae's delightful 1939 story "Hŭngbo-sshi" (A man called Hŭngbo) is one of the fruits of that project and is included in the present volume. It is our hope that *Sunset: A Ch'ae Manshik Reader* will lead to subsequent collections showcasing individual writers from modern Korea who thrived in a variety of genres.

Major credit for the research for the introduction to this volume goes to Ju-Chan Fulton. We wish to thank authors Ch'oe Such'ŏl and Kim Sŏn'a for procuring for us the volumes of *Ch'ae Manshik chŏnjip* (Collected works of Ch'ae Manshik) that we used as source texts for our translations; poet Kim Hyesun and playwright Yi Kangbaek for assistance with the stage directions for *Shim pongsa*; Professor Kwon Youngmin for addressing our queries about certain of Chae's works; and Ms. Eiko Cope and Ms. Miki Hayashi for assistance with Japanese terminology.

We gratefully acknowledge support for this volume in the form of a Translation Fellowship from the National Endowment for the Arts as well as a translation grant from the Daesan Foundation, Seoul. We also wish to reiterate our thanks to Paul La Selle for commenting on a draft of "Mister Pang." Finally, we thank the editors of *Asia Pacific Quarterly* ("Mister Pang"), *Rat Fire: Korean Stories from the Japanese Empire*, published by the Cornell East Asia Series ("Mister Pang"), Asia Publishers, Seoul ("Juvesenility"), and *Acta Koreana* ("Angel for a Day"), for issuing earlier versions of three of the stories anthologized here.

SUNSET

INTRODUCTION

EARLY IN 1937 CH'AE MANSHIK, IN AN INTERVIEW WITH *Paekkwang* magazine, was asked, "Do you know any foreign language well enough to read a text in that language?" The answer was no.[1] This brief exchange opens a window onto a murky scene that has engaged scholars of modern Korean literature both in Korea and abroad since Liberation from Japanese colonial rule in 1945: the elephant (imperial Japan) in the room (colonial Korea). For young intellectuals in colonial Korea, Japanese was of course not a foreign language but a second language, the language in which they had been educated. The problem that scholars of modern Korean literary history grapple with is how to incorporate the bilingual, bicultural, and—the issue that is especially thorny—binationalist tissue of this gargantuan elephant in an understanding of the anomaly of Korea as arguably the first sovereign state in the modern era to be colonized by a non-Western power even as it launched itself on a course of modernity and modernization that has culminated in its present status as a first-world nation.

The elephant in the room is by definition a beast whose presence one must suffer but would rather not acknowledge in public. What tends not to be discussed about Ch'ae Manshik in reference works on modern Korean literature is a chronic pathology resident in the imperial Japanese manifestation of this elephant—collaboration with Japanese rule (*ch'inil*). Where the elephant does appear, it tends to dominate the discussion.[2] In the case of Korean writers during the colonial period, collaboration is likely to be gauged by such indices as the number of times they published in Japanese; the number of times they published in Korean during the last years of Japanese occupation, when publication in Korean became increasingly difficult; and the number of supporting-our-troops (that is, the imperial Japanese military) journeys in which they took part.[3]

Couple the elephant in the room with the penchant of the Korean literature power structure (*mundan*) for categorizing writers in terms of their "representative" (*taep'yojŏgin*) works, and it becomes easier to understand why an incomplete and/or unbalanced view of a major writer lingers more than half a century after his or her passing. The tag usually affixed to Ch'ae's work is satire (*p'ungja*), and his 1934 story "Redimeidŭ insaeng" (A ready-made life), a panorama of the program of colonial modernity bought into by young Korean intellectuals, is cited in at least one prominent reference work as a milestone in his establishment as a creative writer; what he produced until then, starting in 1923—a dozen stories, as many plays, a similar number of critical essays, and some two dozen anecdotal essays (*sup'il*)—are regarded as apprentice works.[4] Ch'ae's reputation continues to rest on this story and four other works: *T'angnyu* (1937–38, Muddy currents), about a woman's downfall amid vanishing traditions, set alongside grain speculation in the author's home region of North Chŏlla, a novel praised for its accurate representation of contemporary realities; the novel *T'aep'yŏng ch'ŏnha* (1938, Peace under heaven), a satire of wealthy landowners and the purchasing of upward mobility; the 1938 story "Ch'isuk" (My innocent uncle), which satirizes not only an impotent socialist intellectual but also his assimilationist nephew; and the post-Liberation novella "Minjok ŭi choein" (1948).

Such is the hold that the colonial period, and the role of public intellectuals during that time, continues to exercise on scholars of modern Korean literature that "Minjok ŭi choein" has come to occupy a central place in the oeuvre of a writer who in a career spanning a little over two and a half decades left enough works to fill ten bulky volumes. Published a year and a half before Ch'ae's death from tuberculosis in 1950, and a mere two months after the creation of the Republic of Korea on August 15, 1948, "Minjok ŭi choein" (literally, "a sinner against the people"; Ch'ae likely had in mind Henrik Ibsen's play *An Enemy of the People*) is a semiautobiographical apologia of a writer who was eminently successful while Korea was a colony of imperial Japan, and who during the benchmark period of the early 1940s had more than a dozen works of fiction published. By contrast, another novella written in 1948, "Nakcho" (Sunset), avoids the labored confessional narrative of "Minjok ŭi choein" but describes through implication and self-deprecating wit the challenge faced by a colonial period intellectual—to live a double life of personal artistic fulfillment also imbued with ethnic pride and cultural nationalism. That "Sunset" (and Ch'ae's works from the post-Liberation period in general) receives significantly less attention than "Minjok ŭi choein" reflects the tendency of scholarship to date to evaluate Ch'ae's output from the mid-1930s through the 1940s more in terms of how it reflects a creative writer's ethics (*chakka yulli*) than as literature per se.

That this estimation of Ch'ae Manshik survives well into the new millennium is obvious in a 2015 interview in which Hwang Sŏgyŏng, one of present-day Korea's most important writers, observes that ever since the post-Liberation movement of writers from south to north and north to south, Ch'ae has pretty much been forgotten.[5] Himself a profoundly intertextual writer who has penned novels inspired by the legend of Pari Kongju, the abandoned princess, and by the paragon of filial piety, Shim Ch'ŏng, Hwang professed astonishment upon reading Ch'ae's 1947 play *Shim Pongsa* (translated here as *Blind Man Shim*). Whether Hwang's surprise originates from the focus of the play (Shim Ch'ŏng's father more than Shim Ch'ŏng herself) or from the intertextual nature of the story, it suggests that in the new millennium much of Ch'ae's oeuvre continues to be little known and/or underappreciated. In fact, by this late stage of his career, Ch'ae had published several intertextual works, ranging as far back as his 1933 story "P'allyŏgan mom" (Sold into servitude), based on the well-known folktale of herder boy Kyŏnu and weaver girl Chingnyŏ, and his 1933 novel *Inhyŏng ŭi chip ŭl nawasŏ* (Out of the doll's house, the title echoing Ibsen's *A Doll's House*), and also including the novel *Paebijang* (1941–42), whose protagonist, an official named Pae, is the focus of one of the twelve works in the standard *p'ansori* repretoire, and a novella, "Ho saeng chŏn" (1946), inspired by Pak Chiwŏn's Choson-period fictional narrative of the same name.

If, however, Kong Chonggu's 2015 essay "Ch'ae Manshik ŭi sanmun yŏngu" (A study of Ch'ae Manshik's prose) is any indication of current scholarship, there is reason to believe that Ch'ae's works will ultimately receive the more balanced assessment they deserve.[6] Though Kong's article nominally concerns prose (which would include Ch'ae's entire oeuvre; he did not publish verse[7]), he focuses on volumes 9 and 10 of Ch'ae's collected works, which consist of plays, film scripts, travel essays, book reviews, anecdotal essays, miscellaneous writings, roundtable discussions, and critical writing (including several pieces focusing on his own works). These writings, as we will see, offer valuable insights into Ch'ae's outlook as a creative writer and public intellectual.

Further grounds for optimism with respect to a reconsideration of Ch'ae's career lie in Hallyu, the wave of Korean popular culture sweeping the world in the new millennium. In its manifestations of television dramas, role-playing online gaming, film, and idol-centric, EDM-influenced popular music, Hallyu has brought renewed attention to the performance tradition in Korea, and in the case of literature, to the venerable oral tradition. One of the most influential elements of that tradition is the oral performance, partly sung and partly narrated, by a single performer (the *kwangdae*) called *p'ansori* (literally, voices/music in an open space).[8] Ch'ae had the good fortune to have been born in Chŏlla Province, where *p'ansori* originated, and he more than any other Korean fiction writer in the modern period has captured the rhythms and rhetorical techniques—repetition, litanies, intertextual references, wordplay—of a *p'ansori* performance. In the present volume this style is reproduced most vividly in "A Man Called Hŭngbo" (Hŭngbo-sshi; "good ol' Hyŏn," the protagonist, is reminiscent of the good-natured Hŭngbo, subject of one of the most frequently performed works in the *p'ansori* repertoire), "Sunset," and the two plays *Whatever Possessed Me?* (Yesu na an midŏttŭmyŏn) and *Blind Man Shim*.

Scholars who can resist the urge to look down their noses at Hallyu will realize that much of it is fundamentally intertextual and intermedial, employing a variety of media in drawing on a wealth of core stories, lyrics, myths, legends, and historical figures from a millennia-old cultural tradition. In addition to Ch'ae, some of the most distinctive fiction writers and playwrights of modern Korea have mined the Korean oral tradition for core stories to which they apply a contemporary approach.[9] Ch'ae drew repeatedly on one of Korea's best-loved stories, that of the filial Shim Ch'ong. In 1936 he wrote a seven-act version of *Shim pongsa*.[10] Ch'ae based this play on *Shim Ch'ŏng chŏn* (Tale of Shim Ch'ŏng), a Later Chosŏn fictional narrative, and follows the core story in terms of situating the ending in China, but he departs from it in not resurrecting the sacrificed Shim Ch'ŏng for a reunion with her father. Instead the play ends with Blind Man Shim, upon realizing his beloved daughter is dead and that he's been duped, gouging out his newly sighted eyes in chagrin. In November 1944 Ch'ae began serializing a fictional work titled "Shim Pongsa," in *Shinshidae*.[11] This work was presumably intended to be a novel, as Shim Ch'ŏng is still a newborn by the end of the last installment. Ch'ae's shorter, 1947 dramatic version of *Shim pongsa* (the one translated here) focuses not so much on Ch'ŏng as on her blind father taking responsibility for the impulsive act that leads his dear daughter to sacrifice herself. Taking into account Ch'ae's distinction as the only "friendly to Japan" author who in a post-Liberation work explicitly reflects on his accomodationist posture during the colonial period,[12] one can't help but wonder if this play involved an oblique attempt to ask the intellectuals of his generation to likewise reflect upon personal responsibility at a time of conflicting loyalties (to Japan, the erstwhile colonial master; to the United States and the USSR, stewards of the Korean peninsula south and north, respectively, in the wake of Japan's withdrawal in 1945; to a united and independent Korea; to a pair of imported ideologies, capitalism and communism).

For a comprehensive understanding of Ch'ae's accomplishment as a writer it's also essential to consider his work in genres other than short fiction, novellas, and plays. The *conte* is a distinctive genre of modern Korean fiction, in length somewhere between flash fiction and short fiction. Unlike the French *conte*, which is usually a tale of extraordinary and imaginary events, the Korean *conte* (pronounced in Korean as a two-syllable word, k'ong-ttŭ) often focuses on everyday life, in which sense it might be considered the fictional counterpart of the personal (as opposed to critical) and often anecdotal essays termed *sup'il*. In the present volume the *conte* are "Skewered Beef" (Sanjŏk), "Egg on My Face" (Hŏhŏ mangshin haettkun), and "Angel for a Day" (Sŏllyang hagoshiptŏn nal). The young male protagonist beguiled by feminine modernity in "Egg on My Face" and in Ch'ae's first published story, "In Three Directions" (Segilllo), will be familiar to readers of colonial period fiction by men such as Yi Kwangsu, Na Tohyang, Kim Tongin, Yi Sang, and Hwang Sunwŏn.[13] "Skewered Beef" is a sketch of a destitute intellectual and his resourceful wife (different from the wives in several of his other stories, who are dependent on their husbands) that brings to mouth-watering life the interior of an urban drinking hole. "Angel for a Day" offers a heartwarming glimpse of one of the true heroine occupations of modern Korea—the bus girl (ch'ajang), who survived into the 1980s.

Though Ch'ae is not usually discussed alongside modernists such as Pak T'aewŏn and Yi Sang, that he was profoundly interested in the possibilities of narrative is evinced not only by the two dozen plays he left (most of them dating from the early 1930s) but also by experimental works of fiction such as "Juvesenility" (Somang), a dialogue between sisters in which we hear only the voice of the younger one. (The title of the story is a portmanteau word that combines the first syllable of sonyŏn, boy, with the second syllable of nomang, dotage, Ch'ae's intent presumably to indicate that the narrator's husband, in the view of his good wife, may be displaying early symptoms of dementia.)

This story was especially dear to Ch'ae's heart. Nine months after its publication Ch'ae mentioned in his essay "Saibi nongch'on munhak" (Pseudo-agrarian literature) that he considered it a better story than the canonic "Ch'isuk." And already by then, in another essay, "Yuǒn" (Last words), Ch'ae had reproduced the headnote: "A grown man should be able, if he wants, to plant himself smack dab in the middle of Chongno in the dog days of summer, then march right past the grain shop that's got him on credit." That quote, Ch'ae wrote in the latter essay, reflected his frustrations to the extent that he could find no better answer if someone were to ask him then and there for his last words. (His last will and testament, made public only in 2015,[14] specified that his corpse be draped in wildflowers and taken to a crematorium in a cart drawn by his friends with hemp ropes—the idea of being transported in a bier previously used for other corpses horrified him—and that his ashes, which he would otherwise have liked to be scattered at sea, be interred opposite the grave of his grandmother. The whole affair, he repeated, must be carried out with an absolute minimum of ceremony.) This frustration, and the contrariness of the husband in "Juvesenility," are embodied in characters throughout Ch'ae's oeuvre, ranging from the morphine addict in "Ungrateful Wretch" (1925) to the aggrieved and cantankerous Hwangju Auntie in "Sunset" (1948) and the feisty narrator of the posthumously published "Angel for a Day." The headnote to "Juvesenility" is strongly reminiscent of the last line of Dr. Stockmann, the central figure in Ibsen's *An Enemy of the People*: "the strongest man in the world is he who stands most alone."[15] Combine this posture with Ch'ae's choice of Ibsen's *A Doll's House* and its strong-willed protagonist, Nora, as the model for his very first novel, *Inhyǒng ǔi chip ǔl nawasǒ*, and it is tempting to conclude that by 1938 and the publication of "Juvesenility" Ch'ae had long since found congenial as a literary persona that of the subversive Ibsen, "father of the modern drama."

It is also fruitful to read "Juvesenility" for the light it sheds on Ch'ae's ambivalence toward women. Images of women in his fiction and drama range from the bold and independent (again, exemplified by Hwangju Auntie in "Sunset") to the self-sacrificing, passive, and dependent (the mother of the morphine addict in "Ungrateful Wretch" and the narrator's aunt in "Ch'isuk"). The narrator of "Juvesenility" tends toward the dependent end of the spectrum, her estimation of her husband and his unrealized potential posing an added burden to the man's load of frustration.[16]

Ch'ae also ventured into children's literature (a genre, along with short fiction, widely considered to be a Western import).[17] "The Grasshopper, the

Kingfisher, and the Ant" (Wangch'i wa sosae wa kemi) is a bravura example of the form, a fable complete with the author's characteristic insights into personality.

Of the two roundtable discussions included herein, the first, "Challenges Facing Contemporary Writers" (Hyŏndae chakka ch'angjak koshim haptamhoe), offers a rare glimpse from the colonial period of the practical problems involved in creative writing (punctuation, titles, plotting, writer's block, even stationery—apparently by 1937 it was becoming difficult to find quality writing paper!) as well as the workings of the mundan, the Korean literature establishment. In this discussion Ch'ae takes a back seat, allowing his younger and lesser-known companions to speak at length. In doing so he may have been mindful of the declining health of Kim Yujŏng, a writer seven years his junior, who was soon to meet his maker, and whom Ch'ae would memorialize four months later in a short essay, "Yujŏng and I" (Yujŏng kwa na).

The second roundtable discussion, "A Three-Way Conversation on Kungmin Literature" (Kungmin munhak ŭi kongjak chŏngdamhoe), brings us closer to the elephant in the room, here masquerading as a literary genre. Kungmin is a two-syllable word that literally means "people (min) of a country/nation/state (kuk)." Kuk as a prefix means "national/Korean." Thus "kungmin literature" would seem to mean the literature of the people of a country/state/nation, in other words national literature. The problem, of course, is that "national" presupposes sovereignty and autonomy, a status formally yielded by the Chosŏn kingdom (or more specifically the Great Han Empire, as Chosŏn was called in its last years) in the annexation treaty signed with Japan in 1910. By 1941, then, when this roundtable took place, "kungmin literature" had come to mean the literature of the subjects of a larger kuk, the Japanese imperial realm.[18]

Ch'ae is more active in this roundtable, speaking bluntly about an issue that would become ever more burdensome to Korean writers during the amhŭkki, the "dark period" from the late 1930s through 1945—the need to negotiate the pressure from imperial Japan as it faced increasing exigencies during the Pacific War, to produce a "wholesome and cheerful" kungmin literature in accordance with wartime emergency policies regarding cultural production. Ch'ae, along with Yi T'aejun and Yu Chino—three authors schooled in a European tradition of realist short fiction by masters such as Turgenev, Chekhov, and Zola—struggle to address the issue of whether it is possible to produce quality works of literature deemed uplifting in an era of total mobilization by the imperial center.

Is Ch'ae's 1940 anecdotal essay "Na ŭi 'kkot kwa pyŏngjŏng'" (translated here as "My 'Flower and Soldier'") an example of "wholesome and cheerful" kungmin literature? Is it grounds for labeling Ch'ae a writer "friendly to Japan"? The answers to these questions may be surmised in the structure of this short piece, which comprises two distinct sections. The first, constituting about one third of the essay, commemorates the historic and divine nature of the mission that has lately landed imperial Japan in the Pacific War, and is presumably the basis for scholar Kim Chaeyong's description of this as the first of Ch'ae's writings to clearly show the influence of "pro-Japanese fascism."[19] The remainder of the essay concerns an encounter, mediated at a distance by the narrator's nephew, between the narrator and a young soldier headed for the front lines. The inspiration for this second section was likely a pair of novels by Japanese infantryman Hino Ashihei (one of the authors referred to in the roundtable discussion of kungmin literature): Mugi to heitai (Wheat and soldiers, 1938) and Hana to heitai (Flowers and soldiers). The question for readers and scholars, then, is whether to engage with this essay primarily on the basis of the glorification of imperial Japan in the first section or on the basis of the personal experiences and the image of the selfless soldier in battle that won a mass audience for Hino's novels in the metropole and in colonial Korea.[20] Either way, it should be obvious where Ch'ae's heart lay.

Apart from "Minjok ŭi choein," Ch'ae's works from post-August 1945 have received comparatively little attention from scholars. And yet the three years between Liberation and the establishment of North and South Korea were an exceedingly rare period of literary production on the Korean peninsula unconstrained by state ideology. Scholarship on modern Korean literature has tended to emphasize the importance of socially engaged literature (ch'amyŏ munhak), and post-Liberation fiction is replete with examples. Ch'ae's "Mister Pang" (Misŭt'ŏ Pang) and "Sunset" illuminate in a way few history texts could the upheavals taking place on the Korean peninsula after 1945. "Sunset" in particular has the immediacy of reportage, and the narrator's comments about the likelihood of civil war are eerily prescient.

How then did Ch'ae Manshik in his relatively short lifetime produce a body of work that is one of the most imaginative and intertextual in modern Korean literary history, yet earn a reputation primarily as a satirist who only late in life came to grips with his role as a public intellectual during the colonial period? Yi Chuhyŏng's informative essay on the life and times of Ch'ae, combined with Ch'ae's own essays about his life as a writer, offer ample detail on the first part of this question. For Yi, Ch'ae must be understood in light of (1) his long experience as a reporter; (2) his experience of poverty; (3) his involvement in gold mining; (4) his conflicted marital life; (5) his submission to Japanese rule; (6) his neutral political and ideological stance during the post-Liberation period; (7) his fastidiousness; (8) and his faithfulness to his profession as a writer.[21]

Ch'ae's career as a journalist spanned approximately a decade, and his journalistic flair is evident in the panorama of colonial modernity he paints in section 3 of his signature story "Redimeidŭ insaeng." But even though his years in the editorial offices sharpened the writing skills he would need to bring his already distinctive voice fully alive, he regretted what he referred to in his 1938 essay "Irŏbŏrin 10 nyŏn" as "ten lost years." They were not of course lost entirely; several of his best-known works date from this period. The problem, in Ch'ae's eyes, is that he focused not on writing but on "other things."

Among those "other things" were the straitened circumstances that beset Ch'ae and his family for much of his life. Like the husband in "Juvesenility," who abruptly quits the kind of editorial job prized by an entire generation of colonial period intellectuals, Ch'ae left the *Tonga ilbo*—already by then possibly the premier Korean-language daily in the land—in October 1926 after all of 15 months on the job. Not until 1930, when he began work at *Kaebyŏk* (Genesis) magazine, did he return to full-time editorial work. But from 1936, when he resigned from the *Chosŏn ilbo*, until his death in 1950, he would attempt to support himself and his family primarily through his writing. Early on he adopted a publish-or-perish approach: as he mentions in "Ten Lost Years," when a manuscript deadline loomed and he had yet to settle on a title, nothing cleared the cobwebs more quickly than the realization of his stark living situation. Even after Liberation, when he returned to his home province of North Chŏlla, he continued to maintain a spare existence. From 1946 to 1948, when he produced his most important post-Liberation stories, he occupied a tiny room in his brother's home in Iri, its only furnishing a jury-rigged desk with barely enough room beneath to accommodate his folded legs. He had never had a home of his own, he was wont to lament.[22]

Ch'ae was also involved in a gold-mining venture that did not turn out well. Gold fever raged through colonial Korea in the 1930s.[23] In "Kŭm kwa munhak" (Gold and literature), an essay from early 1940, Ch'ae recounts the months he spent in the hills observing the lifestyle of the gold miners. This on-site research was done primarily to manage his own claim, but it also provided background for his 1937 novella "Chŏnggŏjang kŭnch'ŏ" (Near the bus station) and his 1941 novel Kŭm ŭi chŏng'yŏl (A passion for gold). The brother of the husband in "Juvesenility" (like a brother of Ch'ae's) is a gold miner, and a group of gold miners add a bit of color to "Angel for a Day." It is obvious from "Kŭm kwa munhak" that Ch'ae was fascinated with the colonial Korean gold rush but was also aware of its inflationary potential, just as he recognized the potential economic fallout from the grain speculation he described so realistically in T'angnyu. This article offers a case study in the rigor of Ch'ae's research. Not only does he mention gleaning gold-mining jargon from a book, but also he tells us that when asked by Yi Kwangsu and Kim Tongin about the accuracy of his graphic depiction of morphine addiction in "Ungrateful Wretch," he replied that his descriptions were based on firsthand observation. Likewise, he learned through observation and explanations from specialists about the intricacies of trading for grain futures.

The ambivalence evident in the images of women in many of Ch'ae's works, along with the occasional glimpse of a strained marriage in such important works as "Redimeidŭ insaeng" and "Maeng sunsa" (Constable Maeng), may reflect the author's own experiences. His first marriage, when he was still in his teens, was to a traditional woman and was urged upon him by his parents; it seems to have been a loveless affair. He subsequently married a university graduate. He had two children by the first spouse and three by the second. In this volume the ambivalence is mirrored in the relationship between the wife and the concubine in Whatever Possessed Me?, Ch'ae's delightful take on the traditional kajŏng sosŏl, or story of household intrigue.

As for Ch'ae's submission (kulbok) to Japanese colonial rule, the husband's silent but very public one-man battle against the summer heat in "Juvesenility" tells us that intellectuals in colonial Korea—at least those who remained on the peninsula—must have accommodated themselves to imperial power in a variety of ways. Anecdotal evidence suggests that not a few among the privileged were outwardly model colonial subjects while secretly supporting the Korean provisional government in Shanghai and/or more active forms of resistance against the Japanese. Outwardly Ch'ae paid lip service to the demands of the total mobilization of the Japanese empire during the war years: in a 1941 essay, "Munhak kwa chŏnch'ejuŭi" (Literature and totalitarianism), he tells himself that his first order of business is to purge himself of all vestiges of liberal ideology. Inwardly he acknowledged this stance. In the words of his alter ego in "Minjok ŭi choein," perhaps as accurate a description as any of the fate of so many of Ch'ae's generation: "I was neither clever nor courageous, and before I knew it I was one of that class of mediocre, bungling, submissive men, but deep down inside that's not how I wanted it to be."[24]

After 1945, free of the constraints of total mobilization, Ch'ae resumed the keen critique of his society begun in works such as "Redimeidŭ insaeng" and "Ch'isuk." All were fair game: wealthy and powerful collaborators (Squire Paek in "Mister Pang" and Pak Chaech'un in "Sunset"), the colonial period constabulary ("Constable Maeng"), educators (the narrator of "Sunset" and the protagonist of the posthumous "Ch'ŏja"), officials responsible for returning Japanese-held land to the former Korean owners ("Non iyagi" [A tale of two paddies]), blind followers of Yi Sŭngman, first president of the Republic of Korea (Hwangju Auntie in "Sunset"), and those who benefited from the American military occupation of the southern sector of the Korean peninsula before the establishment of the ROK and the Democratic People's Republic of Korea (North Korea) in 1948 (Pak Ch'unja in "Sunset" and the protagonist of "Mister Pang"). At a time when writers and other artists were aligning themselves with left-wing or right-wing organizations, Ch'ae remained ideologically aloof. He was not among the more than 100 established writers, including such luminaries as the aforementioned Yi T'aejun and Pak T'aewŏn, who moved permanently from the southern sector of the peninsula to the north—the wŏlbuk ("gone north") writers, the publication of whose works was subsequently banned in South Korea until the democratization of the political process there in the late 1980s.

In his 1935 anecdotal essay "A Writing Worm's Life" (Munch'ung iran chonjae) Ch'ae asked, "Why . . . does literature have such a tight hold on me?" It was a question he would revisit for the rest of his life. The last two of the characteristics mentioned by Yi Chuhyŏng—Ch'ae's personal fastidiousness and his professionalism as a writer—may help to explain. Contemporaries such as Yi Muyŏng observed obsessive-compulsive tendencies in Ch'ae, such as his habit of wiping down spoon and chopsticks when dining away from home. Ch'ae urged a similar precaution upon literary critics in an early essay, "P'yŏngnon'ga e taehan chakka rosŏ ŭi pulbok" (An author's protest to a critic): the critic should take the same approach to a literary work that a doctor takes with a patient. This inclination seems to have prompted the two-year bout of writer's block Ch'ae mentions in his 1939 essay "Chajak annae" (A guide to my works): from July 1934, when he published "Redimeidŭ insaeng," until July 1936, he published no fiction except for the mystery novel Yŏmma (The enchantress)[25] preferring instead to ruminate about himself and the viability of his works. Afterward, for example, he came to think of "My Innocent Uncle" as a healthful by-product of his 1936 story "Myŏngil" (Tomorrow), itself an outgrowth of "Redimeidŭ insaeng." The work of his that contained the healthiest outlook, he wrote in "Chajak annae," was the play *Chehyangnal* (Memorial day).

On the other hand, Ch'ae's compulsiveness certainly contributed to his prolific output once he began writing full time—only in 1945 and 1947 were there notable lapses in his output. Early on, he tells us in "Irŏbŏrin 10 nyŏn," he adopted the goal of turning out twenty manuscript pages a night (he routinely stayed up until 3 or 4 a.m., and sometimes throughout the night). But the effort came at a cost, as he relates in an earlier essay, "Shinbun chapch'o" (A few particulars about yours truly): the nervous exhaustion he'd experienced as a middle school student cramming his brain with English vocabulary had become chronic, he had tried and discarded sleeping pills, he was subject to racking headaches and auditory hallucinations, and sleepless nights had become the norm.

Why then did literature—which by 1940 he had come to describe as caustic soda[26]—exert such a grip on Ch'ae Manshik, why was he so faithful to a calling that led him to the verge of psychosis and left him in constant penury? As an educated young man in a colonized society in which as many as 90 percent of the populace may have been illiterate, did he inherit the Intellectual Man's Burden born by centuries of his forebears dating back at least to Shilla times? He seems to have been born to the task. In 1910, the year Chosŏn was formally colonized by imperial Japan, he entered primary school. Already by then he was being home-schooled in classical Chinese.[27] After graduation from secondary school he spent a year at Waseda University in Tokyo, following in the footsteps of Yi Kwangsu and preceding another giant of modern Korean literature, Hwang Sunwŏn. Returning to Korea after the Great Kanto Earthquake of 1923, in the wake of which Korean residents of Japan were attacked and killed, Ch'ae launched his writing career and worked at a succession of editorial posts before turning to creative writing full time in 1936.

Or was his a "ready-made life," mass-produced, albeit in ever decreasing quantities, for public life in a modernizing colonial society? Did he relish his role as a public offender, one who could satirize both those who were "friendly with Japan" and the ineffectual intellectuals who weren't, who could critique both modernity and tradition, both Christianity and native religiosity? As persuasive as these possibilities may be, one might wonder, after reading the works in this volume and perusing the iconic photographs of the author in soccer gear as a schoolboy or dressed to the nines (like the husband in "Juvesenility") as an adult and smiling a radiant, peace-under-heaven smile, if the strongest hold that literature had on him was simply the joy of producing a story well told.

Works Cited

Ch'ae Manshik. *Ch'ae Manshik chŏnjip*, 10 vols. Seoul: Ch'angjak kwa pip'yŏng sa, 1989.

——. "Chajak annae." *Ch'ŏngsaekchi*, May 1939; *Ch'ae Manshik chŏnjip*, vol. 9, 516–21.

——. "Chehyang nal." *Chogwang*, November 1937; "Memorial Day," trans. Jinhee Kim, in *Korean Drama Under Japanese Occupation: Plays by Ch'i-jin Yu and Man-sik Ch'ae* (Paramus, N.J.: Homa & Sekey, 2004), 137–74.

——. "Ch'isuk." *Tonga ilbo*, March 25–30, 1938; "My Innocent Uncle," trans. Bruce and Ju-Chan Fulton, in *Modern Korean Fiction: An Anthology*, ed. Bruce Fulton and Youngmin Kwon (New York: Columbia University Press, 2005), 95–111; and *The Norton Anthology of World Literature*, 3rd ed., vol. F (New York: Norton, 2012), 418–30.

——. "Ch'ŏja." *Chugan Sŏul*, nos. 34, 35 (1948); "The Wife and Children," trans. Bruce and Ju-Chan Fulton, in *Land of Exile: Contemporary Korean Fiction*, rev. and exp. ed., trans. and ed. Marshall R. Pihl and Bruce and Ju-Chan Fulton (Armonk, N.Y.: M.E. Sharpe, 2007), 3–12.

——. "Chŏnggojang kŭnch'ŏ." *Yŏsŏng* 2, nos. 3–10 (1937); *Ch'ae Manshik chŏnjip*, vol. 5, 291–364.

——. "Irŏbŏrin 10 nyŏn." *Chosŏn ilbo*, February 18–26, 1938; *Ch'ae Manshik chŏnjip*, vol. 9, 503–15.

——. "Kŭm kwa munhak." *Inmun p'yŏngnon*, February 1940; *Ch'ae Manshik chŏnjip*, vol. 9, 526–32.

——. *Kŭm ŭi chŏng 'yŏl*. Seoul: Yŏngch'ang sŏ'gwan, 1941; *Ch'ae Manshik chŏnjip*, vol. 3, 193–516.

——. "Maeng sunsa." *Paengmin*, February 1946; "Constable Maeng," trans. Joel Stevenson, in *Waxen Wings: The Acta Koreana Anthology of Short Fiction from Korea*, ed. Bruce Fulton (St. Paul, Minn.: Koryo Press, 2011), 21–33.

——. "Minjok ŭi choein." *Paengmin*, October–November 1948; *Ch'ae Manshik chŏnjip*, vol. 8, 414–58.

——. "Munhak kwa chŏnch'ejuŭi," *Samch'ŏlli*, January 1941; *Ch'ae Manshik chŏnjip*, vol. 10, 226–32.

———. "Non iyagi." In Yŏm Sangsŏp et al., *Haebang munhak sŏnjip* [A selection of post-Liberation literature] (Seoul: Chongno sŏwŏn, 1948); "Once Upon a Paddy," trans. Robert Armstrong, in *My Innocent Uncle*, trans. Bruce and Ju-Chan Fulton, Kim Chong-un, and Robert Armstrong, ed. Ross King and Bruce Fulton (Seoul: Jimoondang, 2003), 81–113.

———. "P'allyŏgan mom." *Shin kajŏng*, August 1933; "Sold Into Servitude," trans. Theresa Joo, University of British Columbia, 2008, manuscript.

———. "P'yŏngnon'ga e taehan chakka rosŏ ŭi pulbok." *Tonga ilbo*, February 14, 15, 17, 20, 21, 1931; *Ch'ae Manshik chŏnjip*, vol. 10, 20–27.

———. "Redimeidŭ insaeng." *Shindonga*, May–July 1934; "A Ready-Made Life" in *A Ready-Made Life: Early Masters of Modern Korean Fiction*, trans. Kim Chong-un and Bruce Fulton (Honolulu: University of Hawai'i Press, 1998), 55–80.

———. "Saibi nongch'on munhak." *Chogwang*, July 1939; *Ch'ae Manshik chŏnjip*, vol. 9, 522–25.

———. "Shim pongsa." *Shinshidae*, November 1944–January 1945; *Ch'ae Manshik chŏnjip*, vol. 6, 165–204.

———. "Shinbyŏn chapch'o." *Chungang*, September 1936; *Ch'ae Manshik chŏnjip*, vol. 10, 547–51.

———. *T'aepy'ŏng ch'ŏnha*. *Chogwang*, January–September 1938 (therein titled *Ch'ŏnha t'aep'yŏng ch'un*); Seoul: Tongji sa, 1948; *Ch'ae Manshik chŏnjip*, vol. 3, 7–192; *Peace Under Heaven*, trans. Chun Kyung-Ja (Armonk, N.Y.: M.E. Sharpe, 1993).

———. *T'angnyu*. *Chosŏn ilbo*, October 13, 1937–May 17, 1938; *Ch'ae Manshik chŏnjip*, vol. 2, 7–469.

———. "Yuŏn." *Chogwang*, November 1938; *Ch'ae Manshik chŏnjip*, vol. 10, 568–70.

Hwang Sunwŏn. "Nŭp." In *Hwang Sunwŏn tanp'yŏnjip* [Stories by Hwang Sunwŏn] (Seoul: Hansŏng tosŏ, 1940); "The Pond" in *Lost Souls: Stories by Hwang Sunwŏn*, trans. Bruce and Ju-Chan Fulton (New York: Columbia University Press, 2010), 3–14.

Kim Tongin. "Sajin wa p'yŏnji." *Wŏlgan maeshin*, April 1934; "The Photograph and the Letter" in *A Ready-Made Life: Early Masters of Modern Korean Fiction*, trans. Kim Chong-un and Bruce Fulton (Honolulu: University of Hawai'i Press, 1998), 81–88.

Kim Yujŏng. "Ttaraji" [Worthless]. *Chogwang*, February 1937; *Wŏnbon Kim Yujŏng chŏnjip* [Collected writings of Kim Yujŏng: From the original editions], rev. and exp. ed., ed. Chŏn Shinjae (Seoul: Kang, 2012), 302–23.

Na Tohyang. "Yŏibalsa." *Paekcho*, September 1923; "The Lady Barber" in *A Ready-Made Life: Early Masters of Modern Korean Fiction*, trans. Kim Chong-un and Bruce Fulton (Honolulu: University of Hawai'i Press, 1998), 17–22.

Yi Kwangsu. *Mujŏng, Maeil shinbo*, January 1–June 14, 1917; "The Heartless," trans. Ann Sung-hi Lee, in *Yi Kwangsu and Mujŏng* (Ithaca, N.Y.: Cornell East Asia Series, 2006), 75–348.

Yi Sang. "Nalgae." *Chogwang*, September 1936; "Wings," trans. Kevin O'Rourke, manuscript.

NOTES

1. "Munin ment'al t'esŭt'ŭ," in *Ch'ae Manshik chŏnjip* [Collected writings of Ch'ae Manshik], ed. Chŏn Kwangyong, Yi Sŏnyŏng, Yŏm Muung, Yi Chuhyŏng, Ch'oe Wŏnshik, and Chŏng Haeryŏm (Seoul: Ch'angjak kwa pip'yŏng sa, 1989), vol. 9, 499.

2. See, for example, the weblog essay "'Ch'ae Manshik sosŏlbi' e haedangdoenŭn kŭl" [About the "Monument to Ch'ae Manshik's Fiction"], whose author (screen name Nattal) begins with a two-sentence acknowledgment of Ch'ae as a satirist in the tradition of *p'ansori*-influenced fictional narratives but devotes the remainder of the essay to his "friendly to Japan" conduct: http://blog.ohmynews.com/ 99447/tag/%EC%B1%84%EB%A7%8C%EC%8B%9D%20%EC%86%8C %EC%84%A4%EB%B9%84.

3. See, for example, Kim Chaeyong, "Ch'inil munhak chakp'um mongnok" [Inventory of collaborationist literary works], *Shilch'ŏn munhak*, autumn 2002; accessed at www.artnstudy.com/zineasf/Nowart/penitence/lecture/03.htm#36. The list of 42 writers includes such luminaries as Yi Kwangsu, often cited as the father of modern Korean literature; Sŏ Chŏngju, one of modern Korea's most accomplished poets; Kim Tongin, a founder of early modern realist fiction; Pak T'aewŏn, a prominent modernist; the literary historian Paek Ch'ŏl; Mo Yunsuk and No Ch'ŏnmyŏng, stylistically different but equally iconic women writers; and Ch'oe Namsŏn and Chu Yohan, exemplars of the "new poetry." The entry for Ch'ae Manshik lists 13 suspect writings, published between 1940 and 1944—during the depths of the *amhŭkki*, or "Dark Period," when imperial Japanese rule, conditioned by the demands of the Pacific War, became increasingly burdensome and opportunities for publishing in the Korean language dwindled significantly.

4. Kwŏn Yŏngmin, ed., *Hanguk hyŏndae munhak taesajŏn* [Encyclopedia of modern Korean literature](Seoul: Sŏul taehakkyo ch'ulp'anbu, 2004), 941.

5. Hwang Sŏgyŏng and Shin Hyŏngch'ŏl, "'Piroso ch'ungmanhan i Hanguk munhaksa rŭl utchimara': 'Hwang Sŏgyŏng ŭi Hanguk myŏngdanp'yŏn 101' e puch'inŭn int'ŏbyu" [Laugh not, Korea finally has a literature to be proud of: Interview

marking the publication of *Hwang Sŏgyŏng's 101 best Korean short stories*], *Munhak tongne* 82 (spring 2015): 534–70. (The "i Hanguk munhaksa" in the title of this interview derives from the title of a 1965 essay by Kim Suyŏng, one of the most influential poets of modern Korea.) In their disproportionate coverage of Ch'ae and his contemporary Yŏm Sangsŏp (the two of them are referred to by Hwang in the interview as the twin pillars of colonial period fiction), for example, two standard reference works on modern Korean literature seem to bear out Hwang's observation. Whereas Yŏm is the subject of more than seven pages of reference materials in Kwŏn Yŏngmin's *Hanguk kŭndae munin taesajŏn* [Directory of early modern Korean writers] (Seoul: Asea munhwasa, 1990; see 692–99) and six and a half columns of reference materials in Kwon's *Hanguk hyŏndae munhak taesajŏn* (549–52), scholarly works on Ch'ae constitute less than two pages in the former (1196–98) and a column and a half (945–46) in the latter. A more balanced view of Ch'ae's oeuvre may be found in the interpretive essay appearing at the end of his collected works: Yi Chuhyŏng, "Ch'ae Manshik ŭi saengae wa chakp'um segye," [Ch'ae Manshik's life and literary world], *Ch'ae Manshik chŏnjip*, vol. 10, 618–31.

6. Kong Chonggu, "Ch'ae Manshik ŭi sanmun yŏngu," *Hyŏndae sosŏl yŏngu* 60 (December 30, 2015): 5–31. For an updated list comprising 476 items of Korean critical writing on Ch'ae, see: http://www.riss.kr/search/Search.do?colName=re_a_kor&query=%EC%B1%84%EB%A7%8C%EC%8B%9D.

7. Yi Chuhyŏng, "Ch'ae Manshik ŭi saengae wa chakp'um segye," 618.

8. See Marshall R. Pihl, *The Korean Singer of Tales* (Cambridge, Mass.: Harvard University Press, 1994); and Chan Park, *Voices from the Straw Mat: Toward an Ethnography of Korean Story Singing* (Honolulu: University of Hawai'i Press, 2003).

9. Pang Minho devotes almost one third of his study on Ch'ae to the intertextuality in his works: *Ch'ae Manshik kwa Chosŏnjŏk kŭndae munhak ŭi kusang* [Ch'ae Manshik and the embodiment of a Chosŏn-ist earlymodern literature] (Seoul: Somyŏng ch'ulp'an, 2001), chapter 3. See also the feature "Parody in Modern Korean Fiction," ed. Ross King and Bruce Fulton, consisting of an overview by King and Fulton, essays by King, Fulton, Dafna Zur, and Leif Olsen, and stories by Yi Munyŏl (translated by Yi So-Jung) and Chu Insŏk (translated by Jenny Kim), *Acta Koreana* 8, no. 2 (July 2005): 1–95, 139–66.

10. Published posthumously in *Hanguk munhak chŏnjip* [Collected works of modern Korean literature] (Seoul: Minjung sŏgwan, 1960), , vol. 33; reprinted in *Ch'ae Manshik chŏnjip*, vol. 9, 28–101.

11. Publication was suspended early in 1945, the magazine having apparently ceased operation: editors' headnote to "Shim pongsa," *Ch'ae Manshik chŏnjip*, vol. 6, 164. Yet another work titled "Shim pongsa," an unfinished story published in the short-lived monthly *Hyŏptong* in March, May, July, and September 1949, is cited by Ch'oe

Yunyŏng in "1930-nyŏndae hŭigok ŭi kojŏn kyesŭng yangsang: Ch'ae Manshik ŭi <Shim pongsa> rŭl chungshim ŭro" [Legacy of the classical in 1930s drama: Ch'ae Manshik's Blind Man Shim (1936)], Midia wa kongyŏn yesul yŏngu 7, no. 3 (2012): 3.

12. Kelly Y. Jeong, Crisis of Gender and the Nation in Korean Literature and Cinema: Modernity Arrives Again (Lanham, Md.: Lexington Books, 2011), 46.

13. See, for example, the works by Yi Kwangsu, Na Tohyang, Kim Tongin, Yi Sang, and Hwang Sunwŏn in "Works Cited."

14. Kim T'aewan, "Ch'oech'o konggaehanŭn Ch'ae Manshik ŭi yuŏnjang" [Ch'ae Manshik's last will and testament, made public for the first time], Wŏlgan Chosŏn, December 2015; http://monthly.chosun.com/client/news/viw.asp?ctcd=F&nNews Numb=201512100053.

15. Henrik Ibsen, An Enemy of the People, in Four Great Plays by Ibsen, trans. R. Farquhar-son Sharp (New York: Bantam Books, 1967), 215.

16. See Bruce Fulton, "Genie for My Hopes," afterword to Ch'ae Man-Sik, Juvesenility, trans. Bruce and Ju-Chan Fulton, Bi-lingual Edition Modern Korean Literature 101 (Seoul: Asia Publishers, 2015), 65, 67, 69, 71, 73, 75.

17. See Dafna Zur, "Children's Literature in Late Colonial Korea," Azalea: Journal of Korean Literature and Culture 5 (2012): 347–53.

18. On the slippery concept of kungmin literature see Serk-Bae Suh, Treacherous Transla-tion: Culture, Nationalism, and Colonialism in Korea and Japan from the 1910s Through the 1960s (Berkeley: University of California Press, 2013), 96–98.

19. Kim Chaeyong, Hyŏmnyŏk kwa chŏhang: Ilchaemal sahoe wa munhwa [Cooperation and resistance: Society and culture late in the Japanese colonial period] (Seoul: Somyŏng ch'ulp'an, 2004), 99. "Na ŭi 'Kkot kwa pyŏngjŏng'" is the very first entry in Kim's inventory of Ch'ae's "friendly to Japan" works: Kim Chaeyong, "Ch'inil munhak chakp'um mongnok." The discussion of Ch'ae's "Na ŭi 'Kkot kwa pyŏngjŏng'" in Nattal, "'Ch'ae Manshik sosŏlbi' e haedangdoenŭn kŭl," is lim-ited to the first two sentences of that essay, where the glorification of imperial Japan is most obvious.

20. See David M. Rosenfeld, Unhappy Soldier: Hino Ashihei and Japanese World War II Lit-erature (Lanham, Md.: Lexington Books, 2002). Mugi to heitai was made into a film in 1939 and the same year was translated into Korean by Nishimura Shintaro as Pori wa pyŏngjŏng (Barley and soldiers). Nishimura was a well-known government censor in colonial Korea; see Pak Kwanghyŏn's study of this figure, "Kŏmyŏlgwan Nishimura Shint'aro e kwanhan koch'al," Hanguk munhak yŏngu [Research on Ko-rean literature] 32 (June 2007): 93–127.

21. Yi Chuhyŏng, "Ch'ae Manshik ŭi saengae wa chakp'um segye," 619–20.

22. Ku Chungsŏ, "Sanghwang ŭi hyŏngsangjŏk inshik" [Perception conditioned by circumstance], in Munhakchŏk hyonshil ŭi chŏn'gae: Ku Chungsŏ p'yŏngnon sŏnjip [The

development of a literary reality: Selected critical essays by Ku Chungsŏ] (Seoul: Ch'angjak kwa pip'yŏng sa, 2006), 71.

23. For a volume of "nonfiction novel" anecdotes about gold mining in 1930s Korea, drawing on contemporary press accounts as well as recent research on historical figures and events from that decade, see Chŏn Ponggwan, *Hwanggŭmgwang shidae* [Age of the gold craze] (Seoul: Sallim, 2005).

24. "Minjok ŭi choein," *Ch'ae Manshik chŏnjip*, vol. 8, 434; translation ours.

25. *Yŏmma* was serialized in 124 installments in the *Chosŏn ilbo*, from May to November 1934, and reprinted in *Ch'ae Manshik chŏnjip*, vol. 1. It is rarely mentioned in critical writing on Ch'ae's works.

26. "Munhak ŭl na ch'ŏrŏm haesŏnŭn" [Don't take up literature like I did, or else], *Munjang*, February 1940; *Ch'ae Manshik chŏnjip*, vol. 9, 533–34.

27. For an outline of Ch'ae's personal history see *Ch'ae Manshik chŏnjip*, vol. 10, 601–3.

1

SUNSET

(Nakcho, 1948)

I

There we were, working up a sweat over our bowls of kalguksu, the noodles boiled in honest-to-goodness chicken broth.

"How I wish your auntie from Hwangju could feast on a bowl of this, oh yes I do," muttered Mother, the way she did when something was eating away at her. "She didn't come out and say it, but I can tell she won't bring herself to boil up some baby hens to keep herself nourished during the dog days. Just goes to show you, folks are getting squeezed harder by the day."

"Well, she's more plentiful than she used to be," sniped Father.

Mother was on good terms with Hwangju Auntie, but Father had never really taken to her.

"My dear husband, whatever do you mean? Didn't you hear she had to put her home on the market, that nice Japanese house, and she's only asking 300,000 hwan? And with the proceeds she looks to find herself a monthly rental or a little place away from downtown, and she'll have to live off what's left."

"Still, she's plentiful in several ways. She's gained weight, right? More snobbish, right? More of a nuisance, right? A sweeter sweet-talker, right? And her esteemed daughter is more, ah, enlightened, shall we say, in the ways of Westerners? The lady would make a great campaign speaker, that's for sure."

"There you go again," chuckled Mother.

"I'm serious." Father smiled in spite of himself. "She makes more racket than a bunch of tin cans. Gives me a headache."

"Land sakes, even tin cans are good for something. Everything and everyone in this world has a function, a way of doing things." Mother was so easygoing. Otherwise, at this juncture she would have put her foot down and said something like, *My dear husband, would you please be quiet? You say she's gained weight, is more snobbish, more of a nuisance, and more of a sweet-talker, but look at you—you're gaining in peevishness and prejudice. You're so sarcastic about others, you're so spiteful, so cold-hearted, it gives me a headache.* Which would have led to a back-and-forth, then built to a squabble, and then a fight, and ultimately a deep rift.

Thank god for Mother's goodwill hunting—her disposition was our family's blessing. Serving our stingy, unfeeling father, avoiding discord and keeping the peace—it was all thanks to her refusal to pick on others for their faults and mistakes, and instead to give them the benefit of the doubt.

Father blamed me for taking after Mother in not making waves and looking at the world in a positive light—which in his estimation meant that, grown man though I was, I had a shallow understanding of things and was short on initiative.

True enough, I believe I inherited more of Mother's generous and easygoing nature than Father's narrow mind and cold heart, and I tended to look on the sunny side, as a result of which maybe I was a bit shallow and lacking in get-up-and-go. But I always considered it a blessing that I took after Mother more than Father.

If only Father weren't so intolerant and heartless. The poor man gets involved in something that has nothing to do with him, but he can't stomach it, he hates the sight of it, he has to say something nasty or sarcastic, and people don't want to be around him, so he gets shunned. Whether the issue is petty or important, he doesn't try to view it from a different angle or exercise tolerance. Saying something's wrong or he can't stand it is one thing, but he doesn't leave it at that and instead adds spiteful, cynical comments—it's like a perverse pastime.

Until Liberation we somehow convinced ourselves Father was born that way, that his mean-spiritedness, perverse though it was, was only a habit. But as the wheels of Liberation cranked forward, his sardonic traits were aggravated by economic changes that hit us where it hurt.

Here's what our family had before Liberation: enough land to produce 300 sacks of grain a year, and a whale-size tile-roof house in the heart of Kye-dong in Seoul, consisting of two structures separated by a spacious courtyard.

The 300 sacks of grain took care of our food and household expenses, and though you couldn't call us extravagant, you wouldn't catch anybody saying we were stingy to others, and as far as debts were concerned, well, we hardly knew what they were. We were comfortable and content with our life.

And then one day, boom! Liberation was here.

The annual yield from our land, after we deducted one third of the crop for our tenant farmer, dropped from 300 sacks to 200. We had to adjust our annual household budget accordingly.

But while our share of the harvest shrank, the prices of goods went through the roof. Adjusting our household expenditures to 200 sacks of grain was only a remote possibility. Why? Because the 200 sacks of rice you sold to the government brought a government-set amount, but what you paid for commodities was the going rate on the private market.

Now don't get me wrong, government-controlled prices for grain were also in effect at the end of the colonial period. We had to offer up the entire harvest to the empire at 10 wŏn a sack, but because the gap between the set price for grain and the market prices for everything else wasn't that great, we were able to pluck our feathers to fill it.

But after Liberation? Forget it.

Last fall, the price we got for our 200 sacks of rice from the land worked by our tenant farmer was on the order of 250,000 wŏn. Subtracting land tax and all the other taxes, we ended up with a little over 200,000 in our pocket.

Even after tightening our belts for everything except food, we still have to spend 40,000 a month, and that's right now, in 1948 currency. Do the math—200,000 gets you through five months.

So what do you do the other seven months?

As for me, I get 7,000 or 8,000 a month as a grade school teacher. That money goes to little old me, for tobacco, books, a pair of new socks, an occasional lunch or hot drink if I happen to run into someone—but I'm no wastrel, I steer clear of booze—and guess what, I still feel short, and I sense hard-up days on the horizon. Hell, I can't even think of contributing a measly 100 wŏn to the family larder.

Though he didn't come right out and say it, Father made no secret of his wish that as long as I fancied myself a salary man, I should swap my dead-end job as a grade school teacher for a position as a civil servant: that way

I could always pick up a few extra *wŏn* under the table, get a much more generous food ration, and throw my public official weight around, and if I played my cards right and caught a royal straight flush, then one fine morning I'd wake up to find myself in charge of a new destiny.

The problem was, I had no intention of bending to his wishes.

I don't mean to say that being a civil servant was bad. But using your position to write recommendations in return for under-the-table payments? That's not the way for a shining prince like me.

I can't speak for others, but far be it from me to commit the injustice of misusing my position to exceed my authority or, worse, exercising my power for the sake of ill-gotten gain. Unrighteous fame and riches are to me like drifting clouds, said Master Gong—precisely my feelings and attitude, and they will never change.

Committing such injustices as a public servant—not only had it never crossed my mind, I considered my teaching job a heaven-sent vocation. Taking innocent children under my wing and teaching and guiding them was my one and only mission as a human being.

A new day had dawned, a time to establish a new nation. Those who would ultimately shoulder our nation's responsibilities were the very children I was now nurturing. I could not have been more proud and joyful that I was teaching and guiding that workforce of the future.

Even if my family were to sink further, even if our fortunes declined, even if I had to cut down on my meals and go around in rags, I would keep to my heaven-sent calling.

My family began to accumulate debt. In the two-plus years from spring 1946 to now, the sum grew to over 300,000 *wŏn*.

When we tried to sell our farmland, our tenant farmers slashed their offer but gave no indication of buying—an understandable calculation on their part, because they smelled land reform and redistribution in the air.

And so our only option for retiring the more urgent debts was to sell the Kye-dong home and buy our present house in Kahoe-dong, a single building with three rooms.

Selling off the grand home and settling into a smaller one to pay off our debts, were we then able to return to a stable life and maintain a balanced budget? you might ask. Well, no—because our expenses continued to exceed our income. By next year we'd be facing another few hundred thousand *wŏn* of debt.

There was nothing left but to sell this house too, or else dump the farmland at a rock-bottom price. I could see it now—in less than three years our family would be among the poorest of the poor—no land, no home or home site, clinging to a sheer strand of fate.

Of course we had to cut our household expenses, but Father had to eliminate some of his spending as well. His spring and fall sightseeing jaunts with his friends lurched to a stop. He occasionally skipped the monthly poetry club social, and more recently was attending every other month. And then there were the half dozen or so gatherings a year, centered in the new year's and harvest festival holidays, and also including the *hanshik* and *tano* festivals, the ninth-month-ninth-day and winter solstice days, and finally his birthday on lunar October 3—events for which he set out fine spirits and plentiful *anju*, invited his good buddies, occasionally hired a *kisaeng* for eye candy and entertainment, and by the end of the night had everyone reciting poetry and kicking up his heels. First to go were all the events save his birthday and the new year's and harvest festivals. And then the latter two were jettisoned as well. That left only the birthday celebration, with the food presentation simplified to the extreme. The *kisaeng* were history.

When a buddy stopped by to cadge a drink and a snack to greet the sunset, Father couldn't help feeling flustered.

The loves of Father's life, which had lit up his later years in pleasure— friends, spirits, poetry, scenic wonders—went up in smoke, most of them. And along with them his solace and joy.

With our household growing more straitened by the day, Father felt doomed. With no friends, no spirits, no poetry, no scenic wonders to grace his last years—in short, with no pleasure in life—he was riddled with dissatisfaction.

Whatever matter came up, large or small, whether it directly concerned him or not, he viewed it as unjust and unreasonable, wrong and nonsensical. Words and actions, whether of acquaintances or strangers, got under his skin and didn't sit right with him.

And so he complained. But whether it was his discontent, his grievances, or his dissatisfaction, where could he rant and rave, where could he release his pent-up anger, his gripes and complaints?

Father was by nature narrow-minded and warped. What was worse, albeit understandable enough, his twisted temperament grew more severe in his discouragement—through no fault of his own, for external reasons, the household was collapsing, everything was going wrong, and for his bottled-up rage, his gripes and grievances, there was no reasonable outlet, no proper target.

Among those who were closest to Father was Yun, who knew him especially well. "Look, man, just because you never became top dog is no reason to be cantankerous till you're in the grave. So the family's hard up and the economy's going to hell—why can't you take it like a grown man instead of getting a stick up your ass? Why are you always so mean to everyone? Where's the pleasure in that?" Such was Yun's speech, half advice and half scolding.

A man such as Father couldn't help taking a dim view of Hwangju Auntie. She came across to him as a noisy, unladylike, smooth-talking busybody.

2

Speak of the tiger, who should arrive then but Hwangju Auntie herself. As soon as her sumo-size bulk had settled inside the gate, she blasted a greeting that could have awakened the entire block: "Oh my little sister, where have you been all this time, locked up here? I've been *soooo* worried."

Actually Auntie dropped by a good three times a month. Not so much because of matters she needed to attend to but because she missed my mother like she would have a blood sister.

She could carry on all she wanted about Mother not budging from home, but the fact was, Mother paid her a monthly visit.

Inevitably, therefore, the two ladies got to see each other at least every week and a half, and at most every five or six days. Such were the intervals that made Hwangju Auntie *soooo* worried, or as Father was wont to say, turned her into a crybaby.

My mother sprang up at the sight of her. "Aigu! Come on in, my big sister. We were just talking about you."

By the time she'd waddled across the yard, Hwangju Auntie was talking a blue streak: "No wonder my ears were so itchy. . . . And oh look, my dear brother's here too. How are you surviving this heat? It's so maddening, every day, hot hot hot. . . . Well, goodness gracious, look who's here, my dear nephew—that's right, it's summer break, isn't it—nice to have some time on your hands, eh? . . . And just look, how are you, little baby? Oh, you're so cute I could die! And behaving so nicely for the grownups in this heat—would you look at your mom, she never rests! I feel like such a lazybones, Madam

Peace Under Heaven. . . . And so, my dear little sister—oh heavens, don't you look worn. Every Kim, Pak, and Yi is suffering from this heat, and you too, I bet."

Having gone through the family roster with an oh-so-polite and affectionate greeting for each and every one of us, she stepped up onto the veranda.

To hear the constant "my dear little sister" and "my dear big sister," you would think they were close relatives, but in truth they were umpteen degrees removed, so distant you could hardly call them family, so remote the two women's children could have safely joined in marriage.

For all the emphasis that's put on degrees of distance in a family relationship, the fact is, if you live near each other and visit frequently, and if it happens that you tend to agree on things, it's only natural you'll become closer, and that's pretty much how it was with Hwangju Auntie and us.

It was back in the *kisa* year, which would have been 1929, that she moved to Seoul with her kids from Hwangju in Hwanghae Province. In the *kyŏngjin* year—1940, that is—she followed her oldest son, Chaech'un, and his wife back home. Finally, just two years ago, the *pyŏngsul* year, she crossed the 38th parallel, the newly drawn dividing line that had come with Liberation the preceding year, and returned to Seoul. Since then, with our two families living in the same city, we've enjoyed relations every bit as close as those of first cousins, aunts and uncles, nephews and nieces.

Even back in Hwangju she had enjoyed making two or three trips a year to Seoul, toting boxes of the famous Hwangju apples—she *soooo* missed her dear little sister (but surely not as much as she missed her oldest daughter, Songja, who had married into a family in Seoul). Mother, for her part, though she rarely had an opportunity to travel, had managed a few visits over the years to her big sister in Hwangju.

Mother and Auntie were quite the opposite in personality and looks, and in fact had very little in common. Auntie was large and heavy-set, and if her broad, bumpy face were to sport a beard, she might very well be taken for a man. Mother, on the other hand, was slender with a soft and feminine face. For a woman of fifty-two she retained much of her tender youth. Temperament followed looks, with the one being spirited, dynamic, and active like a man, the other calm, passive, and introverted like a woman.

These two mothers who had nothing in common, only their differences in personality and looks, hit it off at once and forevermore were like two peas in a pod. They also got along so well because of Mother's tolerant and condoning personality and Auntie's loyalty to our family, and especially to

Mother, for an act of benevolence in once having extended her a small measure of financial assistance.

After Auntie was widowed at the in-between age of thirty-four, she bundled up her children, all four of them—ages sixteen, eleven, six, and one, the last still a nursling—and moved to Seoul, her earnest hope to give the kids a good education. But having left her in-laws' home in Hwangju, she and her brood had no practical means of survival in Seoul, and if not for Mother's prudent care, who knows how much worse off she might have been.

Father's disparagement of her notwithstanding, she had her faults, all right—she was loud, she was vain and snobbish, she was annoying, she talked too much. But that's not to say she was lacking in attributes.

Maybe it's extravagant to call her a household woman warrior, but in general she was incredibly high-spirited and brave. In favorable circumstances and dire straits alike, she confronted life head-on, never retreating and never yielding.

As the fellow says, even a cow needs a place to rest its butt. But if the cow balks, then what's the use? For Hwangju Auntie in the *kisa* year, widowed in the spring and arrived in Seoul in the fall with the baby on her back and her three other children in hand, the resting place turned out to be a house with six rooms, family room included, front and center in Kye-dong and not far from our home, leased for her by Mother with Father's consent.

Out of Hwangju Auntie's money belt came 200 *wŏn* for dishes, meal trays, spoons, and chopsticks, and now she was ready to take in student boarders. But even supposing she managed to fill the five spare rooms with two students each, would the income be enough to feed five mouths? In any event, Hwangju Auntie wouldn't be satisfied merely to eke out a living; her greater hope, as always, was to educate the children.

And so she tightened her belt and went to work. Leftovers from meals for the boarders did not go to waste. Clothing was not a concern as long as it covered bare flesh. She canceled her water-delivery service, saving the one-*chŏn*-per-bucket fee, and began fetching it herself, the bucket balanced on her head. With baby Yŏngch'un strapped to her back day and night, she cooked, set out meals for the boarders, washed the dishes, stoked the five fireboxes of the five rental rooms, brought the water, and did the wash for all ten of her student boarders. She could have hired a laundress but instead put the money toward her own children's tuition and school fees.

By the time she returned twelve years later to her late husband's ancestral home, the fruits of her shrewd, relentless frenzy were apparent. In the *kapsul* year, make that 1934, Chaech'un had graduated with honors from secondary school. He had talent and smarts to begin with; add to those a good helping of his mother's zeal and encouragement and you had one diligent student. The next step was college, which was his mother's ardent wish and his own intention, and he was sorely tempted by the prospect, but smart fellow that he was, he took into account the family's situation and his mother's tribulations and decided at his young age of twenty-one to enter the real world.

And so it was that the year he graduated he sat for the constabulary exam, completed the training, and was assigned to Ponjŏng Police Station in downtown Seoul. Two years later, which would have been the *pyŏngja* year, he married a young lady from the ancestral home whose family owned an orchard with a hundred apple trees.

Then in 1938, the *muin* year, thanks to a series of visits by a distant uncle from Haeju to police headquarters in Seoul, Chaech'un was transferred back home, making the young couple the first among the family to return to the ancestral village. A year later, the *kimyo* year, this smart and talented young man, with solid backing from his uncle, was promoted to chief of the department and transferred to the police station in nearby Chunghwa.

Also in the *muin* year, Songja, the oldest daughter, graduated from secondary school. The following year she married a college graduate who worked for a bank, and they have lived comfortably in Seoul ever since.

And in 1940, the *kyŏngjin* year, when Auntie moved back to Hwangju, number-two daughter Ch'unja was in her second year of secondary school and baby Yŏngch'un, carried on his mother's back all the way to Seoul those many years ago, was already age thirteen and a fifth grader in primary school.

So there you have it, the results of a frenzied and relentless twelve years of insufficient food, a scant wardrobe, sleep deficit, and not enough rest, the aftermath of Hwangju Auntie and her quartet of babes in the woods improvising their way empty-handed to Seoul.

Considering her life as a single mom, you could safely say she rates an 8 or 9 on a 10-point scale of success. All of it is due to meeting life head-on, fighting the good fight, never yielding, and never giving up.

3

A hefty person tends to be affected less by the cold, but this benefit is countered by increased sensitivity to heat and a tendency to sweat like a pig. And today, if not for Father and me, Hwangju Auntie would have dispensed with her thin summer jacket, her skirt, and her underskirt and made herself at home in her bloomers. Instead she made do by fanning herself nonstop.

My wife brought out a bowl of *kalguksu* and a small tray of kimchi and condiments. Placing them before our guest, Mother said, "Here you are, dear sister. I was just about to send you-know-who over to fetch you—food doesn't go down easy when I'm eating by myself."

"Now that's what I'd call devoted legwork," said Auntie, "but thank the heavens my feet knew where to bring me." She guffawed like a man, then dug in. "This is perfect for summer. Hot broth heats you up inside, but then the heat goes away and you're all cooled off."

"Eat up, big sister. There's plenty more."

"Don't mind if I do. Have you ever heard me say 'No, thanks' here?"

Just then Father finished and pushed his tray aside.

"Brother, are you done already?" said Auntie with a glance in his direction, wanting to make sure that an extra mouth at the table wouldn't leave the family members hungering for more.

With a long belch Father said, "Me, I'm not crazy about this stuff. Never used to touch it. But now that we're pinched, I guess my poor old mouth can't be choosy."

"Just you wait, sir. The day is coming, mark my word, when you can rest easy and show everyone who's boss, just like in the old days," Auntie declared, her face suddenly radiant with delight. "You do know, don't you—about Dr. Yi Sŭngman?"

Everyone gaped at her.

"He's been named our president! Radio's been blasting the news ever since, all the papers put out extras. You didn't know? You dear people, minding your own sweet business!"

Guilty as charged—we knew the National Assembly was set to elect a president all right, but had neglected to turn on the radio. Father as head of household could be let off the hook, but I had no excuse.

"Well, then, it would seem your prophecy was accurate," said Father to Auntie.

The jab was obvious, but instead of picking up on it, Auntie gushed, "You bet it was! Do you remember what I said that day?"

Yes, I remembered. The day in question was back toward the end of April, when all you needed was two people and you had a ready-made conversation about the upcoming election. It was around sunset, so Father was home, I was back from school, Auntie had joined us, and sure enough we started talking about the election.

"Don't think twice, just vote for Dr. Yi. Once we make him president, he'll steer us Chosŏn folk down the right path—otherwise . . ."

Boy, was she adamant about it.

Father listened with a blank expression, then said, "Silly me, I thought we were electing the Assemblymen, but actually we're making Dr. Yi president?"

"Well, you'll see. Only ten days to go. We southerners, we Chosŏn folk, we'll vote for him, nine out of ten, and he'll make president, then and there. I swear!"

After dinner, when Auntie had left, Father muttered, "Huh—half-assed knowledge is a dangerous thing, especially when you talk before you think . . . doesn't know when to give up, subtle as a rock wall, bull-headed . . . imagine I'm on my deathbed and she shows up, the messenger from hell—I wouldn't last an hour before she dragged me off." He shook his head with a vengeance.

Even if it wasn't the case that nine out of ten Chosŏn folks voted for Dr. Yi for president on May 10, it was the case that the National Assembly subsequently elected him, so in any event, Dr. Yi Sŭngman was made president.

Which meant Hwangju Auntie could get away with boasting about it now. Dripping with sweat, she fashioned a kind of swagger with her shoulders as she slurped her kalguksu broth with obvious relish.

Father lit his pipe. "Now that Dr. Yi is president, just as you prophesied, is he ready to steer us Chosŏn folk down the right path?"

"You better believe it."

"My good woman, did you happen to visit the grain shops and the firewood peddlers on your way over here?"

"Grain and firewood? Whatever for?"

"Because the price of grain should have dropped from 1,000 to 500 wŏn by now, a cart of firewood should be down to 2,000, and a measure of broadcloth down to 50 or 60."

"Just like that, out of the blue?"

"Good god, I'm talking to a wall. . . . Don't you remember saying that once he's president Dr. Yi will save us 'Chosŏn folk'? And you said just now that he'll steer us down the right path."

"I did indeed."

"So, the people of our country have been driven to the brink—what do you think the reason is? Think about it—a bushel of rice costs more than

1,000 wŏn, a cart of firewood 6 to 7,000, a measure of cotton 400, a bowl of rice-in-soup at a restaurant goes for 100 wŏn—prices for everything are going up. So if, as you just said, we elected Dr. Yi our president and he's going to steer the people down the right path, don't prices have to drop first?"

"Listen to you! You're putting the cart before the horse. For heaven's sake, give the man a chance—he just today became president."

"Well, the way I hear it, when other countries are having rough times, when the people are suffering because of high prices, if a great man becomes king or president, prices plummet immediately, that's what I'm saying."

"We need a *government* for that to happen. But right now the American military government controls everything."

"Oh, now I get it, we need a government—we get ourselves a government and right away the price of grain goes down, and the price of firewood and fabric too, and the people live happily ever after?"

"Of course."

"That's just wonderful. . . . And while we're on the subject, ah, how should I phrase it, those highway robbers, those corrupt officials who think they're above the law, are they being tied up and sent off to jail?"

"You bet, strung up like fish on a line . . . this very moment they're being rounded up left and right. And not just the lower-level guys, this time they landed a big one, No so-and-so. Everybody knows him, chief of some section or other at police headquarters—"

"You mean No Tŏksul? He's a dirty one all right, but this time it's not bribery—a guy died under torture on his watch."

"Really? That's serious. It's not bribery, but still . . .'"

"I heard it was a commie—I wonder."

"A commie? Well, hurray! Good for No, the guy deserved to die. Torture's too good for that bunch, he ought to have been drawn and quartered. And No, he deserves a bonus, they need to set him free. Since when is it a crime to beat a commie to death?"

Good thing the guy hadn't gotten into Auntie's clutches first, else she might have cut him open, the way she was talking.

"Don't get too exercised. You know how it goes—they go in the front door tied up and out the back door free men." Father let this sink in, then said, "Speaking of the commies, I'm thinking to lie low this year and the next, and the year after, I just might join the Party myself."

Auntie practically jumped out of her skirt when she heard this. "Listen to you—how could you *say* such a thing?" Since she had a mouthful of noodles, she gestured theatrically, the movements of her head, eyes, and hands taking up the spiel, before she continued. "I beg you, I beg you, by the grace of god above, don't you *ever* say such a horrid thing again. Of all the . . . what in heaven's name are you trying to say, *what?*"

"You think I *want* to do that? I don't have that much land, but those thugs, they're out-and-out thugs, they figure they'll help themselves and divvy it up among a bunch of ignorant farmhands. It gives me heartburn—so sure, you're wondering how I could possibly join them."

"Of course I am. And they're thugs all right, as nasty as you're going to find."

"This year I'm selling off the house, and next year the paddies, all 200 sacks' worth; I don't see any other way. Sell the house, sell the land, you do what you have to to keep the wolf from the door. . . . The year after next we'll be dirt poor, not a penny to our names. Why be scared of the commies if there's nothing left for them to take?"

"Commies, leftists, reds, whatever you want to call those bastards, they give me the creeps. I'll hate them forever. I could grind them up and swallow them and still not be revenged." Sure enough, Auntie was shuddering, fury in her eyes.

Father pretended not to notice. "The way I hear it, the commies join up with the poor people and take from the rich bastards, and then it's share and share alike, that's their game. So for me, selling off the house, the paddies, being dirt poor, then signing up with them—wouldn't that be wonderful? A man has to know which side of the fence the grass is greener on, right? And it's his stomach that tells him."

"That's a lie!" Auntie barked, and I could have sworn I saw flames coming from her mouth. "A bare-faced lie. That's what they want you to think. They're reds, masters of the bare-faced lie, see? . . . Of course they take from the rich, what did you expect? But the share and share alike? It's an out-and-out lie—what's there to share anyway? The head honchos are the ones who get to share, and then it's their turn to play moneybags. The new moneybags. . . . The ones who fall for the share-and-share-alike line, the folks who are genuinely poor, they're the ones who get left out." She paused, then her voice softened. "Dear brother, stop thinking about all this. Best thing you can do now is join the Korean Democratic Party or the Independence Promotion Committee."

"Huh, for a guy who's going to be out of a house and land by the day after tomorrow, a guy who's dirt poor, what's the use of joining a bunch of rich gossip mongers in some political party or committee? Unless they want to let me be a doorman or something. . . . Those penniless guys who join the Democratic Party and talk like they actually have something to say, they're human garbage, they're dogs, that's what they are. The penniless bastards singing the praises of the Democratic Party are bigger boneheads than the rich bastards who become commies."

"Brother, how can you call yourself penniless? You have a house and farmland."

"Not for long. Check out the Democratic Party and their so-called program—it's all about land distribution. Should we expect anything different from the Independence Committee?"

"They don't just *take* your land. They give you money for it—the farmers get a good price—and then the land is distributed, that's what I heard."

"And the few hundred thousand *wŏn* we get for it is supposed to take care of us the rest of our lives? Maybe it would be different if we had money coming out the yin-yang to begin with and the price we got was tens of *millions of wŏn*."

"For heaven's sake, will you *please* stop worrying? Just place your trust in Dr. Yi. Now that this fine man is our president we'll all find a way to make a living."

"Not a guy like me—not until Dr. Yi boosts the land rental price from a third of the crop to two thirds."

"Still, just be patient, brother. Now that Dr. Yi Sŭngman is president, we'll have our own government and be independent, and then our national guard will march up to the 38th parallel and smash it down. . . . Our Yŏngch'un, once Dr. Yi gives the order, he'll charge and knock it down—that's all he and his buddies talk about, they're waiting for the chance. That's what he tells me when he's home on leave—he broods about it." With a big sigh, she finished up with, "The thought of them beating those commies to death is like three days' worth of food in my stomach."

I've never known Hwangju Auntie to be short on bluffing and blowing up a situation—except when it comes to the commies. The hatred and antipathy toward the leftists now on display were a true expression of her feelings, and not in the least exaggerated.

In July, a month before Liberation, I spent two nights at her home in Hwangju on my way to Seoul from a visit to my wife's family in Ŭnyul and realized Auntie and her family lived a life worth crowing about. I'd gotten a general idea from my mother, who had visited her last fall, but what a shock when I actually saw it with my own eyes.

The home was brand spanking new, occupied a spacious lot, and consisted of two structures with gracefully upswept tile roofs. With commodities in such short supply at that time, it was a mystery to me where she'd found all that good lumber and glass, the fine wallpaper and floor covering. The rooms were furnished in a blend of Korean, Western, and Japanese styles, and the walls bore classic Eastern artworks—all of it, furniture and art, looked rare and expensive. A wall of red brick surrounded the home, and when I saw all the cement that had gone into it I thought ruefully of our house and the outer shell of our cookstove and firebox, which could have used a cement seal. But we had to settle for mud instead.

Sugar, fancy Japanese soy sauce, jadelike rice unmixed with other grains, fresh fish, meat, beer, sake, items difficult to obtain even if the king himself had demanded them were plentiful here. Traditional rubber shoes, Chinese broadcloth, wool fabric for Western-style suits, silks of various kinds, hosiery, fine cosmetics—all present and accounted for.

You wouldn't catch me poking around in her clothing chests to take inventory, but Auntie proudly displayed these items for me to feast my eyes on. At the end of the show she presented me with fine Anju ramie suitable for a traditional topcoat for Father and a traditional jacket and skirt for Mother, and calico sufficient for two dress shirts for me. I've cherished those shirts and still wear them now.

That Auntie and her family possessed such items when the average person couldn't find a decent pair of socks or a teeny herring, a time when people were scraping the bottom of the commodity barrel, had to make you wonder—was there really a war going on, and if so, where?

And the apple orchard—not only were there the 100 trees that were part of the dowry for Auntie's son Pak Chaech'un, there were another 800 besides. The apples were ripening inside their protective bags, and it wouldn't be long till the early crop was picked. Apart from the orchard, there were 4,000 p'yŏng of fertile paddy.

According to Auntie, the house and the 800 apple trees and the paddy land were obtained through the proceeds from the 100-apple-tree dowry; money Chaech'un had saved up—his year-end bonus and leftover per diem and travel expenses; and 2,000 that Auntie had scrounged up before her departure from Seoul.

In 1943, the *kyemi* year, Chaech'un had been promoted again, this time to deputy inspector, and transferred from the Chunghwa police station to the Kyŏmip'o station. In the space of three years he had come to occupy a strategic position in the economic realm.

It was then that he adopted a Japanese name, according to imperial policy. His new family name, the Chinese characters for which would have been pronounced "Pakch'on" in Korean, was Bokuson.

Deputy Inspector Bokuson proceeded to purchase the home, orchard, and paddy in Hwangju, establishing himself as a large landowner, while at his workplace in Kyŏmip'o he and his wife set up modest housekeeping in a public officials' residence.

Deputy Inspector Bokuson heard of my visit, and the evening I arrived he picked me up in his automobile and took me back to Kyŏmip'o, to a fancy Japanese restaurant, where he put on a feast complete with geisha and *kisaeng*—it was quite a welcome. Deputy Inspector Bokuson, when he was good and tipsy, emphasized the following, over and over: that the people of Chosŏn could not live on their own, apart from Japan; that therefore the people of Chosŏn should become Japanese wholeheartedly and as soon as possible, and could just as quickly become happy; that he would darn well make inspector by age thirty-three and would darn well make superintendent by thirty-nine. All this he solemnly swore.

At the time he was thirty-one.

He also made it known that he was prepared to take the College Equivalency Examination that fall and the High Civil Servant Examination come spring. His sparkling wit and his intelligence, his quickness on his feet, and his overflowing mettle—I couldn't help but admire these qualities. Here I was two years older and yet when I took inventory of myself—big-deal college graduate, no brilliance, no ambition, barely latched on to a primary school teaching job, and I was satisfied with it—I felt ashamed of myself. I was more like a kid compared with him.

Once the feasting was over, he tried every trick in the book to fix me up with one of the geisha, and not a bad looker at that. The times I drank I tended to drink alone, and during my thirty-three years, not once had I canoodled with a woman other than my wife. Whoring wasn't to my liking, and that evening I had to work like hell to weasel my way out.

As for daughter number two, Ch'unja, Auntie reported that last year she had graduated from a girls' secondary school and was now preparing to get married. Unlike her siblings, she took after her father more than her mother, and had always been pretty. She was seventeen when the family returned to Hwangju, and this was the first time I'd seen her since; I have to say she was excellent bride material. But for some reason she looked downright gloomy.

I was absolutely delighted to see Ch'unja—and almost as surprised at the extent of my delight. In the brief time I was there I was with her more than anyone else, strolling through the orchard, talking and having fun. When Ch'unja saw me she jumped for joy, and while we were together the gloominess vanished and she was cheerful throughout.

And Yŏngch'un, the youngest, was all of a sudden seventeen and commuting to a secondary school for the Japanese in Kyŏmip'o. His brother had forced him to enroll, he complained to me. If only he didn't have to put up with all the bullying and abuse from the Japanese kids. . . .

So there might have been a few fires smoldering, but overall, Hwangju Auntie's four children were doing well, they'd all been educated and weren't falling behind. And Chaech'un, barely into his thirties, had already risen to a good position, with further success lying ahead.

Their assets had accumulated and they were now unimaginably affluent, worth millions. Auntie couldn't help but be moved at the thought that sixteen years earlier, in the kisa year, she had arrived in Seoul with three children in hand and the baby on her back, with no firm plans. The groundwork for her present success had started that day, to be followed by years of insufficient food, a scant wardrobe, sleep deficit, and not enough rest, Auntie scrimping even on water, toting it home on her head with the baby on her back to save the one-chŏn delivery fee, and at the same time taking in ten roughneck boys as boarders—day in and day out she had done this, for twelve years. And so it was only natural that looking back, she felt it more meaningful and precious that her efforts and hardship had laid the foundation of her present stability and accomplishments. And it was likewise only natural that her sense of loss and rage would be all the greater for the nightmare of having it all go up in smoke in a single morning.

In Hwangju there was a former student of mine named Ch'oe. I'd had him in fifth and sixth grade in primary school, and he went on to the same secondary school I'd attended. This added up to a rather special relationship. Young Ch'oe had been born in Seoul, but hated the deceitful oppressiveness of imperial Japan and was loath to bend or assimilate with the ugly, irrational world. Wanting especially to avoid being drafted as a student-soldier, he dropped out of college on the pretext of illness and through connections with his buddies acquired a small orchard in Hwangju, where he kept a low profile, reading and contemplating and taking care of the fruit trees with his widowed mother, all the while waiting until the time was right.

I found young Ch'oe tending to the saplings. It was a surprise visit, and he was glad to see me. A modest tray appeared, and soon we were exchanging shots of *soju* and reaching out to the nearest tree to pick the not-quite-ripe apples to snack on while we caught up on the years we'd been out of touch, recalling stories from primary school and griping about current affairs. The hours flew by.

With Germany having lost the war and no longer Japan's partner in the East-West two-front offensive, young Ch'oe declared, and considering how rattled and tuckered out Japan was, fighting on its own—there was solid evidence of this, mind you—and now that the Soviet Union was getting into the act, it was only a matter of time before Japan threw in the towel, he was sure of it.

All along I'd figured young Ch'oe had taken the passive route, avoiding the world by looking after an orchard and killing time reading and speculating. How wrong I was. The orchard tending was a camouflage. I sensed Ch'oe was up to something, but exactly what, I wasn't quite sure.

Some time ago in Seoul I'd heard a fantastic story: in the Yenan area of China there was a Korean group called the Independence Alliance, a red-influenced group fighting for liberation from Japan, and they were in contact with none other than Yŏ Unhyŏng here on the peninsula. To me at the time it sounded like the vainglorious nonsense of people trying to grab onto a star.

And now here was young Ch'oe talking about that same Independence Alliance. He wasn't speaking as a third party, and he wouldn't have sounded so ardent unless he was at least minimally involved—his entire being radiated what he was saying. In his presence I couldn't help feeling pained at what a worthless person I was, not unlike how I'd felt the previous night at the restaurant in Kyŏmip'o in the presence of Deputy Inspector Pak Chaech'un, who had already made a name for himself. The difference was, Young Ch'oe, my student and a graduate of the same secondary school, some ten years younger than me, was bright enough to have a sharp and detailed understanding of current affairs, both here on the peninsula and in the world at large. I felt like an idiot in comparison, a simpleton who took as an article of faith the pronouncements from Japanese imperial headquarters: several enemy battleships sunk, dozens of aircraft shot down, hundreds of soldiers killed and thousands captured, whereas "damage to our side was minimal."

I don't know how much influence he could exert against Japan the invader, but even if it was feeble, even if in the end he had nothing to show for his reckless ambitions, even if his expectations were not met, one thing was for sure—young Ch'oe was doing his part on behalf of the liberation of our people.

I, on the other hand, was a meek and powerless specimen, one who had felt compelled to teach the young people of Chosŏn that the Japanese takeover of our land was the right thing to do. I had reprimanded them for using our language instead of Japanese, I had forced or cajoled them into abandoning the notion that they were people of Chosŏn and accepting that they were people of Japan, I had made them recite the Imperial Prescript for Loyal Subjects and chant "Long Live the Emperor."

I was a mediocre guy, going through the motions, my grand notion of teaching and guiding the young people of Chosŏn stymied in the face of history, transformed into an obstacle I could not shake off in order to stand on my own.

It was getting dark before we knew it, and inside we went. Over dinner young Ch'oe asked me in an offhand way if I was close with Pak.

"Well," I said just as casually, "it's our two mothers who are close. As for me, how close can you be to a guy who's a distant cousin. . . ."

"Aha, so he's more or less a stranger."

"I guess you could say that."

Young Ch'oe lapsed into a thoughtful silence, then said, "You're here for a few days."

"I was planning to take the train back tomorrow morning, but they keep telling me to stay on a little longer."

"Sir?"

"Yeah?"

"Stick to your plan—you don't want to wear out your welcome." There was a decisive tone to this.

I gaped at him. "Wear out my welcome? At their place?"

"No, not at their place, of course not. In the eyes of others, I mean."

"Others? What others?"

"It's a case of hate me, hate my dog. And Pak and his family are hated not just in Hwangju but in Chunghwa and Kyŏmip'o. So it stands to reason that their relatives and their houseguests will be hated too."

"Oh my!" Why hadn't I thought of that?

"I realize it is heartless of me to say this to your face, sir, but regardless of kinship ties, and even if your esteemed mother has a close relationship with that family, the fact is that Pak Chaech'un has made some mistakes, and before long he'll be wishing he was dead. You remember that big shot Min, who lined his pockets during his term here? Pak Chaech'un has him beat, hands down—he's harsh, he doesn't give up, he's got his fingers in every pot, and he's mean-spirited. Remember when he was a constable here, how he used to shake down the guys who sold *ch'amoe* melons at the train station?"

What could I say to that?

"You know he and his family have two apple orchards, and you've seen the big one, right? It used to belong to a Kyŏmip'o man, and Pak nailed him on something or other and more or less snatched it from him. Probably the finest orchard in the entire Hwangju area. If it was an above-board sale, the owner wouldn't have settled for less than 100,000. . . . Hell, the man gets a 40-something-*wŏn*-per-month salary, he gets a 100-tree orchard as a dowry but it produces only a third- or fourth-rate crop, and great god above, you're telling me he can afford to build a monster house and buy a 100,000-*wŏn* orchard and 4,000 p'*yŏng* of prime paddy? How is he able to eat and dress better than an emperor?"

He had a point, I had to admit it. Pak's salary, the proceeds from the smaller orchard, Hwangju Auntie's 2,000 in savings—add it all up and it didn't come close.

"In all of Hwangju, Chunghwa, and Kyŏmip'o, you won't find a single guy who likes this Pak Chaech'un character. You wouldn't believe how many people he's wronged who would like to stick a knife in him. . . . On the surface we act like everything's peachy, but inside it's a different story—if we don't watch our step we'll get screwed. To be honest, I see him pretty often, we play *paduk*, we drink together, I bow and scrape to make him feel good, I always remember to take him something nice over the holidays, I make like everything's cozy between us. And in turn I haven't been nabbed for the military or factory work, they leave me alone, and I've been able to keep my nose clean all this time. But heaven help us if Pak Chaech'un can keep that estate of his and live out his life and die in peace in his own bed. . . . You know his nickname, don't you? Yi Wanyong's Bastard Son. Yi Wanyong's Sack-of-Shit Servant. Why Yi Wanyong? Well, Pak's the kind of guy who cleans up the mess left by that traitorous bastard who sold out Chosŏn to the Japanese. You won't catch him speaking our language—you ought to hear him chattering away in Japanese with the little woman. Anything that has to do with

Japan is great—he worships it. People of Chosŏn, they're no-good thieves, that's what he thinks."

Again young Ch'oe had me at a loss.

"Three weeks ago I got a letter from a friend of mine in P'yŏngyang. He asked me to fill him in on the family of Pak Ch'unja. Apparently she's involved with someone there, and I get the impression the lucky guy belongs to my friend's family. You can see that put me in a fix. What am I supposed to do, lie and screw up the poor guy's life? So I wrote back, told my friend the truth. And for all I know, that's one marriage that's not going to happen. I feel sorry for her, she's more or less blameless, but what I am supposed to do?"

"Was it to be an arranged marriage, or did they actually like each other?" I had to ask because I recalled how gloomy Ch'unja had looked, telling me about the preparations for her marriage.

"I wouldn't feel so bad if it was a love marriage. If there's actually a relationship between the couple, then even if there are problems with the two families, even if there's opposition, the man and woman can stand their ground and go ahead with the marriage. But my understanding is both families were going full steam ahead, formal family meeting and all."

The following morning I left for Seoul as planned, in spite of Hwangju Auntie's regrets at my departure. Ch'unja ended up going with me. I was all packed and ready to go when I noticed she was prepared for a trip as well, duffel bag in hand and all dressed up, and she followed me out. Auntie hesitated, then asked me to take her along, take her in for a month, then send her back home. So saying, she stuck a wad of bills inside the duffel.

Ch'unja was with us for two weeks, and then the day she wrote that letter she took off. I didn't feel right about a young lady wandering off with anger in her heart, but though I felt awful for Auntie, I couldn't very well keep her daughter chained up when she was champing at the bit.

And then a few days later, August 15, 1945, Liberation arrived and the Line of Interference, the 38th parallel, came into being. Songja, who was living in Seoul, began visiting us practically every other day, desperate and crying, having had no news from home and fearing the worst.

And then the news began to trickle in. But there was no way to confirm the reports; the later accounts didn't necessarily jibe with the earlier ones, and it was difficult to put all the pieces together. The only thing the reports had in common was a lack of anything that seemed auspicious.

I didn't let on to anyone, but at odd moments I'd recall young Ch'oe's remarks about Pak Chaech'un wishing he were dead, which brought graphic and gruesome scenes to mind. And sure enough, it turned out that Pak Chaech'un and his wife, though they were able to escape with their lives from Kyŏmip'o, met their fate in Hwangju—he suffered a cruel death, beaten beyond recognition. Not until the following year, when Auntie came to Seoul with Yŏngch'un, did I get the gory details.

Auntie's house was ransacked, and she tried to hold on to what was left of the homestead and land. But with her assets confiscated and an order forcing her to vacate, she took the 100,000 wŏn she'd tucked away and left Hwangju for Seoul, never to return.

For most people there are causes as well as inevitable consequences of their actions. The problem, and it's only natural, is that they tend to overlook the causes and then bewail the consequences. Auntie too was tethered to this mind-set. Why had Chaech'un and his wife suffered such a cruel death? Why had she been stripped of her assets and driven out? She made no effort to understand the causes, but only resented and raged at the slaughter by a mob of rioters of the robust son she had worried herself silly raising, the son whose prospects were so bright and shining.

And the assets that had set her up for life, assets to be bequeathed to the next generation and the next, assets accumulated through every manner of hardship—to have them seized in a single morning was a nightmare that continued to vex and mortify her.

And so the commies, the leftists, the reds, they were Hwangju Auntie's mortal enemies. They had no place in her universe, she could pulverize them, but never would her grudge be assuaged.

4

A few days later.

I'd dropped by a used-book shop in Chin'gogae (it's in the Chungmuro area; you might remember it from the colonial period by its Sino-Japanese name, Old Ponjŏng Street), near Myŏng-dong, and on my way home I ran into Yŏngch'un, in uniform—he was now a lieutenant in the national guard. He was glad to see me and said he'd been meaning to look me up; he had something to ask me about. So down a nearby alley we went, and found a teashop.

Yŏngch'un no longer had a big brother, I didn't have a younger brother, and so I became as affectionate with him as if he were a blood sibling, and

Yŏngch'un looked up to me and trusted in me. From time to time when something complicated came up, he liked to consult with me.

I regarded him across the table. He had just the right amount of weight on his lanky frame, and he wore a determined expression—the result, I figured, of three physically demanding years in the army. His physique and his spirit were equally impressive, and he was still only twenty—he looked much more mature than his age. Yŏngch'un, so manly before I knew it—when I thought of the babe of nineteen years past, who had just had his first birthday, who was bawling his eyes out; when I thought about him strapped to Hwangju Auntie's back as the family set out from their ancestral home for a new life in Seoul, but with an uncertain future confronting them, I couldn't help being amazed at the look of him now, and at the same time deeply moved.

Unusual for a twenty-year-old, he'd already gone through a succession of ups and downs. An infant when he had lost his father, carried piggyback to a vague future in Seoul, starting out on a difficult life, he was already experiencing a fate that was far from usual. Raised by a mother who for twelve years struggled with poverty and menial labor, he grew up in hardship, eating leftovers and wearing hand-me-downs.

The five years back in Hwangju, until Liberation, were as comfortable as you could want, economically. But it was also a dark period of constant uncertainty, owing to his having been sent to the primary school for Japanese students his big brother had attended, and then to a secondary school also for Japanese. He was bullied by the Japanese kids, who called out to him, "Hey, Senjin," or "Hey, yobo," but otherwise shunned him, not including him in their games. Some of the kids called him a "stinking Senjin," saying he smelled of garlic, and wouldn't go near him. When he drew praise from the teacher for homework assignments, the other students were jealous and the harassment went up a notch. If he got into an argument, then regardless of who was at fault, the Japanese kids would side with their own and gang up on him.

And then came 1945, when Yŏngch'un advanced from the third to the fourth year of secondary school. Headed to school on the train one day, he was doing some last-minute preparation for class, writing in his notebook, and his pencil tip broke off. He turned around and it was just his luck that he noticed a Japanese girl in the back of the bus sharpening her pencil. He figured her for maybe thirteen or fourteen. He borrowed her little sharpening knife, got his pencil back in working order, and returned the knife. After school that day a dozen or so Japanese students took him down a secluded alley and beat him to a pulp. The charge? A secondary school kid, especially someone still wet behind the ears, shouldn't be messing around, it didn't look good, who did this kid think he was anyway? A lame pretext, considering that these same kids were always up to blatant shenanigans with the girl students.

"Senjin scum," said the Japanese kids as they beat him. "Messing with our Japanese girls—who does he think he is? Stinking *yobo* needs to learn some manners."

An obvious case of ethnic conflict tinged with sexual jealousy.

As indignant as he felt, Yŏngch'un had to swallow his rage. If he had told Chaech'un, then his big brother would have retaliated. But getting even with those kids would have come at a cost—Chaech'un would have lashed out at him, saying something like, "You idiot, you had to go and get yourself in trouble," and followed up with a worse beating. Better to take his lumps by himself and put up with it. For there was a precedent—back in the first year he'd been beaten up by some Japanese kids, but when he got home from school and reported it to his brother, he caught a scolding and a merciless beating. In any case, young Yŏngch'un, while he had nothing against studying, hated the school and thus this gloomy period of constant uncertainty.

And then came Liberation. Yŏngch'un was among those who welcomed it with a bone-deep joy. As for the heartless and unyielding Japanese kids, they packed up and disappeared, spiritless and without a peep. And just like that, Yŏngch'un was purged of the lumps of rancor he had been forced to swallow.

But the joy of Liberation was short-lived. His big brother Chaech'un and his wife were slaughtered. The family didn't even think about trying to retrieve the bodies, and then their home was ransacked by the mob. Mother and son escaped to the surrounding hills, and when they returned two days later, all that was left of the house was the roof and skeleton.

With no one to turn to, they lived in a state of constant fear and unease, as if in a jungle teeming with beasts. The new year came and went, and in February 1947 their assets were seized and they were ordered to evacuate.

And so it was that again they had to make the tiresome journey south, this time mother and son, a journey they could not have anticipated. It was Yŏngch'un's inborn temperament, along with this life of unusual hardship and vicissitudes from early on, that had made him so mature for his age.

Arrived in Seoul, Yŏngch'un in short order joined the national guard. Just because he'd come south with a bit of money didn't mean he could blithely

live on that money and content himself with further study, and so it was time
to look for a job. But how many jobs awaited a young man who hadn't even
completed secondary school—why not be a soldier instead? He had once
posed that question to me, the nearest thing to a big brother he had.

Be that as it may, I'd said, wouldn't he be better off continuing his studies? Well, he'd keep his options open and think it over, he'd replied, but then
sure enough, he'd ended up joining the national guard. With his three and a
half years of secondary school as a foundation, combined with his strong
constitution and a certain toughness, he'd risen quickly through the ranks,
and now here he was, a lieutenant.

Over a refreshing cup of tea we inquired about each other's family, then
turned to current affairs. He still had that Hwanghae dialect and accent that
was music to my ears.

And then he got down to the business at hand. "What I wanted to see you
about is . . . I really think I need to move out."

I didn't know what to say. I knew that Yŏngch'un wasn't in sync with his
good mother and the two of them sometimes clashed. Better to hear what
came next before venturing an answer.

"As you know, hyŏngnim, when I joined the guard, I didn't have a clear objective or a strong belief in what I was doing, I just kind of said, why not,
you know? . . . And now that I've got a little more sense of what's what, and
now that I've got a firmer idea—whether you call it recognition or self-
awareness—of what it's like to be a soldier, that's how I want to serve my
country and I'm determined to do it. But damn it all, Mom's been on and on
about quitting the guard, and it's getting on my nerves."

"She has?" I could feel myself frowning as I said this. It was just the day
before yesterday that Hwangju Auntie had been slurping noodles with us
and saying, Now that Dr. Yi Sŭngman is president we'll have our own government and
be independent, and then our national guard will march up to the 38th parallel and
smash it down. . . . Our Yŏngch'un, once Dr. Yi gives the order, he'll charge and knock it
down—that's all he and his buddies talk about, they're waiting for the chance. That's
what he tells me when he's home on leave—he broods about it. Didn't this show that
deep down inside she was proud that her Yŏngch'un was a member of the
national guard? Was there any indication she was unhappy with that? No.

"For Mom it's like this—it won't be long before the national guard attacks
North Chosŏn, and if I get killed, then who's she going to depend on? So I
should get out while I can."

"Well, considering her circumstances—"

"Hyŏngnim," he broke in, "Mom's attitude, what she's thinking, it's cor-
rupted, that's how I feel. She's always harping about wanting Dr. Yi to hurry
up and give the order to attack North Chosŏn so our national guard can over-
run the 38th parallel and kill those commie bastards, those murdering robbers, and get even with them for Brother and get our property back. At the
same time she doesn't want me getting killed in North Chosŏn, so I should
sneak out while I can. It's all she talks about. I weasel out when things get
dangerous, I sit tight while others are sweating blood, and then whee, good
for us—that's cunning calculation on her part. Isn't it, hyŏngnim?"

I didn't know what to say.

"It's not just Mom. It's one of our worst traits as a people—you find yourself a nice, safe place to watch what goes on, and when the smoke clears you
come out and have yourself a feast. What a crooked mind-set—it's how our
country went to hell in the first place. And unless the people of Chosŏn
dump it, the country will go to hell again, even if it's independent. Tell me,
how can a people who have no spirit of self-sacrifice or nationalism expect to
stay independent?"

I had no answer for that.

"And there's something else about Mom that's twisted—she's always carrying on about South Chosŏn attacking North Chosŏn and slaughtering the
commies, and that gets us even with them for Brother, and we can get our
house back, and the orchards and the paddy, we'll get it all back, it's all she
talks about, night and day, hurry up and attack North Chosŏn. So for Mom
it's the results she's interested in—revenge for her son, getting back what
belongs to us, that's the heart of the issue. What's actually involved in the
south attacking the north, that's of no concern to her, doesn't interest her in
the slightest. And what's more, the south attacking the north, is it the right
thing to do? She couldn't care less. . . . So, like the fellow says, you let someone else cook your crabs for you, you win without putting any effort in—isn't
that how she's calculating it? She's afraid her precious son will get killed, so
she wants him to weasel out and sit tight and wait for others to sweat blood
on his behalf, and all so we can get even and get our assets back and whoopee,
good for us—sneaky and sly wins the day. . . . Isn't that right, hyŏngnim?
Mom's actions, the way she thinks, it runs in the blood of Chosŏn people, it's
a trait of a people whose country has gone to hell. Don't you see that?"

There was more to come, so I kept silent.

"Me, well, of course I'll grab my rifle and go once the order comes down.
Smash the 38th parallel and attack the north. But there's a reason I'm

taking part—we have a mission to be unified and independent, and attacking the north is the means for carrying out that mission. That and nothing else. Avenging Brother and all the rest, that's not the issue. Sure, I have feelings. . . ."

Before I knew it, his emotions had subsided and he was speaking more thoughtfully.

"I'm angry about my blood brother's death, it was awful, and it's not like I didn't feel it. But revenge is not on my mind—heaven knows, he made some mistakes, he did some very bad things. It's cruel how they killed him, but that's the price he paid. If I was one of them, I'm not sure I could find it in myself to forgive him either. As for our assets, what can I say? All that we came by legitimately is the 2,000 *wŏn* that Mom brought back from Seoul, and the 100-tree orchard he got from his in-laws. Somehow those two assets grew into the 100,000 she brought south—what does that tell you? And the house, the paddy, the big orchard—it's criminal to even think about recouping them. Even if we had the opportunity to get them back, I wouldn't accept them, absolutely not. . . ."

A sigh of admiration escaped me, and I couldn't help nodding. I was happy that I'd gauged him so well. On the other hand, I was dismayed by his *If South Chosŏn invades North Chosŏn.* . . . For all I knew, North Chosŏn would attack first, but either way, the day that happened we'd have ourselves a large-scale civil slaughter and end up in the bloody, tragic vortex of a dog-eat-dog war. What had happened in Cheju earlier this year would spread throughout the peninsula.

"Yŏngch'un."

"Yes?"

"You and I could mope over this situation till the cows come home—the south attacking the north, I mean—but what good would it do? Is there no other means to unify the two sides? No other way to keep our people from spilling the blood they share and killing each other?"

"That's a sad prospect for sure. But if that's the only way to unite south and north, then so be it."

"Clearly the two sides have to be united, I'm absolutely firm on that, but does it have to come at the expense of bloodshed?"

"As for me, I believe in our supreme leader, I believe in Dr. Yi Sŭngman. I believe in his wisdom and insight, that he'll try every peaceful means at his disposal, and only when all else fails will he resort to emergency measures. And when the order comes down, I'll place full faith and trust in him—that those measures are inevitable, unavoidable—and I'll pick up my rifle and head off to the 38th parallel. We're better off unified, even if bloodshed is the price we pay."

While I was thinking about how to answer, Yŏngch'un followed up.

"*Hyŏngnim*, what are you thinking?"

"Yŏngch'un."

"Yes?"

"What if the south attacks the north but there's still no unification?"

"Well—I don't see how that could happen, but—"

"You don't? On what basis? You figure the Americans will remain stationed here in the south?"

"*Hyŏngnim*."

I saw a new resolve in Yŏngch'un's expression.

"*Hyŏngnim*, how long are you hoping the Americans remain here? We have a government, we have independence, we have recognition from the international community, recognition as the independent state of Chosŏn. And still you're hoping the Americans stay here?"

"I'm not hoping anything. . . . It's just that the way things are going now—"

"But how can we be independent if there's a foreign military presence on our soil? That makes us a protectorate, doesn't it—and not an independent nation?"

"Of course, but—"

"I know, I read the article in the newspaper—Dr. Yi says that even though we have an independent government, he's asking that the American forces remain. But as much as I trust Dr. Yi, I just can't bring myself to believe he would say something like that. I doubt he really thinks that way. What I think is that the Americans might have cooked this up themselves, as a political expedient."

"Really?"

"Well, it's clear to me that someone's come up with the notion that the so-called North Chosŏn People's Liberation Army will attack the south. . . . *Hyŏngnim*, let's suppose those rumors come true, but even if the two sides are opposite in their ideology and their political stance, oppression is oppression and shame is shame, and both sides are on the receiving end. Is this how we have to live, under the sword and the rifle of a foreign military force occupying our land, independent in name only, living in a protectorate? You know, there are still people moving down from the north, and there's something I want to ask them straight out—which is better, a life in the south, where you get gunned down like dogs or pigs by American jet fighters, as happened on the Tok Islets last June; where you're subject to murder, robbery, rape, contempt, degradation, slander, defamation, you name it; or life in the north, where you're persecuted by a dictatorship of the workers and the farmers? Which side is more distressing, which side leaves you more resentful, which is more sorrowful? That's what I'd like to ask the people who come south."

I might have taken this as narrow-minded and overly emotional, if not for the fact that it was coming from Yŏngch'un. Time for me to take a new tack.

"All right, then, ideally the foreign military force should withdraw and the south should rely on its own power to attack the north, and then north and south can be unified fair and square—that's the ideal situation. So, let's suppose the Americans do leave. And then the south attacks the north. . . . But, sad to say, the attempt to unify ends in failure. Then what?"

"Well, that's something to think about. But I'm confident."

"Sure you are—because you're a soldier. But in war, winning or losing comes down to military strength, not emotion or hope. We can hope all we want that if the south attacks the north it will win—and that's the way it should be—but at the moment, the south's military strength is a question mark, and so is the north's, which means the outcome is also a question mark. And so if luck should have it that the south attacks but fails, then what? Isn't that an issue we have to consider?"

"If the south wins, then the government will rule the peninsula all the way north to the Amnok and Tuman rivers. If it fails, then the North Chosŏn regime will reach all the way south to Cheju Island. . . . The day warfare breaks out, the 38th parallel will disappear, no matter what—we'll never see it again. And just like the American Civil War and the unification war between Shilla and Paekche, the fighting will continue until one side is decisively beaten, and whether it's the south that disappears or the north, only one Chosŏn remains—there's no way both sides could remain, is there?"

"Naturally we hope it's the north that disappears, but if, heaven forbid, the northern regime ends up reaching all the way south to Cheju, then what? . . . That would be regrettable, wouldn't it?"

"But we'd still have unification as a result."

Surprised to see a grin on his face, I stared at him, which earned me another grin.

"Don't worry, hyŏngnim, I'm not turning into a red. I hate the commies, count on it." He paused, then continued. "But the fact that I hate communism, what does it mean, really? It's like hating the summer heat because it makes you physically uncomfortable—but that's what summer is, hot. So no matter how much I hate communism, if the north ends up reaching all the way south to Cheju, then what can I do, I'll have to accept it, at least in theory."

I couldn't argue with that.

"So in my heart I'll hate it if it's our bad luck that the north reaches all the way to Cheju, but in theory I'll accept the Democratic People's Republic of Korea. On one condition, though—that it not be a satellite state of the Soviet Union but rather an autonomous, independent state free of interference and control by the Soviet bloc."

He had more to say, so I heard him out.

"And that applies to southern Chosŏn, the Republic of Korea, as well, hyŏngnim. Take the Philippines—how can you call them independent when the real power is still held by the American conglomerates? And Manchukuo under the Japanese—would you call it independent? . . . If some son of a bitch put together a government like that, basically selling out the country and the people to a foreign power, then sat back fiddling with his mustache and saying we're independent, if we had someone like that ruling us, I'd never forgive him, I'd put him down first before marching off to attack the north."

His fists resting on the table shuddered; they were clenched so tight I thought they'd burst. There was fire in his eyes.

"If I'd been around when the annexation treaty was signed, I wouldn't have let those guys live—Yi Wanyong, Yi Yonggu, Song Pyŏngjun, and all the rest."

I had more tea brought, and then we lapsed into a long silence. I realized once again what a mediocre, run-of-the-mill guy I was in comparison with my scary protégé. It took a while before he spoke again, and this time his tone was softer.

"What am I going to do about my sister Ch'unja?"

Ch'unja—inevitably I had mixed feelings about her.

"As her brother I feel sorry for her, but I wish I could feed her cyanide or something."

What could I say to that?

"She's in too deep, she's gone bad, she's rotten."

I couldn't respond.

"I told you when you came to Hwangju three years ago, didn't I, what a painful time I had at that school for the Japs? And how those Jap kids beat the shit out of me just because I asked one of their girls to borrow her pencil sharpener? You heard about that, right?"

I nodded.

"Well, I didn't understand till now what made them want to beat me like they did. . . . If it was a Chosŏn guy Ch'unja wanted to go out with, or even have fun with, what the devil would I have to say? But it's those you-know-who bastards—how could she . . ."

Ch'unja had been playing around since the winter before last. I'd run into her once on the street, arm in arm with an American. Should I acknowledge her or not? While I was trying to decide, she marched past me, head held high, for all the world to see. And I'd seen her a few times in a jeep, also with an American. People were constantly telling me they'd seen a jeep parked outside her place.

And then in June, I think it was, the news got around that she was pregnant. True or not, she disappeared from public view, and I hadn't seen her since.

Truth be told, I can't deny that I'm partly to blame for Ch'unja's degradation.

It was clear that the breaking off of her relationship with the P'yŏngyang man after the formal meeting of the two families in Hwangju had hit her hard. Even if love wasn't a factor, Ch'unja seemed to be taken with the man, and when you go through with the family meeting and the marriage negotiations look promising, an announcement by the other side that it's all over can't help but be an unbearable disappointment to a chaste young woman who is old enough to know what's going on.

During the two weeks she spent with us in Seoul her attitude toward me developed into something peculiar. Thinking about it now, I can see that in the wake of the breakup with the P'yŏngyang man her feelings for the opposite sex had gone dormant, but when she was with us she suddenly grew despondent and despairing, she was upset about what had happened, and that led to a kind of rebound, a what-have-I-got-to-lose approach, and perhaps that's when her feelings really ignited for the first time.

And then the morning she ended up leaving, my wife was in the kitchen with our housekeeper, preparing the various breakfast trays, and I was in our room by myself reading, when I heard Ch'unja's voice:

"Oppa, could I see yesterday's paper?"

And the sliding door to our room opened just enough to admit her arm. Through the gap I could see her perched on the edge of the veranda. She was wearing a polo shirt, and the arm extending from the short sleeve was nice and fleshy. It wasn't the first time I'd seen her bare arm, but somehow that morning I found myself sorely tempted by the sight.

I found the newspaper on my desk and as I passed it out through the opening of the door, something fluttered in—a bulging envelope. My heart dropped and I felt the blood rush to my face. The next moment the door slid shut. A letter! I was delighted on the one hand, but scared on the other—that envelope was like a hot coal, and my hand shrank from it. The tempting sight of the arm extending from Ch'unja's polo shirt and now the envelope I saw on the floor made me aware of a peculiar feeling that had been sprouting inside me for some time. You'd have to call it love, amorous love. It was a feeling I hadn't experienced for more than thirty years. And I could no longer deceive myself—it was a feeling I had had for Ch'unja.

Maybe it had started back in the summer of 1945, when I had gone to Hwangju. Or maybe earlier, the year she had returned to Hwangju from Seoul at the age of seventeen—she used to follow me around, vivacious as a minnow, a sweet young thing.

With a trembling hand I picked up the envelope. On the front was written *My Dear Mr. Song*, on the back *Ch'un*. Suddenly I lost all courage to open it. Inside I was sure there was a splendid world I had never visited before. But it was also a frightening world. I closed my eyes. I had made a conscious effort to be upright, a model for my young charges. To stray from the path of righteousness while I was teaching those children would be a mortal blow to my conscience.

Plus, I had a wife. Ours was not a love match, and we hadn't been especially fond of each other. She'd only made it through primary school, and there wasn't much to recommend her, mentally or physically. But she was my wife, there was no getting around it, and I was her husband, no way around that either. For better or worse, you have a wife, and to become amorous and whatnot with another woman, that was something my sense of ethics would not allow, it was immoral.

To fully appreciate a lovely rose, should I get pricked by its thorns? Should I cast that rose aside? I must have been at it less than half an hour, but what a fight it was, a battle hidden from view.

I tucked the envelope inside a sheet of paper and took it across the yard to the room where she'd been staying. When Ch'unja saw me standing there at the shoe ledge, her cheeks reddened and she dropped her head. The lowered head, the furious blush that had spread to her ears—she had never looked so pretty.

"What are you playing around for?" I said, keeping my voice down. Then I deposited the letter and turned away. The next moment I was surprised at how harsh and frosty I sounded—I'd never intended to come off sounding so cold.

Others may think differently, but to me, amorous love is something very peculiar. Even though I'd sliced off that rose at the stalk, from that morning, from that hour, Ch'unja's image was branded on my heart—maybe because I myself wasn't aware of my feelings for her, so that when she made the first move it was like pouring fuel on a fire.

I tried to forget her, but she wasn't to be forgotten. Thoughts of her popped up now and then, and the worst times were when I found myself wishing I could get even a glimpse of her. I was always wondering about her, worrying about what she was doing. So when I learned of her degradation it choked me up, and I felt all too painfully my share of the responsibility.

That same morning Ch'unja packed her bags and left—I'm not even sure she had breakfast—and never visited again. From the time Hwangju Auntie came south, there were several occasions when I saw her—with family or with mutual friends. We would say hello and we would talk, but it was always superficial. And if we happened to find ourselves together, just the two of us, the best she could do by way of greeting was a snort and a "Look who's here, Prince Upright."

5

It was July 20 when Hwangju Auntie had visited and over kalguksu had voiced her expectations, our conversation like fresh water quenching our thirst. Once Dr. Yi took office and an independent Chosŏn government was in place, she had declared, the way forward would open for the people of Chosŏn. True to her word, Dr. Yi was elected president, and a few days after her visit, a prime minister was selected; then in early August a cabinet was formed. On August 13 the United States and China recognized the government of the Republic of Korea.

And on August 15, that blessed day on which, three years earlier, we had been liberated, the Republic of Korea held a grand ceremony to formally announce Korean independence to the Korean people and the world. Among those in attendance was General MacArthur, who arrived from Tokyo. And with that, Chosŏn, or the southern sector anyway, became an independent state with its own government.

The north, for its part, announced that on August 25 it would hold a general election. It would not be held just in the north but would include a so-called underground election—that is, a secret election—in the south, so that it would cover the entire peninsula.

At almost the same time the southern reaches of the peninsula were hit with heavy rains that flooded the paddies and dry fields, swept away homes, and left many casualties in their wake. It was a large-scale disaster, the scope of which was rare in recent years.

These various developments, visible and invisible, and the flush of emotion that followed brought to the hearts and minds of the people a surge of strife and anxiety and commotion and restlessness and unease—you could glimpse it in their eyes, sense it in their hearts.

Early on the morning of August 15 I handed out our new national flags to the children and off we went to the celebration, where we added our felicitations for Liberation and the birth of the Republic of Korea. No matter what anyone might say, for me it was a meaningful and moving day.

That evening, bearing a message from Mother, I set out for Hwangju Auntie's place, a cozy Japanese dwelling with a humble garden, located at the verge of Changch'undan Park. Everything about the home—location, garden, timber, construction—bespoke prudence and care on the part of the family who had originally owned it. Whoever they were, judging from the heart they had put into the home, the exquisite detail of the construction, they must have expected to be living here in the land they had conquered for another hundred or thousand years. I felt a sudden burst of sentiment at the vicissitudes of human affairs.

Auntie had purchased the occupancy rights for 30,000 wŏn in the spring of 1946. Which, subtracted from the 100,000 she had brought with her from Hwangju, left 70,000, an amount that had lasted her until spring of this year.

Someone of her caliber, someone irrepressible like her, should have been out and about with her black-marketing wrapping cloth—it was hard to believe she'd been eating away at her savings, a bit at a time, like nibbling on a skewer of dried, honey-sweet persimmons from the pantry—but instead she was waiting on something.

And that something turned out to be a return to Hwangju and the recovery of all the possessions that had been seized from her. It wouldn't be long, it would happen soon, the 38th parallel would collapse, or so she believed, with the result that she waited day after day, and so the day-by-day draining of her savings didn't leave her feeling needy.

However, she wasn't getting any younger. This year she'd turned fifty-three. From her thirties into her mid-forties she'd grappled with her student boarding-house life, after arriving in Seoul empty-handed with her four children. But she was different now—she just didn't have the same constitution, the same gumption as before.

Today had become tomorrow and then next month and then the month after, and until spring of this year, some two years in all, she'd been waiting, waiting, coughing up her savings a mouthful at a time, to sustain her. Since then, to feed herself she'd been relying on Songja and on the "filthy lucre" brought in by Ch'unja.

And all along, Ch'unja had been sinking deeper into a life of dissipation simply for the sake of it. The breakup of a potential marriage, her rejection in matters of the heart—the disappointment and despair arising from those blows combined with character flaws that had always been there, along with her native curiosity, leading to a lifestyle of loose behavior, playing around, whoring even.

But when times grew desperate, that lifestyle turned into a profession. GI field jackets, along with fabric, cosmetics, cigarettes, sugar, cookies, fountain pens, medication, that and more she managed to get her hands on and then cash in with the "private PX" merchants who operated at the South Gate and Paeogae East Gate markets and whom she would summon to her place for the transactions.

But by June her belly was swollen to such an extent that this source of her "filthy lucre" was inevitably cut off. And now Hwangju Auntie had to scrape by only with Songja's feeble assistance. This was a difficult time, no getting around it. I had heard a detailed account of both Auntie's plight and Ch'unja's situation at the Myŏng-dong teahouse with Yŏngch'un that other day.

As always, Auntie clung to her hopes. And as always, she waited and believed—it wouldn't be long, it was right around the corner, the 38th parallel would open up, and that very day she would rush to Hwangju, now in the north, where the commies had exterminated her family members, recover her home and her possessions and once again live happily ever after. This vision of comfortable life took on a stronger sense of urgency when contrasted with the neediness that now confronted her. Add to this the objective reality of the south holding elections on May 10, the National Assembly being formed with Yi Sŭngman as chair, the constitution prepared, and finally Dr. Yi taking office as president, and Auntie's hopes and beliefs became an article of faith.

But just because you'll resume a grand life in Hwangju doesn't mean you can afford to starve today. Which was a more likely prospect now that Auntie had decided to get by on her remaining funds and sell her home and either purchase a smaller one or else, seeing as how she would soon be leaving Seoul, take out a monthly rental.

It so happened that uphill from our home in Kahoe-dong was a small house that had just gone on the market as a monthly rental. In size it was five k'an, little more than a playhouse, consisting of family room and kitchen and a slightly smaller veranda and guest room, and it required a 60,000-wǒn deposit and 3,000 a month in rent. It was a squat old structure, the yard tiny and the nearest well distant, and that didn't sit well with Mother, but with few mouths to feed there was no reason for Auntie to insist on a large house. Plus, she wouldn't be buying or leasing, so she wouldn't be collared with the responsibility of unloading a home and taking off from Seoul when the time came. So for Auntie it would be a perfect arrangement.

This was the message Mother had charged me to deliver after we had taken a look around the place yesterday. Such places were difficult to find, and Auntie should jump on this opportunity. Mother also told me she knew someone who might pay 300,000 for Auntie's house, and if the price was 250,000 he might very well buy it then and there. From that 250,000, subtract 30,000 for all the paperwork involved in the sale, 60,000 for the deposit on the rental, and 10,000 in moving expenses, and she'd have 150,000 left over—enough to get her through another twelve months. And if in the meantime the 38th parallel opened, it wouldn't hurt to have some money to take with her.

As I opened the gate it occurred to me that Auntie more than anyone else would have welcomed this day, marking the birth of the Republic of Korea, with hope and joy. At the same time I stepped inside the gate, a stomach large as a ripe pumpkin and clothed in a gaudy dress came protruding through the open sliding door to the interior. The next instant that belly flinched and retreated inside and out of sight.

The sight of the monstrously swollen belly was less unpleasant than moving—I couldn't help feeling a burning sensation that practically moved me to tears.

It took me a moment to calm down and then I called out, "Auntie."

But instead of Auntie it was Ch'unja who answered, in a desperate voice: "What are you doing here? Get out, now!"

I called out for Auntie again, and again Ch'unja answered, this time even louder: "I'm going to dump water all over you!"

I gathered that Auntie was out.

I thought it over, then removed my shoes and stepped up onto the veranda—not intending to wait for Auntie, but to talk with Ch'unja. But how was I to effect my goal?

I entered Ch'unja's room, but instead of shrinking back and trying to avoid me she stood her ground and glared at me, panting. Like the face of a woman near term, hers was bloated and lopsided and had lost its luster; her soft eyes had grown sharp and hard. Gone was the pretty appearance I'd always associated with her. When I thought about the blue-eyed, blond-haired thing with the protruding nose that was inside her stomach, wriggling in its desire for its father thousands of miles across the great Pacific Ocean, I felt a surge of hatred and disgust that made me want to gag.

"You'd be better off dead!" I blurted. It was a sad lament, the pitch of my voice as low as I'd ever heard it, the plaintive words unintentional. I felt my eyes welling with tears.

Ch'unja's face took on a spiteful, sardonic expression.

"Well," she snorted, "if it isn't the commendable Prince Upright. So what if I'm knocked up by some you-know-who bastard? So what if I'm carrying his kid? So that makes me dirty. . . ." She snorted again. "So I'm dirty—so what? Tell me. So what if Pak Ch'unja is a bitch, so what if she's a Yankee whore, does that mean I'll spoil the gentleman's chances of getting ahead in the world? Does that reflect poorly on him?"

I didn't know what to say.

Again she snorted. "You're telling me to kill myself? Because I'm dirty? . . . Why? What for? What's dirty about me? How many people in this world are clean? Tell me."

She had me there.

"If selling my virtue to the damn foreigners makes me dirty, then what do you call the 'gentlemen' who sell their integrity to the damn foreigners? If carrying a damn foreigner's baby makes me a dirty bitch, then what about the 'gentlemen' planning to turn their kids into damn foreigners? . . . Tell me. Open that big yap of yours and speak."

Before I knew it she had changed again. Now she had fire in her eyes and was closing in on me.

She snorted once more. "You don't have anything to say for yourself, do you? Then I'll say it for you. . . . Who are the ones who took innocent little children and tried to make Japs out of them? Who are the ones who were always barking about using the Jap language and ditching our own language?

Who are the ones who recited the Imperial Prescript for Loyal Subjects several times a day, who called out 'Long Live the Emperor' day and night? . . . And why stop with the Japs? Once the Japs ran off, who are the ones who cozied up to their replacements, the damn you-know-whos, who are the ones who make our children into slaves for the damn you-know-whos when they're not up to some other dirty tricks?"

What could I say?

"Sure, I'm a whore for the Yankees. Sure, I sold my virtue to the damn you-know-whos. Sure, I'm carrying a damn you-know-who's kid. And sure, that makes me a dirty bitch. . . . But I never prostituted my soul, like others have done. I never prostituted my national spirit, I never sold out our people and their descendants. You want to talk about dirty, you want to know who the really dirty ones are? They're those selfish 'gentlemen,' that's who!"

Well, it was a fair-and-square put-down. You might even call it reasonable.

In early Chosŏn there was a former loyal subject of Koryŏ who held a position in the Yi government. He scolded an unruly *kisaeng* with the old expression, "You eat in the east and sleep in the west," to which the woman replied nonchalantly, "Is that any different from serving the Wangs and then serving the Yis?" She had put him to shame all right.

"I did wrong," I told her in a lifeless tone, looking up at her for the first time, "and what you say is right, but please don't let your anger fester inside you." And with that I turned to leave.

Ch'unja jumped in front of me, and there we stood, eye to eye. Her anger had been washed away, and in its place was a calm sorrow.

"What made us like this? Were we enemies from the start? Is it my fate to be humiliated like this?" she said feebly, almost in an undertone. "You never opened my letter, just tossed it back to me—did you ever think what an embarrassment that was for a girl? If humiliation was on your mind, you did a swell job of it."

Humiliation? I couldn't have imagined it. But listening to her now, yes, it seemed to make sense.

With her tear-filled eyes looking directly into mine, she continued, "I never wanted you to see this stomach of mine. Never, not you. You told me I was dirty and ought to kill myself, and now I'm so ashamed, that's exactly what I should do. You made me ashamed of myself."

She got choked up, and the next thing I knew she had burst into tears and collapsed sobbing onto the floor, hands covering her face.

I felt torn up inside, her crying was so plaintive. It was enough to bring most people to tears, but I just stood there like a moron. My gaze drifted out through the open window and came to rest on a couple of wild rose blossoms, faded and withering, in the garden. Weak rays streamed from the sun lingering above. What a coincidence, the sorry combination of a fading sun and withering flowers.

And then the gate creaked open and a voice bellowed, "Ayu, it's hot as a frypan! Come out, little baby, and help me with this. . . . How in heaven's name can they ask 1,500 for a measure of rice? Everybody's doing it, it's atrocious. . . . Those grain merchants are all a bunch of commies, clear as day."

You can probably guess who was making that racket.

Above the withering blossoms, a heartless crow cawed before disappearing into the last glimmers of the setting sun.

August 15, 1948, interim housing in Iri;
published in Challan saram tŭl, 1948

2

IN THREE DIRECTIONS

(Segillo, 1924)

I BOARDED AT THE TAIL END OF THE TRAIN, FIGURING I'D HAVE more room to stretch out there.

It was quite the spectacle—the huge black train, the platform thronged with passengers pushing and shoving in a frenzy to board first, the porters cupping their hands around their mouths and shouting and screaming in Japanese, "Iri, this is Iri, a five-minute stop, transfer here for Kunsan and Chŏnju," the arriving passengers disembarking in lockstep, with inattentive gazes and settled expressions, while from the windows of the cars shone the placid faces of through passengers at ease with the world.

Not far from the door where I stood, a lady student dressed in clothing the color of pearls caught my eye. What a refreshing sight. She wasn't a knockout, and she wasn't the only woman on the train, but there's something about the term "lady student" that makes you feel you're looking at the world, you're hearing it, in a different way—perhaps more so out here in the provinces. Maybe that's why she grabbed my attention, and I can't deny that others in the compartment might have felt the same curiosity.

She had a broad, fleshy face and her arms, her legs, everything about her was a bit generous. When she happened to look out the window and ask, "Where are we?" I could have sworn I heard plumpness in her voice. I felt sensuality hovering about her.

Her summer jacket was milky white, as was her skirt—and presumably her underskirt, otherwise I would have noticed the dark shadow—and her knee-length stockings, and her powdered face. Black was reserved for her leather shoes with their high, pointy heels and the lush braid that fell stylishly over her shoulder.

Just the type for the oldest son of a well-to-do family, as we like to say in the provinces. She was sitting to the right of the aisle, facing forward, and across from her was a fiftyish woman who, instinct told me, was her mother.

Directly behind the good mother was a young man, early to mid-twenties, maybe a college student, maybe a trade school student—I couldn't tell for sure because he wasn't wearing the black uniform—but in any event a student, I decided. He had a mean, clever look, and my first quick impression was that he was a bit haughty.

The seat across from him was unoccupied.

At first I assumed the young man was a relative, or else someone from the ancestral village, and he and the two women were traveling together to Seoul. But soon I realized I was mistaken: the way he kept sneaking looks at her, his eyes eager and cunning, told me otherwise. I approached, deposited my bag on the overhead rack, and took the empty seat, then rose to remove my jacket and loosen my tie, which gave me the opportunity to regard the young lady head on.

The way her eyes met mine told me she'd probably been watching me as well. Why me? I had to look away. But the next moment I was thinking, *Why shouldn't one person look at another?* The fact was, I was delighted, pure and simple, that I'd caught her gaze. And it wasn't just her: the good mother turned to look at me, and then the young guy, and then the middle-school boy and the country gentleman across the aisle. *Yes* (but with a touch of uneasiness)!

Passengers were still boarding, eyes darting in search of a seat, and the platform was still in an uproar, peddlers of bento boxes, tea, and whatnot pressing close to the compartment windows and delivering their spiel.

The young lady whispered to her good mother, and the next thing I knew she had taken her purse and gone out. The young guy shot to his feet and followed her. Before long she came back with two of the lunchboxes. The guy, for his part, returned empty-handed and reclaimed his seat, then resumed stealing one glance after another at her.

The departure bell rang, muffling the squeak of the porters' whistles, and with a blast of its steam whistle the train chugged almost imperceptibly into motion. It click-clacked and screeched across the intersecting rail lines and then, as if shedding unnecessary baggage, it took off, free as the wind.

It all felt so comforting—the scenery changing nonstop, the roar of the engine, the familiar sense of ease in spite of the dull pounding inside my skull.

Only now did the lady student unwrap the two bento, and she and her mother began daintily to partake. She was so cute, nibbling like a rabbit, but then I realized the guy was watching *me* and I had to turn away. I pretended to look elsewhere, but actually I was delighted, thinking she was probably still giving me the eye.

Regrettably, hot sunlight was streaming in through the window and coal dust was in the air. The solution? Place my hat on the seat to reserve my claim, and move for the time being a few rows up and across the aisle to a seat that was both shaded and dust-free. From that vantage point I could look at the young lady head on.

Before long the train made its first stop, lurching to a halt, and upon the final turn of the wheels the disembarking passengers rose calmly in unison, faces relaxed, voices quiet—as if it had all been scripted. Out they went and in came others, ripples of activity soon assimilated by my comfortable state of mind and the musty air of the train.

In the meantime the guy had moved across the aisle and sat facing me next to the boy who looked like a middle-school student; probably they were traveling together. And from there he sent a glance at the young lady. The next moment he got back up, approached the country gentleman directly behind him—his other travel partner, so it seemed—borrowed a pencil, then got paper from the middle-school boy, moistened the tip of the pencil with his tongue, and began writing.

Was he penciling a note to her? This I had to see, so, pretending to be passing down the aisle, I sneaked a look. With a sheepish smile I returned to my seat. What I'd seen was a string of figures—7.5 0.5 1.5 0.3 1.8 0.7 0.3—expenses he stood to incur on this trip? So much for clever impressions.

The guy, for his part, crumpled the paper and tossed it aside, then lit a cigarette and began puffing away. The kid lit up as well. Whereupon the guy gave him a pat on the back and brayed for everyone to hear, "Lookie here, schoolboy knows how to smoke." His accent placed him somewhere around P'yŏngyang. The kid grinned and innocently had a peek at the young lady, then gave the guy a look and pouted—"What's wrong with a schoolboy smoking?"—and produced a scornful smile. And that launched them into a bantering jag, their gazes constantly on the move.

The guy got up, passed by the young lady, went to the back of the car and out, then returned, still glancing at the young lady, and said to the kid,

"Wow, you wouldn't believe all the paddy land they got here," before sitting back down, a rooster performing for a hen.

I have to admit, she was beginning to buy into the act. The guy must have expected this, and next would be a heart-to-heart connection and, if he could keep the ball rolling, an actual relationship. But as far as I could tell, the way she regarded him was different from the way she regarded me.

She then produced a watermelon, sliced off the top, and with her mother began spearing chunks of fruit into their mouths. My oh my, did that watermelon look sumptuous! Ripe as ripe could be, the crunchy, crimson flesh studded with black seeds and spurting with sweet nectar had me drooling in no time. In truth I felt no urge to eat it, but I swallowed anyway in spite of myself. Instead I liked the way she carved out sections of fruit that looked ready to melt in her mouth, popped them in, spit out the seeds, and proceeded to nibble away—her mouth was cuteness itself.

The guy gaped at her slack-jawed, then shot to his feet and returned to his original seat, and the next thing I knew he'd opened the window, poked himself halfway through, and was singing. His voice was so scratchy it would have cracked a clay pot. Luckily it could only be heard in between the clacking of wheel on rail.

And in no time we arrived at Kanggyŏng. Again the car became a commotion of passengers coming and going.

Among the new arrivals was a fiftyish woman who didn't look like an ordinary housewife but whose clothing was neat and who sported a gold ring and gold hairpin. She had her choice of seats but squeezed in next to the young lady's good mother, perhaps thinking she'd found a companion to chat with over the course of her journey.

And sure enough, out came her pipe, and then her cloth wrapper of leaf tobacco, and soon she was puffing away and talking, and what do you know, she had a Kyŏngsang accent.

"Aigo, for heaven's sake, I just want to live in peace—is that too much to ask?" she said, eyeing the good mother.

"What seems to be the matter?" said the mother.[1]

Even so, the guy looked at the young lady out of the corner of his eye and wrinkled his nose.

In response to his remarks, the good mother turned to him with a look of admiration and asked, "How far are you going?"

The guy's peeved face softened and in an obliging tone he said, "I'm bound for Seoul." And then he ventured, "And you?"

"Seoul as well . . . which means I transfer at T'aejŏn, yes?"

"Yes, Taejŏn," said the guy, correcting her pronunciation. "After Nonsan, Yŏnsan, Tugye, and Kasuwŏn," he added, counting off the stops on his fingers. "So, after four more stops." His face was the picture of satisfaction.

His gaze, loaded with desire and anticipation, returned ever more frequently to the young lady. Occasionally she returned the favor, her gaze curious.

As we neared Taejŏn I went to my original seat and gathered my belongings. I could see the young lady looking at me again. Instead of meeting her gaze I looked away. Regrettable! But what else could I do? Every time our eyes met, I somehow felt embarrassed.

As I turned away, all I could do was feel sorry for myself. *Why can't I look at her all I want?*

As soon as we pulled into Taejŏn the guy launched into a whirlwind of activity, hailing a redcap for the lady student and her mother and fetching their bags. I watched with even more interest as he purchased express tickets for not only the good mother but also her daughter, and found them both seats on the Pusan-Seoul train, to which we were all transferring. Finally he got himself a seat near them.

I boarded a different car. Seeing all the empty seats around me, I got to thinking about the three of them. I found my way to their compartment and sneaked a look. The guy had left his seat and was right next to the good mother, chatting her up like an old friend.

I observed the young lady. She looked me in the eye, but this time *she* turned away. Her gaze felt cold, but the way she looked at the guy, it seemed she was warming up to him.

And then the guy looked at me. Both his gaze and his expression were tinged with pride in himself as well as mockery toward me.

Well, hell! In a fit of anger I turned away. I felt the energy drain from me as I returned to my seat. Only then did I snap out of my daydreams. I smiled a smile that felt colder than ice.

Under darkening skies I got off the train at Namdaemun Station in Seoul, filed through the busy gates, found a secluded nook, and waited for the young lady and the guy to emerge.

The young lady appeared first. She and her mother climbed into a rickshaw and went off in the direction of Namdaemun. The guy scurried out and stood for a time watching them depart; then he and the boy caught a horse cart driven by a Chinese man and set off toward the Sŏdaemun streetcar line.

As for me, I hopped on the streetcar all by my lonesome and headed for Yongsan.

The next day I encountered the guy on the street. I managed to contain myself and let loose a most suggestive smile. And sure enough, he responded with a grin as he passed me by.

Chosŏn mundan 3 (December 1924)

NOTE

1. The following 23 lines of text in the Korean original were deleted by censors.—Trans.

3

UNGRATEFUL WRETCH

(Purhyo chashik, 1925)

IT WAS AN AFTERNOON IN THE DOG DAYS OF SUMMER WHEN RAYS of fire seared everything under heaven. I was on my way home from school, dripping with sweat, and was turning down the alley to my boarding house when I ran across Ch'ilbok's mother, Ch'oe by name. The moment I saw her, my intuition told me she'd heard the news about Ch'ilbok and come up from the country. At the same time a memory wheel of images began revolving in my mind's eye—Ch'ilbok's face; Ch'ilbok sitting with his pant leg rolled up, injecting himself, his hand white as a magpie's belly; the dismal red walls of Sŏdaemun Prison, within which Ch'ilbok in his dull yellow prison garb, his legs shackled, worked at hard labor, looking more dead than alive.

Several years earlier I'd seen the mother when she came to Seoul to visit him, and already by then she was no longer in a position to have made the trip for some other purpose, say, sightseeing or another matter that needed attending to. Then as now, she looked as if she alone were bearing all the poverty and hardship of this world. It had pained me to see her looking so wretched and needy. The ramie skirt and jacket she had thrown on were little better than rags and they clung to her, pocked with holes, tattered, grimy, and encrusted with sweat. I wondered when they'd last been laundered. Her hair, half white by then, was puffed out like a plaited bamboo container for a deck of hwat'u cards that's coming apart. Her quilted socks were dusty, and she scuffed along in a straw sandal whose heel had worn away and, on her other foot, a rubber shoe that was ripped and split.

Today she was dressed the same, with a splotched and faded bundle under her arm, and was propping herself up with an ancient bamboo walking stick that looked like it would burn to a crisp in the late afternoon sun. She had come to a stop and with dull, listless eyes was searching any and all who came along, sun-seared face making her look old beyond her years and bearing a sad, pathetic expression. It all combined inevitably to envelop her in that characteristic mood of sickening destitution, no matter how she might have tried to outfit and pretty herself up.

Anyone with substance of feeling who might witness the contrast between the grandeur of the noble, wealthy family of Pak Chinsa, Ch'ilbok's good father, some thirty years before, and the cruel downfall that now doomed his descendants would be brought to tears of helpless sorrow at the vicissitudes and uncertainties of life.

I approached her and said hello. She looked at me quizzically, wondering who I was. I'd had practically no contact with her since I'd left the ancestral village to go to school here in Seoul. If I hadn't had such a deep impression of Ch'ilbok, who knows, I might not have recognized her either, and continued on my way. To run into a kid with the square hat worn by college students and the Western-style clothing favored by the Japs, out of the blue, must have been too much for her. While I was trying to figure out how best to remind her who I was, she looked up to inspect me, and finally a vague glimmer of recognition came over her. She took my arm and with an overflowing of that characteristic affection of elderly mothers the world over, and radiating delight, said,

"Ai, you're what's-his-name's little brother . . . uh, Odong, right? My, how you've grown . . . I wouldn't have recognized you. . . ."

"Ah yes . . . that's me."

"Mmm, yes, yes. . . . You're the last-born of Cho Sŏndal in Upper Hollow, yes? . . . I hope your family are all well?"

"Yes—but what brings you here, ma'am?" I knew the answer but had to ask anyway.

It was difficult to make out the change in expression in her sun-darkened face, but change it was, to unspeakable sadness.

"Aigu . . . I'll tell you. . . . Our Ch'ilbok is serving a sentence, he's in jail."
Tears pooled in her eyes and streamed helplessly down her wrinkled face.

I felt a tingle around my eyes and my vision blurred over. I had to look away before I spoke. "In that case, please come with me," I said, intending to guide her to my boarding house. Standing there talking with her, I felt stifled and uneasy.

She remained where she was, uncertain as the prospects of a rain shower on a summer evening. "Where do you mean?"

"My boarding house," I said, mentioning the landlord by the childhood name by which he was known back home.

And surprise, with a look of satisfaction she said, "Mmm, sure thing, not as if I have a choice in the matter—that's the very place I'm trying to find." Showing me a scrap of paper with my landlord's name and address written on it, she added, "Yes indeed, I was wondering where to go. Somehow or other, I had to find someone I know. . . ."

The following day she went with P, my landlord, to visit her son at Sŏdaemun Prison. Ch'ilbok was an opium addict and was serving a five-month sentence for theft. That evening when I returned from school I saw her leaning against the front gate and gazing off into the distant sky, tears streaming down her face. I found myself wishing I hadn't come across her, but I couldn't very well walk inside without greeting her, and I was curious about how Ch'ilbok was doing. So I asked if she had been to see him.

Using the hem of her shabby skirt to dab at her tears, she said in a sunken voice, "Ŏi . . . I saw him all right, but I wish I hadn't . . . *aigo* . . . seeing what a hard time he's having, how can I go on living? I wish I could kill myself so I don't have to witness him in his misery, but even a cruel life is hard to bring to an end." And then with a great sigh she dabbed again at her tears. The effect of her wiping was to remove some of the grime from her face, leaving it looking paler in places.

I didn't think much of it at the time, but later I learned from Ch'ilbok that her face looked that way because she'd walked all the way here from back home—she'd been out in the sun for a week and a half. I wanted to say something to comfort her, but what? All I could offer was, "Is he all right?"

"*Aigo*," she said with a stupefied look. "How could be all right? . . . His face looks like it's never seen a ray of sun in his life, it's a godawful color. . . . He looks like bones inside a leather bag . . . says he's got sores popping open all over . . . says he's practically starving, and they expect him to do such hard labor he feels like his bones are going to snap. . . . He's sure he's going to die there and never walk out alive. . . . *Aigo*, the idea of him dying there . . . seeing him in that shape . . . and all for stealing a *kisaeng*'s ring and pawning it—is that such a capital crime? . . . Why didn't they let him redeem it instead? . . . Why's it their business if he wants to spend his own money on opium and stick it into himself?" So saying, she burst into tears of resentment and sorrow.

I'd lived with Ch'ilbok for some time at P's house, so I understood what she was saying about him. The morning before he was apprehended, he'd bought a seven-*wŏn* bottle of morphine and used it up the same day, breaking it open to get the last drops, but it wasn't enough, and that night he was moaning and shivering like he'd come down with malaria. The next morning the detectives took him away. Knowing the extent of his addiction, I could imagine how painful it must have been to be whisked away and left to his cravings; what his mother had said about him being skin and bones was probably no exaggeration. But the loss of weight was a temporary effect of being deprived of opium, and shortly he'd regain his appetite. The problem was, the prison "repast" would leave Ch'ilbok's innards writhing and demanding more. Already by then he'd developed boils on his bottom, his arms, all over. If only he'd mixed the morphine with distilled water and sanitized the needle—but when he was really craving the drug he'd use dirty stream water if he had to, and a needle that had made the rounds of half a dozen other addicts, so the boils were inevitable.

The infection had turned him into a living corpse for some time before he was jailed. His arms, his legs, his entire body was a hideous infestation of scabbed-over boils surrounded by black-and-blue bruises, along with new boils of mung bean–like protuberances with an angry red halo around them—all of them coated with a gummy black salve. Just to witness this scene, him sitting cross-legged, poking and probing with a sharpened matchstick at the soft, fully ripened boils, pressing down on them with a scrap of newspaper to soak up the dark red blood and the yellowish pus that looks like ground-up mung beans, and to smell the stink, like that of a corpse rotting at the torrid height of the dog days—and then he takes from the wall the already used salve patches and presses them down on the boils, and then he takes a beer bottle (which is the perfect size for mixing up a dose of morphine, and which he always keeps on his person along with the needle), adds cold water, and takes out the packet of morphine, wrapped ever so carefully and kept either in his worn-out wallet or in the cigarette case commonly used by these addicts, carefully mixes it into the water, then draws the mixture into the needle, searches for a fresh place to inject, stabs it in a quick motion, then sinks back against the wall and pretends to snore, pops a hard candy into his mouth and sucks on it, eats some peanuts and leaves the shells all over the floor, glances nervously about, his thieving hands reaching about the floor, rambling on to no good end about the pile of money, as big as Inwang Mountain, that he's going to get his hands on, and bragging about whoring with kisaeng, something he's most likely never actually done, squabbling with K, another resident of our boarding house—his actions and his appearance, so ugly and pathetic and hateful, and sneaky besides, are impossible to express in a single word. And the friends he's made? Addicts, every last one of them. Whenever they get their hands on money, they're full of brotherly love, willing to share with you the food that's already in their mouth, but on the other hand, when they run short of money, they'd sooner die than share their drugs or even a peanut shell—it's standard procedure. And the bald-faced lies that come out of their mouths? Take Ch'ilbok when I caught him shooting up just before he was jailed.

"What do you think you're doing?" I asked him.

Needle clutched in his hand, he scratched his head innocently and played dumb: "Who, me? . . . I'm not doing anything."

All I could do was grin in amazement.

No matter how strong your constitution, how humble your demeanor, once you start in on opiates, within a few years you look like a dead man walking and you carry yourself like scum.

But rather than express all this to Ch'ilbok's mother, I tried to comfort her, saying five months in jail wasn't such a long time, it probably seemed such an ordeal because it was his first time, but he'd find his situation gradually improving. As I went inside she was still standing at the gate weeping, then sighing and lamenting distractedly, oblivious to the setting sun.

That day, after visiting her son, Ch'ilbok's mother had buttonholed one of the guards: "Would you please lock me up instead of my Ch'ilbok? Or else kill me right here and now." She must have wept and badgered the guard and inevitably been shooed away, after which she said to P, "I'm going back there tomorrow, even if the only thing they do is give me a look at him." According to P, who related this to me, she had barely made it back home. But sure enough, at first light the next day, heedless of our attempts to detain her, she went again to the prison and after wrangling with the guards in vain, came back to the boarding house.

Three fruitless days she trudged back and forth, which must have worn her down, because she made no further attempts to visit. Instead she remained at P's boarding house, from time to time doing laundry for the students or going around peddling a basket of something or other, tucking away a copper at a time for train fare so that when Ch'ilbok was released she could take him back home. From then on she was allowed a bimonthly visit and would make sure not to miss the appointed day, leaving at daybreak for the prison. To her the time invariably dragged on, every moment feeling like an eternity.

The tedious summer passed, and then the dreary autumn, and a few days ago the gloomy old year gave way to a new year that brought me a springlike surge of energy. I had been back home for winter break and now, in early January, I returned to Seoul to find Ch'ilbok back at the boarding house— he'd been released the previous day. He had changed almost beyond recognition. Formerly so wasted, he had gained weight in prison and now looked positively flabby. His squat nose was buried between puffy cheeks, and his cunning eyes, which seemed a predictor of his future, were more round. But the limp, sallow, swollen flesh of his face, the reddish scalp shorn of its long hair, the peculiar tinges of fear and anxiety that perhaps unbeknown to him had colored his expression and behavior, combined with the musty smell he'd brought from prison, made him seem not of this world. Still, in his comfy quilted cotton clothing, which was old and worn but freshly washed by his mother, he looked as if he had not a care in the world, in fact looked bored to death, and so he bounced from room to room regaling the students about his time in jail.

That evening I sat him down along with young P, son of our landlord, and heard the tale, which by then Ch'ilbok had repeated so many times it came out sounding stale. He told me the whole story, gory details and all.

"So how do you feel?" I asked after I'd heard him out.

The question obviously moved him, but he had trouble finding the right words; only after several starts did the dam break, and out it all came, in a fervent tone, his expression uncharacteristically honest:

"I'll tell you, it's unbelievable . . . seriously, I can't tell you how many times I wanted to hang myself. . . . That first time she came to see me, Mother, I mean . . . what she said to me, how she looked, my god . . . short on train fare, so she walked a week and a half before she got on a train or a bus somewhere around P'yŏngt'aek, and by then her face was baked by the sun and peeling all over . . . *aigu*, if I'd had a knife I would have slit my wrist, I mean it. . . . Dammit all, how I could I have put her through all that trouble? I'm the only one she has . . . look what I've done to myself . . . and to my mother besides, who raised me on her own for almost thirty years, look what I've put her through. . . . It's a wonder I haven't been struck dead by lightning for my sins. . . . I just can't believe what I've done. . . . I can't look my friends in the face, not to mention Mother and my family."

He heaved a sigh, looked up at the ceiling, then lapsed into a thoughtful silence. I wondered if that was all. But no—after a time he slowly looked back at me and in a grave tone resumed.

"Well, well . . . here I am looking at age thirty, and I can see Mother aging by the day. . . . I have to straighten up and fly right . . . correction—not 'have to,' I'm doing it right now. . . . I feel like I've come back to life, and that's the truth."

His voice was plaintive. I won't deny there was something a bit unnatural about his expression and the way he spoke, but I saw a glimmer of repentance I took to be genuine. Before I could consider whether it was temporary or permanent, I grew excited and said,

"That's great . . . that's how it should be . . . and not just for your mother's sake, but like you say, you're twenty-nine or thirty, so it makes sense to be thinking about your future . . . and now that you've decided to straighten out, no need to brood over the past and dwell on all the what-ifs. . . . You know, the folks back home say that of all the sinners on this earth—those who have wronged their ancestors, their parents, their offspring, those who have done moral and legal wrong, those who have wronged their society and their countrymen—those who stand the least chance of being accepted are the opium addicts. . . . Anyway, I'm glad and I'm thankful—you're doing the right thing, really."

And that's how I lectured him, even though he was several years older. He listened with downcast eyes, taking my words to heart. There was still that peculiar fervid tinge to him. He kept silent, and even young P, who had never taken seriously a word Ch'ilbok said and who regarded him with ridicule, kept a solemn silence.

"Well, then," I said after a time, "the sooner you can take your mother back home—and then you can do some farming, or if that doesn't work you can hire yourself out to one of the other families, and then you won't have to worry your mother anymore. . . . Would tomorrow be too soon to head down? . . . We'll round up the train fare somehow."

"Mmm . . . yeah, there's the train fare . . . but also, well . . . how should I say . . ." He gave me that look of his, a sheepish kind of smile, but just wouldn't come out with the rest.

"Also what?" I ventured.

Still he hesitated, and then, trying his very best to look sincere: "I'm afraid you'll think this is more of my nonsense, but if I can work out all the angles there's a business deal that might come through for me. . . ."

"Business deal? For you? Now?"

"Well . . . what it is . . . I met this guy there"—by which he meant the prison—"his name is Cho Wŏnbong—and you have to promise you won't tell anyone this—he's the son of a rich landowner, I mean this rich bastard has a lot of land, but he doesn't give his son hardly any money, and so the son's been busy finagling a way to skip on over to Japan, and if he and I can pull together a deal beforehand, then find someone who can fund us or get us an introduction, then we each stand to make at least a thousand *wŏn*. So how'd you like to join me? Thing is, if I go back home now, sure, it sounds good, but I'm empty-handed, what am I going to do back there? . . . But if things work out and some money rolls in, *then* I can go home and get going on some kind of business, and that should be good for some peace of mind, eh? . . . And you know, he got out a few days before I did, and guess who made a point of waiting when I got out? . . . So we agreed that I'll do all the set-up here, and in the meantime he left last night for Kimje and he'll be back in three days at the latest. . . . I want to tell you, this guy knows what he's doing . . . plus he knows the law . . . and watching him deal with those sons-abitches guards, I knew this was a guy to be reckoned with. . . . Anyway, just you wait till this deal works out. . . . So tomorrow I'm off to Tongmak to find us a backer."

And he grinned as if the plan had already succeeded.

It sounded preposterous, but I silently prayed it would work out.

Just then the door opened and Ch'ilbok's mother stuck her head halfway inside. "Ch'ilbok, are you in there?"

Ever since her son had been released she'd been quiet and cautious. She seemed more conscious of the way she dressed. Her face had taken on a modicum of relief and happiness, which, though, were overshadowed by a deep grief and her constant unease. In she came to huddle in the corner, and from there she gazed benevolently into the heedless face of her son.

"How much do you think we'll need for train fare, you and me?" she asked.

"Eight *wŏn* should do it. . . . Why do you ask?"

"Eight *wŏn*? That's 40 *nyang*, right?"

"Yes."

She did some counting on her fingers, considered, then produced a filthy pouch from which she extracted a paper wad that she proceeded to unfold.

Money, I told myself, and sure enough, out came a dozen or so one-*wŏn* notes. One by one she peeled them off, moistening her finger for each, then handed one of them to Ch'ilbok, saying,

"All right, go buy yourself a pack of cigarettes, and we'll use the rest for train fare, then get ourselves a bite to eat—a bento or something—for the trip, that's what we'll do. . . ."

With nary a "thank you" Ch'ilbok accepted the one *wŏn* and tucked it away, then looked at me with a smirk as if to say, *Now how about that!*

"We'll catch the early train out. . . . They say it costs more if you go later."

"What's the rush? . . . Please, can we wait a few days?" And this time the smile he shot me was saying, *Old folks just don't have a clue.*

"*Aigo*, a few days? Tell me, my boy, what's this all about? . . . We need to go now—he has it tough enough without two more mouths to feed," she said, referring to P. "That's too much to ask . . . I'm so ashamed of myself as it is."

"Gee whiz, will you please not worry. . . . It's all going to work out, I tell you."

"*Aigo*, it's beyond me . . . have a heart, son—you're not fixing on getting your old mom burned up inside again?" And with that she left.

Having decided to remain in Seoul until this "deal" of his came through, Ch'ilbok spent every day waiting anxiously for Cho Wŏnbong to arrive. Two days passed and no news—maybe this Cho guy was history, like one of the messengers sent to Yi Sŏnggye in Hamhŭng and fated never to return? And every day Ch'ilbok made the rounds to Tongmak, Map'o, wherever, not returning until dark, and always fretful: "I've got everything all set—what is it with this guy!"

A month passed like this, and the money in his mother's pouch dwindled little by little, one *wŏn* here, fifty *chŏn* there, for cigarettes, snacks, a moving-picture show, a meal of beef-and-rice soup, the streetcar. And all along she hovered about him, faithfully keeping tabs on his whereabouts, with supreme patience looking after all aspects of his life.

Nature never changes, but the landscape of the mind is like night and day. His mother's expectations, five months in jail, pledges and repentance and hardened determination—none could keep Ch'ilbok from transforming yet again. One morning I saw him take money from his mother's pouch—the very last *wŏn* that remained, as it turned out. And then he left; he came right back, but without the snacks or cigarettes I expected to see. The following day he borrowed one *wŏn* from me. I didn't feel right about it, but decided to wait and see. And then three days later K, who shared my room, grumbled that someone had taken three of the five *wŏn* he had in his pocket. In addition to the two of us, Ch'ilbok had slept there the previous night. I didn't need to ask to know Ch'ilbok was the culprit. But I didn't say anything and just let it slide. Two or three days later several *wŏn* went missing from my wallet.

A few more days passed, and a couple of nice brass rice bowls disappeared from the kitchen. I've forgotten what the next missing item was, but after that one of the other boarders lost first his wallet and then his overcoat. And so it was that less than a month after he'd lost control of himself—granted, it's silly to speak of control in connection with opium addicts—and started shooting up again, he was once again hooked on morphine. According to him, he'd developed a cyst on his bottom that was so sore he couldn't walk, he had to crawl around instead, and then he remembered seeing my injured hand get better after I applied iodoform to it, so he grated some iodoform, mixed it with grains of steamed rice, and applied the salve to the sore, and once again he could walk around. And then he ran out of money and couldn't buy his morphine, so he got a gleam in those crafty eyes of his, grabbed his Korean topcoat and his hat, neither of which was much to look at, and went to try to pawn them.

It was a bitter experience. Once the drug wore off there was nothing anyone could do—he was like a malaria victim, lips turning blue, shivering, wrapping himself up in his quilt, moaning that he was sick to his stomach, his chest was sore, he was dying; to believe him, if left alone he'd die on the spot. And then his mother, dripping tears, for she knew exactly what was happening, would set out to scrape together as best she could 20 or 30 *chŏn*, which she then gave to him. Still trembling, he would hunch up and crawl off somewhere, and when he came back there was life in his face and spring in his step.

And then for a time, every few days his wallet grew fat with folded money and he could afford morphine, and his snacks upgraded to hard candy and fruit. Every time I witnessed this I'd say to myself, *Here we go again, he must have swiped something and gone straight to the pawnshop,* wondering by what means he was coming into money. His appearance was back to the way it had been before he went to jail—actually it was even worse. The color leached out of his sallow face; the flesh disappeared from his leathery, wrinkled skin; his bones poked out sharp as thorns; his hair grew long and stringy; his eyes sank deeper into the bottomless sockets of his haggard face.

Anyone seeing him in this condition, stretched out like a rag doll, barely breathing, could be forgiven for assuming he was dead.

It's said that a desire for sexual satisfaction is among the reasons for injecting opiates, but in the end the addict's sexual capability wastes away. Ch'ilbok too lost all interest in sex. He hadn't remarried after his wife passed on, but even if he'd wanted to, what would have been the use? For his mother's desperate attempts to find him a new match were met with comments such as, "Why not let the poor bastard croak instead of babying him the way you do?" and she too lost the sympathy of the neighbors, who considered her an eyesore. Not that she didn't have her own grievances. When she was by herself her worries churned inside her and she cried until her eyes were inflamed. *Era*, she must have been thinking. *This cruel world, I ought to do away with myself.* . . . *He's not my son, he's an enemy from my previous life.* . . . *I don't care if he lives or dies, I'm going my own way.* But one look at Ch'ilbok's ravaged face and out came another shower of tears to wash away her determination in the blink of an eye, rendering her so helpless that the only dying she did was in her heart. This is the pinnacle of a mother's affection, the acme of absolute love.

Two months passed and finally, at the end of March, there appeared the person Ch'ilbok had awaited so desperately—Cho Wŏnbong. And the appearance of Wŏnbong meant the appearance of the rich man from Kimje who had mortgaged his land to come up with some money. This brought Ch'ilbok jumping up from his deathbed, as excited as if he was bound straight for heaven, and for several days he was out and about, scurrying all over.

One day he returned smiling ear to ear.

"How's your big project coming along, any news? Any chance you'll be treating me to an evening at the Bright Moon Pavilion?" I said, referring to the finest kisaeng house in the land.

"You betcha . . . everything looks good. . . . We're almost there, almost. . . . The money's coming in the day after tomorrow, yessir . . . just a little longer and the cherry trees are blooming. . . . We'll pile the kisaeng into a car and toot around Ui-dong . . . yeah, I'll show you . . . mm-hmm. . . ."

I listened to his blue streak, realizing my scorn had failed to register, and then he turned to his mother and after a few words assured her, for no apparent reason, that he'd be back the day after tomorrow. And off he went. Two days later, no Ch'ilbok. And then the following evening, we'd just finished dinner when the paper arrived. In it was a story titled "Self-Proclaimed

Millionaire Fraud Ring." Next to it was the subtitle "Audacious Trio Mortgage Nonexistent Land." The story was as follows:

> A certain Kim, residing in Kimje County, North Chŏlla, together with Cho Wŏnbong of the same address, recently released from prison where he served time for fraud, together with Pak Ch'ilbok, a morphine addict jailed for theft, originally from Kunsan, North Chŏlla, present address unknown, are being held at the Chongno Police Station after their scheme to swindle a massive sum of money with forged documents was uncovered. Among these three, Pak Ch'ilbok is a prime suspect in a rash of thefts starting in January at a number of large businesses, to which he confessed after a search of his person revealed dozens of pawn tickets for a variety of jewelry and other luxury items. A few days hence he will be turned over to Criminal Investigation, along with charging documents.

Spring arrived and Mother Nature was clothed in benevolence, her lovely, merciful dance bringing chirping, song, and dance from every living thing. But unfolding below Inwang Mountain in central Seoul, unable to share its grief, was another world, the somber red brick of Sŏdaemun Prison, and there an elderly woman wept a stream of tears and wailed, "Ch'ilbok! My Ch'ilbok!" as she pounded feebly against the immovable iron gates. Did her emaciated son even hear her, shackled as he was and clothed in dull yellow prison garb, dying for a fix of opium?

Chosŏn mundan 10 (1925)

4

SKEWERED BEEF

(Sanjŏk, 1929)

I

I was in a back-alley drinking place in one of the commercial districts along Chongno. Outside it was dark and dreary and a cold wind nipped at your ears, but here inside it was bright and toasty from the coal brazier.

Looking in from the door, you see on your left a stove with two cookpots practically as big as the Great South Gate, and in front of it a long, narrow table where the proprietor sits tall, like a judge at his bench, dispensing beverages, and next to him the snack selection. Moving to the right, you see a shelf as big as a forage tub in a stable (I know, a shelf is flat and a storage tub is rounded), with bowls of soy sauce—both the plain variety and the one with vinegar—red-pepper paste, salt, and whatnot, and a cutting board with a kitchen knife on it. And right in front of you is the brazier where the drinking snacks are grilled.

And there's the black grime you'll see in any of these places, but because it's nighttime, it doesn't really stand out.

It's still early and the boozers aren't out in full force yet. Two parties have arrived, and each member is grilling snacks with chopsticks stripped of their red lacquer from common use by the lips of the citizens of the capital, slurping a bowl of steaming soup, and quaffing their drink.

"Over here, three *yakchus*."

"Is that all right with you?"

"Cash only, no credit. . . . Here you go, gentlemen."

"And a bowl of soup."

"Let's have one more."

"No thanks, I've had my fill."

Now that the coals are glowing white-hot, the grimy helper brings the grilling brazier over near the door and begins cooking the skewered beef.

Listen to that meat hiss and sizzle.

Take in that savory smell from the rising smoke and feel your nose tingle.

Drinking place: sense of belonging + rich aroma + a helping of good old grime = perfection!

The rich aroma already has you drooling, but add the smell of freshly grilled meat and you'll get those tummy worms churning for sure.

2

Back at home I sent the wife off to the pawnshop, then did some calculating: maybe 10 minutes to get there—hang on, make that 15 minutes, she'll want to stop off elsewhere—5 minutes jawing with the owner, and 15 minutes for buying the rice and bringing it home. There you have it—35 minutes.

Thirty-five frigging minutes? That's forever. When she left I was 27, by the time she gets back I'll look 35. Now there's a scary thought.

But we're not out of the woods yet. Add 40 minutes for steaming the damn rice, for a grand total of 75 minutes. Seventy-five minutes till I get some food in my mouth. That's pathetic. On the other hand, you can imagine my delight at eating that nice, warm, steamy steamed rice.

Before you write me off as some guy with a hunger demon in his stomach, try going all day without a meal and see how you feel.

And if you should ask, "Why should a perfectly healthy guy be starving?" I'd answer, "Because I lost my job."

And if you should ask, "Why did you lose your job?" I'd answer, "Because I cussed out those damned Liberals and wrote bad things about them."

And if you should ask, "Why can't you get another job?" I'd answer, "Because I have about as much common sense as a crab's tail."

And if you should ask, "And so?" I'd answer, "And so what?"

And if you should ask, "And so what next?" I'd answer, "Finding a way not to starve."

And if you should say, "Hmm," I'd say "Hmm yourself."

Fact is, if a guy like me kicked the bucket, there'd be plenty of folks who would say "Good riddance," but I haven't starved yet, I'm still alive and kicking, and you've just heard all the spiteful things that come out of my mouth.

So what next? Hmm, good question.

Everything I said above is beside the point—which is, waiting 35 minutes and then another 40 minutes is *painful*.

So I said to myself, just forget about it and stretch out and read a book or something. Problem is, the book starts looking like a bowl of rice or soup. You ought to hear my wretched stomach growling because there's not a thing in it. And if that's not enough of a reminder, it always comes with a tearing pain in my innards.

I somehow managed to get through the next 30 or 40 minutes, but the little woman still hadn't returned.

And then it was an hour, and still no wife. I went through every possibility: Maybe she'd had her fill of me and flown the coop? Maybe she was run over by the streetcar? Maybe she was still wandering around in search of an obliging pawnshop, shivering in the cold? Or did some dirty sonofabitch . . . ?

As I was entertaining these possibilities I heard footsteps outside the gate and then "Honeyyyy." Boy, was I glad to hear that voice! I jumped up and opened the gate.

"Didja get it?"

She closed the gate behind her. Our rented room was just inside, so coming and going was a breeze.

"How come you didn't start the fire?"

"Fire—what for?"

"For the meat—what did you think?"

"Meat?"

"Mm-hmm." Displaying something rolled up in newspaper, she came inside.

"But I don't see any rice—what the bejesus is going on?"

"I brought some meat, for crying out loud!"

"How did you get your hands on *meat*?"

"It's for skewering."

"Meat for skewering. What about rice—you know, food? Something to fill our stomachs?"

"Food? . . . *Aigumŏni* . . . Oh my. . . ."

We'd been together three years, and in all that time I had never seen her so shocked, regretful, and sad. Once the realization had dawned, that shock, regret, and sadness hit her all at once and she just sat there blankly, nodding stupidly while a line of tears trickled down from each eye.

"What in heaven's name came over you—did something happen?"

"What are we going to do with this?"

"Meaning . . . ?"

"I was so focused on the meat I forgot about the rice. . . ."

Well, how about that! I had to smirk. "My foolish little lady." She had nothing to say to that, merely hung her head, so I followed with, "Say something, for god's sake, how much did you get anyway?"

"Fifty *chŏn.*"

"And?"

Her head was still down, but she managed to flash me a grin. When it comes to womenfolk, tears are cheap. Then again, when you've lived with your husband for three years, there's not much left to hide. Look at her hauling out her woman's bag of tricks—smiling and angling her head from side to side, trying to be cute, playing the coquette.

She must have had a terrible craving. "All right, I get it—you wanted meat, and that's where all 50 *chŏn* went. You little fool! Thirty *chŏn* would have gotten you two measures of rice and you could have used the rest for meat, right?"

"No."

"What do you mean?"

"Well . . . I . . . I . . ."

"I . . . what?"

"On my way home from the pawnshop I went by this drinking place . . ."

"And?"

"And I saw all those men cooking their meat and slurping their soup and drinking their *yakchu* . . ."

"And you fancied yourself a bowl of that *yakchu*?"

"No."

"Then what?"

"That rich aroma . . . it came floating out . . . and then the meat . . . they put a rack of it over a white-hot brazier and cooked it all up."

"Mm." Which meant she had my attention.

"And that smell shot up my nose, and oh myyyyy."

I chuckled. "And?"

"And so I went to the nearest butcher shop and . . ."

And the little lady just sat there with her head down, gnawing on a finger.

I had to laugh. "Fine. All right, then, let's have ourselves some skewered beef." Rolling up my sleeves, I got to my feet.

The little woman gave me an embarrassed look and picked up the meat in its wrapper. "I'm going to return it."

"What are you talking about? He won't give you your money back, and you want to eat it so bad, just cook it up, what the hell."

"And tomorrow?"

"We'll figure out something then." I had myself a belly laugh—a very big belly laugh. And the little woman laughed right along with me.

We didn't have much in the way of seasoning, but that meat sure did taste good.

Pyŏlgŏn'gon, December 1929

5

EGG ON MY FACE

(Hŏhŏ mangshin haettkun, 1930)

IT WAS AROUND SUNSET JUST A FEW DAYS AGO. A FREAK RAIN shower had left the streets a muddy mess.

Just like any other day, I left the print shop in my ink- and oil-stained coveralls, my bento in its cloth wrapper close to my side, and turned down the alley to Kyo-dong.

You've had red-bean porridge at the winter solstice, right? Well, that's what the ground was like, a lumpy mess that made me imagine a guy on the cusp of a nervous breakdown having the time of his life rolling around in it.

The people trying to avoid the mud as best they could resembled babies taking their first wobbly steps.

I made my way to dry land on the east side of the alley and was tiptoeing along, hugging the shop fronts, when I saw, mincing toward me like a dancer, a modern girl—well, maybe four parts traditional and one part modern. *Come come baby baby, come come.*

She lacked the New Woman bobbed hairdo but wore the baggy camel-colored coat that was the latest rage, silk stockings in the same beige color, and Mary Jane shoes (young lady, *where* are your galoshes?), her face half made up, hair two thirds of the way down over her ears, clutching a palm-size lawyer purse—you get the idea.

Such a modern girl wouldn't give the time of day to a print-shop specimen in ink- and oil-stained coveralls with a lunch wrapper slung around his waist.

But of all the strange coincidences, fancy the two of us coming up face to face in front of the smoke shop!

With scarcely a thought, I stepped into the mud to make way for her. The two of us faced each other at an angle.

And that's when it happened.

Miss Modern Girl had just set foot on a board, now mud-slicked, put out for customers, when the pointed heel of her shoe slid off it. Her torso lurched in my direction.

She tried to straighten herself, arms flailing and body twisting, but the laws of physics said, "We're sorry. . . ."

Calamity was in store!

I stepped forward and *plop*, into my bosom she fell, face and honor pawned like a Jesus freak meeting her savior.

And why not? I *accept thee.*

Just then I heard a voice behind me. "Wow, you must've had a lucky dream last night." *Bastard.*

That was the signal for us to liberate each other.

I released Miss Modern Girl, and Godfrey Daniel! she was glaring at me, face white as a sheet. "What do you think you're doing latching on to me like that!" And she hotfooted it down the alley and disappeared.

Well, well—it's like I tried to breathe life back into a drowning woman and she says, "Get your dirty mouth off of me!"

Some lucky dream! Hell, what do I do now?

"Huh-huh, egg on my face!" I had a good laugh.

There was a wave of laughter all around me.

Damn it, as long as people were going to make fun of me, why didn't I get a tasty smooch when I had her in my arms?

Too bad!

1930

6

A WRITING WORM'S LIFE

(Munch'ung iran chonjae, 1935)

I'VE BEEN WRITING ALMOST TEN YEARS NOW. BUT I HAVE TO confess—the last year and a half I've been idling, plain and simple.

With clear eyes and a cool head I have tried to figure out those ten years I've devoted, from my bright and energetic twenties to my thirties, only to realize it's all been in vain—oh my god.

There is of course the inadequacy of the works I've written till now. But the real reason for my remorse is, how can the quality continue to be bad over ten years, to the point where I realize nothing will sprout in the future? Ten years of self-study are supposed to enlighten you, aren't they?

Maybe I was too ambitious, a fragrant wild persimmon that wanted to bear those tasty national-glory apples.

Maybe if I had some old-time greed and bravado instead of my current hesitation and escapism, I would turn something out, whether successful or not. The problem is, regardless of what others might say about a piece I've written, I end up prickling with embarrassment.

I've been courting literature for ten years, a decade-long unrequited love. I can't just break that attachment and walk away.

My obsession isn't limited to literature. There's also my fountain pen— I'm so attached to it, it's so precious. I can't imagine what I'd do if I lost it on the street; I'd probably assume the worst, that someone found it, or it'd been stepped on and broken. So out of habit I'll look down intently on the street or reach into my pocket to make sure it hasn't fallen out. It's a foolish lingering that gets me malingering.

These aren't the only thoughts I entertain as this year comes to a disturbing close, but as I consider my bump-on-a-log life in which I haven't produced a single work in the past year and a half, I so envy others I can't stand it. I feel like it's New Year's Eve and I'm listening to the kids gathered at the head of the alley chattering about what they want for their new clothing the following morning—I feel the desperate loneliness of the servant kid who, forbidden to join them, can only watch from a distance, sucking on his thumb.

Lately, surprise surprise, I've latched on to an idea for a work and it's clear in my mind. So these days I get to thinking that if I can just get it written, whether it turns out to be a story or a play, it'll be quite the achievement. But even though I've several times taken pen in hand, ready to give it a try, my daily life being as it is, I just don't have the wherewithal to execute. And if I force it, it will inevitably turn out to be trash.

I feel the disappointment and horror of a new mother who has given birth to a deformed child. I'd rather be childless forever. I don't want a deformed child.

If I could just spend a year without being a wage slave. . . . I attempt to float this wild thought. If it were possible, I'd spend the first six months traveling, free as the wind, and for the remaining six months I'd serialize that story I was just telling you about, maybe thirty installments in the newspaper. And if it turned out all right I'd devote myself from now on, but if it were trash I'd break my fountain pen in half and be done with it forever.

I've lost my self-esteem, I'm less resilient, I can't tell what's clean and what's murky in my life, and I'm drawn by animal instinct. I see nothing else in my existence. Why then does literature have such a tight hold on me?

"Writing is the work of heroes." As a child I often heard that from the grownups. These days I feel with all my heart that these words are correct.

We should interpret the hero not as a great man but as a man of character, which if we apply it to the writer could mean the "capacity to judge the ways of the world through observation that is not overly skewed." But the more I think of myself, the further from that level I seem to be.

And so I feel I'm more like a writing worm than a writer. I wonder if there are other such writing worms in our literary world. If not, what a relief.

Chosŏn ilbo, December 22, 1935

7

TRAVEL SKETCHES

(Yŏhaeng sup'il, 1935)

I LONG FOR TRAVEL THE WAY I MIGHT LONG FOR A LOVER I'VE never met. And travel is the fuel for my reveries.

But when you add work to travel it's like putting on a suit you haven't paid off yet—it comes with nagging feelings.

This past summer when I went to T'ongyŏng, South Kyŏngsang Province: My train pulled into Shin Masan Station and I had a two-hour wait for the next bus to my destination. I was standing at the stop where the shuttle bus for Ku Masan leaves every ten minutes or so, and the bus girl was a perfect specimen, such a fine sight to see that I took a gander at her every time the bus came back in—not a bad way to kill two boring hours.

Eventually I found myself *waiting* for the bus to return—I was that intrigued by her. I figured her for maybe seventeen or eighteen.

I can't for the life of me figure out how Korean women's looks are handed out regionally. For slender, oval faces with a shapely jaw line, an aquiline nose, and overall intelligence, you look to Hwanghae and P'yŏngan provinces, and for round faces with burning, sultry eyes and thick, dark lashes it's Hamgyŏng women.

Heading south to Kyŏnggi, we find women with faces that look freshly scrubbed but are freckled with a bulge in the middle, and there's just no way you could pick them out in a crowd.

Continuing south to Ch'ungch'ŏng and Chŏlla, you'll see necks that disappear into shoulders; flat, expressionless faces; squashed noses; mouths hanging open; and rough, dark skin. There's not much to look at in these women.

Now turn sharp left and you're in Kyŏngsang, but you might think you're back in Hamgyŏng, so similar are the fine facial features.

How did I get off on this tangent anyway? I noticed the departure time for my bus was only five minutes away. In the meantime the bus girl had noticed I was looking at her, and the last few times her bus had pulled in I had caught her sneaking looks at me and thought I detected a *Who the hell is this guy?* expression. The final arrival: the passengers are getting off, the next load of passengers are getting on, the driver says something to her, she responds with a playful tap on his shoulder, and they launch into a back-and-forth that's quite the performance. And then her bus left, and then I boarded my bus and left, wishing I'd departed fifteen minutes earlier.

I wonder what Freud would think of my reaction—would he call it a kind of jealousy?

Several days earlier—

After sunset on a cold day I had transferred onto the kyŏngp'yŏn tram that runs between what I'll call points A and B. The kyŏng part of that word means light, and that's fair enough, but the p'yŏn, which means convenient, is bogus. The cars are long and narrow and bouncy, and a five-kilometer ride between stations takes close to twenty minutes.

As if that wasn't aggravating enough, there were a couple of hayseeds in my car, a man and a woman, hogging one of the benches that run along the side of the compartment. I don't think they knew each other, but it was difficult to tell from the way they were jabbering together.

And so your humble narrator in his spiffy Western suit proceeded to scrutinize them. I then tried to strike up a conversation, but their response was curt and reluctant, and they kept their distance after that. They were being territorial.

I felt the loneliness of the outsider. It being dark and cold out and me feeling anxious, I got off short of my destination, spent the night at an inn, and the next morning took the first tram to B. Why bother going all the way to B the night before? I'd just have to spend the night there, and it wouldn't save me any time.

Ignoring the complaints of my soon-to-be-emptied pockets, I checked in at a first-class inn that was graced with a sign reading "Hotel." Every time I went to a hot spring I was mortified by the overflowing water—what a waste, why couldn't some of this water be diverted to Seoul? Which got me thinking about the unsanitary public baths in Seoul.

Anyway, I had myself a nice soak in the hot spring there and what do you know, my aches and pains eased up immediately.

My tatami room came with a Western-style glass-enclosed balcony, and there I sank into a chair and looked out on what appeared to be a full moon. The moon floated high in the cold, faintly starlit sky, and stretching out below were vast fields soaking up its light. Somehow this spare scene aroused my aesthetic sensibility. There I sat, enjoying the moon, with no thought of laying my tired body down to rest, and for some reason I felt regretful—something was missing. Just then the maid happened by with my tea. Why had they shown me to the big shared bath? I grumbled to her. The inn had private baths, didn't it? And since I would only be there one night and this was a rare opportunity for me to enjoy the hot spring, I wanted to savor the mood and have myself a nice long soak in a private bath.

"I'm sorry, sir. It's usually the couples who ask for a private bath, and single guests usually use the public bath, so we just assumed. . . . I'm sorry. But if you'd still like a room with a private bath . . ."

Of course—why didn't I think of that!

This experience enlightened me to the fact that no one who relishes life would want to come to an inn with a hot spring unless he's recovering from an illness or needs some downtime.

A radio was squawking in one of the other rooms. Damned thing had tracked me down in a place I had come to precisely to escape such a racket!

The next disturbance was when the night was well along and I'd just gone to bed. From the neighboring room came the voice of a drunken man trying to win over some girl who was saying, "No, I don't want to"; it sounded like she was pushing him away. Well, well, I tutted, maybe she wished she could self-reproduce—there are aphids like that, aren't there? And with that I rolled over in the other direction.

Fall out the door to the inn and you're practically at the entrance to the train station, that's how close they were. And yet the inn people send out a car for the guests, transporting them back three or four at a time, to be greeted upon arrival by the staff rushing out from the inn and bowing, then ushering them to a warm room with silk bedding and a maid who attends to your every need like the tongue in your mouth—you scarcely realize she's there. So here I was, an overnight first-class gentleman back at the station waiting for the tram to point B, shivering in the wind at daybreak.

This preposterous extravagance, staying at a first-class inn, was a kind of pathetic revenge on my part for the oppressiveness of contemporary reality, in which I walk around Seoul curled up in abjection.

Like the sparrow that never bypasses the mill until it's checked for any stray grain, I had stopped at P'yŏngyang on the way back from seeing a friend who had left for Manchuria but come down ill and gotten off the train short of his destination, and was laid up sick. I went down to the Taedong River, and when I saw its ugly, bumpy frozen service I wished I hadn't bothered. On Nŭngna Islet, stark with its bare trees, the woodcutters were raking leaves. I saw no signs of life on Moran Peak, heard only the wind ripping nonstop through the needles of the pines. *Not much into natural scenery, are you,* I said to myself, and with a wry smile I turned back. "Outside the long wall" the ground was a skating rink. "On the great plain with the hills to the east" squat thatched dwellings flinched beneath the bombers flying overhead.[1]

What's best about P'yŏngyang are the public baths, which are plentiful and clean, and the women, who revive your spirits. What's worst are the inns and the roar of propellers disturbing your sweet morning sleep.

Chosŏn ilbo, December 27, 28, 1935

NOTES

1. The quoted expressions are from a *hanshi* by Kim Hwang'wŏn (1045–1117), a Koryŏ literatus.

8

CHALLENGES FACING

TODAY'S WRITERS

(Hyŏndae chakka ch'angjak koshim haptamhoe, 1937)

PARTICIPANTS

YUN KIJŎNG

YI HYOSŎK

OM HŬNGSŎP

YI CHUHONG

NO CH'UNSŎNG

HAN INT'AEK

CH'AE MANSHIK

(representing the publisher) "MASTER THOUSAND-EYES"

For better or for worse, what follows are stories of the painstaking work of Korean writers who are currently active. We invite both aspiring writers and our readers to savor the following accounts of the rigors of writers preparing to serve up their next literary repast.

1. First of all, would you please speak about the challenges you face in composition—for example, adjectives, punctuation, anything that comes to mind?

YUN KIJŎNG: I'd have to say I'm still an apprentice. The challenges are enormous, I could go on and on. Whether my attempts to respond to those challenges are reflected in proper, accurate, or effective composition, I can't say. I myself don't really know. . . .

NO CH'UNSŎNG: Composition is painstaking in the extreme. We can think of composition as art expressed in letters, and in that sense, if there are flaws in my writing, then my art has already suffered a fatal wound. I punctuate for clarity of reading, and I try to use the best adjectives. I review my work several times, replacing adjectives that aren't descriptive enough.

YI HYOSŎK: Instead of aiming for perfection the first time around, I write a draft and then revise it several times, and that seems to work for me. With description, short phrases seem to work better than long sentences, and I tend to avoid modifiers unless I think they're necessary.

HAN INT'AEK: The lack of standardization of our language and its deficiency in modifiers are constant problems for me. Because we as writers have more interest in language aesthetics and composition, and because we have to do extensive research, the times we're writing are extremely painstaking. My habit is not to use punctuation.

ŎM HŬNGSŎP: How can composition not be painstaking? Whenever I publish a work I always ask myself if I've paid enough attention to modifiers and punctuation.

YI CHUHONG: The power of composition is that it makes subject matter come alive as art. Perfecting a work of literature clearly involves a great amount of time mastering the act of composition. When you describe an object you need to select a word, a sentence, that does it perfectly or else comes close, and that's where the hardship comes in. Fortunately we have excellent graphic capabilities—the shapes, lines, and symbols of our type fonts can be as expressive as words.

CH'AE MANSHIK: I find it quite difficult because of the deficiencies and lack of systemization of our language. I don't consider myself very knowledgeable about modifiers, and for days at a time I'll stop writing because I'm thinking about them. I use spacing instead of punctuation, but the print shops don't bother following my spacing when they set the type.

2. Can you tell us about your reading habits and your compositional methods?

YI HYOSŎK: Of course there are times when what I read influences how I write. If you're well read and you keep writing, you tend to develop a distinctive writing style almost without realizing it.

ŎM HŬNGSŎP: I can't say I have the slightest interest in reading someone else and thinking, *Oh, that's beautiful, I'll learn from it.* I don't like chasing after someone else's writing; maybe it's my pride—whether that's good or bad, I can't say. The bottom line is, a creative writer has to establish his own writing style.

NO CH'UNSŎNG: I tend not to do a lot of reading, but I make an effort to read new releases and good books. Once I spent four days at the library reading Sholokhov's *And Quiet Flows the Don*. And I like to buy books—I have quite a few rare books, and if I happen to be short on funds, now and then I'll sell one.

As for compositional methods, simply put, I try to write truthfully and with beauty. I don't have any special secrets, but I've memorized many well-written phrases of others.

YUN KIJŎNG: I try to read as much as I can by Korean writers—mainly short fiction and novellas, and the occasional novel. Every month I remind myself not to slack off in this. I'm learning quite a lot from the authors, but I will try to break new ground with a writing style of my own. It's one of the tasks I've been concerned with all along. . . .

HAN INT'AEK: I read a lot, and I've learned a lot from what I've read.

YI CHUHONG: Like it or not, readers approach reading in a spirit of critiquing it in their own way. It's natural that when you're reading you consciously decide whether the writing appeals to you. For example, if we're talking about the classics, I've never read anything I was influenced by, or took as a model. But it may be that writing I admire somehow finds its way inside me and ends up nourishing me.

CH'AE MANSHIK: Lately I can't say this happens a lot, but when I latch on to an interesting book I can stay up all night reading it. As for compositional techniques, I'm not exactly sure what you mean.

3. Who are your favorite writers?

YI CHUHONG: I'm ashamed to say I haven't read as much as others in the classics. The few I have read tend to be abridged editions or outlines, and maybe a few excerpts I've come across in the journals, and I've seen some film adaptations, and it's only ever the story line that stays with me. I haven't found anybody I particularly enjoy. It's very unfortunate that the current generation, for all their short time on this earth, lack firsthand contact with the classics of our forebears, and it's my plan to make my way through these works for the rest of my life. I envy the erudite who can talk like walking encyclopedias about writers such as Shakespeare, Goethe, Zola, Dostoievsky, and Balzac.

Speaking of which, I've heard people rave about Minch'on's *The Ancestral Home*,[1] and I said to one such person, "I'm amazed at the energy you put into reading it. And granted, it was serialized in the newspaper, but *how* did you manage to get through all of it?"

CH'AE MANSHIK: I tend to read more foreign literature. Lately I've been absorbed in Gorky's writings about literature.

HAN INT'AEK: Lately I'm reading a lot about poetry. Not that I want to be a poet; I just want to see for myself the thought processes poets undergo.

NO CH'UNSŎNG: I've enjoyed Honma's *Introduction to Literature*, Merezhkovsky's book on poetics, Yazaki's *The Human Theater*, *Poems by Heine*,[2] Tolstoy's *Anna Karenina*, and Artsybashev's *Sanin*.

ŎM HŬNGSŎP: The books I've enjoyed recently are the first volume of Minch'on's *The Ancestral Home* and Nosan's *Meaninglessness*.[3] And I enjoy any kind of book on geography and customs. But I'm concerned about books you enjoy to the extent that you lose your sense of self in them.

YI HYOSŎK: What I read tends to change with the seasons. When I'm really into reading I'll go for days without eating and sleeping, but once I start slacking off I'll go months without reading anything.

YUN KIJŎNG: Once I have a book I enjoy, I'll read it two or three times.

4. What do you write about?

CH'AE MANSHIK: I start from something that's real or could be real.

YI HYOSŎK: Unless we have access to life in all its grandeur, and to a variety of exceptional experiences, selecting subject matter will be a huge problem. Apart from what you get from talking with people and reading, the best you can do is use your brain, and with the brain I'm not sure ambition or passion fits in.

ŎM HŬNGSŎP: You have to plant your subject matter in your mind and nurture it. No matter how quickly a subject comes to mind, I don't like putting it to paper right off. The way I see it, you have to wait till that subject sprouts, produces leaves, matures, fills with kernels, and in a burst of ripeness jumps out at you.

YI CHUHONG: Even though it's said that art reflects life, life itself doesn't become art. In the end, great art must be a living picture of the daily life of a certain time, and although that life may be quotidian, it can still be distinctive, typical, and reflective of history all at the same time. The reason a work of popular fiction reaches the end of its life span as soon you put the book down is that its subject matter is not engaging—though you could say that about the writing too. A creative writer is forever seeking a high level of refinement and breadth of knowledge. Wearing the label of a labor writer, pastoral writer, or some such specialization isn't much of an honor. To the extent possible, you have to broaden your horizons beyond the rural and the urban and with a sharp eye seek your subject matter.

NO CH'UNSŎNG: Subject matter is difficult to handle unless it comes from your own experience. Subject matter based on pure fantasy seems dangerous to me, and I don't think it will yield a good work.

HAN INT'AEK: I've had a lot of trouble with subject matter. But lately I've taken quite a few hits in my private life, and I'm thinking that for the near future I might try to find subject matter there.

YUN KIJŎNG: Subject matter is the most painstaking element of writing. Over the course of the six months in which I've pursued creative writing, I've felt like a sailing vessel with no one at the helm, and I'm far from the level of someone like Chekhov, who, as people say, employs more subject matter than grains of sand on a beach. Another way of putting it is that my ideological turmoil renewed the skepticism and agitation in my views on life, ethics and morals, and society, and I couldn't avoid impoverishment of the subject matter of my work. And so I grabbed on to whatever subject matter came to mind.

5. How do you go about titling your works?

HAN INT'AEK: I decide on the title as I'm plotting the work.

YUN KIJŎNG: I used to settle on a title and then write, but nowadays I'll finish writing but have a terrible time coming up with an appropriate title. It's been more than two weeks since I finished my latest story, and I'm worried silly because I still haven't come up with a good title.

NO CH'UNSŎNG: I have to start with the title. Otherwise I can't write a line. Without a title I feel I don't have a course to follow and I might as well not pick up my pen.

CH'AE MANSHIK: I try to make the title the focal point of the content.

YI HYOSŎK: For me the title comes at the end, after I've written the piece. Because the title that first comes to mind can change during the course of writing.

YI CHUHONG: Just like a tool's name, a work's title symbolizes everything about that work. I think we all feel that way, but still I find titles to be quite a challenge. I'm happiest selecting a title and then writing. I know that Hŭngsŏp here often writes first and then hangs a title on the work, but if I don't have a clear title in mind it keeps nagging at me and I just can't write. If the title is too pedestrian and flat, you'll lose a lot of your readers. I always think it's good if the title is original, provocative, stimulating, and offbeat.

ŎM HŬNGSŎP: Because a title is really like a person's name, you can name your work however you like. But I'd have to say that just like a person's name reflects his personality to some degree, the title of the work reflects the character of that work.

6. Tell us how you go about plotting a work.

YI HYOSŎK: That's something I spend a lot of time on—because when your ideas ripen, the writing goes easier. You can't force incipient thoughts onto the story.

YI CHUHONG: For me the best time to do plotting is when I'm taking a walk. Or before I go to sleep. Plotting involves a wordless story taking shape inside my head, and only then does it spill out onto the manuscript page. Many times I've seen two of my characters collide and I end up with two stories inside my head—like a double exposure in a motion picture—and that can be annoying. You can think of plotting as a blueprint, and in that sense it's even more important than the foundation work.

CH'AE MANSHIK: Plotting is a matter of taking a title from the subject matter and then amplifying it.

ŎM HŬNGSŎP: You want to keep plotting as concise and simple as possible. Maybe it's good if the development of the story is complicated, but that's not so effective with readers. I've been working on a novel called The Everlasting Flower,[4] and I think I'll keep it to three or four main characters.

NO CH'UNSŎNG: I haven't written a novel yet, so plotting hasn't become a challenge for me, but even with short fiction, I can't start writing until the plot is set in my mind. Trying to write without plotting is like trying to draw a tiger and having nothing take shape, not even a dog.

YUN KIJŎNG: I do most of my plotting while I'm out on my walks. But sometimes a plot comes to mind that won't let me make any alterations, and I hate that.

HAN INT'AEK: When I start a work I set up two plots against each other, and once they're finalized they become the basis on which I complete the plotting of the work as a whole. It takes time, but using this method I often discover new elements in the work.

7. What's the hardest part about actually starting to write the work?

YUN KIJŎNG: Getting started is pure agony. If I can't look forward to the joy of artistic inspiration along the way or when I finish, or the joy of finishing a perfected work, whether it gets a good or a bad critical reception, then I just don't have the courage to start in.

NO CH'UNSŎNG: Starting itself is hardest. I usually tear up three or four sheets of manuscript before I really get going. When the writing's not going well, I'd rather take a break, lie down in my room, and do some thinking.

CH'AE MANSHIK: It's the most demanding time. Sometimes I end up wasting fifty or sixty sheets.

ŎM HŬNGSŎP: It's quite difficult. But once I've written the first page I feel like I'm half done, or at least a third of the way there. Like they say, well begun is half done. So when I've finished ten pages I get some relief, and after twenty pages I'm positively cheerful.

HAN INT'AEK: Even if I've done the plotting, once I pick up my pen, I have a heck of a time writing—I end up wasting four or five sheets first.

YI CHUHONG: Kijŏng there once said to me something like, "I don't feel melancholy, I don't feel like I'm languishing, I don't feel a sense of urgency, I don't feel uncertain, but what I do have is this weighty feeling, or you might say, it's not pleasant, it's a heavy, oppressive sensation." The truth is, the moment I'm about to transfer what's in my head to paper I feel good, but when I actually pick up my pen, I don't know why, but my head is heavy and I feel strange. But if I get through the first few pages then I unwind and the pen takes over.

8. What if you can't write?

YI HYOSŎK: You can force yourself to write, but it's hard work and you won't end up with a masterpiece.

CH'AE MANSHIK: I can't write if I'm hungry, or sleepy, or too cold, or too hot, or someone's making a racket, or I can't come up with the right words. And if I don't have a clear outline of the work in my mind, then it doesn't get off the ground.

YI CHUHONG: There are several situations in which I can't write. At such times I'll wander around in front of the house or go for a long walk, or I'll try to soothe myself by stimulating my imagination, and then when I sit back down at my desk I stay there. And I write a line or two, even if it takes me an hour or two, and only then is my mind at peace. And then I can en-joy a long walk for what it is—not as a means to an end—and the same with an outing.

And the more I'm unable to write, the more I sit tight and end up strug-gling with this damned can't-write mind set. In the case of my worst work, "Heine's Wife,"[5] I struggled through in this fashion and somewhat managed to finish it over a period of several days.

HAN INT'AEK: When I can't write, it's for one of two reasons: the thought process doesn't work or I have something else to do. Most of the time it's the first reason, and what I do then is lie down and think.

ŎM HŬNGSŎP: When I can't write, it lasts for days at a time. Nothing is as unpleasant as forcing yourself to write when you need money to pay off a debt.

NO CH'UNSŎNG: If I can't write, I'll snack on a crabapple or something and play with the kids, or else take a nap.

YUN KIJŎNG: If I start something but hit a wall, I throw down the damn pen and run outside and disappear somewhere.

9. How many sheets a day do you use, and how many writing sessions per day?

CH'AE MANSHIK: Once I get into high gear, 50 or 60 sheets of 200-letters-to-the-page. And I'll do it at one sitting, or else at intervals.

YI CHUHONG: If I'm feeling good I can turn out about 60 sheets at a stretch. Some days I'll work two sessions, for example if time is tight. Usually I write 50 or 60 pages a day.

HAN INT'AEK: If I stay up all night I can do 50 pages easy. But if the thoughts don't come I can't finish even 10 pages.

YI HYOSŎK: On a good day I'll write 20 sheets of 400-to-the-page. But if it's not going well, maybe five pages or barely one or two. As for frequency, sometimes I work throughout the day, but if I'm taking it easy I'll break up the day.

ŎM HŬNGSŎP: If I'm not at a job, I can cruise through an entire work in a day. But lately the best I can do is write for a couple hours at night, and I'll end up with no more than 30 pages.

NO CH'UNSŎNG: In a day I'll write 12 pages of 400-per. I write in the morn-ing and again in the afternoon, but never at night.

YUN KIJŎNG: 40 to 50 pages, and two or three times a day.

10. Is there a secret to ending a story?

YUN KIJŎNG: After I come down from the tension and excitement of writing the story, I try to be as cool as possible.

NO CH'UNSŎNG: I don't have a secret method, but if I did it would be to end the story where it's most impressive—the payoff point, you might say. I don't want any extra trimming.

CH'AE MANSHIK: No method, no secret—the end takes place where I planned it.

ŎM HŬNGSŎP: I don't have a secret. It seems customary with writers of popular fiction who want to draw reader interest to end after a juicy part, to stick in a lot of unnatural coincidences so as to avoid the ordinary, and work up to a climax and end there. But with literary fiction it's not that cut-and-dried.

YI HYOSŎK: I don't have any secrets to speak of. I end at the appropriate place, and what's appropriate depends on the work. And unless you make a really clean break, the ending drags out and overflows with sentiment. Once you find the right place, you finish with one cold-blooded slice.

HAN INT'AEK: The ending depends on how the story turns out—there's no real secret involved in that.

YI CHUHONG: There's really no secret method to ending a work. The ending depends on the nature of the story. But it's all right to end after the climax, as long as you don't get carried away and end with melodrama.

11. When and where do you like to write?

YI HYOSŎK: No fixed time, but I prefer late at night. And I usually write at the desk in my room.

HAN INT'AEK: After ten in the morning, at home.

ŎM HŬNGSŎP: Two hours a day, at home, at night.

NO CH'UNSŎNG: Morning is best for me, and my favorite place to write is a nice warm, sunny room.

YUN KIJŎNG: During the day if I'm at the library, in the middle of the night if I'm home.

CH'AE MANSHIK: I use a room at a boarding house and I usually write late at night.

YI CHUHONG: Occasionally during the day, but generally after 10 p.m. One or two in the morning is even better. I just can't write when it's noisy and chaotic. No fixed place, but wherever I happen to spend the night. I wish I had a study. I've heard Minch'on does his writing at home in the one room he and his wife and kids have—what a racket that must be. And Song Yŏng writes outside, sitting under a tree, using a serving tray for a desk. I'm afraid I'm not up to their level.

12. What kind of manuscript paper do you prefer?

YUN KIJŎNG: I use 400-per, regardless of the quality. I guess I'm peculiar like that.

NO CH'UNSŎNG: I don't use the manuscript paper supplied by the newspapers and magazines. Instead I use Samwŏl paper, the premium variety, 400-per.

YI CHUHONG: Anything is fine with me. But I don't use paper from the newspapers and magazines, the quality's bad. The most important thing is quality, and it's good if the letter boxes have clean outlines and are large enough. Manuscript paper affects my mood—if I like it, my writing goes much better. I prefer 200-per, but I don't see much of it in the shops.

ŎM HŬNGSŎP: I generally use paper from the magazine I'm writing for, but most of it is coarse, and I don't like having to write on it with a metal-tip pen.

HAN INT'AEK: My mood changes depending on whether the paper is good or bad. I won't use paper that makes the ink from my pen run.

CH'AE MANSHIK: I used to use paper from the newspapers and the magazines, but these days I buy it—400-per. So I no longer get supplied by the publisher, but I get better results with this blessed stuff.

YI HYOSŎK: I use 400-per because all the shops carry it. Lately my favorite is what they sell at Hwashin Department Store, because the letter boxes are larger.

12. Was there perhaps a tearful experience associated with your maiden work?

YUN KIJŎNG: I guess you could call "Memories of Christmas Eve"[6] my maiden work. It was published in the Chosŏn ilbo sixteen years ago. When I think back to that time, instead of tears my recollection makes me wonder how I had the nerve to lay this story out for the world—combined with a sense of shame that felt like heartburn, shame that the story was so wretched.

YI HYOSŎK: I can't really point out any one work as a maiden work. In the case of poetry, I had poems published during my second year of preparatory school; with fiction, I was first published when I was at the university.

CH'AE MANSHIK: My so-called maiden work would be "In Three Directions,"[7] which came out in *Chosŏn mundan* the first year that magazine was published—it was issue number 2 or 3, I can't remember which—and Ch'unwŏn[8] was the adjudicator. I don't recall anything tearful about it.

HAN INT'AEK: I don't have anything I would call my maiden work, but when I look back on my early days as a writer, I often find myself wishing I did. Back then everything was full of yearning and hope, but now that I'm confronted with worries related to writing, I think that if I wrote about those days, I would depict the world with a funny story that contains nonsense, humor, excitement, and fantasy.

ŎM HŬNGSŎP: No tears I can remember.

YI CHUHONG: Since I don't have a maiden work, I can't say I have a debut period. At age 17 or 18 I was undecided among literature, art, and music. About ten years ago it happened that a work of mine caught the attention of the *Chosŏn ilbo* and was entered in their new year literary arts competition, and I remember that two of the adjudicators, Ch'oe Tokkyŏn and Pak Yŏnghŭi, said some nice things about it. So once again I contemplated literature as a future—but that was all. And then five or six years ago I ended up working as an editor for a magazine, and since then various poems and stories of mine have been published in magazines.

So when it comes to literature, I feel like I'm somewhere between a recluse and a philistine. I've lost literature, art, and music, and all that remains from that time in my teens is my physical self.

NO CH'UNSŎNG: Because I never wrote a play I'd consider worthy of being called a maiden work, I have nothing to brag about. But back in my twenties when I was a head-in-the-clouds writer-to-be, I had a fair amount of zeal for literature; I was ready to offer up my life for it. Back then I used to submit to the *Kidok shinbo*, and finally a long poem of mine was published there, "A Figlike Life,"[9] and that's my debut work.

13. Which of your works brought you to the attention of the literary world?

YI CHUHONG: Again I'm not really qualified to answer this question. There's a big difference in how I'm viewed by the pure literature people and how I'm viewed by journalists. I can't say I've written anything yet that's captured much attention. And I don't know if I ever will.

ŎM HŬNGSŎP: I'm hoping it's the one I'm thinking of writing now.

NO CH'UNSŎNG: Sad to say, I don't have one yet.

HAN INT'AEK: I completed the manuscript of *The Stormy Age*[10] within a month, if you can believe that. My passion has waned, but if I were to write that novel now, it would take two to three times longer but be a better work.

CH'AE MANSHIK: An attention-getting work—that's an appetizing prospect, but I don't think I've written it yet.

YI HYOSŎK: For me, perhaps that work is my story "City and Specter."[11] Due to a foul-up by one of the editors, it wasn't published till a year after I wrote it.

YUN KIJŎNG: For me, nothing so far. But soon I hope to have published something that others might stamp with the "worthy-of-attention" seal. If not this year, then it should be next year. . . .

Thank you all very much for sitting through this long session. This brings our discussion to a close.

Sahae kongnon, January 1937

NOTES

1. The novel *Kohyang*, by Yi Kiyŏng.
2. *Hai'ne shijip.*
3. *Musang*, a collection of anecdotal essays by Yi Ŭnsang.
4. *Kuwŏnch'o.*
5. "Hai'ne ŭi anhae."
6. "Sŏngt'anya ŭi ch'uŏk."
7. "Segillo" (the second work in this volume).
8. Yi Kwangsu.
9. "Muhwa kwa kat'ŭn saengmyŏng."
10. *Sŏngp'ung shidae.*
11. "Toshi wa yuryŏng," trans. Youngji Kang, *Acta Koreana* 10, no. 1 (January 2007): 103–13; and *Rat Fire: Korean Stories from the Japanese Empire*, ed. Theodore Hughes, Jae-Yong Kim, Jin-Kyung Lee, and Sang-Kyung Lee (Ithaca, N.Y.: Cornell East Asia Series, 2013), 89–104.

9

YUJŎNG AND I

(Yujŏng kwa na, 1937)

I'M IN TEARS OVER YUJŎNG'S DEATH, AND YET I ENVY THE MAN.

I became aware of his works first at the offices of *Genesis*, where I was seeing to some business or other. It was later that I met him face to face, at An Hoenam's place, where I'd gone to shoot the breeze, and it's the face I remember. In comes this young man who looks a bit naïve, and his clothing wasn't doing him any favors, and he was already cracking a har-de-har joke for An's benefit, but when he saw me his face turned sullen and he looked put out, which I chalked up as a territorial thing. And that was Yujŏng.

The truth was, and I found this out later from An, that Yujŏng knew who I was, but he was a bit tipsy as he trudged in and he thought An was the only one home. So when he noticed me he got embarrassed and tried to hide it, which gave me, your abnormal, neurasthenic narrator, the impression he was a sourpuss.

And sure enough, once we'd had the chance to properly introduce ourselves and I'd seen him once and then met him again, I felt the flush of recognition that if ever there was a man who didn't need the law to tell him how to live, it was Yujŏng, a true gentleman. He displayed courtesy, but not the showy variety; he was warmhearted, with an emphasis on "heart"; and there wasn't an iota of snootiness to the man. He was a true Tolstoy. (I should mention that Tolstoy is a character in "Worthless," one of his last stories.)

I didn't respect his works, I *loved* them—and more, the joy of doing so. But I loved Yujŏng the person even more. Or perhaps I should say I *wanted* to love him but couldn't, because I wasn't as sincere a man as he.

He'd taken ill while I was still in Seoul, but it was only after I moved that I looked him up. I told him how sorry I was for being a heartless bastard. Then I followed up with a letter offering some concrete suggestions about benefiting from treatment and saving on the costs, and he wrote right back, saying for sure he'd give it a shot and promising he'd do his damnedest to beat the disease.

Yujŏng died a miserable death. What a waste. If only I could trade in a dozen hacks like me and bring him back.

Chogwang, May 1937

10

WHATEVER POSSESSED ME?

A Play in One Act

(Yesu na an midŏttŭmyŏn, 1937)

CHARACTERS

MASTER OF THE HOUSE: pawnshop owner, about fifty
HIS WIFE: about forty-five
HIS CONCUBINE: about thirty
EVANGELIST: a married woman, about forty
MAID: about forty
TWO OR THREE NEIGHBORHOOD CHILDREN

Early summer, present day, the capital.

A traditional ⊏-shaped dwelling with the opening facing the audience. At the near right corner, a guest room, and behind it the main gate, the kitchen, and in the far right corner the family room. In the center, the yard, and to the rear, the veranda. To the left of the veranda, the side room. At the far left, the red-brick back wall of a two-story pawnshop, which adjoins the home, its back door opening into the yard. Facing the audience is the side room's sliding door, its glass panels removed for the summer, that opens onto the yard. Both that door and the sliding door to the veranda are open, revealing in the side room a wardrobe and other furnishings. On the strip of veranda outside the sliding door to the yard lie a reed mat and a wooden headrest. The small double door at the back of the veranda is wide open, and visible through it, close enough to touch, is the back wall of the neighboring house. On the veranda are a hutch and rice chest, and atop the rice chest a gramophone. The family room likewise has separate doors to the veranda and the yard, and both have been slid open, revealing to the rear of the room a clothing chest. In the yard are a soy-crock terrace and a faucet.

It's just before noon as the curtain opens onto the maid wiping down the veranda floor. She works rhythmically with grand gestures, as if she's performing rather than doing a household chore. From the family room comes the ticking of a clock.

MAID (*pauses in her work, eases back, and counts along with the chiming of the clock*): One, two, three, four, five, six, seven, eight, nine, ten, eleven—aiii? Twelve—twelve o'clock!? Already twelve o'clock—how can that be! That clock is bonkers, it's gone crazy! It's not even eleven. Bonkers, crazy clock! Crazy as the lady of our fine house, who's always out attending to her Jesus! Lady of the house is crazy, the clock of the house goes bonkers, that must be it.

(*The noon siren blares.*)

Aiii? The noon siren? Then it must be noon—damn it all to hell! Already twelve noon. Cleaning's not done and I gotta start lunch. After lunch, it's starch and hang the laundry. Damn it all to hell! Now that she's moved in, the little lady or whatever you want to call her, my workload's doubled—twice as much damn work to do. Why's there so much consarned laundry? Twice as much, that's no lie. Damn it all to hell. If there's twice as much work, then I oughta be worth twice as much—twice as much pay, twice as much to eat, sleep twice as long, have twice as many clothes to wear. But I still get only three wŏn, and they still only feed me one lousy bowl of rice a meal. Yeah, more food sure would be nice. And I only have from eight in the evening till seven in the morning to sleep or whatever I want. Damn it all to hell. (*getting up with her rag and looking at the gramophone perched on the rice chest*) Darn it, how come I can't listen to this little contraption—it sure would be nice to turn it on, especially now when I'm all by my lonesome. Ei, you little devil. I'm so mad I could die! The little lady or whatever you want to call her, long as she's gonna buy a contraption like this, least she could do is get something that makes a sound. Then I could turn it on and (*clearing her throat*), "Down by the riverside, where the willows grow and a pair of doves frolic" (*looks away and giggles, embarrassed, then, much louder*), "Paeg'yŏn Falls"—aigumŏni, that's too loud! Master bastard, if he hears, with his rabbit ears he'll know for sure it's me. If only he didn't have such sharp hearing—then I could have some fun with that gramophone! Aigu, damn it all to hell. What's the use of standing here looking at it, it's rice cake in a picture, pie in the sky. (*turning around*) If she comes in now, oh is she gonna bitch when she sees I haven't cleaned her room yet. Our lady is bonkers, she's crazy! Darned if I know why she brings in his mistress and they play like we're one big happy family! (*looking into the side room*) Hmph, some people have all the luck! She has it so comfy—lazing around, decking herself out and dolling herself up, going out on the town, and if she doesn't wanna do that, she can stay right here and hum along with that gramophone. And if she doesn't wanna do that, she can take a nap. Damn it all to hell, if I was a little younger and a little prettier, if I'd gotten widowed back then, I'd be a concubine having the time of my life too. (*pause*) Let's see if I can doll myself up. (*checks the gate and the door to the pawnshop, sticks out her tongue playfully, enters the side room, and plops herself down in front of the vanity, where she applies beauty lotion, pats cream all over her face, adds powder, and finishes with rouge on her cheeks*) Well—look how pretty I am, la-di-da! Oh no, I overdid it with the rouge. Then again, a lady's got to have her rouge.

EVANGELIST (*dressed in white sneakers and socks, knee-length skirt, long jacket; wears glasses and carries a velvet bag, holds a black parasol over her head; she goes through the gate and looks around*): This is the house. Is anyone home?

MAID (*startles visibly at the sound of the visitor and comes out onto the veranda, vigorously wiping off the makeup with her rag*): Oh, it's a peddler! If you got any of that ku-rim stuff, leave me some and I'll pay ya next time.

(EVANGELIST, *amused by the maid but irked by her words, thrusts her head high and stares at her*)

MAID: Ain't got any? C'mon, just one bottle. Next time they pay me, I'll make it up to ya.

EVANGELIST (*enraged*): I AM NOT A PEDDLER. I have come to visit the lady of the house.

MAID: Ah yes, yes, the lady. You're a guest, are you? Yes, yes. Would that be the big lady? Or the little lady?

EVANGELIST (*confused*): Big lady? Little lady?

MAID: Ah yes, we have the big lady, and we also have the little lady.

EVANGELIST: All right—I mean the one who attends the church.

MAID: Ah yes, yes. (*aside*) I knew it, a Jesus freak. (*to* EVANGELIST) Yes, yes, the big lady, she's at the neighbor's out back, I'll go fetch her, please wait. (*steps down to the yard*) Your legs must be sore, please have a seat and make yourself at home. (*goes out the gate*) And please keep an eye on things. (*exits*)

EVANGELIST: Is she demented or what? (*quickly looks about the house*)

MAID (*aside; looking behind her as she comes through the gate*): Rotten little bastards! Who do they think they are, making fun o' me! (*to* EVANGELIST) She says she'll be right back, and for you to make yourself at home.

NEIGHBORHOOD CHILDREN (*peering inside the gate*): There she is. (*giggling*) Look, there she is.

MAID (*shooing them away*): Scoot, ya rotten kids!

NEIGHBORHOOD CHILDREN (*exit; from offstage, giggling*): Didja see her? What a sight! Ugly hag puts flour on her face! Slaps rouge on her cheeks and her forehead! (*giggling*)

MAID (*aside*): Little bastards, wait till I get my hands on one o' ya. I'll rip yer crotch apart fer ya. (*to the children*) They oughta lock ya little bastards up! Don't your mommies powder their faces? Ya little bastards!

NEIGHBORHOOD CHILDREN (*from offstage; giggling*): Gotcha, didn't we? (*giggling*) Ya old bag, slapping on rouge, whatcha showing off for, you getting married or something? (*giggling*) What a sight—what a plug-ugly sight!

MAID: Ei! Rotten little bastards!

EVANGELIST (*taking in the scene*): Well, look at you! What are you doing putting on makeup at your age? No wonder the children are teasing you!

MAID: Ain't none o' yer concern. At least I'm prettier than you. (*exits to kitchen*)

WIFE (*rushing in*): Oh, there you are—I was wondering who it was! For heaven's sake, you came all this way just to see me. (*takes* EVANGELIST *by the hand*) Let's go in. How have you *been*?

EVANGELIST: I'm well, thank you. And your good self?

WIFE (*steps up onto the veranda and beckons her guest*) Please. (*toward the kitchen*): Auntie!

MAID (*from offstage*): Yes?

WIFE: Has the master had his lunch? If not, then hurry up and prepare his meal. And what happened to your face? What an embarrassment! The neighbors are falling down laughing. (*to* EVANGELIST) You must join us for a bite to eat.

EVANGELIST (*steps onto the veranda and sits down with* WIFE): Who, me? I had lunch at home just now.

WIFE: Even so. How about some cold noodles, then?

EVANGELIST: No no no. Next time.

WIFE: Ai! What now? You made a special trip. Ai! Then what can I offer you?

EVANGELIST: Please, don't worry. I feel you've already served me.

WIFE: Ai, even so. Then let's play some music for you. (*puts a record on the gramophone: the phrase "crying in my sake"[1] is heard*)

(EVANGELIST *frowns.*)

WIFE: Isn't that great? I simply *adore* his voice. Makes me feel like crying myself. Great, isn't it?

EVANGELIST: Well . . . it's all right, I guess.

WIFE: If it's not to your liking, then let's try something different. *(putting on a new record)* This one's "The Yiyang Song"—guaranteed to put a wiggle into you. I really like it. *("I don't want to forget you" is heard.)* What do you think—great, isn't it? *(following along with the song)* I absolutely love it. And I almost have it down. *(chuckles)*

(EVANGELIST frowns.)

WIFE: Ai, you don't like that one either! Then what should I play? *(lost in thought)*

MAID *(sticking her head out of the kitchen)*: Oh lady, lady—play her "Down by the Riverside"—she'll love it.

WIFE: Hush now, we can do without your suggestions—my goodness, whatever did you do to your face?

(MAID withdraws her head from view.)

WIFE: Oh, that's right—I know just the thing. *(looks through the records; aside)* Where is that darned thing? I marked the cover with my fingernail. *(finally locates the record and puts it on)* I tell you, this one is *really* good. Let's give it a listen. *(Chŏng Mongju's shijo "Though I die, though I die a hundred times" is heard.)* What do you think?

EVANGELIST: Mmm, that's more like it. Not afraid of death—praise be the martyr spirit that we Christians uphold. Mmm, yes, that's better.

WIFE *(delighted)*: You like it? I sure do.

EVANGELIST *(hearing the phrase "My undivided heart for thee," frowns)*: Aeng! I thought I liked it, but did you hear that? Aeng, aeng! That's obscene!

(MAID looks out from kitchen, shoulders shaking in silent laughter.)

WIFE: Oh my, you don't care for that one either?

EVANGELIST: Whether I like it or not isn't the issue—it's for people with dirty minds, not us holy Christians.

WIFE *(startled)*: Good heavens, what should I do? I had no idea. *(pauses the record)* I'm a sinner in the eyes of our lord! I only started believing last week, and now I'll be punished—oh, what am I to do?

EVANGELIST: Our lord forgives those who repent.

WIFE: Oh yes! Ai, thank you so much. So I will never, ever listen to such songs again. *(pauses)* But . . .

EVANGELIST: How can you not listen when you still have the record? You must destroy it.

WIFE: Ah yes, of course. Actually, though, it's not mine. It belongs to my master's little lady.

EVANGELIST: Little lady? A concubine, you mean.

WIFE: Yes. Well, you know, our master wants a child and I haven't been able to give him one, so he took a concubine. We've saved some money, and now we can live just like rich folks. So as far as money is concerned, we get along just fine.

EVANGELIST: I see there's something you still don't understand. You've only been a believer for a few days, and you're not yet familiar with the Bible, but in that Good Book you will find these words: "It is easier for a camel to pass through the eye of a needle than for a rich man to enter the kingdom of God."

WIFE: A camel? Like the one in the zoo? How could such a large animal go through the eye of a needle?

EVANGELIST: Well, that's the point—rich men don't go to heaven.

WIFE: Oh my, what now? That is a *huge* problem.

EVANGELIST: And that's why you need to encourage the master to believe in Jesus. If you use all of your assets for God's work, then your sins will be forgiven. What's worse, your master has taken a concubine.

WIFE: Yes.

EVANGELIST: That will not do—it's adultery. It's a cardinal sin!

WIFE: A cardinal sin? Oh my, what now? He said he's doing it because we don't have a child.

EVANGELIST: But not having a child is God's doing.

WIFE: How could that be? I thought children were a blessing of the Three Spirits that govern childbirth.

EVANGELIST: That's superstition. In the Ten Commandments, God says that you shall have no other gods except Him.

WIFE: Oh? Yes?

EVANGELIST: Meaning you should worship none but God.

WIFE: Oh yes, of course. I will most definitely serve only God. But then the concubine—what about her? He told me he would set up a separate household for her! So I said, why waste money, we can live together? So she stays in the side room there.

EVANGELIST: Good for you, but . . .

WIFE: Well, we want to get along and we call each other Big Sis and Little Sis, but sometimes I get mad and I absolutely hate her! When I think about how she might have a baby and then win his heart over, and all we own would go to her, then she's like my enemy.

EVANGELIST: As the Bible says, you should love your enemies.

WIFE: Oh yes, love your enemies, yes! If I love my enemy then she won't be my enemy anymore—that's good.

EVANGELIST: Yes, indeed.

WIFE: Yes, I'll get right to it. Oh, I forgot, you know that gramophone of hers—well, she also bought the records.

EVANGELIST: I see. But even so, you should get rid of them now—break them or else throw them away. True Christians should not listen to such indecent songs.

WIFE: All right, I'll do that. (takes record from gramophone and flings it out the door at the back of the veranda, breaking it)

EVANGELIST: Well done. (rises) Well, I must be off.

WIFE: Oh, won't you stay just a bit longer?

EVANGELIST: I have someone else to visit. Please lead your master down the right path and have him repent. And tomorrow don't forget to come to the worship and the Bible study.

WIFE: Yes, I will. (accompanies EVANGELIST to the gate)

(MASTER OF THE HOUSE emerges from back door of pawnshop.)

MAID (face cleaned; looking out from kitchen): Master, your lunch is ready.

MASTER: Mmm, take one over to the shop too, will you? (stepping up onto veranda) Is the little lady off somewhere?

WIFE (returning from gate): When you don't see her, you're always looking for her!

MASTER: I don't have to look for you—you're always at home.

WIFE: I do go out sometimes. In fact, I just came back. (steps onto veranda and sits)

(MAID serves MASTER his lunch tray.)

MASTER: Where did she go—tell me!

WIFE: This morning she set out that mat and headrest and had herself a nap, and after that I don't know. The bitch was snoring loud enough to shake the neighbors' houses.

MASTER: I didn't hear her, and I was right next door in the shop.

WIFE: You think I'm making it up, you think I've got it in for her?

MASTER: No way. Snoring can be music to the ears.

WIFE: Well, my snoring is better than hers.

MASTER: Until you overdo it, and then it gets ug-ly!

WIFE: Sure—everything the little woman does is cute, isn't it? And everything I do is the opposite.

MASTER: What are you talking about!

WIFE: What's so pretty about her anyway? The way her nose sticks up?

MASTER: Mmm, can't say as how it looks that bad.

WIFE (*pointing to her face*): What about mine?

MASTER: Mmm, the way it flares out makes you look quite the good-hearted sort.

WIFE (*pleased*): What about her eyes?

MASTER: All right, she's kind of slit-eyed, but they're not half bad.

WIFE (*indicating her eyes*): And mine?

MASTER: Mmm, there's talent in those eyes—no one would take you for a fool.

WIFE (*giggling*): What about her mouth?

MASTER: Her mouth? Well, it's kind of small, gives her a noble look.

WIFE: And mine? (*points to her mouth*)

MASTER: Your mouth? Well, all right. It's kind of big, which brings good luck, and the fact that I have a good life is all thanks to you.

WIFE (*giggling*): You know, we just had a visit from the evangelist, that An woman.

MASTER: Ah yes, now that you believe in Jesus you can go to heaven?

WIFE: Well, speaking of heaven . . .

MASTER: If you go to heaven, maybe I ought to tag along—you wouldn't mind, would you?

WIFE: Well, please hear me out first.

MASTER: What's the matter—is there a problem?

WIFE: Well, I'm afraid I can't go to heaven.

MASTER: Huh! Is that such a big deal? What does it take to go to heaven anyway? I can set up pawn heaven anywhere and we'll do just fine.

WIFE: I should still go to heaven.

MASTER: What's stopping you?

WIFE: Well, the evangelist, she told me the Bible says it is easier for a camel to pass through the eye of a needle than for a rich man to enter the kingdom of God.

MASTER: What was that again?

WIFE: A rich man . . .

MASTER: Mmm, a rich man . . .

WIFE: Going to heaven . . .

MASTER: Mmm, going to heaven—is difficult, you say? Then I'll ride first class.

WIFE: No. A camel . . .

MASTER: A camel what?

WIFE: It is easier for a camel to pass through the eye of a needle.

MASTER: A camel passing through the eye of a needle? You mean that zoo animal?

WIFE: Yes.

MASTER: Well, of course it can't do that! Are you sure it wasn't a needle passing through the eye of a camel?

WIFE: Yes, I'm sure. You still don't get it.

MASTER: Well, then. A rich man going to heaven, a camel, and the eye of a needle. Mmm, so it's more difficult for the rich man, all right, sure. A needle can pass through the eye of a camel, but a camel passing through a hole so narrow, no way! But why is it difficult as all that for a rich man to go to heaven?

WIFE: You got me. But that's what the Bible says.

MASTER: Mmm, in that case I have an idea. Mmm, yes, a good idea.

WIFE: Which is?

MASTER: It might cost some money, see, but we'll custom-order a *humongous* needle from an ironworks. Now listen carefully—it'll be bigger around than a camel. And, bang!—when it's time to go to heaven we'll load it on a truck and take it along with us, see? And the gatekeeper at heaven will say, "You're a rich man, and just like a camel can't pass through the eye of a needle, you can't pass through these gates," right? So if he blocks the way, we'll take out that damn needle and he'll see it, and we'll poke a big old hole in those gates, you get it? So now we got a hole. Next we say, "Let's try a little experiment—we'll see whether a camel can pass through this opening," and we don't budge till we get an answer. What do you think—that should do the trick, eh?

WIFE: Well! Not a bad idea. You know, it makes sense.

MASTER: No worries, now we've got a trick up our sleeve. But don't tell a soul—keep it to yourself.

WIFE: Of course. Who would I tell, anyway?

CONCUBINE (*comes flouncing through the gate, folding her parasol*): My god, it's hot!

WIFE (*in a welcoming tone*): Come on in.

MASTER: Where have you been?

CONCUBINE: I went to Samch'ŏng-dong.

MASTER: Again? Praying for a baby?

CONCUBINE: Yes. (*sits down on the veranda, unfolds her handkerchief to reveal a pack of cigarettes, and lights up*)

WIFE: Seeing as how you were there, maybe you prayed for a baby for me too?

CONCUBINE: Yes, Big Sis, I prayed for you first, then I asked them to bless me too, but if they didn't want to, fine.

WIFE: Ai! That's no good. You should have one and I should have one—that's how it ought to be.

CONCUBINE: It's all up to the will of our benevolent three gods.

MASTER: All right, you two, have yourselves some lunch. (*exits through back door of pawnshop*)

WIFE: Dig in.

CONCUBINE: Go ahead, I need to cool off first. (*gets up and goes toward the door at the rear of the veranda*) Who the hell broke my record! (*goes out and gathers the pieces, then re-enters; to* MAID) You!

WIFE: No need to call her—I'm the one who did it.

CONCUBINE: But why?

WIFE: I was told that if I listened to those songs I couldn't go to heaven, and God would punish me.

CONCUBINE: That's the damnedest thing I ever heard. (*tossing the pieces of the record toward* WIFE *and going into the side room*) Why did you have to do that, why! Who do you think you are, breaking my stuff!

WIFE (*patiently, to herself*): I shall love my enemy. (*kindly*) My dear little sister.

CONCUBINE: "My dear little sister." You mean, "Woman I want to beat to death," yes?

WIFE: Dear heavens, don't be like that. But I love you even so.

CONCUBINE: I don't want to hear any more. You're disgusting!

WIFE: Please stop. I love you even so. (*ponders; to herself*) Wait a minute—if I love that bitch, she won't be my enemy. And if she's not my enemy I don't have to love her. (*jumps to her feet*) You bitch. Listen to me, bitch. How dare you run off your yap at me, you bitch. (*rushes to side room*)

(CONCUBINE *jumps at the* WIFE.)

WIFE (*grabbing* CONCUBINE *by the hair*): You bitch, you damnable bitch!

CONCUBINE: So? You're the bitch.

　　(*All tangled up, the two of them fight.*)

MAID (*enters from kitchen, chortling*): Atta girl! That's my mistress, good for you.

WIFE (*letting go* CONCUBINE's *hair*): Wait—hold up. Let's stop and calm down. We shouldn't be doing this—whatever am I thinking?

(CONCUBINE *lets go* WIFE's *hair and steps back.*)

WIFE (*aside*): If we're fighting, then we're enemies again. That's right, enemies. And I shouldn't fight with my enemy, I should love her. (*looks tearfully at* CONCUBINE) Look, I love you, I really do. I've done wrong. I love you.

CONCUBINE: The little woman's lost her mind.

WIFE: No, no I haven't. (*entering family room*) I love you, I really do. (*turns and faces veranda; aside*) I must love my enemy. But wait—if I love her, then she's not my enemy anymore. Right, that's right. Then it's fine if I hate her and beat her. Yes, of course. (*attacks* CONCUBINE *again*) You bitch! I'm going to tear you apart, you bitch! Tear you limb from limb!

CONCUBINE (*wide-eyed*): The bitch has really gone off the deep end! All right, bitch, go ahead, bring it.

WIFE (*stops suddenly; aside*): No no no. She's my enemy again! My enemy, yes she is. And I can't do this to my enemy, no I can't. I must love my enemy. (*to* CONCUBINE) Listen, my dear little sister, I love you, I really do. (*turns back toward family room*)

CONCUBINE: The little woman is mental—makes me want to throw up.

WIFE (*aside*): That's right, I must love my enemy. I really must. Mm, right now. (*ponders*) But if I love her, she's not my enemy? Then it's all right if I take everything out on her and beat her? Because if I love her then she's not my enemy. (*turns back toward veranda*) You bitch, you deserve to die. (*aside*) Wait, then she'll be my enemy, and I can't do that. (*turns back and forth between family room and veranda*) What am I going to do? Mmm? What am I going to do? (*rips open her jacket*) Aigu, I just can't put up with this. I'm about to die! Whatever possessed me to believe in Jesus? Aigu, I can't put up with this anymore.

(Curtain.)

Chosŏn munhak, May 1937

NOTE

1. From "Sul iran nunmul inya han sum inya," the Korean title of a 1931 Japanese trot song, translated and made popular by singer Ch'oe Kyuyŏp.

11

JUVESENILITY

(Somang, 1938)

A GROWN MAN SHOULD BE ABLE, IF HE WANTS, TO PLANT HIMSELF
smack dab in the middle of Chongno, dressed in his winter suit in the dog
days of summer, then march right past the grain shop that's got him on
credit. . . .

"Ai, I'm so stirred up, dinner's the last thing on my mind."

"No, it's not the heat, that's the least of my worries."

"It's that husband of mine. Whatever am I going to do? It absolutely irks
me to think about him."

"Cold noodles? No, like I said, I'm not in the mood for anything. On second thought, how about some fruit juice—and you have ice, right? So you
already ate, Sister? Isn't it kind of early?"

"I guess Brother-in-Law's out on a house call? I didn't see his rickshaw
outside, and he wasn't in the clinic either. . . ."

"See, I'm right, process of elimination. If he's not in his office and he's not
glued to your side, then he has to be out seeing a patient, otherwise look
out—trouble brewing."

"Your looks, Sister dear? Then I swear, he must be cross-eyed. What do
you expect from those hicks, anyway? Darn, I forgot his name, it's so long
since I read it—Shwarl, is that it?—you know, the one who's married to
Madame Bovary?"

"Little bitch? Listen to you. I'm not a little girl anymore, hahaha."

"Yes, outwardly I'm laughing, but inside it's a different story."

"Oh yes, you said you ordered a new wardrobe—and look, it's already here. Wow, *very* nice, and it's a perfect fit."

"Darn it all. I only get to visit you once in a blue moon, and looking at you two lovebirds living it up—I'm so jealous I could die."

"What—you want to buy me one? Sister, really! Thanks but no thanks."

"No, I'm fine with the one we have. It's old, but we still get some use out of it."

"I can live with being poor, that's all right with us."

"Well, I'll tell you—here we are, you and me, born of the same father, conceived in the same womb, we grew up together, went to school together, and when I see you and your peachy life, not a single worry, I think, *Why not me? Why do I have to suffer on his account?* My insides are churning, it's just so unfair. It makes me mad as heck!"

"I guess that's why old wives always talk about what sign you were born under, your fate, stuff like that."

"Now that you mention it, superstition or not, I almost feel like calling in a *mudang* to do her thing."

"Well, it's not as if he's crippled or something—actually he's intelligent, he's a capable man and he knows it, he doesn't have to take a back seat to anyone. He wasn't born with much of an inheritance, but is that his fault? Anyway, we'll never be rich, no matter how we try to save."

"Are you kidding—how can you say that?"

"Can you guess what he said about *your* husband? He's a lower form of life, all he knows is squeezing his patients for money just like he squeezes pus out of them. The world has turned upside down, people act like animals, but what does he care? As long as he eats well, dresses nice, and has a cute, plump wife to make things comfy for him at home, everything's ducky, right? Hahaha. Don't deny it, Sis."

"Well, like they say, when you marry you start taking after your husband, yes? When we were young, *you* were the fussbudget, you were so anal and thin-skinned, and I was the happy-go-lucky one. Isn't that right? And now we're the exact opposite."

"The point is, if I'd married a doctor like you did, Sis, I wouldn't be envying you. Gee whiz, I wouldn't worry about anything."

"Yes indeed, right you are, Sister dear, this time you have won. Not in terms of values, only that you're better off than me at this moment in time. And I'm not going to hide it—there's a part of me that envies you."

"Anyway, I don't have the foggiest notion what to do. This is something—"

"I've been thinking every which way, and decided I need some advice from Brother-in-Law, so I dropped everything and rushed over here thinking I'll spill it all out, all of what's happening between the two of us. I've been keeping it to myself because if he knows, he'll start thundering at me, and I know what he's like, he'll say I'm making a sane man out to be a lunatic."

"I *do* want to roll up my sleeves and get to work on him—but how? He's acting so scary I have to do *something*."

"Well, doesn't Brother-in-Law have a classmate or a friend who's a psychiatrist?"

"You think it's a neurosis?"

"Well, yes, a neurosis, kind of. But today I think he went a step beyond that."

"Sis, you're probably not aware of this, since you only moved up here a little while ago, and I haven't had a chance to lay out the whole story. I thought he'd gone downhill as far as he was going to go, he couldn't get any worse, maybe he'd even get better. So I've been half worrying and half optimistic."

"All right, I'll tell you. This afternoon took ten years off my life, I swear. My heart's been galloping ever since. For heaven's sake, it just doesn't add up."

"It wasn't quite two o'clock. I was busy in the kitchen, and I heard him behind me."

"Well, I wasn't really thinking about it, but when I wheeled around, here's this guy all dressed in black, I didn't even recognize him. *Who the hell is this?* And then I realized it was him. And he had his *winter* suit on—can you believe it? It's the dog days, for crying out loud."

"'Oh my god'? No, Sis, it was worse than that, I practically fainted."

"Well, it's obvious, isn't it? No one in his right mind would do *that*. I'd washed and ironed his white summer suit and hung it in the wardrobe—didn't he see it? It's so steaming hot out, what's he thinking? And it wasn't his homespun, but that *black* one; the wool threads are as thick as your fingers. Plus, he must have walked right past his panama hat and his white leather shoes, because instead he's wearing his fedora and his dark shoes. Add the dress shirt and the necktie, and there he was, dressed to the hilt for winter."

"Which is the last thing I need, considering my heart's always going pitty-pat these days. I mean, imagine a person like me witnessing a scene like that, what a shock it was."

"Well, my heart dropped—I mean, what was I supposed to do? I felt like a quaking aspen, I was shivering from my lips to my toes."

"*Good heavens*, I said to myself. *Look at him.* My voice sounded like a death rattle. I was just standing there like I'd lost my mind. And the next moment he's out in the yard, standing like a statue, eyes on me, and guess what—he flashes a grin. A grin, for god's sake!"

"No, not since last fall, not one smile in almost a year. Before that, if something pleasant happened, something that cheered him up, sure he'd grin. Just like he did in the yard."

"Of course I was glad. On the other hand, my heart was pounding like crazy. Can't you see—here's someone who hasn't cracked a smile in a year, and suddenly the smile is back. We little women just love our smiling husbands, but what if he's gone off his rocker, you know?"

"How could I calm myself down? I was crying like a river, and the next thing I knew I'd jumped down to the yard and grabbed his arms, I was so choked up. I'm sure I turned white in the face; I must have looked like death warmed over. He didn't know what to make of it, me jumping down to the yard, crying, and he made a face. Thank god he must have realized what a sight he was. He glanced down at his outfit, and it must have embarrassed him, because out came a smirk. And *that* got me burning up again."

"'What's wrong with you?' he says. 'Are you going to croak just because I'm dressed for winter in the summer?' The way he clucks—you know, tsk-tsk—the look on his face, his tone of voice, they're just like before, he's nonchalant as ever. Apart from the clothing and the smile, nothing's different, no holes in the armor. When someone gets deranged, there are signs, right? The way they sound, the attitude, you can see the person coming apart at the seams."

"'You're so low-class!' he says to me. 'Don't be such a snob! The world's turned upside down and for you it's peace under heaven, so why the fuss if I want to dress out of season?'"

"Low-class—that's what he always says, it's like he's laying a curse on me, but I tried to forget all that while I gave him the hawkeye—don't they say if someone's getting loopy, his eyes give it away?"

"No, the more I search those eyes, the more bright and shiny they look, just like before, the same spirit and energy—nothing's changed."

"A load off my mind? I *wish*."

"Well, I grab his arms and shake him and say 'Yŏboooo!' and he barks at me, 'What the hell!' just like he always does. And I say, 'Oh my god, where have you been, rigged out like that?'"

"*Obviously* he'd been somewhere—I mean, he's red as an apple and dripping with sweat. There's something definitely wrong with him, I'm sure of it."

"Don't you see? Out of the blue, he puts on his winter suit, the whole nine yards, nice and neat and proper, and off he goes. Just looking at him scared the devil out of me. How in creation . . . ?"

"If you ask me, it all goes back to early last fall when he quit his job at the newspaper. He's been holed up in his cave ever since, flat on his back. Go out for a walk? Heck no, he doesn't go out, period! With one exception—every five or ten days he heads over to Hwa-dong to see his friend Sŏ, or so he says. And that's about it."

"Not much. Unless he's got his nose in a book or he's flipping through his newspapers and magazines, he's laid out on the floor. Regardless, there's no smiles, no talk, his mouth is clamped shut, it's all he can do to give a yes or a no, and that's only if he's in the mood. Once in a while he really gets irritated and takes it out on me, and that's the only time Mister Eloquent from the old days comes out. So here I am, the lamb before the slaughter."

"Get over what! I mean, there's nothing tying him down—he ought to feel thankful. Chungang School's right behind us, he could cut through their back garden and in no time he's at Samch'ŏng-dong and the swimming hole. And with little T'aeho off from kindergarten and bored out of his mind because there's no one to pal around with, he could roll up the straw mat, take the kid in hand, and off they go—just think, it's the one thing he could do any day he wanted. They could play in the water, and when they get tired, find a shady little spot beneath the pines to stretch out, and he could read to the boy. It's good exercise, you can beat the heat, and besides he could see people he knows, make a new friend or two, and forget about everything under the sun—what more could you want? I've worn my tongue out trying to get him to budge, but do you think he listens? Instead he snaps at me, 'You're so obtuse, you're such a snob!' says I'm all wrapped up with a bunch of jerks. He curses me, saying I want him to live like a pig."

"Well, there's more to it than that. As you know, Sis, Mother's been writing us since early last summer, four letters by now. In the first three she kept saying, 'If nothing's tying him up, why not come down? There's a beach nearby, it's better than Seoul, you can get fish right off the boat. And though we aren't that well off, there's a woman we can send up to take care of the house for the summer while you're here, she's dependable, she knows her way around Seoul, and we could set her up with you?' She really wants us to spend the summer near the water where it's not so hot, all three of us, especially the little one, she's dying to see him. So in the latest letter, number four, that is, it sounds like she's assuming we can't go down because we can't afford it, but if we *were* to go down she'd send money for that woman to look after the house, and we should let her know right away."

"Well, we all know the mother-in-law coddles the son-in-law, more than her daughter or her grandson. It's her precious son-in-law who's the apple of her eye, isn't it true?"

"That's what I mean. Other people are dying to get away for the summer, they spend *money* to do it. But not us—even though Mother is practically begging. Think about it, Sis. How sweet it would be if you and your family could go somewhere, but you can't, right? Brother-in-Law's too busy. Wouldn't it be wonderful if we could just drop everything and go?"

"I just don't get it. There's only Mom and Dad, no brothers-in-law for him to worry about, he'd get all the pampering he needs—what's so difficult about that? To tell you the truth, he'd be a whole lot freer down there than he would with his own family."

"Oh yes, I keep after him. But he's like a little kid, the way he shakes his head no. And you ought to hear him talk—'You can cut my head off, but my butt's staying right here in Seoul.'"

"That's precisely what I asked him—'How come you're so in love with Seoul that you'd rather die than leave?' Guess what? He lashes out at me: 'A lower form of life like you, a blockhead, would you understand even if I explained it to you? You're hopeless. If you can understand an explanation, then you don't need the explanation in the first place.'"

"No, when he gets sick of my pestering he tells me to get lost, says to take T'aeho and go down by ourselves. Or for that matter, just disappear once and for all. Now that the world's going to hell, who cares about family, marriage, children? You tell me, Sis, have you ever heard such a thing?"

"Why not go down by myself? Sis, I wish you wouldn't talk like that."

"As a matter of fact, I've told myself that very thing, more than once."

"No—as much as I would like to, I can't simply drop everything and take off. You think I should leave him behind, the way he is? If he was a *no-mal* person—you know, *no-mal*, English *no-mal*—well, maybe. But he's a sick man, he's sick—where do I get off dumping him on someone else?"

"Sister, for god's sake! If it was *your* husband, you'd be walking on eggshells, you'd pamper him. Hahaha, listen to me, running off at the mouth—I guess that man of mine's been rubbing off on me."

"No, it wasn't a clash with somebody or a difference of opinion, he just up and quit—turned in his resignation to the editor-in-chief and left. I'd call that a distress signal, wouldn't you?"

"Well, I guess they had second thoughts. First they send him a letter, and then the political affairs editor shows up at our door, and finally the editor-in-chief mails him a business card with a message from the owner himself, and all along they're saying, come on back."

"Nope, he didn't budge, kept giving them excuses—his health isn't good, he can't handle the workload, blah blah blah."

"I mean, look at him. All these university graduates, three, four years later they still don't have a job, they're having a heck of a time, and he comes back from studying in Tokyo and the minute he arrives he lands the job with the newspaper, and in five years' time he's kept his nose clean, everybody likes him, the owner's taken him under his wing. And he throws it all away. . . . In fact, this is what he said—'Anybody with two eyes can see this is no way to make a living.' And you know, around that time he was looking absolutely miserable."

"How are we making a living? Well, we're managing. The 300 *wŏn* they sent him off with got us through last fall and winter, and this spring and then early in the summer his folks sent us 100 *wŏn*, so we put on a happy face and pretend we're scraping by."

"No—we can't depend on them. His little brother runs a gold mine, you know, but it's a small-scale enterprise. He feels sorry for his big brother, because he lives away from home too, so he sends us 100 *wŏn* from time to time. It looks now like he's fixing to sell it off, and that would probably bring him tens of thousands of *wŏn*, but there's some kind of hold-up and for a couple months now the sale keeps getting pushed back to tomorrow or the next day, and in the meantime there's no money coming in. We keep waiting, and our debts keep piling up—I feel like the porcupine with everything caught in its quills."

"Don't worry, we'll survive. If we're really hard up we can sell the house, pay off the debts, and have enough left over to live on for a while—and we could always move outside of town and get ourselves a shack. Actually I'm kind of resigned to the idea. I've decided to take things as they come and not get too worked up about how we're going to get by."

"I mean it, I don't worry that much, and I'm not threatened by the prospect. If only he can get back on his feet and get out and about, job or not . . . if he can do that much for me, gosh, I could take in laundry, and if we only eat once in three days, well, I can handle that too."

"No lie, Sister, I'm serious. It's so frustrating! Like I said, I told him to go out somewhere, the Samch'ŏng-dong swimming hole or wherever, but at this point that's really not a priority. Darn it all anyway!"

"Sister, you've been there, you've seen it for yourself, that room of his—room, how can you even call it a room? In summer it's not fit to live in. It faces west, and by afternoon it's practically burning up in the sunlight. And with those galvanized zinc eaves, the way they overhang and heat up, it's like a steam bath. A north-facing window would be nice, but there's only that tiny little door off the veranda, so it doesn't get any breeze. It's a *cauldron*, for heaven's sake. Ten minutes in there would be the death of me. The idiot who built that house, did it ever enter his thick head . . ."

"I don't understand it either—he just figures he'll put up with it, I guess. It's all right in fall and winter, and spring too. But now it's the *dog days*, and he won't budge from that steam pot. If the heat can wear down a healthy man, imagine what it's doing to *him*. It's like he's trying to kill himself."

"'For heaven's sake, will you *please* come out on the veranda.' I can recite that to him all day long, but do you think he listens? I know, the veranda's no miracle cure, but at least it's not as hot as that room. Plus, it gets a cross breeze if we open the door to the family room. So why can't he strip down and make himself comfortable and find a nice cool place to lay himself? There's nobody to gawk at him except the two of us."

"Well, I could understand if it was a huge annoyance. But all he's got to do is roll over once, and he's out of his room and onto the veranda; flip over again, and he's practically at the back door of the family room. But he won't move a muscle. Instead he sticks to his cauldron. It's like he wants to make things worse for himself. Either he's awfully bull-headed or he's scheming something."

"Well, my heart's about to burn a hole in my chest—I'm worrying myself silly."

"Oh yes indeed, he's always had a stubborn streak, he's not very flexible, and he's a bit eccentric, I'll grant you that, but the way he's behaving now, no way is it stubbornness or eccentricity, he's showing about as much sense as a rock or a log. Meaning he's sick—how could he not be sick and act the way he does?"

"A clinic? A checkup?"

"Hmph! I let out one little peep about getting help for him and he'll kill me, your innocent little sister. No way. Let me get back to what I was saying before—if your good husband happens to know a neurologist, maybe they could put their heads together and cook up something, and then they drop by and see him, but not make it too obvious. Instead they act it out, you know, 'Hey, how are you?' Because, tough as I am, under no circumstances could I wrestle him to a clinic—I'm no superwoman, you know."

"Sister, I *have* tried. I even pulled a little trick of my own today."

"Well, it was just before noontime, and I empty T'aeho's piggy bank and what do you know? Out come a couple of one-*wŏn* notes and maybe three or four *wŏn* in change. 'A jackpot!' I say to the boy, and we talk hush-hush, and then over we go, mother and child, to our fine gentleman in his steam pot—he's all in a dither about something or other, but we march right in."

"So I say to him, 'Wow, isn't it hot, dear. You know, our boy's been pestering me for days to go somewhere—so why don't we go down to Anyang and have ourselves a watermelon and take a dip in a swimming hole? From what I hear, it's not so crowded and you can find a nice quiet place just about anywhere.' I kind of pumped everything up, setting him up for T'aeho, but when it's time for the kid to say his lines, guess what the little scamp comes out with—'Let's have some *Anyang*, let's go to *watermelon*'!"

"No, it didn't get a rise out of him at all. In fact, he didn't say anything at first. So I sat myself down and kept after him and finally he says, 'Go ahead, *you* take him.' Can you believe it?"

"No, he just turned over. And what a godawful sight—all he's wearing is his summer pajama bottoms and he's sweating like a hog, the sweat is dripping off his back and puddling on the floor. I had to fetch a rag and mop it up. Heaven help us!"

"I knew it wouldn't work, but I said it anyway: 'Why don't we *all* go? Some fresh air would do wonders for you. And without you it's no fun. Come on, will you *please* get up, let's get some cold water and wipe you down.' I was practically rubbing my hands together, begging that big baby."

"No, he didn't say a word, not at first. But then he says, 'Fun?' and I say to myself, *Here we go, he wants to pick a fight.* And he follows up with, 'Fun, huh? Fun for you two and suffering for me?'"

"Well, I'd had it by then and I couldn't help saying, 'What a mean thing to say—I wish you wouldn't force the issue. My god, since when did a family outing turn into suffering? Let's suppose you suffer a bit, as you say, and let's forget about me for the moment—if we give the boy a day to run free, is that too much to ask?'"

"And he says, 'A play day for the boy is supposed to make the world a better place?'"

"And I say, 'You're helpless!' He doesn't say a word. 'Come on, *yŏbo*.' Silence. And finally I say, 'Keep this up and you're going to drop dead. What then?'"

"And he says, 'When my time comes, it comes. And the notion that human life is precious is beginning to sound like a myth to me.'"

"And I say, 'Would you *please* shut up. What if I went *poof* somewhere! Is that what it's going to take for you to come to your senses?'"

"And he says, 'You might actually be good for something if you'd stop yapping. Frankly, my dear, chattering like you do is really aggravating.'"

"And I say, 'Well, there's the proof, I really do need to drop dead—so my dear husband won't be aggravated, and so he comes to his senses. Just say the word and I shall die for you.'"

"And he says, 'For my sake? You'd die for me?'"

"And I say, 'Try me if you think I'm joking.'"

"And he says, 'Look at all the people who died in vain for someone else. Do you have any idea why the Yankees have been living high on the hog ever since World War One? Listen to the chorus of twenty million dead souls! What are they singing? "Wasted lives," that's what. Think about it—twenty million able-bodied men in the prime of life.'"

"And I tell him, 'Aigu, you're so dense, how can I get through to you! Will you *please* move yourself to the veranda, or the family room? Please?'"

"And then he barks at me, 'Can't you shut your mouth? You're such a grub.' And lo and behold, it's like he rises from the dead—he actually sits up, he's so angry. 'You imbecile! You think I *like* shutting myself up in here? Did it ever occur to you there might be a reason? You probably don't see it, but I'm involved in a *war*. It's me against the heat, and we'll see who's left standing. I'm fighting, damn it!'"

"Now can you see what I'm up against? God almighty, it's ridiculous."

"Well, all that bickering just worked him up, it was making his nerves worse, so I cleared out. My insides were churning, and the way he was behaving, I thought, *Why not fetch up T'aeho and take him to Anyang, like he said.* But the way he is, I couldn't leave him alone. It's such a mess, I'm exhausted just thinking about it."

"Well, it dawned on me that today's the last of the dog days. The whole summer he's been stuck in that furnace of a room; I haven't even been able to feed him a chicken to help him handle the heat, he's nothing but skin and bones, and these last few days T'aeho's come down with diarrhea, you ought to see his sunken eyes. *For heaven's sake,* I think, *why not go to Namdaemun Market and buy a couple of chickens?* So out I go with the boy."

"Yes, I told him that, told him I was going out to buy some chickens, told him nicely, and as I'm going out he calls to me. And guess what he says—I'm to tell the grain shop owner that he came back from the countryside a couple of days ago, but he's sorry, things didn't work out, and could he be patient till the end of the month? Well, that's not something a crazy man would say, is it?"

"It's down the street from us and we owe about twenty *wŏn.* We've been putting off payment since spring, and late this past June he tells the owner he's going down to the country to get some money together and he'll come right back and square things with him. But the end of July comes around and he still hasn't left, and guess what—it was all a bunch of malarkey, and now he feels so guilty that whenever he visits his pal Sŏ, instead of going past the store and straight over Kahoe-dong, he goes way out of his way, behind Chungang School. He should have found a better way to stall the guy. Then he wouldn't have to feel leery about showing his tail in front of the grain store. What do you make of a man that timid? What it tells *me* is, he's the biggest coward under the sun."

"Who cares, I just went to the grain store and said what he told me to say, then I took the streetcar to Namdaemun and bought three chickens, nice young ones, plucked and cleaned out, and by the time I was done it wasn't quite one o'clock—I probably spent less than an hour there. But when I got back home the gate was shut and the place was empty. He was gone."

"I figured he took off to see Sŏ—nothing suspicious about that. When he does go out, it's always spur of the moment, he grabs his jacket and scurries off, any hour of the day."

"So I thought, Sis. Who would have dreamed he'd deck himself out in his winter duds, from hat to shoes?"

"There I was running around in the kitchen, boiling the chickens, kneading dough for *kalguksu,* slicing and boiling the noodles and putting them in the strainer. I put together the seasoning, and everything was pretty much ready, the only thing missing was him, and speak of the goblin, that's when he made his appearance. Suddenly there he was, and you should have seen him!"

"I was at the end of my rope, any more of a shock and I would have gone over the side—and you know, Sister, I'm no shrinking violet. Sure I'm concerned for his family, but if *Mother* knew, she'd faint."

"Well, I managed to snap out of it long enough to sit that big baby down on the edge of the veranda, and I took off his hat, his jacket, his vest, I tried cooling him off with a fan, and I kept asking where in god's name he'd been, and can you believe it, he was in Chongno, right in the heart of downtown."

"I didn't know *what* to do—I was laughing and crying at the same time."

"When someone gets senile before his time, you have to fix him. Like they say, whack the oak tree with a stick. But I couldn't get the words out of my mouth. So what do I do, whack him with that rolling pin for the *kalguksu* dough! It was right there on the veranda where I'd put it."

"So I say to him, '*Yŏbo*, you've got a nice neat summer suit, whatever made you take out *that* one, and *what* were you doing in Chongno?'"

"And he says, 'Don't talk like an ignoramus. So what if I go out in *this* suit and *this* hat and fry in the sun? You want me to be like all those clowns who raise the white flag and surrender to the heat? You ought to see them, huffing and puffing, and they're hardly wearing *anything*. Me, I go smack dab to the center of Chongno, in my winter clothes, and stake out a place there—did *that* feel good! I was proud of myself. It was absolutely triumphant!'"

"What a blowhard, waving his arms around and putting on a show."

"So I say, 'No one laughed at you?'"

"And he says, 'What do those worms know? I was kind of hoping somebody might say, "Look at this guy, now *that's* style for you." But no, not a one of them, the sons of bitches. If they weren't smirking at me, they were looking up with their jaws hanging open, wondering if I was out of my mind.'"

"And then I noticed his suit jacket was practically oozing sweat—imagine, he must have been boiling."

"And then he says, 'Oh, and you'll get a kick out of this—on the way home I thought I'd swagger right past the grain store.'"

"And I say, 'What did they say?'"

"And he says, 'Nothing much, just "Hello, having a good day?" And I thought, *Now that's more like it*.'"

"And I say, 'You should have done that in the first place.'"

"And he says, 'Yeah, maybe you're right. No detour this time, I just took it easy, held my head high, marched right past the place carefree as all hell, and proud as could be. You bet! What a feeling of liberation! I tell you, liberation feels *good*!'"

"Oh, he was full of himself all right. Still had some of that hangdog look, but overall he was cheerful as a baby."

"Maybe it was that triumphant feeling, or just that he felt *good*, but after I added the chicken broth to the *kalguksu* he ate a whole bowl full—out of my little bowl—then half a bowl more out of his big bowl."

"You know, I can't be sure. If he's turning the corner, then great! But if it's a sign of a relapse, then what?"

"In his family? No, not in his lifetime, and not in his ancestors' either. You know, it's seven years we've been married, but I lived with his family the three years he was in school and the first two years after he got a job—that makes five years—and don't you think I'd know by now if insanity runs in his family?"

"Right you are, Sister, yes. Actually, I thought about that too. He's not a man's man, that's for sure—talk about getting slapped around in Kwach'ŏn and not bitching about it till you get to Seoul. Darn it all anyway. Why can't he just go out and show the world who's boss, huh? That's what he should do, right?"

"As far as I'm concerned, the issue now isn't how he got sick in the first place or what the root cause is."

"What I want to know is, is he beyond hope, or is it just temporary? And if he really is having a breakdown, then how can I make him better? Beyond that, I don't see where I can stick my nose in. And you're telling me I don't understand him? Where have you been all this time—haven't you been listening? How could I *not* understand him?"

"Well, guess who's here—and it's about time."

"As long as I've dragged my rear end all the way over here, why can't I sit myself down with him and pick his brain, then we take it from there?"

Chogwang, October 1938

12

A MAN CALLED HŬNGBO

(Hŭngbo-sshi, 1939)

I

A Japanese lunchbox in one hand and a pint bottle of *chŏngjong* in the other
. . . bet you're thinking this story's about the gentleman in the derby and
morning coat—or is it a frock coat?—with the artificial flower pinned to his
lapel, his face bearing a healthy sheen and a ruddy glow, a toothpick in his
mouth; a man on his way home from some commemorative event, a public
servant of note or a neighborhood worthy. But actually we'll be concerned
instead with the doings of good ol' Mister Hyŏn, the odd-jobs man at XX
Primary School.

The esteemed principal had arrived at school that morning in his *hurok
kotto*, which is Japanese for "frock coat," which led me to believe he had a
function to attend, and sure enough he had stepped out briefly after the
lunch hour and was now returning with the lunchbox and *chŏngjong*. But this
man, a confirmed teetotaler, had left the bottle capped and taken only a
couple of nibbles from the fixings in the bento lunch.

"You come, Hen"—this was how he pronounced Hyŏn's name—"this sea
bass nice," he says, offering the lunchbox and *chŏngjong*.

The steamed rice was prepared with polished grain, white as jade and
glossy like oil, with thick, tender grains, but it was the *fixings*: so savory, so
precious, they'd make good snacks for children, and Hyŏn couldn't help
thinking of his little girl, Sundong.

Day in and day out, Hyŏn returned home around dusk, stepped inside the roofed, pillar-flanked gate, and *ahem*ed to announce his arrival, but before he could call out "Sundong-*a*!" she had recognized his footsteps, hobbled out to the threshold as fast as her gimpy little legs would take her, called out "Daddy!" and latched on to him. So pathetic and yet so lovable, she was his little cripple, Sundong, always happy to see him at the end of the day. So imagine her delight and excitement if he arrived unannounced, sneaking into the yard with these precious, tasty snacks in hand! Oh, how she would savor them!

As luck would have it, an opportunity had come up for him to hurry to the post office and post a document.

It was not far from Chae-dong, where the school was located, to the main intersection in An-dong, so all he had to do was stop by the house on his way back to school.

Parents as a rule try to be fair to all their children, and so his thoughts turned belatedly to his boy, Sunsŏk, at which point thoughts of his wife crept in as well (she *loved* fish cakes).

But if it had been his intention to do something special just for young Sunsŏk or his wife rather than his little girl, he wouldn't have gone to the trouble of squeezing in this side trip and making extra legwork for himself, and besides, since today was the twenty-first, the monthly payday, he could bide his time and before long he would have his pay envelope and make the customary evening return home from "work."

(Come to think of it, parents *are* fair to their children, but ultimately it seems difficult to get around the fact that it's a matter of degree. Just like fingers both long and short can come out of the same mother's belly at the same hour on the same day.)

In any event, although it contained someone else's leftovers, and notwithstanding its origins in Hyŏn's poverty, this was now a good, solid bento lunchbox jam-packed with love and affection.

So at this very moment good ol' Hyŏn was on his way to the Chae-dong intersection, walking briskly along the avenue that led past Unhyŏn Palace, the lunchbox in one hand, the bottle of *chŏngjong* in the other.

It was already the twenty-first of May, the breeze was past being pleasantly warm, and he was downright hot in his black Western suit (imagine that, a suit!) of heavy cotton.

And the sky: the quintessential May sky, as clear and blue as you could want.

Outside the gate and within the walls of the palace there was everywhere the dazzling green of new growth—the grass, the sculpted pines, the willows, everything!

This was the scenery good ol' Hyŏn saw during his daily comings and goings, but now, as he bustled along, it caught his attention and he couldn't help turning his gaze to the verdure that graced the old palace so conspicuously.

This first greenery, ringing in summer and seeing off spring, was as ripe as a pert young Buddhist nun, and as he passed by, good ol' Hyŏn thought he felt the vague stirrings of his own youth, which had passed so suddenly and so long ago.

As he gazed up at the immaculate sky he fancied himself back in those youthful days, and the thought excited him almost enough to make him forget for the moment that his hair was flecked with gray and that he was well north of forty.

It didn't take long for good ol' Hyŏn's presence to botch this splendid scene and aggravate everything in sight. His forty-odd years of exposure to the sun, wind, and rain had left him with a leathery, ashen-colored face blotched with liver spots, and on this foundation were sleepy, shifty eyes that eluded contact; a feeble attempt at facial hair, consisting of a few faded whiskers that would barely have distinguished him from a eunuch; meager lips; a deflated nose resembling a starving bedbug—all of which combined to lend him a wistful air—ears so grandly huge (read "deformed") they seemed bound and determined, if only out of spite, to compensate for the insufficiency in every other area; and too much white hair to hide. How pathetic to think that with these hoary, grotesque features, which must have generated many a complaint from the finery silently suffering this considerable indignity, he could feel his bygone youth as his heart thrilled to the May sky and the emerald colors. But this was not the half of it. . . .

His jet-black suit with its shiny splotches of starch, plus the pockets, like ox testicles drooping in the heat of the season, positively bulging with what he'd squirreled away, were hardly so heavy as to bow him over. His manner of walking bent over with knees flexed was one thing, but the way the soles of his olive-colored training shoes dragged along, so that his heels kicked up twin trails of dust that made a cloud even worse than an aerial smokescreen, could not help but tarnish the crystal sky of May.

Good ol' Hyŏn himself was well aware it was a very bad habit, this heel dragging.

And come to think of it, it amounted to a considerable waste of money when the heels wore down to the soles even though the shoes were otherwise quite serviceable, and scuffing his heels wasn't the best way to make a good impression—what self-respecting person would slog along like that in public? And so when he walked down the street he would from time to time hear insults—"Look at that poor sap"—but what could he say, since he was the one who kicked up all that dust. . . . The list goes on and on.

As long as we're on the subject of insults: people on the street were the least of his worries, for once his own wife (née Kang) lit into him, she would always start by heaving a sigh and saying, "Ayu! Just look at these heels—can't you pick up your feet when you walk!" and then it was on to his eyes, nose, mouth, whiskers, ears, waistline, legs, even his belly button—well, there was plenty more where that came from.

Insofar as good ol' Hyŏn was sufficiently aware of this bad habit, it was not as if he was never mindful of the need to desist. But (and of course this might have been a question of his fate) ever since he was old enough to know better, and in spite of a good thirty years of constant reminders to himself, he just couldn't kick the habit, and apart from those sporadic occasions when he felt compelled to pay attention to the way he walked, he would be going along with something else on his mind only to realize in a rare moment of clarity that there it was again, that same old bad habit.

And sure enough, right this moment, a pair of nice, puffy billows of dust were rising from good ol' Hyŏn's feet every time his heels scuffed along the dirt road (and wouldn't you know it, they were coming off a long drought and the road was bone dry, and there was a soft breeze in the air), and the result was a sight to behold.

"What's with the dust storm!" someone barked.

Starting at this sudden assault on his ears, good ol' Hyŏn whipped around and found himself looking the Chae-dong police box square in the façade, and there sat Constable Kim grinning at him.

"Heh-heh. . . . I was wondering whose dulcet tones I was hearing, sir! . . ."

Good ol' Hyŏn lifted one hand to remove his hat, realized it held the lunchbox, then lifted the other hand only to realize it held the bottle of chŏngjong, and finally he settled with bending at the waist in a bow.

"How are you, Kim Chusa?"

"How in hell can you walk around like that? Look at yourself!"

"Heh-heh. . . . Now mind that sun, sir, don't want it blinding you in the performance of your duties!"

Good ol' Hyŏn and Constable Kim were on such an equal footing that they could talk with each other in this completely unaffected way. Goodness knows, the one was a lowly gofer at a primary school while the other was a provincial constable for the Government-General who at least occupied the lowest rungs of Japanese officialdom, but even if you want to ignore lineage and status, there is such a thing as social standing, and people are going to raise an eyebrow, or maybe get downright indignant, at the notion that lack of ceremony translates into equality. Yet on the other hand, granted that lineage and status are a fact of life and there are inevitable distinctions between high and low, is it not the case that every so often humanity prevails in a relationship?

Now if that notion rankles you, then feature this:

Good ol' Hyŏn and Constable Kim were neighbors, their front gates opening onto each other across a slender alley, and the year before last, when Constable Kim had moved in, Hyŏn's daughter, Sundong, despite her game leg, had become fast friends with Kim's daughter Chŏngja, who like Sundong was five years old, and within half a year the womenfolk had struck up a friendship, and through this agency the two men's nodding acquaintance had grown chummier.

And then this past March, when Constable Kim was attempting to enroll Chŏngja at good ol' Hyŏn's primary school and everyone was having a devil of a time getting even their seven- and eight-year-olds registered because of the usual enrollment squeeze, good ol' Hyŏn had done some fast footwork, thanks to which Chŏngja was admitted without incident.

"This here girl's the daughter of a cousin on my mother's side, so you've got to find a place for her even if that means turning away ten other children."

Of course he told the principal and vice-principal this, and he even went out of the way to make several appearances before the school board because he happened to know one of the clerks there. And even if the constable wasn't actually a cousin, a good neighbor is worth his weight in cousins, as the saying goes, and so it's not as if good ol' Hyŏn was a pathological liar.

Be that as it may, liar or not, after all this fuss and bother the constable's darling little girl was admitted. And so the family was grateful to good ol' Hyŏn, and this gratitude could only mean a cozier connection between the two men.

To make a long story short, it would not be out of line for me to say that this lowly gofer and a certain constable were on the most liberal of terms (with due allowance for their different pedigrees), and enjoyed a relationship free of pretension.

2

The constable gave the bottle of *chŏngjong* a meaningful look and with a twinkle in his eye teased good ol' Hyŏn: "Lucky you. Later today, eh?"

It would be unseemly of me to say that he was salivating as he said this, but the constable was a drinking kind of man, and although he would be above blatant ogling of the vulnerable vessel in good ol' Hyŏn's hand, the mere sight of the bottle triggered his drinker's hankering, a yen that couldn't help but play across his face.

They say good ol' Hyŏn's a little slow on the uptake, but insofar as he had served a considerable apprenticeship in the ways of drinking ever since he was a wee lad, he could not possibly misread such a telling hint from a fellow tippler.

"Heavens! You didn't think I was planning to drink this by myself, did you? Where's the fun in that? Eh, Constable Kim?"

So saying, good ol' Hyŏn flashed the constable another look-see at the bottle, along with a wink and a grin.

"Are you out of your mind? On duty?" His words sounded solemn enough, but the attendant grin suggested that the constable was only too happy to be tempted. He continued, upping the ante: "We can do better than that lunchbox, though. . . . What a bottle like that needs is for your wife to whip us up a pound of sukiyaki meat, which we wash down with a drink while we watch the sun set."

Needless to say, these instructions to good ol' Hyŏn were seasoned advice from a fellow boozer.

But good ol' Hyŏn didn't dare.

"Then why don't I drop the bottle off at your place, Constable Kim?"

"No no no. No need for that."

"Come on, you're just saying that. . . . Tell you what, you get home for supper and have yourself a drink, how's that?"

"Oh, fine, then. I'll buy some meat and after it's cooked up and we sit down to supper I'll give you a shout, all right?"

Now it was good ol' Hyŏn who felt a powerful temptation. Even so, he said, "Who me!? You know damn well I can't drink."

"You mean you're not *allowed* to drink. . . . You want to, but your old lady's got you spooked. You just get yourself over when I holler. Leave your wife to me—I'll make something up."

"Heavens, no!" Good ol' Hyŏn chuckled sheepishly. "How could I? How about I just take this bottle on over right now?"

Thus was good ol' Hyŏn saved the trouble of disposing of the offending pint bottle of *chŏngjong*.

The principal had made a point of giving him the bottle as a sign of gratitude (he knew that although good ol' Hyŏn rarely drank, he had it in him to do so). Granted, it was just a small bottle, but for good ol' Hyŏn it was precious indeed. On the other hand, as Constable Kim was always joking, good old Hyŏn's wife, née Kang, was such a terror when it came to alcohol, he could not bring himself to partake; instead, even a fleeting glimpse of it, or a momentary possession, was a source of pleasure and excitement. And this was why good ol' Hyŏn had felt so uneasy just then while reverently escorting the cursed bottle and attendant lunchbox to his home.

Anything involving booze, even the mere sight of it, triggered antipathy in the wife, along with the anxious thought that her husband might up and drink the stuff, so she felt compelled to let loose with a double-whammy two-for-one barrage of bitching about the here-and-now bottle and any yet-to-come partaking thereof.

He'd taken nary a whiff from the bottle, but it was enough for him to realize what a precious windfall it was. The notion itself worked him into a tizzy, but if he took it all the way home there would be hell to pay for his transgression, and therein lay the problem. And he mustn't forget his esteemed principal. Half-eaten bento or not, food it was, and one just doesn't go and throw it in the ditch. That was no way to thank the principal, besides which it might incur the wrath of heaven; it was simply beyond the pale.

That being the case, to be on the safe side, both business-wise and personally, what if he ran into an acquaintance and simply handed over the bottle? That way he'd keep up appearances and come off looking like a great guy. Now *there* was a capital plan. Such was good ol' Hyŏn's intention when he happened upon Constable Kim (I plumb forgot to mention this earlier, but he held the constable in great esteem), and when shortly after the fact he reflected on how the two of them had disposed of the bottle he decided that all in all, the outcome couldn't have been better.

And so it was, with the delight of being relieved of a major headache, together with the satisfaction of finally being able to do something for

Constable Kim in the way of a little neighborly assistance, that with a bounce in his step (alas, preoccupied as he was, he had once again lapsed into dragging his heels) good ol' Hyŏn was hustling toward the six-way main intersection of An-dong.

He had picked up his pace with the intention of making up for the time he had lost dallying with the constable at the police box, when he found himself sidetracked yet again. A couple of girls were coming his way, book bags strapped to their backs, arms around each other's shoulders, swaying back and forth, tittering and chattering and generally carrying on. These two were third-year students at the primary school. They didn't recognize good ol' Hyŏn until they were practically upon him, whereupon one of them giggled, "Eek, it's the vice-principal!"

"The vice-principal!" said the other. "Salute!" And just like the schoolboys would have done, they both held their little hands to their short, bobbed hair in a salute.

Good ol' Hyŏn came quickly (if somewhat clumsily) to attention and returned their "Salute!" bringing the bottle to his visor in the process. Then followed an amused chuckle.

It's late in the game to be mentioning this, but at school good ol' Hyŏn was known as "good ol' Hyŏn," as "the odd-jobs man," "the gofer," and—catch this—"the vice-principal"!

There comes a time when an odd-jobs man who has worked long enough at a company will be nicknamed "Vice-President." Or if he's worked long enough at a police station, "Deputy." It's the same at a school: a longtime odd-jobs man just one day ends up with the moniker "Vice-Principal."

This was good ol' Hyŏn's nineteenth year running as the odd-jobs man at XX Primary School. Those years had seen the principal replaced six times and the schoolhouse renovated three times, and good ol' Hyŏn had received medals for ten years' consecutive service, and then fifteen, to be followed in turn next year by the medal for twenty years.

Given all those years, good ol' Hyŏn was thoroughly versed in the ins and outs of the history of the school. He knew Principal Joe was appointed at such-and-such a time of year, that Principal Shmoe was transferred to such-and-such a place and at what time of year, and that's just for starters. He had the lowdown on all the various instructors, from date of hire to date of retire; he knew the number of graduates; he knew about the renovations to the schoolhouse, the results of sports events—you name it.

And the power of recall he had over all that goes in those two ears of his was simply phenomenal. This powerful memory not only helped him remember past events but also came in even handier in the present, such that he could recite the name of every single student from third grade on up. On the street, or wherever, no sooner did he see you then he'd let you know who you were, without a moment's hesitation: "Yep, grade such-and-such, So-and-so's homeroom," and any other pertinent details.

And that ain't the half of it: he knew where practically every one of them lived too.

Which brings us back to the two girls. Well, they were both third graders, both in the Pine homeroom; the one with the big eyes was Yun Sunae, the one with the mare's face was Ch'oe Pokhŭi, and they lived across from Hwimun Academy, in Wŏnkkol to be precise, and they were neighbors. . . .

Like I told you, this guy knew his stuff.

That alone qualified him for "Vice-Principal," but hell, for my money you can get rid of the "Vice."

There should be no doubt, of course, that "Vice-President," "Assistant Chief," or "Vice-Principal," spoken in reference to a gofer who's seen better years, is a jocular yet not altogether kind appellation tempered with a mixture of pity and contempt, the type of thing one's betters might say of a mere underling whose fate it is never to ascend to such a position. For good ol' Hyŏn, though, just as for the great majority of the boys and girls at the school, calling or being called "Vice-Principal" held no subtle or underhanded meaning but in truth was a term of endearment infused with the innocent purity and artlessness of these young children. In other words, this was all because good ol' Hyŏn loved these children to pieces.

3

Good ol' Hyŏn shook with laughter as the two girls flanking him, each clutching one of his thighs, giggled hysterically. . . . And then, as good ol' Hyŏn looked down solicitously at the two little dears looking up at him with their adoring, fawnlike eyes and their grinning faces, he was struck with a thought. These third-grade girls in the Pine homeroom had been dismissed from school way back at two o'clock already, and here it was just shy of four and all this time these girls had been out and about on the streets—boy, were they in for it!

"Now—now just a minute here, you two," good ol' Hyŏn said with concern, bending over and peering into the two faces. "Where you girls been— you oughta be home by now."

Sunae, the one with the large eyes, was the first to answer: "Playing. . . ."

Followed by Pokhŭi: "At our friend's house."

"At your friend's house? Playing?"

"Mm-hmm."

"Mm-hmm."

The two of them nodded furiously.

"Heyyyy! That's no good."

"How come?" each girl asked in turn.

"How come? Well . . . you're supposed to play with your friends at school. . . . And when school gets out you scoot on home!"

"But we got out early today."

"And Okcha said we could play at her house, so we went to Okcha's."

"Heyyyy! That's still no good! . . . What if Mommy, Daddy, and Grandma are waiting for you? What if they're all worried, saying, 'Oh, what's happened to our little Sunae?' 'Why isn't our little Pokhŭi back from school yet? Did she get hit by a bike? Did she catch a scolding from her teacher and have to stay after school?' Look—those big, huge buses, those cars charging along, those bicycles whizzing by, those pony carts—see 'em all? What if you get hit? And here you are playing in the street. . . ."

"No problem here." Sunae giggled, shaking her head and indicating the street surface with her foot.

"Yeah!" said Pokhŭi. "This street's only for people. No cars allowed, not even cats! . . . Long as we walk here we won't get hit—our teacher said so!"

This brought a laugh from good ol' Hyŏn. "Well, aren't you two remarkable!" Good ol' Hyŏn had an urge to pat the girls on their bobbed heads, but with the lunchbox in one hand and the bottle of *chŏngjong* in the other, the backs of his hands had to stand in for the palms. "The things you two know already—that's just remarkable."

"What does 'remarkable' mean, Vice-Principal?"

"Vice-Principal, where did you get that bento?"

"Huh? Oh! . . . Oh yeah, 'remarkable.' Well, that means you're good girls and smart too—"

"Ooh, liquor!"

"Ah, this? The principal brought it back for me from some function."

"Are *you* going to drink it, Vice-Principal?"

"Vice-Principal, you *drink*?"

"Drink? Not me!"

"It's bitter, isn't it?"

"Yes, very bitter—nasty stuff!"

"So why do you have liquor?"

"Well, ah . . . I got somebody in mind for it—"

"But the bento's good, right, Vice-Principal?"

"It's *real* good, Pokhŭi—isn't it, Vice-Principal?"

"You bet it is! Pokhŭi, you've never had a bento lunch?"

"Nope."

"But you have, Sunae?"

"Yep. . . . When Father takes me down-country . . . to Grandfather's place . . . on the train."

"Well . . . you don't say! But this here bento is tastier than any bento they sell on any train. . . . Want a taste? I'll give you some if you want."

You could tell the girls wanted to, but they didn't immediately respond. Instead they eyed each other, all the while grinning sheepishly at good ol' Hyŏn.

"There, have some, mmm? . . . Maybe just a smidgeon of the fixins, mmm?"

Good ol' Hyŏn set his bottle on the ground and began to unwrap the lunchbox.

"My mom'll cuss me out. . . . Eating on the street, and all."

"My mom too. . . . She says only beggars eat on the street."

"Well, I'll—gosh, hadn't thought of that!" Good ol' Hyŏn could barely control the emotions accompanying this revelation. "Why, yes indeedy. . . . I clean forgot. . . . Yes, yes! No eating on the street, no sirree! Only bums do that!"

Good ol' Hyŏn chuckled, but what a shame not to share. And the girls, in spite of what they'd said, struggled to keep their composure, eyeing all the while that scrumptious bento lunch—if only they could have a taste of it!

How could good ol' Hyŏn, seeing those expectant faces, just turn and walk away? But just as the girls said, to pick at morsels from the bento on this busy street—why, that's like taking these precious kids and making urchins out of them. . . . *Plus, what would people think of me?*

Might be better to send Pokhŭi off home with a bit of the fixins, since she's never tried one of these lunchboxes, but that obviously wouldn't sit well with her parents either, seeing as how it's not fresh out of the box—another awkward situation. . . . But he wasn't about to dwell on it because it had been his intention all along to take the lunchbox home to his own little Sundong.

Wish I hadn't met the girls in the first place; shouldn't have opened my big mouth either. Good ol' Hyŏn was about to scratch his head in bewilderment when an idea occurred to him. A quick gander around revealed a bakeshop nearby.

Sad to say, good ol' Hyŏn didn't have so much as a copper in hand (not like he ever wandered around with spare change in his pocket anyway).

Oh yeah, that's right! . . . payday's comin' up—darned if isn't today—I'll just tuck away 20 chŏn before handing over the rest to the old lady, and tomorrow or the day after, I'll buy each of the girls one of them 10-chŏn cookies...yeah, that's what I'll do. . . . Once this decision was firm in his mind, his otherwise uncooperative feet turned in the direction of home.

He took a few steps before looking back and offering one last reminder: "You girls run on home now, you hear?"

"Yes, Vice-Principal, *gut-bye.*"

"*Gut-bye*, Vice-Principal."

"Yes, *gut-bye*, and we should go straight home, right?"

"Yes indeedy."

"That's right, we'll both go straight home."

"Of course! And every time we cross the street we'll be extra careful and look both ways for cars, buses, bikes, and pony carts."

"That's my girl!"

"Vice-Principal, you be careful crossing the street too, all right?"

"You betcha," good ol' Hyŏn chuckled.

4

Down his alley he went, and at the gate to his house good ol' Hyŏn hesitated— go on in, or pop over to Constable Kim's first? Needless to say, his druthers would've been to hurry on in to his little Sundong and everything else he held dear. But that pesky bottle in his hand—you just can't keep a good bottle down. Since he was going to give it to the constable anyway, no point in catching hell at home first. The old lady had an uncanny knack for ferreting out contraband, and the moment she caught sight of him coming in, devil's brew in hand, he'd catch hell from the old bag before he even had a chance to come clean.

Without further ado, good ol' Hyŏn eased open the inner gate to Constable Kim's house and announced himself with a shallow cough.

"Pongja, anybody home?" So saying, he ventured into the courtyard.

The sliding doors to the family room were wide open, revealing Constable Kim's wife dozing inelegantly on the warm part of the floor, her upper torso clad in an *appappa*. She must have heard good ol' Hyŏn enter, for she sat up,

woozy, passed one hand over her bulky bun and rubbed the cottonseed-size
sleep from her eyes with the other, then lumbered out on elephantine legs to
the edge of the veranda before letting loose a couple of healthy yawns that
would have done a hippopotamus proud.

"Good afternoon to you, Mrs. Kim!"

"Who's that? Oh, it's you. I must have dropped off."

"Uh, actually I, uh, thought Constable Kim might like. . . ." He offered up
the bottle, and wouldn't you know, she stretched out not only one hand for the
bottle but the other hand for the bento. Evidently it wasn't unknown for the
man of the house to return home bearing a bottle in one hand and a bento in
the other, which would explain her presumption that her husband had flagged
down good ol' Hyŏn passing by the police box and said, "Be a good fellow, will
you, and run these home for me, if you're going that way anyway."

Once good ol' Hyŏn had unraveled her thoughts thus far, a sinking feeling
hit him in the stomach—*Oh no!*

Sure enough, she blurts, "So nice of you to run this errand!" and opens
her palms wide.

A fine pickle good ol' Hyŏn found himself in now. Good ol' Hyŏn that he
was, he couldn't for the life of him muster the nerve to pull the hand holding
the lunchbox behind his back and say, "No ma'am, it's just the bottle I'm
delivering." When good ol' Hyŏn realized he was nigh on losing the both of
them, he felt like plopping himself down and bawling. All the pains he had
taken, all the hustling he'd done just to be able to enjoy the sight of little
Sundong eating the bento—the prospect of having it taken away from him
was crying shame enough, and in light of the situation with the girls just
now, it was adding insult to injury.

So there you have it: on the one hand, since good ol' Hyŏn had gotten the
lunchbox as sloppy seconds from the principal, if Constable Kim's wife were
to open it now it would be clear in an instant that someone had already par-
taken. . . . On the other hand, she might think nothing of it and assume that
her husband had taken a few nibbles before sending it along, but when the
constable came home it would be only a matter of time before they suspected
good ol' Hyŏn himself of having had his hand in the cookie jar. At some
point she'd almost certainly say to her husband, "Wait a minute, I thought
you had taken a few bites before sending it along with Hyŏn." And then the
constable would say, "What! You mean someone's already been eating it? Of
all the low-down. . . . So he's giving me bento leftovers that he's already been
rooting around in. That weasel Hyŏn!"

Annoyed they would be, but it wasn't the possibility of verbal abuse that worried him, rather the prospect of a sound spanking on his bare behind.

The more he thought about it, the more helpless he felt, the more hopeless he became.

For the life of him, good ol' Hyŏn couldn't fathom how a lunchbox could rear its measly head and from the first moment on the street with the girls till now cause him so much grief and trouble.

"Your wife's not home? I haven't seen her. . . ." As if good ol' Hyŏn weren't feeling sorry enough for himself already, these parting words from the wife of Constable Kim (polite chitchat though they were) ushered him out the gate. "Looks like little Sundong is all alone at home. Shouldn't you go check on her? You're not intending to go out again, are you?"

"Yes, ma'am, I'll be sure to do that."

"I sure do wish that husband of mine wouldn't go sending you on errands like this all the time."

"Don't you mention it! At your service. Say, is Pongja back yet?"

"Mm-hmm, school got out just before lunchtime. She's probably out playing somewhere."

5

Sundong, knowing as she did from the sound of his footsteps that her father was home, and given the proximity of the two houses—how could she not know that her daddy was home? And so just as good ol' Hyŏn was pulling shut behind him the gate to Constable Kim's house, little Sundong, hobbled by her crippled leg, was flinging open their outer gate to meet him, taking dainty little hops on her good leg.

Father's "Sundong!" was met with Sundong's "Daddy!"

Good ol' Hyŏn swept his daughter up and gave her cheek an affectionate rub. He managed to say "I'm going to buy my little girl a bento" before he got choked up—he had to do something about this wretched lunchbox business, and that's when this idea struck him.

Sure enough, good ol' Hyŏn had stumbled upon a wish fulfilled, and the dark cloud lifted from his face in an instant and a bright smile filled it instead. It was this revelation that choked him up, not sadness.

But it was all a mystery to Sundong—what was this about a bento? Usually the best he could do was a cookie. And what's more, for Sundong, "bento" could only mean the few measly fermented beans on rice that she and her brother took to school every day for lunch in a tin container.

"A bento? You're buying me a bento?"

"Yes, indeedy, just you wait."

"Yippee! So you can buy bento too?"

"Yessiree."

"Where?"

"Uh, for starters, at the train station."

"Yippee! Are they good?"

"As tasty as can be!"

"Oh goody—I can't wait to try one!" And she wasn't just playing cute either—that she really wanted to try one was written all over her face.

Atrophy from the waist down, the overall wasted appearance, the bulging eyes, her long skinny neck, the narrow, bowed shoulders—scrofulosis, is that what they call it?

Good ol' Hyŏn really ought to have been feeding her cod liver oil or calcium supplements, but even if we were to allow as how he lacked the means, this much he surely could have afforded, so it was due to his ignorance that the girl was left untreated, with the result that she looked like a plucked bean sprout and suffered from perpetual hankerings. Besides which, because of her deformed leg, even though she'd turned seven that year, she couldn't run around outside and take in the sun, let alone go to school, so all she did was sit cooped up at home day and night, with the result that she didn't grow properly.

As far as good ol' Hyŏn was concerned, cripple though she might be (and this was precisely why her future was so bleak), it wasn't that he didn't want to send her to school—which, if she finished, would mean doing something better than being a glorified errand boy like her father. But thus far, say what he might, and because she was still too immature, at the mere mention of the word "school" she would complain that people were mean to her and kids made fun of her, and she couldn't bear the thought of it. What could he do—you can't force these things.

Good ol' Hyŏn was so wrapped up in little Sundong and the bento that he was oblivious to the fact that little Spotty had followed the girl out the gate. A speckled terrier cross with black spots on a white background, Spotty was his second most favorite thing in the world after little Sundong. When little Spotty, wagging his tail in greeting, went unnoticed, in a bid for attention he began humping good ol' Hyŏn's leg. This caught good ol' Hyŏn's attention.

"Oh Spotty, didn't see you." Good ol' Hyŏn lowered little Sundong to the ground and stroked Spotty's head. Spotty lay down on his back, ears perked up, and wagged his tail like he couldn't get enough of it.

"All righty, then, let's all go inside."

Supporting little Sundong with one hand and guiding Spotty, he led them both through the gate.

"Where's Mommy?"

"She went out to pray!"

"To pray? Is somebody else sick now?"

"Yeah, somebody or other."

"Your brother home yet?"

"Nyuh-uh."

"Really. Weren't you bored all by yourself?"

"Yeah. . . . But me and Nabi and Spotty—the three of us—were playing. Nabi was playing with the marbles, and me and Spotty were watching."

As if on cue, a black cat with a white mouth, underbelly, and legs perked up at the edge of the veranda and produced a cute meow.

"You don't say." And then good ol' Hyŏn addressed the cat: "Hello there—did you have fun playing with my baby?" He stroked the cat's back. Nabi was his third most favorite thing in the world.

Seeing little Sundong all alone and bored like this, good ol' Hyŏn couldn't help feeling exasperated: *If only I didn't have that pesky bento taken away, I could have given it to her. And if only I could have given little Spotty and little Nabi a morsel or two each, boy, would they have lit up!*

Good ol' Hyŏn was momentarily lost in thought when little Sundong called out, "Daddy, Daddy!"

"Yes, dear, what?"

"The swallows. . . ."

"Oh shoot, I almost forgot," said good ol' Hyŏn, looking up at the swallows' nest under the eaves of the room across the way.

These first nestlings were almost ready to fly and that morning had been bunched up at the edge of the nest, taking turns trying out their wings, when one of them had misjudged and fallen to the ground below. Good ol' Hyŏn had rushed over in alarm, scooped up the fledgling in his hands, and placed it back in the nest. When the mother swallow came back with food in her beak she unceremoniously evicted the poor thing. Thinking this strange, good ol' Hyŏn picked it up and replaced it, and once again the mother swallow pushed it out. This sequence was repeated several times.

Good ol' Hyŏn did not realize that swallows have the peculiar habit of never returning to a nest that comes into contact with a human, and always pushing out of the nest and refusing to rear any chick that smells of a human touch.

"So what happened?" Good ol' Hyŏn looked hopefully up at the nest and counted the chicks.

"She pushed it out again!"

"Again? So then what?"

"I made a nest for it out of cotton and brought it inside."

"Really. Good for you. . . . And then?"

"I gave it a teeny bit of rice, but it won't eat."

"It won't? . . . It must be awful hungry. What should we do?"

Good ol' Hyŏn looked around for a fly, but not finding one, headed into the kitchen, emerging some moments later with a catch. In the meantime, little Sundong fetched the swallow chick, still swaddled in cotton, and father and daughter joined forces to pry open its beak and feed it (the wretched thing struggling all the while). Whether from hunger or confusion, swallow the fly the swallow did.

Good ol' Hyŏn was so taken with the little chick he forgot he had to go back to school, and so obsessed was he with fly hunting and swallow feeding that he was having the time of his life. But wouldn't you know, here came the mother swallow, who, seeing her chick in human clutches, flew into a rage, chirping and flapping like you've never seen.

"Oh, jealous are we. Here, be my guest. And next time, don't go pushing it out of your nest," said good ol' Hyŏn, as if admonishing a person, and then placed the chick back in the nest.

But damned if in the next breath that mean old mother swallow, in cahoots with the male, who had just flown back to the nest, didn't push the little fellow right back out again.

"Of all the miserable creatures!" Utterly perplexed and exasperated though he was, there was nothing much that good ol' Hyŏn could do about it; on the one hand he felt sorry, and on the other hand it drove him nuts.

6

Once your day decides it's got it in for you, it's just one nasty surprise after another. For starters, at the crack of dawn this swallow chick went and fell out of its nest, and there'd been no end of trouble ever since. *And then for the life of me, why did this cussed lunchbox and bottle of* chŏngjong *show up in the middle of the street, and lead to more grief at the hands of those two kids, and the next thing I know I'm giving sloppy seconds to my neighbor, which means I'm in for it now with Constable Kim's finicky old lady (which also means I've got a lot of fence mending to do).* . . . Not to mention all the hassle involved in going out to the South Gate to buy a bento, because he felt so badly for little Sundong. . . .

And that was the easy part.

Of all the people, who should he run into on his way back from buying the bento but that no-good Yunbo; there was no escaping his clutches without first downing at least three drinks apiece—and so, in went good ol' Hyŏn behind him, and there they were polishing off drink number one, when who should go marching by but his good wife, who must have had some informants in the spirit world, and good ol' Hyŏn was caught in the act. No doubt if he had consulted a fortune-teller he would have learned that spiteful ghosts and mortal danger awaited him in the southeast quadrant—it doesn't get much worse than that.

Just a little while before, he'd gone back to school to pick up his pay envelope, and after giving a lick and a promise to a couple of errands, he scurried off to the South Gate, asked around in the market area outside, and managing to find a stall still selling bentos, and after buying one he huffed and he puffed his way back to the six-way intersection at An-dong, by which time it was well past seven in the evening. In late spring the days are long, and it hadn't even thought about getting dark yet, but good ol' Hyŏn had eaten breakfast at seven and had a poor excuse for lunch, and for the next seven hours he'd been on his feet, constantly on the go—this was one hungry man. Seeing as how he was no stranger to the bottle—even though he had suffered a prohibition decree, never had he sworn off the stuff—how could the effervescent jolt of downing a drink on an empty stomach not have tickled his fancy?

In fact, good ol' Hyŏn had been quite the drinker until something like early in his thirties, when his wife, née Kang, had found Jesus and demanded that he become a good God-fearing Christian and swear off tobacco and drink. (At least those were the orders she handed down.)

Even if we grant that from where good ol' Hyŏn sat, his wife's dictatorial demands carried the force of law, they constituted an emasculating act of violence that took no consideration of the humanity of the oppressed—i.e., the husband.

The way good ol' Hyŏn saw it, believing in Jesus was about the same as hiking up to the shrine at the top of Samch'ŏng-dong and watching a *mudang* do her song and dance; it was so repugnant to him, he couldn't bring himself to do it. Think about it—all a *mudang* does is deck out one corner of her shaman shrine all colorful-like and install the titular spirit and worship her—bow to her, pray to her, give her a song and a dance, and supposedly if you're sick you get better, your luck improves, and your path to the next world is free and clear. Now think about this—in Christianity, instead of a shrine you've got a big brick house where you install some naked guy on a couple of crossed logs in the shape of the Chinese number 10 and instead of bowing, you get down on your knees in front of him, and instead of banging a drum and chanting, they sing things called hymns to the tune of a pump organ. . . . The purpose is the same: if you're sick you get better, your luck improves, the path to heaven is free and clear. The only difference would be that you make a big deal out of going around asking for forgiveness (by saying "I repent!"), and speaking just of this sinning and forgiveness bit, good ol' Hyŏn through firsthand observation had developed a pretty good idea of how it worked: the Kang woman, his wife, would sin up a storm and then head off to the chapel, where she would get down on her knees and bawl and wail and swear up and down, "Lordy, Lordy, I have sinned; I promise I won't do it again; please forgive me," and then come home all smiles and titters. The next time it would be the same all over again, and again and again. . . . If she took out her frustrations on Spotty by pouring scalding water over him, she would run off to chapel to wail and pray and collect her forgiveness; if she cussed out little Sundong and smacked her, saying, "You little bitch, you deserve the leg screws; better yet, why don't you go get yourself run over by a streetcar?" she would run off to chapel to wail and pray and collect her forgiveness.

But once you've done that a couple of times, once you've gone and committed your sin and wailed and prayed and collected your forgiveness, you need to stop committing those sins. She could smack little Spotty ten times in a month, and wail and pray and collect her forgiveness every time, and cuss at and spank little Sundong fifteen times, and wail and collect her forgiveness every time. So in the end, as long as you cry and pray you can collect your forgiveness, so basically you can sin as much as you like. It didn't take long for good ol' Hyŏn to realize what a sweet deal that was. *Sin as much as you like, 'cause as long as you pray you'll be forgiven.*

Good ol' Hyŏn had gotten so fed up observing all this that once upon a time he had even lit into his wife: "Quite generous this God of yours, eh? Different from the old God of Chosŏn times, who would strike a man dead with a lightning bolt if he sinned. For all I know, a disgusting crook like Chŏn

Yonghae could set up his White-White Bright-Light cult and commit his sins and collect his forgiveness and go to heaven and all he has to do is believe in Jesus."

In any case, it was only natural that good ol' Hyŏn with his limited wisdom, and knowing only what he saw in terms of spiritual practice among his wife and her small circle of coreligionists, would be unable to distinguish between religion and superstition, and therefore it should be no less surprising that for him, believing in religion was no different from a bunch of womenfolk with a mean streak finding solace and future happiness in visits to the local shrine to take in a *mudang* song and dance.

For good ol' Hyŏn, shamanism was as appealing as insects crawling along his inner thigh, and understandably enough he couldn't bring himself to believe in Christianity, which he found just as distasteful. For a good year and more the climate on the home front was stormy practically day in and day out, but finally husband and wife came to an understanding. Good ol' Hyŏn was damned if he would believe in Jesus Christ, but he would quit drinking and smoking. And there you have it: booze was forbidden. And somehow he'd been dry for a decade now.

And so good ol' Hyŏn had avoided the fate of becoming a lush. His salary wasn't much, barely 40 *wŏn* a month, but he was still able to send his boy Sunsŏk to XX Commercial Secondary School, he was able to keep his family of four in food and clothing without being a tightwad, and he could keep making the two-*wŏn* and one-*wŏn*-fifty-*chŏn* payments on two insurance policies for little Sundong.

At the odd times when he considered how his fate had taken a turn for the better, he felt a profound upwelling of gratitude for his wife's tough love—even though at first he had had to be dragged kicking and screaming into abstinence. And since it was only ever a case of prohibition rather than the water wagon, and seeing as how his wife couldn't very well follow him around all the livelong day to keep him honest, on a day like today when he was feeling hungry and hankering for a drink and happened to meet an old drinking buddy, good ol' Hyŏn just didn't have it in him to fend off the temptation of a nightcap.

7

It was a delightful place—up past the six-way An-dong intersection, find the alley on your left that skirts the palace wall, and half a dozen steps in, just before the pawnshop on your right, is a sorry excuse for a building cobbled together from dilapidated tin and wooden siding and straw matting—and you'll find the tastiest soybean mash and makkŏlli in town.

And here came good ol' Hyŏn looking resolutely to the south and doing his damnedest to avoid the sight of this peerless drinking hole and skedaddle on by, the heels of his tired legs dragging along the pavement and the arm holding the bento torquing him along.

As good ol' Hyŏn fled this otherwise dearest of places, as if it were an archenemy, his head spun from the dizzying battle of wits.

And suddenly, "Ah, brother!"

Good ol' Hyŏn didn't have to look up at the pockmarked mug of the giant towering before him to know that the husky, cheerful voice belonged to Yunbo, already pickled on rotgut, and none too displeased to see him.

"Ah, Yunbo!" For his part, good ol' Hyŏn was pleased as punch to meet a comrade in arms.

"Fancy meeting you here—what's up?"

"Oh, nothing in particular. . . . How's about your good self?"

"You know me, always on the move."

"And how's the missus and the little ones?"

"Eating me out of house and home. . . . And how's your good wife?"

"Oh, just . . ."

"And, your little girl, Sun . . . Sundongi?"

"Sundongi? Well, all things considered, what's a fella to do?"

"I hear you," Yunbo tsk-tsked. "Say, instead of standing out here in the street, what say we . . . ?" Scanning the surroundings, Yunbo grabbed good ol' Hyŏn by the arm and led him off in the direction of said drinking establishment.

"Come on, brother, in we go!"

"Oh, this place—I really shouldn't. . . ."

"Speak no more, brother, I know your troubles. . . . But jeez, we meet so rarely, what kind of pal would you be not to let me stand your good self to a snort?"

And with that, good ol' Hyŏn's urge to backpedal dissipated on the spot.

"Cheers, brother, bottoms up!"

"You bet—here's looking up your old address."

They had just raised their bowls of makkŏlli, refreshing at room temperature (albeit better if on ice), and glug-glugging it down when . . .

At the best of times her protuberant eyes were like all-seeing searchlights, so you can well imagine how fearsome she looked with those orbs half rolled back in fury. With those same eyes good ol' Hyŏn's wife, née Kang, flanked by the reverend and two Bible women, stopped short for four or five seconds and glared at good ol' Hyŏn as he imbibed the devil's brew. And not just the eyes, but her lips, thick as a newlywed's quilt, and indeed her limbs and all of her, trembled like a *mudang* possessed.

Needless to say, if she had been by her lonesome, unaccompanied by a respected reverend and the Bible women, a battle scene worthy of *The Romance of the Three Kingdoms* would have ensued. Such not being the case, she martialed superhuman forbearance, suppressed her awful ire, and discreetly rejoined her entourage.

<h2 style="text-align:center">8</h2>

Here we are back at good ol' Hyŏn's sweet home.

It was getting on eight in the evening but still bright as day.

Little Sundong sat expectantly on the yard side of the veranda, and parked in the yard Spotty gazed up at her as if she were the empress of all canines in this world. Both were hungry, and so little Sundong waited ardently for her father.

When Mother was late coming home it was Father who got the rice going, but now Father too was late, and little Sundong's face drooped lower and lower. He'd said he would buy her a bento, but there was no bento and on top of that no father—what a mean father! To make things worse, her big brother was sprawled out back in the family room cussing up a storm—he was so annoying!

"Ya little bitch, you're seven years old, make me something to eat."

"Why can't you do it yourself, Brother?"

"Men don't cook!"

The way little Sundong snorted at him would have done her mother proud. "Worthless bum!"

"Who you calling a bum—you little bitch!" He jerked himself to a sitting position and glared at her. It's normal in this world of ours for the son to resemble the mother, but heaven help us if this young man wasn't the spitting image of her: protuberant eyes, a disappearing forehead, bulbous nose, and a pair of fleshy lips that must have weighed a pound if they weighed an ounce. The face of this eighteen-year-old boy was plastered with pimples, and the collar of his black school uniform bore the two horizontal strokes of the Chinese character for two, indicating he was in grade 2 at the commercial secondary school. It was taking him two years to get through each of the grades (such is life when you want to master the course material!), and if he kept up the good work he just might make it all the way through a commercial college.

"How come Father's not back?" After spouting off, Sunsŏk plopped down on his back again.

Sundong pouted, then said, "Should I tell Father to make dinner?"

"Yeah, why not?"

"But you said men don't cook."

"Father's not a man, he's a devil!"

"What do you mean? Why do you talk like that? Why is Father a devil?"

"Think, ya little bitch—since he doesn't believe in Jesus he's a devil!"

"Why does he have to be a devil if he doesn't believe in Jesus? . . . I'm gonna tell on you."

"Go ahead, ya little bitch, I'm not afraid o' him."

"I'll tell him to give you a whipping."

"Huh—*Father* whip *me*? Do you know how strong I am, ya little bitch!"

"Huh yourself—just because you're strong doesn't mean you're number one!"

"You know how good I am at boxing, ya little bitch! . . . Oh, shit." He jerked himself back up, and the next moment he was like a different person. "Did Father get paid?"

"Who knows, brown nose!"

"Hmm, today's gotta be payday. Hmm, I gotta tell him to buy me a pair o' boxing gloves, hmm."

"Huh, even after I tell him you cussed him out?"

"No way! I was just pretending—can't a guy have some fun? . . . So come on, no tattlin', huh?"

"I can't hear you, did you say something?"

"Cut it out! I'm serious! . . . Father's a good dad all right!"

And that's when all hell broke loose. *Thunk thunk thunk* came the sound of hurried footsteps and with no preliminaries, "Aiguuuu!" followed by the *crash!* of the gate being kicked open, then, "Aiguuu! Lord save me!"

Son and daughter flinched, and then Sunsŏk scooted for the yard; little Sundong crawled, trembling, to the corner of the veranda; Spotty hid beneath the veranda, tail between his legs; from the threshold of the family room Nabi looked out with eyes wide as saucers; and the entire neighborhood was up in arms.

"*Aiguuuu!* Lord save me!"

"Mother! Mother!"

"*Aiguuuu!*"

Getting an assist from Sunsŏk and staggering into the yard, bawling all the while, their mother, her bun coming apart and her hair trailing every which way, her jacket ties undone and a goodly amount of her cargo exposed, one of her rubber shoes still on its foot and the other in her hand—you get the idea (and did we mention her period started yesterday?). Helped up onto the veranda, the moment she was laid down, she stretched out arms and legs and with fists and heels began pounding on the floor—*bang bang . . .* !

"*Aiguuuu!* That no-good—what am I to do with him? Tell me! That no-good!"

If you, dear readers, had just moved into the neighborhood you'd have had to assume that the no-good in question had just taken a concubine and the poor wife, née Kang, had flipped. And needless to say, if you'd heard the first verses of this lament, you'd look at each other and say, "Now *that's* a laughing matter."

The bawling was if anything more energetic, while for his part Sunsŏk had parked himself in the far corner of the veranda, and from there he shot a hot rebuke to his sister.

"Sundong!"

No response.

"Go fetch the Pak woman, the Ch'oe woman, Sŏpsŏp's mother, tell them to get over here—now, ya little bitch!"

Silence.

"If I get my hands on you I'm gonna wring your neck!"

Still no answer from Sundong.

"You little bitch, move! Or I'll put the leg screws to ya!"

9

It's May, but when it's the middle of the night and you're out in the open it can get a bit nippy.

And here was good ol' Hyŏn, squatting with his back against the gate, the precious bento tucked against his side, Spotty clutched to his chest, nodding off and waking up the whole night through.

As long as he wasn't going inside, why, you might ask, couldn't he sleep in the night-duty room at his school? The answer was, not that he preferred spending the night all by his lonesome, but when he thought of his little Sundong crying herself to exhaustion waiting for her father, then curling up and falling asleep, he felt much more comfortable seeing out the night crouched outside the gate with his worries keeping him company, shivering though he was.

And lucky man that he was, he'd been sniffed out by Spotty, who had come outside to huddle in his bosom, and oh did that leave good ol' Hyŏn feeling safe and sound.

The moon had passed over the horizon and the stars were once again free to twinkle.

Ttaeng, ttaeng. Inside the house the clock struck two. It was quite chilly now, and good ol' Hyŏn kept hunching his shoulders to conserve body heat. It would be another couple of hours before the sky began to brighten, but when it did, he'd be sure to softly call for his little Sundong and give her the bento. And when he thought of the happy look on her face, with a beaming grin of his own he rubbed his cheek against Spotty's head.

The night was dead still, and a shooting star streaked far across the heavens.

Once again good ol' Hyŏn nodded off.

Inmun p'yŏngnon, October 1939
Translation by Ross King and Bruce and Ju-Chan Fulton

13

MY "FLOWER AND SOLDIER"

(Na ŭi "Kkot kwa pyŏngjŏng," 1940)

THE THIRD ANNIVERSARY OF THE JULY 7, 1937, INCIDENT—SO much to be said! A long-cherished desire of the Yamato people, and its inevitable consequence, was the historic and divine work of building and developing the mainland with its 100 million subjects, united in pursuit of this goal, the first step of which was that single gunshot on the Luguo Bridge in Beijing at that hour on that day—and we are about to enter the fourth year since.

It was the resounding prelude for the new order spreading throughout East Asia, a majestic current of history that flows to this day, forceful and true to its course.

During these years the effort from top to bottom was never the least. Still, the effort and sacrifice continue, and will be demanded till the war is over.

Regardless of time and place, an unfortunate amount of sacrifice has accompanied the mass-scale pan-national divine workings, and the Incident resulted in the new Reorganized National Government led by Wang Jingwei, which is entering its third period and has manifested clearly the intended goal and also the effects, one step at a time. In other words, the new order will soon be established throughout East Asia with The Great Japanese Empire as leader, together with the Reorganized National Government and Manchukuo, a joint economic bloc to support each other for friendly coexistence, internationally to defeat the European and American invasion and exploitation, ideologically to offer protection from communism and con-demnation of the reds. Soon to come will be the shining day of glorious pay-back for the Japanese people's sacrifice.

In preparation for that historic, glorious day and to mark the beginning of the fourth year since the Incident, we the people behind the lines must intensify our strength in a new fashion and appreciate from deep in our hearts the front-line soldiers and the soldiers who have fallen in the line of duty to protect the fatherland.

When the war broke out, countless soldiers were transported ever north to the front lines. Living on the hill across from the station, we could see them close by, even if we didn't join the well-wishers.

One day—I presume it was sometime in August, since the zinnias were in full bloom—just like on any other day, the convoy trains were coming and going from early in the morning, and around sunset another train arrived, spilling out the soldiers, a rest stop long enough, it seemed, for groups of them to stretch.

After stretching, the groups of soldiers dispersed among the bustling well-wishers and received treats prepared by the middle and elementary school students and various business organizations, or they mingled with the younger students as they were swinging the Rising Sun flags and singing "Teni kawarite . . ." (On behalf of the sky) or watching *kisaeng* performances on the stage; a few were shouting "Hayaidoko, Arirang butte tsutegureyo!" (Hurry up, you can skip "Arirang"). Some of the soldiers came up toward our hill along the stream; a few of them spread out on the grass and rolled down the hill for fun; others beckoned the neighborhood kids who were gathered there watching, and chatted with them—it must have been quite a respite for the soldiers heading to the war front.

Just then my seven-year-old nephew, who was playing next to me while watching the interaction, said he wanted to go join them and grabbed our Rising Sun flag. He was about to set out toward them when I was struck by an idea: I picked zinnias of various colors and handed him a bouquet, saying, "How about giving these flowers to one of the soldiers, your pick?"

The boy was so excited, he chased after the soldiers, kept scanning them, and finally stopped in front of one of them and bowed.

I was too far away to hear what they were saying, but I could make out and guess their expressions—the soldier pulled the boy close to give him a hug, asked questions as he looked down at the boy's face and smoothed his hair, then kept nodding as he looked toward our house and back toward his comrades.

The strange emotional impact I felt then didn't go away for a long time, and I often think about it.

Even today I think about that soldier whose name I don't know and whose face I wouldn't recognize.

Maybe he is fighting bravely at the front and thinking about the bouquet from the boy and falling into reminiscence.

Or he might have made a glorious homecoming and rejoined his wife and kids and shared the story with them.

Or unfortunately, he may have fallen while protecting the country and be now only a spirit. . . . Arriving at this thought, I can't help feeling a lump in my throat.

I wish I could visit the foremost front line; I am desperate to write a story about zinnias and a soldier. The truth is, I feel that if I visited the front line it would be more emotional and give me more dynamic subject matter. However, that's not the only motive for my desire. . . .

Inmun p'yŏngnon, July 1940

14

THE GRASSHOPPER,

THE KINGFISHER, AND THE ANT

(Wangch'i wa sosae wa kemi, 1941)

THE GRASSHOPPER'S HEAD IS BALD AS A BILLIARD BALL, THE kingfisher's bill sticks way out, and the ant's waist is pinched like a wasp's. How the grasshopper got its bald head, the kingfisher its long bill, and the ant its pinched waist is quite a story.

Long, long ago in a far-off place, a grasshopper, kingfisher, and ant lived together under one roof. Ant that he was, the ant was an industrious little fellow. The kingfisher could be out of sorts and unfeeling, but was basically a clever, diligent type who knew how to care of himself and then some.

Pity the poor grasshopper, so weak it couldn't get a rise out of a fly. All it did was loaf around and stuff itself. With its big belly, it ate twice as much as its housemates. Only the belly grows when all you do is loaf and stuff, and the grasshopper, thoughtless and obtuse, felt no shame about its double-the-intake food consumption. You have to be stupid to have that much nerve.

It would be one thing if this were a story about parents and siblings, or more distant relatives, but our tale instead concerns three unrelated creatures, and inevitably their differences came out in the open. By nature the ant was generous, forgiving, and too optimistic to find fault. But the fussy kingfisher couldn't stand the sight of the grasshopper and seized every opportunity to turn solemn and abusive and make the poor grasshopper keep a weather eye out for him.

It was autumn—and not just any autumn, but one whose ample harvest could satiate ample appetites. One day the kingfisher suggested to the grasshopper and the ant, "Now that it's autumn, why don't we have ourselves a little old feast?"

"That's a terrific idea!" said the gluttonous grasshopper, jumping on the suggestion—for who doesn't like a feast?—but not knowing this was actually a cutting remark meant to shame him.

The ant was silent, but betrayed no hint of opposition.

They agreed that "the little old feast" would take place for three days and that each of them would be responsible for one of those days—if the kingfisher took on the first day, for example, then the grasshopper would follow and the ant would finish up with the third day. The grasshopper was cowed by the prospect of being solely responsible for one of the three days, but rather than admit to his worries he gave an evasive "Mmm-hmm." *Why not?* he thought, relishing the prospect of feeding off the other two for the other two days. So what was new? Such nerve had gotten him through his life thus far.

It was the first day of the feast and it was the ant who set out for the fields, where all were busy with the harvest. It so happened that one of the village women was bringing out a snack basket, balancing it on her head in the usual way, making it look like her neck was compressed. "Well, lookie here!" said the ant to himself, and he skittered right up to her, crawled up toward her crotch, and chomped down mercilessly on her thigh.

"*Aigumŏni!*" she cried, and slamming the basket to the ground, she ran for dear life.

Oh, you should have smelled the steamy white rice, the fresh, tangy kimchi, the rich bean-paste stew, the salted chunks of hairtail, the piquant shrimp garnish. . . . All of it the ant took back home, where the three of them gathered and ate deliciously, a feast you don't often see.

The next day it was the kingfisher's turn. Down to the stream he went. The water was so clear you could see the bottom. The minnows were jumping and the snakeheads frolicking. But unlike other days, he wasn't on the lookout for minnows, snakeheads, and such. Instead he parked himself beside a hitching post and waited.

Presently a golden yellow carp came along and worked its way to the surface. The moment its head broke water, the kingfisher took aim, swooped down, and with its long beak skewered the poor fish in the eye.

The kingfisher was welcomed home with a round of applause from the grasshopper and the ant. Imagine once again the savory taste of a special meal, this time a carp fresh out of the water. And so this second day of the feast likewise passed with an abundant repast.

And finally it was the third and last day. The grasshopper marshaled every pretext at his command, hoping to brazen out the situation, but when he noticed the sharp eyes of the kingfisher looking daggers at him he thought better of it. *What a price I'm paying for two days of gluttony.* With this thought but no plan in mind, out went the grasshopper.

First he tried the fields. Everywhere he looked, as far as the eye could see, grain was ripe on the stalk, but the harvest was still in progress, and with all the farmers busy reaping there were slim pickings for the grasshopper. No, a measly few grains of rice wouldn't do.

So off he wandered, with no destination in mind, and lo and behold, the first place he stopped, he heard the one-eyed taffyman drumming on his board of taffy and proclaiming for all the world to hear, "Get your taffy, get your walnut taffy!"

Hold everything! Up sprang the grasshopper onto the taffy board. It was heaped with a sumptuous array of taffy. If only he could take it all back home, the whole kit and caboodle, oh what a coup that would be—but how?

Asking himself what might work, he peered about every which way, and before you knew it, there he was perched on the taffyman's shoulder.

"What the hell, ya little nuisance." And with a slap of his palm the taffyman came oh so close to delivering the grasshopper a cruel death.

With his heart in his mouth, the grasshopper flitted off in terror.

He came to the hills at the far end of the fields and had a look about. The pheasants were skittering, the rabbits were hopping, and there among some rocks were honeycombs. The honey aroma got the grasshopper's innards churning. But they were pie in the sky, beyond his reach.

In a grassy field he came upon a cow with its calf, grazing. The mother was too big, so the grasshopper hopped onto the back of the calf, which commenced bucking in an attempt to dislodge its tickly rider.

How can I lure this big lunk home? wondered the grasshopper. But no workable scheme presented itself. Moving to the calf's forehead, he grabbed onto a tuft of hair and pulled gently. But the untamed calf reacted by shaking its big head and the grasshopper was sent flying.

I'll show you! thought the indignant grasshopper, and he settled onto the calf's flank and began tickling it—"Koochie koochie koo."

The calf, thinking it was a fly, swished its tail, slapping the grasshopper in the side and sending him flying. Helplessly the grasshopper slunk down to the streamside. There he found the minnows jumping and the catfish splashing about. Sure enough, the makings of a feast, but how was he to catch them?

In the meantime, the afternoon passed and before long it began to get dark. But to return home empty-handed would be disgraceful, no ifs, ands, or buts about it. That said, how long could the grasshopper keep wandering about? It was so gosh-darned frustrating, the grasshopper parked himself and bawled.

Just then a golden carp, similar to the one brought home by the kingfisher the day before, finned its way to the surface. Resolutely the grasshopper stilled his tears and poised himself. *What am I doing, a big strapping grasshopper, sitting here bawling?* He resolved to catch the carp, come what may, and sprang toward it. The carp happened to break water just then and the grasshopper landed square on its snout.

Bless me, what do we have here, thought the carp, who just happened to be hankering for a bite to eat, and its tongue flicked out and captured the grasshopper and down the hatch it went, no need to chew.

Back home, meanwhile, the kingfisher and the ant wondered about the grasshopper, who had set out early that morning. Now the sun had completed its circuit across the sky—when would he ever return?

The ant began haranguing the kingfisher: "You and your sharp tongue— whatever compelled you to send that nitwit out? What if he sticks his neck out and gets hurt, and heaven forbid, what if he should die—what do you propose to do then?"

Finding himself on the defensive, the kingfisher struck back: The grasshopper was a gutless eyesore—what else was he supposed to do in that situation? If he hadn't said anything, the nincompoop would have made himself nice and comfortable and never ventured out—he would have come up with some excuse or other and weaseled out of contributing his share of the feast. Who would have thought he'd race outside like that? Anyway, they had to hope he'd get back safe and sound. There was no end to the kingfisher's rationalizations and regrets.

The day having passed and no feast in the offing, the two of them decided they could wait no longer, and off they went in search of the grasshopper.

The ant went out in the fields, but nowhere did he find a trace of the grasshopper. The kingfisher went down to the stream, but of course there was no trace of the grasshopper there either, what with him ensconced in the belly of the carp.

By now dusk was creeping across the landscape; the search became futile. The kingfisher, anxious as could be, gave himself a good upbraiding and decided there was nothing to do but return home, banking on the slender hope that somehow the grasshopper had found his way back on his own.

Just then as he was swooping over the water he noticed a golden carp working its way to the surface. Well, why not? Down he dropped, and with his long beak speared his prey through the eye.

Back home went the kingfisher, to find the ant already returned and waiting without a clue. Surely something had befallen the grasshopper, they decided. Heaving a ground-shaking sigh, they realized that even if they'd wanted to resume the search, by now it was too dark. Nothing for it but to postpone their efforts till first light the following day.

Home felt empty without all three of them there, and in that desolate atmosphere the two survivors began to partake of the carp brought by the kingfisher. With their banquet in plain view, they felt choked up thinking how much better it would be to have their missing comrade by their side.

So you can imagine their surprise when halfway through their meal they heard a buzzing of wings and out popped the grasshopper from the belly of the carp. By the most mysterious good fortune, the carp speared by the kingfisher was the very same that had swallowed the grasshopper alive.

Delighted though they were, the kingfisher and the ant were sent reeling by the shock, while the grasshopper in mid-flight let loose with the performance of his life:

"Gosh! It was so hot in there! Eat up, mates! Look what I caught for ya! Boy did I work hard for this! So damn hot! Come on, eat up!" Along with the chatter he mopped his sweaty brow.

As happy and surprised as the kingfisher was, he couldn't help feeling annoyed. Obviously it was *he* who had caught the carp, thanks to which the grasshopper had been saved from an anonymous death. And now listen to him. How brazen can you get, yapping about his hard work, urging them over and over to eat up, taking credit for their feast—the gall of it! And so he sat silently, twitching eyes downcast, long beak hanging morosely.

The ant, meanwhile, recovering from his shock, took in the other two and practically laughed himself unconscious at the sight of them. Just look at the grasshopper wiping the sweat from his forehead. Yes, it was true, if you grow up expecting handouts the rest of your life, you end up bald as a billiard ball.

And look at the kingfisher with his beak drooping down.

It was sooo funny—the ant rolled around, beside himself with laughter, until he almost came apart at the waist.

And that's how the grasshopper got its big, bald head, and the kingfisher its long beak, and the ant its pinched waist.

Munjang, April 1941

15

A THREE-WAY CONVERSATION

ON *KUNGMIN* LITERATURE

(Kungmin munhak ŭi kongjak chŏngdamhoe, 1941)

PARTICIPANTS
YI T'AEJUN
YU CHINO
CH'AE MANSHIK

PURE LITERATURE AND PEOPLE'S LIVES:
WITH A FOCUS ON THE WHOLESOME

REPORTER: If we all agree that as a matter of course we should focus on the goal of what is known as *kungmin* literature as the path for literary activity in Korea, then as a writer, how do you interpret *kungmin* literature, what is your philosophy of it, and when you actually get down to writing, what are your ambitions and your methods—in short, what are your current views on establishing a *kungmin* literature? This is our primary objective in inviting you three gentlemen here tonight, and we ask that you discuss these issues openly and unreservedly. I will merely be a listener, and the three of you are free to conduct what we hope will be a cordial three-way conversation.

YI T'AEJUN: Perhaps our first order of business should be to delve into what constitutes a *kungmin* literature.

CH'AE MANSHIK: Indeed. Because we need to establish our specific views on *kungmin* literature before we can convert those thoughts into action.

But for a thick head like myself, I need specific examples rather than theories, because even in the Japanese literary world you don't hear people trying to make a case for a work as a good example of *kungmin* literature. I try to scour new publications and the journals for these examples as a way of learning theory, and although I occasionally come across a work that might fill the bill, I'm often suspicious of whether there actually is something we can call "*kungmin* literature."

YU CHINO: Shouldn't we first be talking about what defines "*kungmin* literature"?

YI T'AEJUN: That's a job for the critics, but . . . these days, doesn't it seem that what's called *kungmin* literature is, strictly speaking, a literature driven by national policy?

CH'AE MANSHIK: Then what would we call works such as Hino Ashihei's *Barley and Soldiers* and Ueda Hiroshi's *Yellow Dust*, which incited a big stir in the Japanese literary world after the Manchurian Incident?

YI T'AEJUN: War literature, wouldn't you say?

CH'AE MANSHIK: Couldn't they also be called *kungmin* literature?

YI T'AEJUN: In the sense that they were written in accordance with national emergency policy, sure, it would be correct to call them *kungmin* literature.

CH'AE MANSHIK: If they're written in accordance with national emergency measures, then both are *kungmin* literature, but in journals like *Kisogu* and *Shinch'ŏngnyŏn*, we can find many works that go beyond simple accordance with national emergency policy. Can we call them examples of *kungmin* literature?

YU CHINO: The quality's bad for sure, but they're *kungmin* literature—what else would you call them?

YI T'AEJUN: Yes, because it's natural that the meaning and mission of *kungmin* literature will be different in times of emergency from normal times.

CH'AE MANSHIK: In that sense, the works of the writers involved in pure literature in the past simply can't keep up in popularity with the popular fiction carried in journals like *Kisogu* and *Shinch'ŏngnyŏn*. And if we think of the effect of political coloring, then popular fiction has a much greater influence on readers.

YU CHINO: But following on that, we can't then say this is the correct path of a *kungmin* literature, can we? Because from a literary standpoint these works are trash. What we don't need in a *kungmin* literature is a degraded literature. A genuine *kungmin* literature is first a literature of the people, and at the same time it has to be accomplished. So, strictly speaking, works of low quality can't qualify as *kungmin* literature.

YI T'AEJUN: Now that this sense of purpose has come into being in our literature, can we really say in general that the quality of literary works has declined?

YU CHINO: *Kungmin* literature is by definition a literature of the people, a literature in which we look for better and better works, but the bottom line is that authors haven't yet met this demand, and it's because they can't write such works. Works are being written in accordance with national policy, but it would be preposterous to think of them in terms of literary quality, and none of them can be called *kungmin* literature. In any event, if we interpret only as policy-geared fiction those works of inferior quality published in journals such as *Kisogu* and *Shinch'ŏngnyŏn*, then it will be difficult for a *kungmin* literature to develop.

CH'AE MANSHIK: This discussion is all over the place. . . . How am I supposed to find the examples I said I'd need?

YU CHINO: Well, we hear a lot about wholesome entertainment. And isn't it one of the suggestions for the *kungmin* literature we're talking about that from now on, writers will depict a more wholesome environment in their works? Writers in an age of freedom have traditionally been intrigued by the unwholesome in life, and many such depictions have come down to us in literature, but from now on such depictions should be done away with. Instead, authors should imbue their works with something more wholesome and cheerful, and once you settle on subject matter that is more wholesome and cheerful, that will be something that is demanded by *kungmin* literature, and such works will become so-called national-policy literature as well.

CH'AE MANSHIK: Well, what do you expect? Literature has always looked on the gloomy side of human existence.

YI T'AEJUN: As for works being imbued with wholesome and cheerful thought, if they stand out in effectiveness in this way, then it's essential that these two aspects be contrasted with the unwholesome and the gloomy. But then the situation gets very complicated. Is the work to be wholesome and cheerful from beginning to end, does the theme have to be wholesome and cheerful? I'm not sure we can always do that.

YU CHINO: I assume that will depend on the attitude of the writer.

CH'AE MANSHIK: It's a matter of degree—*how* wholesome and *how* cheerful.

THE GAP BETWEEN LITERARY WORKS AND REALITY: REALIGNING NATIONAL POLICY AND LITERATURE

YU CHINO: A short time ago, in the literary arts competition sponsored by the National Federation of Total Mobilization, I was in charge of adjudicating twelve submissions in the fiction category, and as many as ten of them could be referred to as national-policy fiction. I found them overly colored with contemporary affairs and rushing to accommodate national policy, and they were low-quality works. Apart from the prize-winning story, "Awakened from a Dream" [J. "Yume wa samerumono"], they could scarcely be considered fiction. One of them, "Patriotic Platoon" [K. "Aegukcha kongdae"], written by a young woman, received honorable mention, but I don't consider it worthy of discussion. So in my adjudicator remarks I wrote, "Fiction must above all else be fiction." But if we take the prizewinning story as an example, its subject is praise of the new ethics in the business world, and in comparison with the other works, at least its expression and description are worth mentioning. Because the story line can appeal to anyone, it can touch the reader's heart. This got me thinking that if in the future we write something characteristic of *kungmin* literature, we must write of life so that anyone can empathize with it— namely, we must write of progressive sentiments that are imbued with the reality of the lives of the people. Then we can create successful works of literature.

YI T'AEJUN: Regarding national policy, if we try to overly accommodate by imbuing our works with too much contemporaneity or coloring them with the present age, the works will end up crude. With writing, instead of consciously forcing ourselves to imbue our works in a certain way, we must allow the works to ripen in our heart, and if we use artistic form they will inevitably mature and emerge in and of themselves. In the most recent national drama competition sponsored by the Theater Association and the *Maeil shinbo*, my first impression was that the submissions were solid in terms of character and dramatic composition, but when they tried to emphasize national elements, then by the end there was a ridiculous amount of current events coloration and the majority of them ended up falling apart. And so when I begin reading I'll think, *Hmm, this one has potential*, but by the end my expectations are spoiled. This situation isn't new; we experienced it in the past in the case of fiction that displays an awareness of society, and it would seem we're experiencing it again now.

CH'AE MANSHIK: Well, I guess that means we should look at what's cheerful, constructive, and productive, but until now the tendency has been to look at the opposite—what's gloomy, pathological, and wasteful. The fact is, an in-depth look at literature shows us that there are more of these negative aspects. So it would be good if we could meet midway between fitting in with national policy and satisfying our creative desire [dismissive chuckle], but since we're not at that point, *kungmin* literature is national only in a narrow sense—the obvious logic is that it's something that has to accommodate to national policy.

YU CHINO: In that sense you're absolutely right.

CH'AE MANSHIK: I'm not sure if this relates to the topic of *kungmin* literature, but when I read Tokutomi Roka's *The Cuckoo* in Tokyo [J. *Hototogisu*; trans. K. *Puryŏ kwi*], the French hairstyle was in fashion for the women there, all the women wore their hair in a chignon, but to me, the Japanese version of it—the curled hair of the young woman in this story—is better. So if I encountered someone like this young woman on the street, I would think of the story and perhaps take to her for that reason, you see? And not so long ago I was on a train passing by the city of Atami and everybody got up and started making a fuss—"Look, Atami." I wondered what they were looking at, but all I saw were the neon signs of inns. I'm guessing Kan-ichi and Omiya[1] are engraved in everyone's mind and even though there's nothing in particular to be seen, the Atami seaside by itself creates a kind of sentiment in them. These are examples of how everyday people become attached to traditions that have come down to them from long ago. And it's this kind of popular sentiment that forms the foundation of a great *kungmin* literature. And it's not just a matter of sentiment shared by one people; the sentiment should be easily understood by other peoples as well, and moreover it should be worth understanding. At the risk of conjecture, among other things, don't Britain and America have in common their readers' appreciation of the works of Shakespeare?

YU CHINO: Well, both countries use the language the works were written in—English. But thus far we've been talking too much about *kungmin* literature as national-policy literature, and our writers have been asked to accommodate excessively to national policy, but if in the end that doesn't work, we're left with writing that's not good and policy that's not carried out. As for the popular sentiment you spoke of just now, if we think about the meaning of that in broader terms, then the writers have to work hard to differentiate their new works from their previous works. In other words, because we've been looking at the negative aspects of life included in their previous works, authors should from now on view constructive aspects of life and bring to life in their works a heightened and thriving people's spirit. Only by taking this broad interpretation can we benefit from the development of a kungmin literature itself. If we think too narrowly, then the path ahead will disappear.

CH'AE MANSHIK: Everyone outside the literary world is discussing kungmin literature, but if it's only their comments we seek, we're doing injury to the prospects for a kungmin literature, and literature as we know it can no longer exist.

YU CHINO: Whatever the cause, there are always people who go to extremes, as well as people who are less concerned, all sorts of people. You don't get progress unless you hook all these people up so they work together, and then something will come of their efforts.

CHEERFULNESS, BEAUTY, AND UGLINESS: THE HARMONY AND COMPLEXITY OF LITERATURE

YI T'AEJUN: More than anything, literary production requires delicate artistry; treating writers like manual laborers and scolding them for not working hard won't work. Those who are outside literary circles shouldn't attack writers for being passive or uncooperative, the writers themselves shouldn't overemphasize current affairs, and everyone must make an effort, in whatever way, to make a pan-kungmin literature to be read by anyone. The lives of writers, like those of scholars, must include the leisure to plant oneself in one's study and contemplate, and only then will we see fine works that can indeed by called a proud kungmin literature. Otherwise, we can't hope for good literature.

CH'AE MANSHIK: The beliefs of politicians and the beliefs of writers are different—what I'd like to know is which side we should respect.

YI T'AEJUN: Of course we have to respect the beliefs of those who have long devoted themselves to their field. In the field of politics, we writers respect the beliefs of politicians. . . .

CH'AE MANSHIK: On my way here I was reading the book review column of the Choil shinmun and saw a short piece titled "Quality Is Low." The columnist said that these days the quality of all sorts of items is going down, and what worries him more than anything else is the decline in quality of anything associated with "the nation." This is only my thought, but as for the so-called national-policy fiction of the *samp'a* magazines, which emphasize quantity over quality, the decline is really severe. The decline in literary quality of these works is indescribable. They aren't literature, and even as propaganda they're embarrassing.

YU CHINO: When *kungmin* literature is discussed abroad, don't people always include writers such as Tolstoy, Goethe, and Balzac?

CH'AE MANSHIK: They represent a mature, fully realized *kungmin* literature. So that literature has to be distinguished from the national-policy literature we see during wartime.

YI T'AEJUN: We should study carefully the works coming out lately from writers in Japan. Because they are our seniors in terms of their theory and the acumen with which they create their works, and because they hold certain beliefs about *kungmin* literature, I think we need to learn how they put those beliefs into practice.

CH'AE MANSHIK: I've read widely, but believe me, I haven't found anything I'd want to apprentice myself to. It looks to me as if those writers are still fogbound.

YU CHINO: Instead of fussing about what's right and wrong, it's best for us to understand *kungmin* literature more broadly and try to engender a pan-*kungmin* literature, a literature that all people can cherish. Otherwise, if we keep overemphasizing national policy alone, then our writers won't be able to write and it will be difficult for literature itself to develop. The fact is, until now we've been overly focused on "I-fiction." That this is a negative development can't be denied, and so from now on, literati have to take as their guiding principle the engendering of a great and powerful literature that can bring alive and sustain the work in which we are involved.

CH'AE MANSHIK: I feel the same. Only then can genuine development of literature become possible. To get to that point, maybe we should experiment with production literature—even something like a reportage style of literature, for example, *Barley and Soldiers*, which I mentioned earlier.

YU CHINO: That would be good. In any event, if we go in the direction of a *kungmin* literature, it's best to do some study.

CH'AE MANSHIK: That would be more likely if our situation as writers were to see some real improvement, and if we can travel freely, all the better.

HOPES FOR A GUIDING PHILOSOPHY:
AN ACTION PLAN FOR WRITERS

YU CHINO: This too depends on how each of us tackles his subject matter. For example, if you're depicting love, and the work is more beautiful and it leaves an impression on any reader . . . well, that's good.

CH'AE MANSHIK: If you want to make a love story interesting, then you have to have conflict, you have to have ugliness and evil, and the question becomes, how do you handle those elements?

YU CHINO: *Romeo and Juliet* and *Mignon*, by Meister, are both examples of pure love, but contemporary literature is distancing itself from this. Many works depict immoral elements, and naturally that's become a tendency in our works as well.

YI T'AEJUN: There are classic love stories that are tragic, and they have sentiment, but they're not all pure.

YU CHINO: There are those who ask, what is the meaning of love in our current situation? But we can't look at people's lives so narrowly. Only if it's wholesome and cheerful can love be sufficient as subject matter for a *kungmin* literature.

YI T'AEJUN: You mention wholesome and cheerful, but among the techniques of fiction it's effective to contrast the pure with the ugly and the cheerful with the dark; otherwise the cheerfulness doesn't come alive. This is a difference in thinking between writers and those outside literary circles. By asking only for the cheerful the outsiders are also asking for none of the dark, and I think we need to make them understand that. Take contemporary fiction—the writer plans a cheerful scene and to set it up writes a very dark scene; if people want to make a stink about that, it will become very difficult for writers to write, you know.

CH'AE MANSHIK: I wouldn't go so far as to say they can't write, but I *would* say that literature has gone sour. The tragedy-won't-work approach to people's literature is a difficult issue.

YU CHINO: Literature can't establish itself without a tragic element, can it?

YI T'AEJUN: It all depends on how you work it in. . . .

CH'AE MANSHIK: Regarding the two literary competitions mentioned previously, the results fell short of expectations and there were all sorts of complaints.

YU CHINO: I can imagine. The first condition is whether the works themselves measure up as fiction or drama.

CH'AE MANSHIK: Well, of course—the culture section of the National Federation of Total Mobilization is presumably looking for literary works; they couldn't possibly be expecting research papers. Which goes to show that any attempt to eliminate the boundaries between current-affairs pieces and artistic literature would be incredibly difficult.

YU CHINO: Perhaps the thinking of the culture-section people is more progressive, but for authors it's a daunting question. The best we writers can do is study hard and make a good effort.

YI T'AEJUN: It would be good if those authors who in normal times took the lead in working their philosophy into their writing would guide us now. Because then we writers would follow along.

REPORTER: This concludes the discussion. Thank you all.

Maeil shinbo, November 7, 10, 11, 1938

NOTE

1. Subjects of the Meiji writer Ozaki Koyo (1868–1903)'s novel *Konjiki yasha* (Gold demon).

16

MISTER PANG

(Misŭt'ŏ Pang, 1946)

HOST AND VISITOR ALIKE WERE GROWING QUITE TIPSY. THE host—Mister Pang; the visitor—Squire Paek, a man from the ancestral village.

Mister Pang was exultant as could be these days, and his tipsiness and exuberance went hand in hand until the sky looked just like a single large bank note.

"I'm not bragging, no sir, but nothing can stop me now, nothing. Hmph! No son of a bitch is going to find fault with me, no son of a bitch is going to look down on me, not now, not ever. Hmph! No sir, no way."

You might have thought someone was actually there beside him, finding fault with him, looking down on him. For why else had his protruding eyeballs grown so animated? Why else had his nose, which bent a good thirty degrees to the left, kept twitching as he carried on?

"I may not look like much, no sir, but I'm Pang Sambok, and I've tasted everything the three kingdoms of the East have to offer." The Chinese characters for *Sam* and *Pang* in his name, by the way, meant "three directions." "Don't I speak Chinese? Don't I speak Japanese? And English, of course. . . ."

Mister Pang rediscovered his glass of beer, hoisted it, gulped it down. Sweeping the back of his swarthy hand across his lips, taking a piece of kimchi between his fingers and plopping it into his gaping mouth—such had been this man Pang. Still these habits survived, whether you called him "Mister Pang," "Gentleman Pang," or simply "sir," but now it was beer foam he wiped from his lips and Chinese-style deep-fried chicken he picked and munched.

"When it comes to drinking, beer is the thing, yes sir."

If anyone had provoked him just then, or looked down on him, he was ready to seize the fellow on the spot and chew him out as if he were a piece of chicken. But suddenly his indignation disappeared in favor of a eulogy on beer.

"The Americans are civilized when it comes to drinking. We Koreans have a long way to go."

"Indeed we do," echoed Squire Paek, humoring his host as he refilled Pang's glass. Paek's mousy face with its sparse, brownish beard was tiny as a Chinese date seed.

"Drink up, Paek-san!"

"I've had enough."

"Listen to you! I know your capacity, Paek-san. Even though it's been a long time since we drank together."

"That was back when I was young. Now I'm—"

"You know, I was just about to ask—how old are you, anyway?"

"I was born in the kapsul year, which makes me forty-eight."

"How about that. Eleven years older than me. Well, you don't look it, Paek-san. Hahahaha."

"What are you talking about? Look at my hair."

"Prematurely gray—that's all."

As Squire Paek kept up the banter, he hid his true feelings—namely, that he couldn't stomach Mister Pang's behavior.

According to the etiquette of their ancestral village, you performed a full bow, prostrating yourself, to anyone ten years or more your senior. You addressed such a person with courtesy and respect, sitting with knees bent. Normally you didn't smoke or drink in his presence, but if circumstances compelled you to drink, you turned away and did so discreetly. Pang's manner of speech was disgusting: "Paek-san," "Drink up!" "Prematurely gray," and the rest, as if Paek were a close, same-age friend or else a stranger. Crossing his legs, staring him in the face when he drank, sucking on cigarettes— never had Paek seen such insolence. And it wasn't just a matter of age. If you took lineage and family background into account, then such behavior was utterly unforgivable.

You might not know it from looking at me, thought Paek, but I come from a distinguished clan. My grandfather was a chinsa (I can show you the certificate), his grandfather was revenue minister (you can look it up in our family register), and his grandfather was prime minister of the nation (you can look that up too). Yes, a distinguished clan. And one of my distant cousins was a county magistrate, and one of his sons was a village headman in Manchukuo. But now this cursed "Independence," or whatever they call it, and look at how things have turned out. Until two months ago, wasn't I the respected father of Section Chief Paek, head of accounts at a police station, a recipient of the Eighth Order of Merit, a man you wouldn't dare cough in front of? Two months ago I would have dressed down a man like Pang, could have had him drawn and quartered on the spot. And now things have come to this pass. If only. . . . Where had those good old days gone?

In any case, compared with his scintillating pedigree, that of Mister Pang was nothing to brag about.

Mister Pang's great-grandparents, it was rumored, were outsiders of no distinction who had floated into town from who knows where. His grandfather was a petty clerk in the village bureaucracy, his father a peddler of straw sandals. The father had grown infirm, but even now, at the age of seventy, this Old Man Pang was the villager you went to for a beautiful pair of straw sandals. And then there was Pang Sambok. . . .

He had been an unskilled laborer who knew no life other than eating, sleeping, working as a beast of burden, and turning out the little ones. Crooknose Sambok, who, closer to age thirty than twenty, still migrated from house to house working as a farmhand. And of course he was utterly ignorant, couldn't have copied the native script if his life had depended on it.

If you're going to do unskilled labor, you might as well be a tenant farmer and get yourself a parcel of someone else's land to work for yourself. But not Crooknose Sambok. And so, pushing thirty and still hiring out as a farmhand, he decided one morning to earn himself a bit of money. Leaving the wife and children with his parents, who had trouble enough feeding themselves, he disappeared to Japan, free and easy. Twelve years earlier, it had been.

There must not have been a miraculous windfall, for he sent not a penny home during the next seven or eight years. And then one day, from out of the blue came word that he was in Shanghai. Nothing further was heard from him until three years later, when he popped up in the ancestral village. For a good ten years, as he liked to say, he had tasted everything the three kingdoms of the East had to offer. And yet he looked as unsophisticated as ever, and rather more shabby now—his suit in tatters, his leather shoes mended— than when he had left in his cotton jacket and short pants, which, though patched in places, had at least been washed and ironed.

For a year he loafed and idled, eating or starving on the proceeds of the blood and sweat of his aged parents and his young wife. But then he must have done some soul searching, because he left again, this time for the capital, and this time taking his wife and children.

In Seoul the family occupied a cramped servants' room in a hillside neighborhood in Hyŏnjŏ-dong. For the first year he lived a hand-to-mouth existence working at the Japanese camp for Allied prisoners of war in Yongsan, at the same time building on the broken English he had acquired in Shanghai.

For another year or so, using this same broken English, he worked at a shoemaker's and managed to scrape by. But with the shoe supply dwindling because of the war Japan was losing, shoe leather became extinct. Shoemakers large and small closed down, and Pang felt compelled to strike out as an itinerant cobbler.

It was only natural that as a cobbler, whether he made the rounds of the alleys with his box of tools or parked himself along the main thoroughfare of Chongno, he would from time to time catch the eye of someone from back home. And so it was that the news spread to the ancestral village, but not a soul had anything good to say of him—all you could hear were cynical remarks:

"The no-good spent ten years in Japan and China, and that's all he has to show for it?"

"Chip off the old block. Dad sold straw sandals, Sonny mends leather shoes."

"Bound for the Shoe Hall of Fame."

Such was his humble background—nothing to his name, no position, desperately poor. For his livelihood he squatted on the street patching the worn-out, stinking leather shoes of passersby, fixing them with heel plates, polishing them. Such was Crooknose Sambok's wretched occupation.

These thoughts made Squire Paek indignant. *Hmph! This frog doesn't remember he was once a tadpole! Ill-bred son of a bitch! Uppity bastard!*

But on the other hand, he had to admit that Crooknose Sambok, whether due to this "Shoe Hall of Fame" business or to some freak of nature, had enjoyed great good fortune in the space of only a few months, had become rich, had become "Ass-wipe Pang"—well, that's what it came out sounding like when the Japanese tried to say the English word "mister"—that this "Smelly Pang" had all the comforts of life, had nothing to fear in this world, could prance and strut to his heart's content. It was, if you thought about it, partly amazing, partly enviable, partly annoying.

Deep inside, Squire Paek felt a sincere wonder that he couldn't deny: when it comes to a person's fate, you just can't tell.

This dazzling metamorphosis of Crooknose Sambok was not some miraculous vicissitude, was not, as Squire Paek had wondered, a freak of nature or the result of being destined for the "Shoe Hall of Fame." Rather, it was something extremely simple and easy, though in Pang's case a kind of special condition: he was resourceful after a fashion, and bright enough not to have forgotten the bits of English he had picked up early on.

August 15, 1945—a historic day.

Cobbler Pang Sambok welcomed Liberation Day as he had any other, by squatting in the shade across Chongno from Pagoda Park, fitting shoes with heel plates. He knew no deep emotions, no joy, though. To Sambok the sight of utter strangers embracing each other on the street, reveling, weeping, was alien to him; it was just rather unseemly. He found the surging throngs annoying, the hurrahs painful to his ears; it was enough to make him scowl.

With everyone shouting "*Mansei!*" and jumping up and down in mindless abandon, business was slow to nonexistent.

"Hell! Is independence supposed to fill your stomach?" he groused, full of animosity.

But in the space of a few days Sambok was partaking of the benefits of Liberation, such as they were for a cobbler.

For there were no policemen now to dress him down for overcharging, and he received fifty *chŏn* for a heel plate that used to be ten or fifteen *chŏn*. With no police around, he could swagger free as he pleased, get away with any sort of mischief, and have nothing to fear.

"Well, they're right. This independence is something to crow about after all," he muttered to himself. Nail ten heel plates and he had himself five *wŏn*.

But within another few days Sambok was obliged to curse Liberation once again. His decision to charge more money was not as harmless as it seemed—the wholesalers, for their part, had increased the price of materials. Heel plates, leather, rubber, thread—everything became five, ten times as expensive. No matter how much a cobbler charged his customers, he had to pay dearly for his materials. In the end, only the wholesalers grew fat; Sambok's net earnings were no greater than before.

At sunset he shouldered his cobbler's box and in a fit of pique went to a *makkŏlli* house, where he drained several bowls of the milky rice brew.

"They can go to the devil! Did they all drop dead, those damned economic ministers? What the hell use is independence, anyway!"

In the meantime August passed, and then a week and a half into September the streets of Seoul grew thick with American soldiers and their jeeps.

Sambok saw the frustration of these soldiers when they couldn't communicate while sightseeing or shopping, and eureka!

Sad to say, however, his prospects were hopeless as long as he continued to present himself in his grimy, sweat-soaked rags.

There must be a way. All morning long he mulled it over, and finally at noon he saw the light.

He hastened home and had his wife bundle up his cobbling tools and materials, along with a quilt and his worn-out clothes, and take them to a local pawnbroker. There she consigned the items for a month and returned home with a hundred *wŏn*, repayable at 3 percent interest.

Sambok took this money to one of the secondhand shops you could find all over the city and spent the lot of it on something they called a suit, along with a hat. As for footwear, he was compelled to swap his own shoes for his landlord's army boots, with the understanding that he return them in five days and resole them in due course.

The following day found Sambok setting forth rather later in the morning than when he was a cobbler. Even in his worn-out suit, worn-out hat, and worn-out boots, he was more smartly turned out than he'd ever been. But as he was about to leave, his wife suddenly tugged at his coattail, his one-eyed wife who since the previous night had been pouting, who had done little in the way of waiting on him or answering him.

"Out with it—what are you up to?"

"Are you crazy? Let go!"

"Look at yourself, blockhead—who is she, huh?"

"Shows how much you know. Don't get notions, you idiot."

"Over my dead body!"

"Keep this up, woman, and the first thing I'll do when I get me some money is find myself a concubine."

"More power to you! Go ahead, then, get rid of me—"

"Bitch—I ought to put the leg screws to you!"

He knocked her down with a punch that was something to see, then left their cramped hovel and set out for Chongno.

If a slave is going to be sold, can't he at least be free to choose his own master?

Sambok got off the streetcar at Chongno and ambled east, looking for someone—someone with a good appearance. A common soldier wouldn't do; it would have to be a lieutenant or higher.

In front of the YMCA he came across a man trying to buy a pipe. A stout man, he didn't appear to be a common soldier, and his face looked as good-natured as could be. Sambok immediately took a liking to him. Playing the curious onlooker, he approached unobtrusively.

The man, an American officer, picked up the pipe and examined it with great interest.

"How much?" he asked, peering at the pipe peddler. "How much?"

The old man shouted the price, which the officer, of course, couldn't understand. Cocking his head in puzzlement, he asked again, "How much?"

Here was Sambok's chance. "Tutty *wŏn*," he said in a low voice.

The officer's head whirled around. "Oh—can you speak?" he said with a look of such delight that Sambok thought he was about to be embraced. He then shook Sambok's hand raw.

Sambok was on the verge of disgust.

What did Sambok do? the officer asked.

He'd just lost his job, came the reply.

Well, then, how would Sambok like to be his interpreter?

That would be fine.

Then and there he boarded the officer's vehicle not as Crooknose Sambok the cobbler but as Mister Pang. And so he became an interpreter for a second lieutenant in the American occupation army, at a salary of fifteen dollars, or two hundred forty *wŏn*, a week.

Most days the routine was the same, Mister Pang taking the lieutenant sightseeing during the day and guiding him to drinking houses with serving women at night.

Once, while observing the tower at Pagoda Park, the lieutenant asked how old it was. Whenever the place in question dated back thousands of years, Mister Pang gave the same answer: "Too tousaind eels."

Another time the lieutenant asked about Kyŏnghoeru, the pavilion where kings took entertaining women to drink, dance, and sing.

Mister Pang answered without hesitation: "King doo-ring-kuh wa-een enduh dahn-suh end-uh shing, wi-duh dahn-sah."

It looked to him, ventured the lieutenant, that Korean women's clothing was lovely and graceful. Why, then, did some of them wear Western clothing?

They wanted to marry Westerners, Mister Pang answered.

Seeing the excrement that fouled the streets, including Seoul Station, the lieutenant asked if Korean dwellings lacked toilets.

By no means—every house certainly had one, Mister Pang replied.

When the lieutenant said he wanted to buy a very good Korean painting, Mister Pang bought him a five-*wŏn* reproduction of the sort you often see hung above the door—deer feeding on an elixir of life, a Daoist wizard seated.

What was the best-known and most interesting Korean work of fiction?

Ch'oe Ch'anshik's *Hue of the Autumn Moon* was Mister Pang's reply. The lieutenant said he would like to buy a copy, and after several days of searching, Mister Pang was finally able to obtain one from a neighbor for two *wŏn*.

Such was the general outline of Mister Pang's new position, though he rendered great service in many other ways as well while introducing the lieutenant to his country.

Mister Pang grew more excellent by the day, in direct proportion to these services. He had moved to his present house—said to be the company house of a bank director before Liberation—from the Hyŏnjŏ-dong rented room three days after becoming an interpreter for the lieutenant. Upstairs and down, it was decorated half in the Western style, half in the Japanese— altogether a palatial mansion. The garden featured colored foliage and autumn plants at their loveliest; carp frolicked in the fish pond.

The room where host and guest sat drinking was the best of the several in the house, a bright, sunny room that led out to a balcony. But inside, there wasn't a single picture on the walls, not a single piece of furniture. It was merely a vast, tasteless chamber. Mister Pang still had little idea of such things as interior decoration.

At first Mister Pang kept a housemaid. Next he added a seamstress. And then an errand girl.

Gentleman Pang received several visitors a day. The bulk of them arrived in motor vehicles, but quite a few came in rickshaws as well. It was the rare person who arrived empty-handed. A box of Western cookies would be brought, an envelope of money inevitably attached to the bottom.

His metamorphosis from the cobbler Crooknose Sambok to Mister Pang was so very simple and straightforward.

"Kimiko!" shouted the host as he prepared to pour Squire Paek another glass of beer.

"She's running an errand," came the voice of his one-eyed wife from the ground floor. The tone was pointed.

"What about the snacks?"

"*That's* what she went out for."

"Do we have any *chŏngjong*?"

Instead of an answer there came steps on the stairway, and then a head of permed hair, a pinched forehead, a single eye, a powdered face, a dress worn over a mammoth bust, and finally a pair of massive, tablelike legs sheathed in silk stockings.

"Squire Sŏ left this for you." She handed her husband an envelope.

"Let's see what we got here." Mister Pang opened the seal and a single bank draft appeared—ten thousand *wŏn*. "Is that all?" Mister Pang's temper flared and he tossed the draft to the tatami-covered floor.

"Don't ask me."

"Worthless son of a bitch, just you wait. I know his game—buy a hundred-thousand-*wŏn* property from the government, resell it for a million-*wŏn* profit, easy, and this is all I get? Damned son of a bitch—he doesn't realize that one word from me to the MPs and he's up the creek."

"Shall I bring the *chŏngjong*?"

"Doesn't realize that one word from me means life or death. Hmph! Son of a bitch is going to learn the hard way. . . . Heat up the *chŏngjong*—it's a tad chilly outside."

More drinking snacks arrived, and the two men exchanged several rounds of the warmed rice brew.

Finally Squire Paek broached the reason for his visit.

Squire Paek had a son, Paek Sŏnbong, who could boast of seven years' service as a constable until the day before Liberation. During that time he had rotated among three substations and two station houses and had accumulated land enough to provide him with two hundred sacks of rice annually, had put away ten thousand *wŏn* in the bank, had silks and other fabrics worth more than that amount, and had provided his wife with another ten thousand *wŏn* worth of jewelry.

While others were tightening their belts and starving, his granary was piled with straw bags of polished rice that resembled jade, and not a day passed that his table didn't contain meat and fish—items that others wouldn't see for half a year, for a year even.

Over the previous two years, when he was head of accounts at a station house, he had been even more the deluxe edition. On the night of August 15, Liberation Day, when the masses raided his house, the items that poured out of it, not to mention the sacks of rice, were as follows:

6 bolts of cotton cloth
23 pairs of rubber shoes
8 pairs of Japanese-style shoes

3 boxes of laundry soap
50 pairs of socks
13 bottles of *chŏngjong*
1 sack of sugar

So it was reported. And of course there were his wife's jewelry, his fabrics and silks, and his bank account, each worth ten thousand *wŏn* or more.

Every last one of these articles was seized, his house and furniture laid waste. Paek Sŏnbong himself had his arms broken and barely managed to escape with his life to the ancestral home, leaving behind a concubine with half her hair plucked out.

There in the home village Squire Paek, through the misdeeds of his son, had accumulated land and taken to treating his neighbors haughtily. He charged his tenant farmers 80 percent of the harvest. He lent out money at usurious interest. And so the night Paek Sŏnbong returned in a state of collapse, Squire Paek, master of the house, had his dwelling raided.

The house and all the furnishings were destroyed, and the wealth of rationed items sent by his son were confiscated in their entirety. The family members were beaten within an inch of their lives, and father and son stole away, to Seoul and the in-laws, respectively, preserving their hides above all else.

In Seoul, Squire Paek went to the expense of rooming and boarding at an inn. He roamed the streets in dejection. How could he get revenge? How could he regain his wealth and possessions? But no clever scheme came to mind.

And then that very morning he had come across Mister Pang. He was walking aimlessly along Chongno when a passing vehicle stopped. The distinguished-looking gentleman riding with a Westerner stepped down, looked him in the eye, and said with delight, "Aren't you Squire Paek?"

He had inspected the man. Without a doubt it was Crooknose Sambok, the streetside cobbler.

"You—you're—you're Pang—Pang. . . ."

"That's right—Sambok."

"But—but—how did you . . . ?"

"Every dog has his day."

And he had let himself be led to the other's home.

To Squire Paek's utter surprise, Mister Pang managed a house complete with maid, seamstress, and errand girl. His mien was completely transformed and his speech seemed rather dignified. Sewers could indeed spawn mighty dragons!

Squire Paek realized his past prosperity was but a dream, that he'd been ruined in the space of a day, and he couldn't help cowering once again—he felt like the wretched dog that's ignored when a house goes into mourning. And now this rascal Pang—when had he become so audacious? It galled him in the extreme. So it occurred to him more than a few times simply to get up and remove himself from this situation. But he endured.

For it had become clear that his host wielded great power. His one remaining hope, it seemed, was to be lucky enough to utilize that power to revenge himself and recover the fortune stripped from him. Revenge, the recovery of his fortune—to this end he would bow his head to fellows even worse than Crooknose Sambok.

"In any event, Misshida Pang. . . ."

Squire Paek, having embroidered a bit to liven things up, concluded his account by saying: "You must round up those scoundrels, every last one of them. The ringleaders deserve to have their heads chopped off, and the others, beat them to a jelly and make them kneel on the floor till they submit. I demand everything back that they stole from me. House, furniture, everything else they destroyed, I demand full compensation. In return, I'll—I'll give you half of all I own. Mark my words, Misshida Pang, you and me, fifty-fifty."

"Don't you worry." Mister Pang seemed delighted to be of service.

"Do you really mean it?"

"Why, right this minute, one word from my lips and a hundred, a thousand MPs with machine guns will swarm down and make mincemeat out of them, mincemeat!"

"Thank you so much!" Envisioning his revenge, Squire Paek clutched Mister Pang's wrist. "I'll remember your kindness until these bones of mine are dust."

"We'll kill off every last one of those scoundrels, just you wait."

"I have no doubt, as long as you have anything to say about it."

"One word from me and Dr. Syngman Rhee himself would be on his knees—this is no lie."

So saying, the host took a mouthful of water and swished it around. It was a kind of habit he'd developed after becoming Mister Pang.

Mister Pang looked about for a place to dispose of the water, then rose and strode out to the balcony. Directly below was the front door.

It happened just as Mister Pang spat the turbid liquid from where he stood on the balcony. By the most unfortunate coincidence the American lieutenant had arrived—had gone up to the door and, hearing Mister Pang above him, had stepped back a few paces to look up.

"Hello!"

"Oh my god!"

But it was too late. The foul liquid had already splattered onto the lieutenant's smiling, upturned face with the force of a torrent.

"You devil!" roared the lieutenant, brandishing his fist.

Mister Pang ran downstairs and out the door in his stocking feet, rubbing his palms together in supplication, only to be met with a curse—"Low-class son of a bitch!"—and an uppercut from that same upraised fist.

Taejo, July 1946

17

BLIND MAN SHIM

A Play in Three Acts

(Shim pongsa, 1947)

CHARACTERS

BLIND MAN SHIM: in his mid-fifties

SHIM CH'ŎNG, his daughter: age sixteen

SONG TAL: about twenty

KWIDŎK'S MOM

MENDICANT MONK

OLD LADY PPAENGDŎK

HONGNYŎ

Setting: Tohwa-dong in the city of Hwangju, at the mouth of the Yesŏng River

Time: mid-Koryŏ, a temperate day midway through the third lunar month

ACT I, SCENE I

(BLIND MAN SHIM's home, a decrepit thatched hut with the kitchen to the rear and the one-room living quarters to the front, giving onto a narrow veranda. Space left and right, bordered by a bush-clover fence.

To the front, a yard and the sagging skeleton of a twig gate. The bush-clover fence separates the hut from the neighboring dwellings.

Beams, rafters, and walls are all askew and soot-begrimed, the eaves dilapidated. The veranda and door frame are crooked. Not many of the household items you'd expect to see in a rural dwelling. Overall, it's the shabbiest, most forlorn home you'd want to *see. On the other hand, the interior is spotless, no trash pile to be seen; not even a stalk of grass has found its way in, showing that in spite of the occupants' poverty the neat and tidy appearance reflects the character of she who manages the household, namely* SHIM CH'ŎNG. *On the flat ground below the veranda are* BLIND MAN SHIM's *straw shoes and, propped next to them, his walking stick. An apricot tree in full bloom leans against the twig gate.*

The curtain opens onto the closed door of the room, from behind which BLIND MAN SHIM's *voice is heard, reciting in a plaintive tone a passage from the chapter of the Mengzi describing one of the master's disciples, Gong Sun.)*

"A man of Song bemoans his stunted plants and gives the tips a tug. Wearily he returns home and says: 'Today I am tired from helping the plants to grow.' His son hurries out to look at them, and of course they are dead and withered. In this world, as for those who meddle in the growth of their plants, there are quite a few."

(The voice draws out "quite a few," then stops. A short time later, "In this world, as for those who meddle in the growth of their plants, there are quite a few. . . ." And again, "In this world, as for those who meddle in the growth of their plants, there are quite a few. . . .")

BLIND MAN SHIM *(from inside the room)*: Not again! Damned if I didn't forget the next part! What's going to happen to me? If my mind goes blank like this, how can I sit for the state examination—even if my eyes should open to see? *(pauses)* "In this world, as for those who meddle in the growth of their plants, there are quite a few. . . ." "In this world, as for those who meddle in the growth of their plants, there are quite a few. . . ." It's on the tip of my tongue, but it just won't come out. Good heavens, how can my mind go blank like this? "In this world, as for those who meddle in the growth of their plants, there are quite a few. . . ." "In this world, as for those who meddle in the growth of their plants, there are quite a few. . . ." What comes next? Damn it, what comes next! "In this world, as for those who meddle in the growth of their plants, there are quite a few, quite a few. . . ." I just can't remember. *(pauses)* Just this one text, I've forgotten so many passages. Goodness gracious, what a disaster.

(The door opens and he emerges onto the veranda, blind as a bat, his pupils covered with a white film. He wears cotton clothing, patched but clean. His horsehair skullcap and cap are neatly positioned.) "In this world, as for those who meddle in the growth of their plants, there are quite a few. . . . In this world, as for

those who meddle in the growth of their plants, there are quite a few. . . ."
The girl is off doing the wash, and here I am pounding my chest in
frustration—what's a man to do? (*sitting down on the edge of the veranda*)
Wouldn't it be nice if someone could read that section for me? (*smacking
his lips impatiently*)

(*enter* KWIDŎK'S MOM *through the twig gate, an earthenware basin of boiled laundry perched on her head*)

BLIND MAN SHIM: Who's there? Is that you, mother of Kwidŏk?

KWIDŎK'S MOM: Yes—something I forgot to pick up.

BLIND MAN SHIM: Your timing is perfect. I'm going to bring out a book
and I want you to read me a section. I started in on it and got stuck just
now.

KWIDŎK'S MOM: Of all the senile things to say! What book could I possibly
read to you, sir?

BLIND MAN SHIM: Ah yes, of course.

KWIDŎK'S MOM: Your kneepads, *saengwŏn*, sir, could you go in and get
them for me, please? The young lady asked me if I could add them to the
laundry I was boiling and I clean forgot to pick them up from you.

BLIND MAN SHIM (*exiting to room*): I'd better go see Song Ch'oshi before the
girl gets back. I've haven't seen him in a while, and he can help me with
that passage I'm stuck on.

KWIDŎK'S MOM (*tutting to herself*): If that doesn't take the rice cake—the
poor master, if only he could see again and sit for the examination, he
wants it so badly. (*tutting*) And at his advanced age!

BLIND MAN SHIM (*entering from room, holding the kneepads*): You mean these?

KWIDŎK'S MOM: Yes, thank you. (*accepts them*)

BLIND MAN SHIM: What use is a man when he gets old? My smarts get
dumber by the day—huh!

KWIDŎK'S MOM (*stepping down into the yard*): But you are a well-read man,
saengwŏn, sir, and if only your eyes would open again, you would have
no worries with the examination. Why, you would be first place,
guaranteed.

BLIND MAN SHIM: Is that so?

KWIDŎK'S MOM: Of course. Well, I will be back. (*exits through the twig gate*)

BLIND MAN SHIM: First place in the state examination, hmm. (*pause*) I
must do it, one way or the other. (*pause*) I must do it. "In this world, as for
those who meddle in the growth of their plants, there are quite a few. . . .
In this world, as for those who meddle in the growth of their plants, there

are quite a few. . . . In this world, as for those who meddle in the growth of their plants, there are quite a few. . . ." (*cocking his head back and forth in thought*) I just can't remember. (*tutting*) I really should visit Song Ch'oshi. (*dons his straw shoes, takes his walking stick, and steps down to the yard*) What wonderful weather—oh, the balmy days of spring, when the flowers are blooming.

(*from backstage, the voice of a peddler of croaker fish*)

BLIND MAN SHIM (*advancing toward the twig gate*): Ah, croaker—the balmy days of spring, how balmy they are. (*exits through twig gate*)

(MENDICANT MONK *peeks through bush-clover fence, hesitates, then, beating his gong, recites his alms song.*)

BLIND MAN SHIM (*from backstage, just when the* MENDICANT MONK'*s song has ended*): Oh, help me! Save me!

MENDICANT MONK: Good heavens, what's that?

BLIND MAN SHIM: Someone help me! Where is everyone? Someone help me!

MENDICANT MONK: That blind man must have fallen into the stream. Of all the bad luck—if I make like I didn't notice, the local yokels will give me shit. Damn it, today just went to hell. (*exits*)

BLIND MAN SHIM: Help me, Ch'ŏng-a! Mother of Kwidŏk, help me!

(*enter* MENDICANT MONK, *supporting* BLIND MAN SHIM, *who is soaking wet and covered with muck*)

MENDICANT MONK (*sitting* BLIND MAN SHIM *down on the veranda*): What were you doing in the stream? It's too early in the year for outdoor bathing.

BLIND MAN SHIM (*sighing in relief*): You have saved me from a certain death, sir; there can be no greater benevolence. You do not seem to be of our village—who in the name of heaven might you be?

MENDICANT MONK: I am a lowly monk of Mirŭk Temple.

BLIND MAN SHIM: Ah, a venerable monk of Mirŭk Temple, you say?

MENDICANT MONK: You should change into dry clothing, sir—we wouldn't want you catching cold.

BLIND MAN SHIM: Yes, I should. Please make yourself comfortable and I will return shortly. (*exits into room*)

MENDICANT MONK (*perching on the edge of the veranda and scanning the hut and surroundings*): I'd be lucky if I got even a handful of grain from these folks.

BLIND MAN SHIM (*enters, having thrown on the first clothes that came to hand*): I can't see in front of my nose, and I don't know what's where. In any event, how may I repay your benevolence, master? You have saved my life. If you had not come along, master, I would have died for certain, yes, yes indeed.

MENDICANT MONK (*feigning nonchalance and speaking as if to himself, in a wheedling tone*): Ah yes, as it turns out, our Lord Buddha foresaw your predicament.

BLIND MAN SHIM: The Lord Buddha? Wonder of wonders.

MENDICANT MONK: To be more specific, our Lord Buddha appeared to me in a dream this past night.

BLIND MAN SHIM: Oh? And what, pray tell, was the nature of this dream?

MENDICANT MONK: Our Lord Buddha instructed me to remember that this afternoon, on my way down here to Tohwa-dong, I would come across an unexpected calamity, a poor soul in mortal danger.

BLIND MAN SHIM: Wonder of wonders—praised be the Lord Buddha! Well, good master, if I say so myself, it is just as you said. Miracle of miracles! If only I had known that the Lord Buddha of Mirŭk Temple is so perspicacious!

MENDICANT MONK: Ah yes, perspicacious he is, and if you serve him with devotion, any and all maladies will disappear.

BLIND MAN SHIM: Any and all maladies?

MENDICANT MONK: The lame shall walk.

BLIND MAN SHIM: The lame shall walk?!

MENDICANT MONK: The withered arm will straighten.

BLIND MAN SHIM: The withered arm will straighten?!

MENDICANT MONK: The mute shall speak.

BLIND MAN SHIM: The mute shall speak?! And the blind?

MENDICANT MONK: The blind shall see.

BLIND MAN SHIM: The blind shall see?! (*taking the monk's arm and shaking it*) Is it really so?

MENDICANT MONK: Shall the deaf speak but the blind not see?

BLIND MAN SHIM: So it is true what you say, the blind shall see.

MENDICANT MONK: To be sure.

BLIND MAN SHIM: If I serve the Lord Buddha with devotion.

MENDICANT MONK: Yes, but with *substantial* devotion.

BLIND MAN SHIM: Would one hundred days of devotion be substantial?

MENDICANT MONK: No, I mean substantial, as in substance, as in grain, as in an offering of grain.

BLIND MAN SHIM: I see, I must make an offering of rice. Indeed, so that's the way it is. Yes, my dear departed wife made many such offerings. For all the good that did us. (*pause*) Good master?

MENDICANT MONK: Yes?

BLIND MAN SHIM: If I should be sure to offer up rice grain to the Lord Buddha of Mirŭk Temple, then will I see again?

MENDICANT MONK: To be sure.

BLIND MAN SHIM: Verily?

MENDICANT MONK: Verily, I say.

BLIND MAN SHIM: Then prepare me the pledge form.

MENDICANT MONK (*rummages through knapsack, produces document, writing brush, and inkpot, dips brush in inkpot, and places it in* BLIND MAN SHIM'S *hand*): Here you are.

BLIND MAN SHIM: And how much shall I pledge?

MENDICANT MONK (*covetously, with pursed lips*): Well, both eyes . . . that should come to at least three hundred sacks.

BLIND MAN SHIM: I'd be much obliged just to have one eye back. All right, then. (*writes*) "Three hundred sacks of rice grain, Shim Hakkyu of Tohwa-dong, Hwangju"—there.

MENDICANT MONK: Save us, merciful Buddha. (*checks the document*) "Three hundred sacks of rice grain, Shim Hakkyu of Tohwa-dong, Hwangju." And this is truly written?

BLIND MAN SHIM: What do you mean?

MENDICANT MONK: This you should know: among humans, if one lies to or deceives another, it is a crime. But if a human attempts to deceive our Lord Buddha, a terrible punishment awaits him.

BLIND MAN SHIM: I should think so!

MENDICANT MONK: If perchance there is any deceit, your blind eyes will rot away.

BLIND MAN SHIM: My blind eyes will rot away?

MENDICANT MONK: The tongue of the mute will curl up.

BLIND MAN SHIM: The tongue of the mute will curl up?

MENDICANT MONK: And the arm of the cripple will wither.

BLIND MAN SHIM: And the arm of the cripple will wither?

MENDICANT MONK: And when you die you will suffer for eternity in the burning fires of hell.

BLIND MAN SHIM: And when I die I will suffer for eternity in the burning fires of hell?

MENDICANT MONK: If you commit the sin of deceiving our Lord Buddha.

BLIND MAN SHIM: If I commit the sin of deceiving our Lord Buddha.

MENDICANT MONK: So, is this truly written?

BLIND MAN SHIM: It most certainly is.

MENDICANT MONK: When may we expect your donation?

BLIND MAN SHIM: Within a few days.

MENDICANT MONK: Verily.

BLIND MAN SHIM: Make no mistake about it.

MENDICANT MONK: Well then. (*places the document and the rest in his knapsack and slings it over his shoulder, and takes his gong and mallet*) Your humble servant departs.

BLIND MAN SHIM: Go in peace, good master. How can I ever repay your benevolence?

MENDICANT MONK: Save us, merciful Buddha. (*exits through twig gate*)

BLIND MAN SHIM (*animatedly*): Well well, look who's going to get his sight back. And how many decades has it been? Well well, my eyes will snap open, and there before me, once again, heaven and earth, bright and shining. I will sit for the state examination, I will win first place, I will have an official position. It's never too late for glory. I shall bring honor to my forebears and my family name. (*shoulders swaying in excitement*) Yippee! Good for me! How happy our dear Ch'ŏng will be, and my dear departed wife could not be happier.

(*enter SONG TAL, who rests his backrack with its load of firewood against the bush-clover gate and stares incomprehendingly at BLIND MAN SHIM's antics*)

SONG TAL (*finally*): Hello.

BLIND MAN SHIM: Who's there.

SONG TAL: It's me, sir—Tal.

BLIND MAN SHIM: Ah, Tari. Glad you're here. Guess who's going to get his sight back?

SONG TAL (*in surprise*): You'll be able to see, sir?

BLIND MAN SHIM: Yes, these blind eyes of mine are going to snap right open, I'll be able to see again, yes I will. (*chuckles*)

SONG TAL: Did you find some miracle cure, sir?

BLIND MAN SHIM: Yes, but not a medicament. It's all thanks to the Lord Buddha, thanks be to him.

SONG TAL: So you went to the temple and offered up a prayer of devotion.

BLIND MAN SHIM: No, not that. I left a short time ago to visit your esteemed father, and I stumbled into that stream back there and nearly drowned. I hollered for help, but do you suppose anyone heard me? I was going to die for sure. But then what do you know, a man comes running and fetches me out of there. Darned if it wasn't a monk from Mirŭk Temple.

SONG TAL: Must have been one of those bald-heads looking for a handout.

BLIND MAN SHIM: Uh-uh. He brought me back home and got me nice and comfortable and then he told me he had a dream about the Lord Buddha last night. The Lord Buddha told him that the next afternoon, on his way down here to Tohwa-dong, he would come across an unexpected calamity, a poor soul in mortal danger. The Lord Buddha is all-knowing and all-seeing, yes he is.

SONG TAL: Well, I'll be darned.

BLIND MAN SHIM: The Lord Buddha of Mirŭk Temple has long been known to be all-knowing and all-seeing, yes indeed. Anyone who offers up rice grain will be cured of any disease, and any handicap will be fixed, that's what he said.

SONG TAL: I never thought that temple was anything special.

BLIND MAN SHIM: It may not look like much. But if the Lord Buddha is all-knowing and all-seeing, what more could you ask? Guess what—the cripple shall rise, the withered arm will straighten, the mute shall speak, and get this—the blind shall see. The blind man will open his eyes and see heaven and earth, bright and shining. How's that for all-knowing and all-seeing?

SONG TAL: Darned if I know.

BLIND MAN SHIM: So right then and there I signed—no ifs, ands, or buts. I make an offering to the all-knowing, all-seeing Lord Buddha, and I'll be able to see again, it's guaranteed.

SONG TAL: I'll be darned. (pause) How much did you pledge, sir?

BLIND MAN SHIM: Three hundred sacks of rice grain.

SONG TAL (his jaw drops): Three hundred sacks?

BLIND MAN SHIM: You bet. I signed that pledge right off—three hundred sacks of rice grain, Shim Hakkyu of Tohwa-dong, Hwangju. In a few days I'll deliver it.

SONG TAL (looking intently at BLIND MAN SHIM): Where will you find three hundred sacks of rice grain?

BLIND MAN SHIM: Where, you say?

SONG TAL: Between your home and ours, you know full well we don't have three hundred handfuls of rice grain, much less three hundred sacks.

BLIND MAN SHIM: Good heavens! (*ponders*) You're right—good heavens!

SONG TAL: Even thirty sacks would be a problem. By the way, where is Ch'ŏng?

BLIND MAN SHIM: Doing the wash.

SONG TAL: So you were by yourself, sir—that's how all this happened.

BLIND MAN SHIM (*embarrassed*): Say, Tara.

SONG TAL: Yes?

BLIND MAN SHIM: I have a huge problem. What do you think I should do?

(SONG TAL *smacks his lips nervously.*)

BLIND MAN SHIM: Yes, what should I do? We don't have even a handful of rice grain and here I am pledging three hundred sacks and signing that pledge on the spot. Yes, what will I ever do, what should I do?

SONG TAL (*tutting*): Nothing. But it's not as if you had grain to offer up in the first place.

BLIND MAN SHIM: Goodness me, how is it possible I never thought of that? Mm-hmm. Whatever possessed me to say I'd offer up three hundred sacks of rice grain? In all my life I've never caught onto anything good, my little girl Ch'ŏng does sewing and takes in laundry so we won't starve— and I can afford to donate three hundred sacks of grain? Even though a person doesn't know himself, there should be a limit to his stupidity.

SONG TAL: I think I can see how it happened, sir. When he said the Lord Buddha is capable of such miracles, that he can restore your sight, you focused everything on that and didn't think about what would follow— that's what happened.

BLIND MAN SHIM: Huh—ever since I was little, I've been someone who can't think long term, can't think deeply when I run up against a problem like this. I forget everything, and so I've had many failures; I was born that way and I can't fix it. So here I am again, something like this was bound to happen. (*heaves a great sigh*)

SONG TAL: Please don't worry, sir. If you can't give it, you can't give it— what are they going to do?

BLIND MAN SHIM: If it's a crime to deceive one another with idle talk or lip service, then do you think I can get away with deceiving our Lord Buddha?

SONG TAL: If the Lord Buddha is really the Lord Buddha, then he will be aware of the circumstances of the poor and the pitiable.

BLIND MAN SHIM: Poor as I am, I should have sat tight and kept my mouth shut—how could I have been so obsessed that I ended up deceiving the

Lord Buddha? Powerless as I am, *how* could I have pledged three hundred sacks of grain? If that isn't a trick to deceive the Lord Buddha, then what is? If I were the Lord Buddha, I could never forgive such a person.

SONG TAL: If I were the Lord Buddha and a gentleman like yourself offered up even the tiniest measure of grain, I would restore your sight, I would bestow on you many blessings, I would do all that and more.

BLIND MAN SHIM: I've earned my punishment. I've earned my punishment, and there's no way out.

SONG TAL: Oh? What punishment?

BLIND MAN SHIM: If you knew the full story, you wouldn't ask such a question. Now look here, boy, if a blind man deceives the Lord Buddha, his eyes will rot away, yes they will. (*begins to tremble with fear*) And after his eyes rot away, his tongue will curl up and he will become mute. (*flustered and fidgeting*) His arm will wither and he will become crippled. (*begins to wail*) And when he dies he will suffer for eternity in the burning fires of hell. Yes, yes, he will suffer for eternity in the white-hot flames of hellfire. Being blind is difficult enough, but now the blind man's eyes rot away, his tongue curls up and he becomes mute, his arm withers and he becomes crippled, and when he dies, he suffers for eternity in the burning fires of hell. (*wails*) Oh, I'm scared. (*wails*) I'm scared. How can I face that punishment for my sin? Better to hang myself here and now, yes, yes. I should kill myself right now, I should kill myself in that stream where I almost died, I should kill myself. (*staggers down to the yard*)

(SONG TAL *jumps down to the yard and detains him.*)

(*Curtain.*)

ACT 1, SCENE 2

(*Setting is the same as for scene 1. The apricot tree has shed its blossoms and sprouted tender leaves. Daytime early in the fourth lunar month. As the curtain opens,* BLIND MAN SHIM, *dressed for an outing, is standing in the yard with* SHIM CH'ŎNG, *who is seeing him off.* BLIND MAN SHIM *is quite cheerful, while* CH'ŎNG's *face is ridden with concern.*)

SHIM CH'ŎNG: Father, I'll go with you halfway.

BLIND MAN SHIM (*smiling*): Afraid I'll fall in the stream again? You needn't worry.

SHIM CH'ŎNG: But Father, still. . . .

BLIND MAN SHIM: It only happens once in a while, not all the time. I've walked that road all my life.

SHIM CH'ŎNG: Yes, Father, but you did fall in.

BLIND MAN SHIM: Truth be told, I think the Lord Buddha was playing a trick on me. To see how devoted I am. Well, I'm off.

SHIM CH'ŎNG: All right, be careful, Father.

BLIND MAN SHIM (walking toward the twig gate): All right.

SHIM CH'ŎNG: Don't get caught out in the dark, Father.

BLIND MAN SHIM: All right. (suddenly stops and turns) Ch'ŏnga.

SHIM CH'ŎNG: Yes?

BLIND MAN SHIM: When you go on the boat with those whaddyacallem to Nanjing, it's four months—two there and two back?

SHIM CH'ŎNG (face noticeably more clouded, her tone alone calm): Yes.

BLIND MAN SHIM: Is it the eighth you're leaving? That's coming up fast.

SHIM CH'ŎNG: Yes.

BLIND MAN SHIM (thinking): You're so young, still a maiden, how will you survive such a long journey over rough seas? The decision's been made so there's no turning back, but I think you're making a mistake.

(SHIM CH'ŎNG manages to hold back her tears.)

BLIND MAN SHIM: And, I'll have to wait four months until I see you again.

SHIM CH'ŎNG (speaking with difficulty): When I think of all the trouble you'll have, waiting for me day and night, all by yourself, I can't bring myself to do it, but then if only you can see again. . . .

BLIND MAN SHIM: Anyway, it's four months, and it's not till the eighth month that you return.

SHIM CH'ŎNG: Yes.

BLIND MAN SHIM: All right, then. I'm off to see Song Ch'oshi, I have a matter to settle with him.

SHIM CH'ŎNG: Oh? What about, Father?

BLIND MAN SHIM: About you and Tal marrying. I'm going to suggest we have the ceremony in the ninth or tenth month.

(SHIM CH'ŎNG lowers her head meekly.)

BLIND MAN SHIM: As you know, in my eyes he's a nice boy, a decent sort, and even though his family's circumstances are such that he has to sell firewood, he hasn't been polluted by the life of a commoner, and he's diligent enough to spend nights studying under his father, so he's not bad at reading and writing—not to mention he comes from good stock. And

Song Ch'oshi has promised that the boy can come live with us. What more could we ask of a family to marry into? It's almost more than we deserve.

SHIM CH'ŎNG: Father?

BLIND MAN SHIM: Yes?

SHIM CH'ŎNG: Can't we take our time on that—until I return?

BLIND MAN SHIM: Sure we could, but since it's already in the works, why not settle the matter once and for all?

(Enter SONG TAL through twig gate. His face is tense and he coughs nervously. CH'ŎNG's eyes meet his.)

SONG TAL: Hello, I hope you are well.

BLIND MAN SHIM: Tal, is that you? Come on in. Is your esteemed father well?

SONG TAL: Yes, thank you. Are you going somewhere?

BLIND MAN SHIM: I was about to visit your esteemed father—he is in, is he not?

SONG TAL: Yes, he is. Actually he's been wondering about you, sir, he hasn't seen you for so long. He was thinking he might pay you a visit.

BLIND MAN SHIM: Yes, indeed, it's been about a month. Well, have fun.

SONG TAL: Why don't I go with you?

BLIND MAN SHIM: No, I'm fine.

SONG TAL: Just part of the way, then.

BLIND MAN SHIM: I said don't worry. (approaches the twig gate) I'm off.

SONG TAL and SHIM CH'ŎNG (simultaneously): So long.

SHIM CH'ŎNG: Be careful, Father.

BLIND MAN SHIM: I will. (exits through twig gate)

(TAL approaches the hut and sits on the edge of the veranda. CH'ŎNG slowly steps up and leans back against a post.) (silence)

SONG TAL: Ch'ŏnga!

(SHIM CH'ŎNG gazes at him instead of answering.)

SONG TAL (looking CH'ŎNG full in the eyes): I just heard—is it true?

(SHIM CH'ŎNG lowers her gaze.)

SONG TAL: So you take a merchant ship to Nanjing, and for three hundred sacks of rice you throw yourself into the Indang Sea as an offering?

(SHIM CH'ŎNG remains silent.)

SONG TAL: It's true, isn't it?

SHIM CH'ŎNG: If I don't, who's going to give us three hundred sacks of rice for Father to offer up so he can regain his sight?

SONG TAL: Are you out of your mind?

(SHIM CH'ŎNG remains silent.)

SONG TAL: Answer me.

SHIM CH'ŎNG: Why shouldn't a useless girl like me give up her life so her father can see again?

SONG TAL: If a donation of three hundred sacks of rice can get a blind man's sight back, then what's stopping all the blind people in the world from seeing again? There's a lot of rich people who are blind. What's three hundred sacks of rice to them, or even three thousand? Are they blind because they didn't make a donation?

SHIM CH'ŎNG: It's not how well off you are, it's how devoted you are.

SONG TAL: Devotion? Isn't that something you do at night, before you go to bed? Throwing yourself into the Indang Sea as an offering, snuffing out a healthy life—how can you call that *devotion*?

SHIM CH'ŎNG: I admit it's extreme, but it's not the kind of devotion that just anyone is capable of. Doesn't a person need that much devotion in order to impress the Lord God or the Lord Buddha?

SONG TAL: All right, then, let's suppose a parent gets to see again—is the return of his sight at the expense of the death of his child something he will rejoice in? Will he be comfortable with himself?

SHIM CH'ŎNG: If three hundred sacks of rice is what it takes for him to get his sight back, I'm happy with that. But what if he doesn't follow through on his promise to donate that rice? For the last three days he's been out of his mind, saying he's deceived the Lord Buddha and that as punishment his blind eyes will rot away, his tongue will curl up and he'll be mute, his arm will wither and he'll become a cripple, and then he'll suffer eternally in the burning fires of hell. He's so scared he wants to do away with himself on the spot. As the child of such a person, I just can't bear to see him going through this. I'm comfortable that in return for my life I have already eased his suffering. And what could be better than getting your sight back? If I had ten lives, I'd do the same thing with no regret.

SONG TAL: Even if he knew that sacrificing yourself to the Indang Sea is the price you're paying for that rice?

(SHIM CH'ŎNG remains silent.)

SONG TAL: Ch'ŏng, I'm not questioning your devotion to your father, it's more than any parent could ask, and I respect you for that. But for heaven's sake, there's a time and a place for everything, even filial piety— there has to be a limit. For a child to take her own life, is that the way to devote yourself to a parent? If that's filial piety, then I'd rather be unfilial.

Do you realize how precious you are? The only daughter of a man who lost his wife three days after you were born, who through blood and tears managed to raise you—he wouldn't exchange you for a *dozen* children. If he knew you would sacrifice yourself to the Indang Sea for three hundred sacks of rice so he can avoid punishment from the Lord Buddha and regain his sight, do you think he would sit back and smile? No, he'd be jumping up and down, he'd faint dead away, it would be the death of him.

(SHIM CH'ŎNG *bites down on her jacket ties.*)

SONG TAL: What do you have to say?

SHIM CH'ŎNG: I haven't told him the whole story. I said that the seamen who journey across the Indang Sea to Nanjing need a sixteen-year-old virgin to perform a ceremony for the Dragon King, and they bought my services for three hundred sacks of rice. I go out to sea with them, I perform the ceremony on the Indang Sea, and I come back with them. The round trip takes four months. That's what I told him. When I'm gone, if you see him moping, please tell him the same thing.

SONG TAL: Well, once or twice maybe. But I can't keep deceiving him.

SHIM CH'ŎNG: Look at it this way—what's better, a person suddenly hurting all over, or that person developing a slow hurt here and a slow hurt there? So, yes, I'm deceiving him, but he gets his sight back and time goes on and on, and when he finally realizes the truth it won't hurt so much.

SONG TAL: Ch'ŏnga.

SHIM CH'ŎNG: Yes?

SONG TAL: Why don't you change your mind?

(SHIM CH'ŎNG *shakes her head.*)

SONG TAL: Never?

SHIM CH'ŎNG: The three hundred sacks of rice have already been delivered to Mirŭk Temple—on the full-moon day last month.

SONG TAL (*waving demonstratively*): You need to go hide for a few days!

SHIM CH'ŎNG (*shakes her head*): That would be dishonorable. Rather than helping a parent, it would bring disgrace upon him.

SONG TAL (*holds his head in despair; after a time*): You're so heartless, so cold. You never sought me out about this—how could you . . .

(SHIM CH'ŎNG *lowers her gaze.*)

(*momentary silence*)

(CH'ŎNG *dabs at her tears with her jacket ties.*)

SONG TA: (*frantic, grabs* CH'ŎNG *by the wrist*): Ch'ŏnga!

(SHIM CH'ŎNG *remains silent.*)

SONG TAL: How about me? Did you ever think of me?

(SHIM CH'ŎNG *breaks into sobs.*)

SONG TAL: Ch'ŏnga, if you go through with this, I'm going too—I'll throw myself into the sea too.

SHIM CH'ŎNG: Just tell yourself we never met in this life—forget about me.

SONG TAL: *Forget* you? Never—not till I'm dead and buried.

SHIM CH'ŎNG: We will meet again in the next world—tell yourself that. (*rests her head against his arm and weeps*)

(*Curtain falls slowly.*)

ACT 2, SCENE I

(BLIND MAN SHIM's *hut, more run-down than in act 1, the yard untidy with dried grass strewn about, giving the desolate appearance of a vacant home. The leaves have fallen from the apricot tree next to the gate post. An afternoon early in the ninth lunar month. The curtain opens on* BLIND MAN SHIM *seated on the sunlit veranda, reciting from the Analects. He recites spiritedly and easily. He wears shabby clothes but no horsehair skullcap or hat, giving him the appearance of a beggar.*)

BLIND MAN SHIM (*finishing a section*): Listen to me, the words flowing from my lips, no hitches today. The day of the state examination is coming, I can feel it. (*ponders*) My eyes are going to snap open any day now. Snap wide open and all under heaven will be bright and clear. (*chuckles, shoulders swaying in excitement*) My blind eyes will once again see the bright light of day, I will sit for the examination, I will earn first place, I will have an official position, and glory be to my ancestors and my family, and my little Ch'ŏng will bask in the lap of luxury. (*chuckles*) I can't wait until she sees me, she'll be so happy she won't know what to say. Wait a minute—what day is it today? (*looks toward the interior*) Hey, woman. (*pauses*) Ppaengdŏk? Hey, where are you!

PPAENGDŎK (*from inside*): You sound like you're about to croak.

BLIND MAN SHIM: What's today?

PPAENGDŎK: It's the day when the swallows take off. (*door to the interior slides open; she eases herself across the threshold and squats, then heaves a great yawn*)

BLIND MAN SHIM: If it's the ninth day of the ninth month, then she's a month late. She left on the eighth day of the fourth month and said four months would be plenty of time to get there and back, so she should have been back on the tenth day of the eighth month.

PPAENGDŎK (*pouting*): You know best.

BLIND MAN SHIM: So she's a month overdue—what's going on?

PPAENGDŎK: Maybe she came down ill?

BLIND MAN SHIM: On a big merchant ship?

PPAENGDŎK: Or maybe the boat sank.

BLIND MAN SHIM: (*flaring up and jabbing her with a fist*) Watch your yap, woman.

PPAENGDŎK (*pokes him back, square in the chest*): Who do you think you're hitting, you old fool? Stop acting like a lunatic.

BLIND MAN SHIM: What do think you're doing, you bitch? I told you to watch your yap.

PPAENGDŎK: You ain't seen nothin' yet!

BLIND MAN SHIM: Your lip is the last thing I need when that girl is on a perilous ocean voyage.

PPAENGDŎK: Hmph!

BLIND MAN SHIM: Don't wag that yap of yours again, or else!

PPAENGDŎK: Or else what?

BLIND MAN SHIM: You can mistreat me all you want, but if you dare slight that girl you'll die by my hand, mark my word. All you do is swill and gorge yourself, day in and day out. You've used up a thousand cash of mine, and that's no pittance, and have I ever given you a hateful look? And still. . . .

PPAENGDŎK: Stop your nonsense, you broken-down idiot. You need to change your way of thinking.

BLIND MAN SHIM: About what, you bitch?

PPAENGDŎK: About a girl who's long gone. (*snorts*)

BLIND MAN SHIM: What! What are you talking about?

PPAENGDŎK: Do I have to make it any clearer?

BLIND MAN SHIM: Long gone? Who's long gone?

PPAENGDŎK: The girl, Ch'ŏng—who did you think?

BLIND MAN SHIM: You bitch, you're asking for it. (*lunges at her*)

PPAENGDŎK: Lookatcha, crawling like a puppy—I knew you came from a family of dogs.

BLIND MAN SHIM: You bitch. Out with it—and stop provoking me.

PPAENGDŎK: You really want to know?

BLIND MAN SHIM: Yes. And your life is at stake.

PPAENGDŎK: Who are you trying to scare?

BLIND MAN SHIM: Are you going to tell me or not?

PPAENGDŎK: What are you getting so worked up about?

BLIND MAN SHIM: Out with it—now!

PPAENGDŎK: Did you hear about those merchants crossing the Indang Sea to Nanjing?

BLIND MAN SHIM: I want to hear it from you.

PPAENGDŎK: When merchant boats going to Nanjing cross the Indang Sea, there's a Dragon King—I think that's what they call him—who always sends out storms, and when those storms hit, the boats sink and people die. So the sailors are more scared of the Indang Sea than they are of hell. You never heard that—ever?

BLIND MAN SHIM: So what's the point?

PPAENGDŎK: So the Dragon King's so nasty he needs a ceremony, a really good ceremony, and only then does he let up on the storms so the boats can cross safely.

BLIND MAN SHIM: And?

PPAENGDŎK: And so the Dragon King needs a sixteen-year-old virgin. Once she's been offered to him and the ceremony is over, the girl gets dumped into the water, into that vast Indang Sea. The nasty Dragon King gulps her down, that satisfies him, and then he calls off the storms and thanks to him, the boat travels safely.

BLIND MAN SHIM: Are you telling me our little Ch'ŏng was sold for that offering?

PPAENGDŎK: That's what I'm tellin' ya.

BLIND MAN SHIM: She was thrown to her death, into the Indang Sea?

PPAENGDŎK: I can't say for a fact she's dead, but the fish must've filled their bellies.

BLIND MAN SHIM: Is it really like you say?

PPAENGDŎK: The stuff about her being part of the ceremony and then coming home—she probably said that so you wouldn't throw a fit.

(enter SONG TAL through twig gate)

If you don't believe me, ask young master Song there.

BLIND MAN SHIM: Is that you, Tal?

SONG TAL: What seems to be the matter?

BLIND MAN SHIM: Is it true our little Ch'ŏng is dead?

SONG TAL (*brandishing a fist at* PPAENGDŎK): How could that be?

PPAENGDŎK: Dammit all, he's gonna find out sooner or later. What's the use of hiding it till the end? Are you expecting a miracle or something?

BLIND MAN SHIM: Tara!

SONG TAL: Yes?

BLIND MAN SHIM: Let me hear the whole story!

(SONG TAL *hangs his head.*)

PPAENGDŎK: Listen, boy, now that it's out in the open, tell him everything. Is she gonna come back to life just because we keep telling him she's not dead? (*disappears inside*)

BLIND MAN SHIM: Tara. I'm going out of my mind! (*pounds his chest*)

SONG TAL: Please, sir, try to calm down.

BLIND MAN SHIM: She's dead? My little Ch'ŏng? Sold as an offering to the Indang Sea?

SONG TAL: I don't know what to say, sir.

BLIND MAN SHIM: So it's true, then, she's dead! Dead? (*writhing in agony*) So it's true! (*shouting at the top of his lungs*) Ch'ŏnga! My little Ch'ŏng! How could it be? You died so your foolish dad could see again—how could it be? Aiguu! (*wails, then collapses, unconscious*)

(SONG TAL *rushes over to him.*)

(*Curtain.*)

ACT 2, SCENE 2

(*A grassy hill and behind it dozens of thatch huts, and behind them trees clad in colorful autumn foliage. An evening a few days later.* SONG TAL *sits upright, facing the audience, hands gathered in his lap, his backrack behind him, still on his shoulders but the supports resting on the ground. Sitting comfortably beside him,* HONGNYŎ. *Apart from a few pockmarks on her face, she's as presentable as a barmaid can be. There's a liquor flush to her face, and beside her hand is a serving tray bearing a porcelain pitcher and cups, and dried drinking snacks.*)

HONGNYŎ: So why the long face? Did he die?

(SONG TAL *remains silent.*)

HONGNYŎ: Hmm? (*takes* TAL's *arm and shakes it*) You're pouting because you don't like me and here I am again?

SONG TAL: Why do you keep coming around and bothering me?

HONGNYŎ (*chortling*): Because I adore you to death and I don't know what else to do.

SONG TAL: Why can't you change your wretched ways?

HONGNYŎ (*chortling*): Not my wretched ways, my lusty barmaid ways. So you hate me, but that doesn't stop me from loving you, so I'll follow you everywhere. And I know my craziness upsets you, so here (*pours him a drink*), drink up!

SONG TAL: Drink it yourself.

HONGNYŎ: Just because you dislike someone who offers you a drink doesn't mean you have to dislike the drink itself. (*drinking the drink she offered him*) Do you know what happens to someone who turns down an offer of food?

(SONG TAL *remains silent.*)

HONGNYŎ: He turns into a beggar—you didn't know that?

SONG TAL: For the love of heaven, I'm happy to be a beggar if only you stop pestering me.

HONGNYŎ: Do you know what happens to a guy who gives the cold shoulder to a girl who wants him?

SONG TAL: He dies a bachelor and goes to hell.

HONGNYŎ: No, he dies a bachelor without ever having touched a woman.

SONG TAL: Look!

HONGNYŎ: Mmm?

SONG TAL: I'm really feeling distracted, so would you *please* leave me alone so I can have some peace and quiet?

HONGNYŎ: Whatever is the matter?

SONG TAL: It doesn't involve you, so you don't really need to know.

HONGNYŎ: Damn it, you don't want to be my sweetheart, and you don't even want to tell me what's bothering you. But you think I'm going to let go of you?

SONG TAL: If I tell you, will you go?

HONGNYŎ: Sure.

SONG TAL: Shim Saengwŏn—Blind Man Shim, it has to do with him.

HONGNYŎ: Your almost father-in-law.

SONG TAL: That's right.

HONGNYŎ: And you're thinking of the girl, and that's why you despise me so.

(SONG TAL *sighs*.)

HONGNYŎ: Good thing she's dead.

SONG TAL: What an evil thing to say.

HONGNYŎ (*chortling*): I didn't mean it—really.

SONG TAL: How can a human being be so warped and twisted?

HONGNYŎ: I was only joking. You only think about her, you treat me like dirt—can't I be a little jealous?

SONG TAL: You shouldn't think that way—else you'll have a hard life.

HONGNYŎ: All right, I won't do it anymore.

SONG TAL: It's such a pity what happened to them.

HONGNYŎ (*tearfully*): Of course—I'm aware of that. But you're so heartless—that's why I came out sounding the way I did.

(SONG TAL *remains silent*.)

HONGNYŎ (*rubbing her hands together*): I'm begging you, release your anger. And then let's talk.

SONG TAL: I'm not to the point of anger.

HONGNYŎ: Really? All right, then, what's happening with Shim Saengwŏn?

SONG TAL: He finally found out.

HONGNYŎ: About Ch'ŏng getting sacrificed to the Indang Sea?

SONG TAL: I think old lady Ppaengdŏk was running off at the mouth again. And I told her so many times to keep her trap shut.

HONGNYŎ: Shim Saengwŏn must have thrown a fit.

SONG TAL: He did—I thought the shock was going to do him in. After he sends his daughter to her death so he can see again, if he doesn't throw a fit then something's wrong with him.

HONGNYŎ (*thinks, then suddenly grabs his arm and shakes it*): Honey!

SONG TAL: Now what?

HONGNYŎ: What if Ch'ŏng came back alive?

SONG TAL: How can a dead person come back to life? If she could, then sure, that would be great.

HONGNYŎ: All right, so what if?

SONG TAL: I'd make her hop onto my back and then I'd do a dance.

HONGNYŎ: Ai, don't be mean!

SONG TAL: Wouldn't you do the same if you were me?

HONGNYŎ: Are you going to listen to me or not?

SONG TAL: Listen to what?

HONGNYŎ: Are you going to be my man?

SONG TAL: You already asked me that!

HONGNYŎ: If you'll just hear me out, then I can save Shim Saengwŏn.

SONG TAL: How?

HONGNYŎ: I've got an idea.

SONG TAL: You're sure?

HONGNYŎ: I'm sure.

SONG TAL: All right, let's hear it.

HONGNYŎ: Really?

SONG TAL: Really.

HONGNYŎ: Ai, goodie! You're not holding anything back.

SONG TAL (nodding): Right—I'm not holding back.

HONGNYŎ: All right, then let me up on your back, and try out your dance.

SONG TAL: What do you mean? You're not Ch'ŏng.

HONGNYŎ: All right, next time for the dance. But for now, how about calling out to me "Oh honey, my sweet wife"?

SONG TAL: Now? Already?

HONGNYŎ: I just want to see how well you can do it.

SONG TAL: First you have to save Shim Saengwŏn.

HONGNYŎ: Honey!

SONG TAL: Mmm?

HONGNYŎ (adopts a serious expression): It was never my intention to be your lawful wedded wife—after all, I'm a barmaid, a floozy. And you're twenty and I'm ten years older.

SONG TAL: And?

HONGNYŎ: So, find a young lady and make her your lawful wedded wife, for all the world to see. And if your circumstances make that a problem, I'll help you out. Once that's done with, then you take me as your concubine. All I ask is that you don't mistreat me.

SONG TAL: If you can save Shim Saengwŏn, I'll do anything you want.

HONGNYŎ: Let's go pay him a visit. On the way I'll tell you my plan, then just do what I say.

(Both rise. Curtain.)

ACT 3, SCENE 1

(Setting is the same as act 2, scene 1. Evening of the same day. Curtain opens; BLIND MAN SHIM is wailing in the direction of the twig gate, calling for SHIM CH'ŎNG. Enter SONG TAL and HONGNYŎ, rushing through the gate.)

(HONGNYŎ comes to a stop and waits.)

SONG TAL (*with forced urgency and tension in his voice*): Sir!

BLIND MAN SHIM: Who's there—is that you, Tal?

SONG TAL: Please listen to me calmly, sir, and don't be too startled, all right?

BLIND MAN SHIM: Whether I listen or not, with my little Ch'ŏng dead, heaven could collapse and I wouldn't flinch.

SONG TAL: Sir, it's Ch'ŏng I'm talking about.

BLIND MAN SHIM: Ch'ŏng? Ch'ŏng who's dead and gone? What about her?

SONG TAL: She's not dead.

BLIND MAN SHIM: *What!* Not dead, you say?

SONG TAL: That's right.

BLIND MAN SHIM: Is it true? You're not deceiving me?

SONG TAL: It was a rumor that she died, and I believed it too. But there was nothing to it.

BLIND MAN SHIM: How do you know?

SONG TAL: Because the boat and the seamen came back.

BLIND MAN SHIM: The boat and the seamen? (*clutching* TAL's *arm*) Then where is Ch'ŏng?

SONG TAL: She came back too.

BLIND MAN SHIM: She did? Where?

HONGNYŎ (*speaking at the same time as* BLIND MAN SHIM): Father! (*rushes to him*)

BLIND MAN SHIM: Oh, my little girl!

HONGNYŎ (*taking his arm*): Father, your little Ch'ŏng is back.

BLIND MAN SHIM (*blinking*): Let me see you, my little girl.

(*His eyes snap open to reveal that the white film is gone.*)

BLIND MAN SHIM: Oh, my eyes! (*Dazzled by the light, he shields his eyes with his hand and plops down onto his haunches.*)

SONG TAL: You can see!?

BLIND MAN SHIM: Yes, I can see, I can see! My little girl, my little Ch'ŏng, let's have a look at you. (*rises and looks about*) Where are you? Where's my little Ch'ŏng?

SONG TAL (*takes hold of* BLIND MAN SHIM *and looks into his eyes*): You can see?

BLIND MAN SHIM: Yes!

SONG TAL: So you can!

BLIND MAN SHIM: So you're Tal—aren't you handsome? But what about my little Ch'ŏng? (*looks about and spots* HONGNYŎ) You're Ch'ŏng?

HONGNYŎ (hesitantly): Uhh . . .

BLIND MAN SHIM: The voice . . . and you look so much older...and those are pockmarks on your face—you aren't my Ch'ŏng, are you.

HONGNYŎ: Well no, the story is . . .

SONG TAL (steps between them): Sir!

BLIND MAN SHIM: What's going on? You said my little Ch'ŏng came back—where is she?

SONG TAL: Finally, her utmost devotion to you has manifested itself. Sacrificing herself to the Indang Sea so you could regain your sight (weeping), donating three hundred sacks of grain—here, finally, is the outcome of her heart, her filial devotion. Rejoice, sir, though you're sorry she's not here, think of her utmost devotion and rejoice. Heaven would not ignore her. And the Lord Buddha is not so heartless that he would prevent you from regaining your sight. Ch'ŏng is but a spirit, but now there is nothing more to wish for. Sir, feast your newly opened eyes on the bright, clear world before you.

Look, sir, look until you want to look no more. The eyes you've waited so long to be able to see with again, they've opened, haven't they? The eyes Ch'ŏng wanted you so much to be able to see with, they've opened, haven't they?

BLIND MAN SHIM (dejected): Well, then. So my little Ch'ŏng is gone forever.

SONG TAL: She may be dead, but for us she lives on. Her devotion to you will live for ten thousand generations.

HONGNYŎ: And I will play the role of your esteemed daughter, all right?

BLIND MAN SHIM (fiercely): Dead forever? My little Ch'ŏng is dead forever? She gave back sight to her old, shriveled-up, worthless dad? So then . . . (raving) my little Ch'ŏng is dead, a living sacrifice to the Indang Sea, and all for three hundred sacks of rice? Hmm? Is that the way it is? (spreads two fingers and points to his eyes) I killed my own daughter on account of these two holes? How could I? Would I have my precious daughter take her life in exchange for all under heaven? Hmm? (Grinding his teeth, he spears his eyes with the two fingers.)

(Too late, TAL and HONGNYŎ rush to him.)

BLIND MAN SHIM (continues gouging his eyes): All this to get you damnable holes to open! (thrashing about, clutching his bloody eyeballs, his face a crimson mask) Wretched holes! (steps down to the yard and collapses) Wretched holes! (TAL and HONGNYŎ try to raise him to his feet as the curtain drops.)

ACT 3, SCENE 2

(A two-story pavilion, its traditional multicolored pattern freshly repainted; attached to the eave is a plaque reading "Dedicated to the Filial Maiden Shim"; in the background, the sea.

Twilight on a late-autumn day. The curtain opens to reveal BLIND MAN SHIM, leaning against one of the posts of the pavilion, facing out to sea, a blind man's walking stick in his hand. Perched on the pavilion steps, facing the audience at an angle, head down, is SONG TAL.

The soothing wash of sea on shore is heard.

The distant sound of a bamboo flute, playing a refreshing melody.)

Chŏnbuk kongnon, October–November 1947

18

ANGEL FOR A DAY

(Sŏllyang hagoshiptŏn nal, 1960)

TODAY IS THE DAY. NO WAY WILL I BE THE MOTHER OF ALL BITCHES, no way will I bite off the passengers' heads.

So much for good intentions. My pledge to be a sweet girl, made as I set out early for work that morning, didn't last till noon.

I got through the morning rush, but then instead of slackening, passenger traffic grew to a flood. What's up with this? I wondered. And then I realized it was Buddha's birthday, April 8 by the lunar calendar.

As always, the load was manageable as we set out from the East Gate, but on the return trip the bus would be packed by the time we got to Kwangnaru. Kuŭi, Mojin, Hwayang, Togyo—every stop looked like a marketplace, so many people had mobbed there. Mobs of people were always getting on and off at Hwayang, but Togyo was a different story—we don't stop there unless people are waiting, which happens three runs out of ten, but today, guess what—there must have been a good dozen people waiting each time. And at Sanghuwŏn, where the Ttuksŏm line joins ours, there's always a throng, so our cargo practically doubles.

Next are Sŏngdong, Ŭlchi, and Wangshimni, and Wangshimni is no problem on the return route because people going downtown can catch the streetcar there. And then it's Majang and Yongdu—two stops where there's often so much of a crowd I have to leave some of them behind.

The people who take my line, the Kwangjang line, are always the same bunch—working stiffs at the lower end of the wage scale, but compared with the sleazy and wretched makeup of the outlying neighborhoods served by our line, they're positively high-class.

Since our line seems to have been put in exclusively for the women going down to market carrying their baskets of goods on their heads, these women get their use out of it, and then some—they use it, they like using it, and they use it exclusively. Great for them, right?

It's a rare day when a bus doesn't break down somewhere in the city, and it's a rare bus line that doesn't have at least a few of these women among the passengers.

We have a lot of passengers coming downriver from as far out as Kwangju—peddlers, farmers, and god-knows-who. Morning and evening we have quite a few students. And then there are the miners—supposedly there's a couple of big mines out in the vicinity of Songp'a, in a place called Mongch'on or something like that, and when these guys have money in their pockets they come into town for a good time.

"Lookie here, don't tell me you're off to Seoul to see the sights"—that's a Chŏlla miner sounding off. "How'd I ever end up a friggin' miner?"—and that guy sounding like a screech owl has to be from Kyŏngsang. You'll always see this bunch with their britches hanging loose, Japanese rubber footwear, either shoes or knee-high boots, and a towel tied around their forehead.

So with the regulars alone the bus is always jam-packed to begin with, and the passengers get jostled around. But today, with all these extra people out and about, it's twice as crowded—can you blame me for being surprised?

Among this bunch who've come crawling out of the woodwork, most are womenfolk—old women and young ladies. The way they're dressed is so gaudy. It kills me the way the young ones fancy themselves. The old ones aren't as bad. Just when I've recovered from the shock of the women in their quilted chŏgŏri of pink Japanese silk and their skirts so dark blue they look like they've been dyed with bugs, along come the ones in their unlined summer jackets. I feel like asking if that's all they have to wear for viewing all the colorful paper lanterns hung on this special day.

Whatever they're wearing, it makes me wonder if until today all these clothes were wrapped up deep inside a hope chest, waiting for their wearer to get married off, but more than the clothing tucked away in the hope chest, it's these women all gussied up for their grand outing, who've been buried off in the sticks somewhere and only today are coming out of hiding to see what the world looks like. For all I know they're mostly healthy, good-hearted, salt-of-the-earth people, but today, with their hairdos coming apart, their grimy, sun-darkened faces, splotched makeup, and claw-fingered hands, there's no way you could consider them beautiful.

Most of them wear straw sandals, a very few have Korean rubber shoes, and believe it or not, there's the occasional woman shuffling around in *geta*. The ones in *geta* are having a heck of a time maneuvering, they're obviously not used to them—you might find it funny, but to me it's a miserable sight. And it's on account of those clack-clackers that a little incident occurred.

The bus had stopped at Mojin, and among those who shouldered the competition aside and made their way on were a young woman who even among the countrified looked as country as you get, and an older woman I guessed to be her mother-in-law.

We took off, but only a short distance later the young one bawled out, "Oh for heaven's sake, my *geta*!"

It seemed her shoe had come off in her panic to board, and only now did she realize it.

Right away I pressed the buzzer and the bus lurched to a stop. The bus was so packed I couldn't have opened the door, so I jumped out a window, saw that clack-clacker lying a short distance off, next to the streetcar track, ran to get it, then crawled back through the window and returned the clog to its owner. I saw gratitude in her face, but she didn't say a word. It was the mother-in-law who spoke up.

"*Egu*—thanks be! Young lady, you are *so* sweet." I could tell she meant it. And could see the passengers nearby were impressed. *Well done!* I told myself.

If it was another day, no way would I have done it. Why would I want to stop the bus? And to think I'd fetch someone a damn clack-clacker. Her crying wouldn't have changed my mind, not even a tantrum. Not even if she'd clutched my arm and pleaded. In that case I would have snapped at her, *Don't want to deal with it!* and followed up by pouting at her and mumbling, loud enough for her to hear, *An outing . . . this is your idea of a damn outing? And I'm supposed to bend over backward for you? Why don't you take your outing money, buy some laundry soap, and scrub that dirty neck of yours? Hmph!*

So far, so good—my morning pledge was holding up, and not just to the young woman with the *geta*. I didn't turn away any of the basket-head peddlers, not a single one. And I didn't double-punch anyone's ticket because of an oversized basket. I tried to accommodate everyone, and if someone with an oversized load volunteered the extra payment, I waved her off. And it was nice to see the thankful faces of people who were probably thinking, *She made my day.*

But . . . do you suppose they made any effort to meet my kindness with kindness of their own? On the contrary, I could tell they saw me as gullible, someone they could string along, and instead of goodwill, it was ill will they had in mind. It wouldn't be long before some guy got on at Kwangnaru, played dumb and didn't pay a fare, and then around Sŏngdong he'd say, "Gimme a ticket for Wangshimi—I got on at Togyo," and hold out a ten-*chŏn* coin. I'd try nicely to get him to 'fess up, he wouldn't go for it, and finally I'd have to bark at him, "What gives, mister? Come on," and that's the only way he'd get the point. An ass like that really deserves a rap on the head.

Little by little I got irritated. How can a person be kind and gentle with human trash like that? The hostility bubbled up inside me.

Back at the East Gate, before my next departure I was in the waiting room and saw a Kwangnaru bus pull in. While everybody was getting off, a guy in a shabby suit waltzed out into the lot like he owned the place—this was before ticket sales had begun—and he headed for the bus. Figured he'd grab himself a seat ahead of time and get nice and comfy. This was around the time I was really getting aggravated.

I followed him out and said, "Excuse me, kind sir?" I managed to be polite in spite of myself.

The guy turned around with an inquiring expression.

"Where are you going?"

"I'm getting on the bus—what do you think?"

"Boarding hasn't started yet!"

"I have a return ticket!"

The guy was throwing a fit, and I could hear myself getting louder too: "A return ticket doesn't give you the right to get on before the other passengers!"

"What!"

"Get mad all you want, it's not going to get you anywhere. All the other passengers are waiting in line. What do you think you're doing, trying to make things easy for yourself? Don't you have any shame?"

"How dare you treat a passenger like this!"

"If you want to be treated well, then you shouldn't step out of line like that!"

"What kind of nonsense is this, you little . . . ?"

He was about to strangle me, I could see it in his eyes, but the other girls stepped in and nothing came of it. But my insides were churning.

The strange thing is, when I get my dander up like this, none of the passengers looks decent to me. Doesn't matter if there are ten or a hundred of them, male or female, young or old, all of the passengers on my Kwangjang line have crooked faces, faces wearing a permanent scowl, only one eye, pockmarks, twisted lips—in short, they're the most ugly and threatening people, no manners or compassion, no kindness or etiquette, pathetic sons of bitches who don't come close to being civilized.

And then on the return trip, we stopped at Sŏngdong. The bus was still packed to the brim, and as always there were a bunch of vendor women waiting, and they all tried to push their way on with their bulky baskets. The woman at the very front happened to make eye contact with me, and she broke out in a fake laugh and said in a treacly voice,

"Let me on, I'll pay extra for my basket."

If she hadn't said anything, all would have been well, but when I saw that sly smile and heard the syrupy words, I barked at her, "No!" and then pushed her and her basket out, closed the door, and hit the button for departure.

The bus took off and the basket came off the woman's head and ended up flipped over on the ground. In spite of myself, I looked back—and saw the eyes of that woman as she stood there gaping forlornly at the tail end of the bus. I don't think I've ever seen a look so sad and despairing. I felt a surge of emotion in my chest and my eyes teared up. I resisted the urge to plop down and start bawling, and when we arrived at Wangshimni I was still not myself.

Yagŏp shinmun, June 18, 25, 1960

Qian Zhongshu, *Humans, Beasts, and Ghosts: Stories and Essays*,
edited by Christopher G. Rea, translated by Dennis T. Hu, Nathan K. Mao, Yiran Mao,
Christopher G. Rea, and Philip F. Williams (2011)
Dung Kai-cheung, *Atlas: The Archaeology of an Imaginary City*, translated by
Dung Kai-cheung, Anders Hansson, and Bonnie S. McDougall (2012)
O Chŏnghŭi, *River of Fire and Other Stories*,
translated by Bruce and Ju-Chan Fulton (2012)
Endō Shūsaku, *Kiku's Prayer: A Novel*, translated by Van Gessel (2013)
Li Rui, *Trees Without Wind: A Novel*, translated by John Balcom (2013)
Abe Kōbō, *The Frontier Within: Essays by Abe Kōbō*, edited, translated, and
with an introduction by Richard F. Calichman (2013)
Zhu Wen, *The Matchmaker, the Apprentice, and the Football Fan: More Stories of China*,
translated by Julia Lovell (2013)
The Columbia Anthology of Modern Chinese Drama, Abridged Edition,
edited by Xiaomei Chen (2013)
Natsume Sōseki, *Light and Dark*, translated by John Nathan (2013)
Seirai Yūichi, *Ground Zero, Nagasaki: Stories*, translated by Paul Warham (2015)
Hideo Furukawa, *Horses, Horses, in the End the Light Remains Pure:*
A Tale That Begins with Fukushima (2016)
Abe Kōbō, *Beasts Head for Home: A Novel*, translated by Richard F. Calichman (2017)
Yi Mun-yol, *Meeting with My Brother: A Novella*, translated by
Heinz Insu Fenkl with Yoosup Chang (2017)

HISTORY, SOCIETY, AND CULTURE

Carol Gluck, Editor

Takeuchi Yoshimi, *What Is Modernity? Writings of Takeuchi Yoshimi*, edited and translated,
with an introduction, by Richard F. Calichman (2005)
Contemporary Japanese Thought, edited and translated by Richard F. Calichman (2005)
Overcoming Modernity, edited and translated by Richard F. Calichman (2008)
Natsume Sōseki, *Theory of Literature and Other Critical Writings*, edited and translated by
Michael Bourdaghs, Atsuko Ueda, and Joseph A. Murphy (2009)
Kojin Karatani, *History and Repetition*, edited by Seiji M. Lippit (2012)
The Birth of Chinese Feminism: Essential Texts in Transnational Theory, edited by
Lydia H. Liu, Rebecca E. Karl, and Dorothy Ko (2013)
Yoshiaki Yoshimi, *Grassroots Fascism: The War Experience of the Japanese People*,
translated by Ethan Mark (2015)